PENGUIN BOOKS

Instinct

Ben Kay was born in London in 1973. He has worked in advertising as an award-winning copywriter and creative director. Since 2006, his blog, ifthisisablogthenwhatschristmas, has provided an 'acid tongued' commentary on the industry. *Instinct* is his first novel.

D1081051

Instinct

BEN KAY

PENGUIN BOOKS

Published by the Penguin Group

Penguin Books Ltd, 80 Strand, London WC2R ORL, England

Penguin Group (USA) Inc., 375 Hudson Street, New York, New York 10014, USA

Penguin Group (Canada), 90 Eglinton Avenue East, Suite 700, Toronto, Ontario, Canada M4P 2Y3
(a division of Pearson Penguin Canada Inc.)

Penguin Ireland, 25 St Stephen's Green, Dublin 2, Ireland (a division of Penguin Books Ltd)

Penguin Group (Australia), 250 Camberwell Road, Camberwell, Victoria 3124, Australia
(a division of Pearson Australia Group Pty Ltd)

Penguin Books India Pvt Ltd, 11 Community Centre, Panchsheel Park, New Delhi – 110 017, India

Penguin Group (NZ), 67 Apollo Drive, Rosedale, North Shore 0632, New Zealand
(a division of Pearson New Zealand Ltd)

Penguin Books (South Africa) (Pty) Ltd, 24 Sturdee Avenue, Rosebank,
Johannesburg 2196, South Africa

Penguin Books Ltd, Registered Offices: 80 Strand, London WC2R ORL, England

www.penguin.com

First published 2010
2

Copyright © Ben Kay, 2010
All rights reserved

The moral right of the author has been asserted

Typeset by Palimpsest Book Production Limited, Grangemouth, Stirlingshire

Printed in England by Clays Ltd, St Ives plc

ISBN: 978–0–241–95211–5

www.greenpenguin.co.uk

Penguin Books is committed to a sustainable future
for our business, our readers and our planet.
The book in your hands is made from paper
certified by the Forest Stewardship Council.

To Gabi.
My ideal reader and my ideal everything else.

Hunger, love, pain, fear are some of those inner forces which rule the individual's instinct for self-preservation.

Albert Einstein

Prologue: The Swarm

The stripped-down jeep rattled, hopped and bumped its way across the rocky sands of the Koh-e-Sufaid. This far into the desert, the roads were harsh, nothing more than tracks of boulder-strewn dirt, flattened and cleared by the tread and sweep of occasional tyres.

With a spray of gravel, the car skidded to a stop. Looking ahead, the driver reached under the passenger seat and pulled out a pair of binoculars. At twenty-two years old, Houshmand Sahar looked closer to thirty, his weather-worn face obscured by a dark, scrappy beard that had never been cut.

Peering through the grease-smeared lenses, he searched for the gloomy arch that marked the entrance to his cave. To the untrained eye, it appeared to be just another dark shape in the mountain rock, but Houshmand had made this journey often enough to recognize the denser shade that meant home.

He placed his binoculars on the seat beside him, shoved his jeep into gear and sent it fishtailing through the grit until the tyres caught and began roaring up the foothills.

At this stage of the journey secrecy was paramount, so headlights were strictly forbidden. Houshmand had made the mistake of forgetting this once before and his back was still criss-crossed with raised lacerations from the hour-long whipping he'd received for such stupidity.

As the foothills steepened they became a lattice of thick ridges that worked every spring of the jeep's suspension. Houshmand looked behind him to check his cargo was still firmly secured. It would not do to come this far and lose such prized items in the last mile.

Reaching the final slope, he slowed to a crawl, the subdued grumble of his engine and tyres the only signs of life for miles around.

His jeep was now poised at the cave entrance. Raising his hands to his mouth, he let out a short, ululating call that echoed into the dim depths of the tunnel ahead. A second later the call received its response: a similar sound, only rounder and lower as it made its way from inside the cave. Houshmand pressed gently on the accelerator and eased the jeep into the darkness.

Then the light burst into his face.

'Speak!' barked the voice behind the harsh white flare.

'The banner of Islam will necessarily be raised when the land is watered with the blood of martyrs!' yelled Houshmand.

'Good,' came the softer reply. 'You can stop there.' The man holding the light was Behnam Azizi. He was three years older than Houshmand, but they were physically indistinguishable: both thin and bearded with an apologetic gait developed from years of cave dwelling.

Behnam hooked the cord on to a rusty nail and walked towards Houshmand. They embraced with a smile, kept a few inches apart by the Kalashnikov that hung across Behnam's chest.

'Good to see you, brother,' he said, looking beyond his friend to the roped-down tarpaulin in the back of the car. 'What have you brought us?'

Houshmand untied the canvas to reveal ribs of dark metal, shaded by the shadow of the tarpaulin. The shapes were not clear, but Behnam could tell immediately what they were. He lifted one of the rifles into the light and a smile spread across his face.

'You got the XM29s?'

Houshmand nodded. He knew he had done well. With its computer-assisted firing system, laser range finder and telescopic sights, the XM29 OICW made the Kalashnikov look like a popgun. This would take their training to another level, readying the cell for its next assault in a matter of weeks.

Behnam looked through the sight, then back down to the jeep. 'What else?'

'Everything,' said Houshmand. There were four large canvas bags under the cache of guns, each full to bursting. He began pulling at the zips.

'Heroin, ammo, fuel, passports and, of course . . .' Reaching into one of the bags, he pulled out several blue boxes. '. . . Kraft Mac and Cheese.'

Behnam laughed. 'You know what? I hate the infidels, but they got that shit just right. Come, let's get it unloaded and take it to the boss-man.'

'Oh yes,' said Houshmand, reaching into his pocket and pulling out a small brown envelope. 'And I've got a message for him from base.'

Taking as much as they could carry, the two men squeezed past the front of the jeep and headed deeper into the tunnel. The original caves had been shallow, stretching no more than twenty yards into the rock, but a dedicated programme of expansion had more than doubled their length.

Grimy, jagged corridors of rock were sporadically lit to show walls decorated with Islamic teachings. What furniture there was consisted of dust-caked planks of rotting wood supported by breeze blocks. The priority here was not comfort. As long as secrecy was maintained and the weapons and explosives were stored safely, the cave's function was fulfilled.

Even the quarters of this cell's leader, Abdullah Faraj Juwei, were basic at best. A thin, filthy mattress and a ball of rags that served as a lumpy pillow were the only indications of his superior status. It was to this part of the cave that Houshmand and Behnam were heading, greeting the other foot soldiers as they went.

Arriving at the thin sheet that separated Abdullah's room from the rest of the cave, Behnam gave a throaty cough and waited with Houshmand to be called in.

'Enter,' shouted Abdullah.

He was a thickset man, both fat and muscular, whose dark eyes were barely visible beyond their flabby, hooded lids. Under his sharp nose, a vast beard spread across his face and neck, covering the top of a khaki jacket, which was wrapped around a dirty-white *chapan*. Neither of the two men had ever seen him laugh, and they lived in nervous fear of his violent and arbitrary rule.

Beckoning them in with a short wave, he did not speak, instead indicating with an impatient glare that Houshmand should place the offering at his feet.

His eyes widening with impressed surprise, Abdullah picked up the weapons and felt their weight. As he looked through the sights and checked the magazines, Houshmand gave a stuttering catalogue of the contents of the jeep.

Abdullah nodded. 'You have done well,' he said without looking up. 'Is there anything else?'

Houshmand suddenly remembered the envelope in his pocket. Yanking it out and handing it quickly to Abdullah, he hoped he had not made a mistake worthy of serious punishment.

With a look of glowering annoyance, Abdullah snatched the envelope and turned it over to look at the front. Recognizing the handwriting, he scrabbled to rip it open.

He moved his lips as he read, occasionally whispering syllables to himself. Houshmand and Behnam watched anxiously as their master's expression changed from concern to panic.

Whipping the sheet aside, he barked the name of his lieutenant, who bolted from the back of the cave, where he'd been napping on a pile of clothes.

'Yes, sir' he yelled, trying to look alert.

'Look at this.' He held the letter in front of his face. The younger man read it at speed and nodded frantically. 'Pack whatever you can into the jeep and prepare to leave immediately. Weapons first, then the drugs, the money and the ammunition.'

'Yes, sir!'

He turned and ran to where the guns were stored, leaving Houshmand and Behnam cowering behind Abdullah. Houshmand knew he had committed a grave error, and he was now certain the beating would arrive quickly and without mercy.

Abdullah looked up, his face a knot of scarlet fury. 'You!'

The fat hand rose and swooped in one swift movement. As it smashed into Houshmand's jaw, it sent his neck whipping round, cracking the other side of his face on the rock behind him.

'You dare to bring me a message of such importance with the speed of a crippled goat?' Another crack.

'Our position has been compromised! You are a fucking fool to wait even a second to tell me this!' *CRACK! 'A fucking fool!'*

Houshmand was on the ground now, conscious thought slipping away. The last thing he heard was a humming in his ears: quiet and distant, but getting louder.

Abdullah turned to Behnam.

The younger man raised his arms to protect his face, while trying to protest his innocence.

'Please, master! I told him to tell you straightaway!'

'Liar!'

A punch this time, forcing Behnam's head to jerk backwards on to the rock.

He slumped to his knees, a scream, loud and high, ringing through his ears.

Abdullah heard it too. Curious, he pulled back the sheet.

They arrived like a cloud of driven evil, their burning drone mixed with the ferocious grinding of flesh that now filled the cave.

Abdullah opened his mouth to scream, but before he could make a sound the sparrow-sized creature flew into his mouth.

It clawed its way deeper to tear at his gums and rip the tongue from his throat. Four more of them gripped at his fleshy belly and back, consuming them from both sides until their jaws met in a mush of chewed intestines.

The first had torn Abdullah's jaw from the rest of his skull, leaving ragged, bloody cheeks hanging like burnt cloth beneath his eyes. It then worked its way upwards, removing the nose with the rampant appetite of a starving pig.

Before it could crawl up to the scalp, the rest of Abdullah's stripped-white bones collapsed to the ground in a broken slop of guts and innards.

Eight more set upon Houshmand, shredding his clothes to reach the skin that covered his meagre flesh. They tugged at it, creating low tent shapes which stretched, then tore, releasing the scent of fresh meat.

Then they burrowed inside, searching with their

mandibles, hungrily dragging the moist organs and tight, gristly muscle into their mouths.

Behnam was next. Through his pained confusion, he heard the helpless cries of terror, then froze as six claws landed on his back, quickly followed by twelve more. Three stingers stabbed into his shoulderblades, infecting his bloodstream with a rush of poison.

His nervous system shut down instantly leaving him unaware of the three sets of mandibles tearing through his neck.

A moment later his head rolled off the strip of skin his trachea had become and thudded on to the ground, rolling forwards until it came to a rest beside Abdullah's fleshless pelvis.

More wasps arrived. They had torn away every scrap of the other soldiers with clinical vigour, and were now hunting for more. Within seconds, there were fifty of them, feasting and fighting to grab at the last of Behnam's calves and ankles.

Shhrrrripppppp. The muscle peeled from the bones, which then clattered to the soaked ground. The three puddles of cherry-red had now joined together, making a wide slick of viscous, congealing blood that covered the floor of Abdullah's quarters.

It had taken no more than two minutes: eighteen men were reduced to pockmarked skeletons which lay throughout the cave in ghoulish poses of horror and thick drippings of gore.

PART ONE
The Head

I

'Show me again.'

'There, Dr Trent. It definitely looks like a whatcha-callit, an *a . . . berration*, like there's something different about this batch.'

'Given the preparations we made, that would be most unexpected, but if you're sure . . .' Laura Trent peered into the microscope, adjusting the focus until she found what she was looking for.

'Karen?'

'Dr Trent?'

'What did you have for lunch today?'

'Um . . . sausage roll, ham sandwich, bag of crisps – cheese and onion, I think. Diet Coke.' Karen Needham was twenty-two, round-faced, with the complexion of fresh porridge. She wasn't particularly interested in working as a lab assistant at the British Entomological Association, but it paid for the rent on her little flat and she couldn't really be bothered to find another job since slipping into this one with her third-class degree in molecular biology.

'Anything else?'

'Um . . .'

'Doughnut, perhaps? Jam sandwich?'

'Oh, yes, now you come to mention it I did have a jam sandwich, but that was more for elevenses.'

'Yes, because this "aberration" is . . . a raspberry pip,' replied Laura, leaning back from the microscope. It took Karen a moment to register what Laura was suggesting. When she finally understood, her face reddened and broke into an embarrassed smile.

'If, in future, you could make sure your hands are clean before working with samples of microscopic cell structures, that would probably help.'

'Er . . . yes, Dr Trent.'

Laura hated the way Karen spoke to her as if she were some matronly headmistress. She was only thirty-seven, for God's sake – she had years left to indulge in the kind of irresponsible behaviour she never quite found time for. And she was pretty, too, with long, bright hair that still held a trace of the natural blond it used to be. Perhaps the stress of being a single parent hadn't been kind to her, but she was still capable of attracting (mainly unwelcome) attention from some of the lab technicians.

She sent Karen to the admin office to fill in the next day's requisition order and started to write up the afternoon's findings on *polistes metricus* DNA. That would take about an hour, giving her a chance to edit some new submissions for the *European Journal of Entomology* afterwards.

Like many people who have lost a spouse, Laura had taken on more work to occupy the hollow left behind. Michael had been gone for over two years now, but she had got into the habit of keeping his absence from her life at bay. As she put in the hours to look through EJE papers and make further headway into her own experiments, she rarely paused to look at the space she was trying to fill. Being there for her son Andrew was her priority; other than that there was little in her life to stop the insects taking it over.

Her vocation had started with a childhood interest sparked by an uncle who took her to London Zoo in the school holidays. It had then been nurtured in a well-taught module in her biology A-level. After a gap year searching southern Madagascar for the giant comet moth she had chosen to pursue the subject in a full-blown degree, during which she had come under the tutelage of Dr David Heath. Seven years with him had allowed her to see the contributions her continued study could make. It was as if he opened one door to a million others, each more fascinating than the last. The quality and quantity of time she spent in his company meant that their relationship surpassed that of teacher and pupil. It had never become physical, but he was never far from her thoughts.

When she acquired her doctorate, it was a foregone conclusion that she would take the subject on as her occupation. As a former pupil of Heath, further opportunities arose with something approaching inevitability, and she soon found herself in the company of the pre-eminent doctors and professors in the field. This, and the number of hours she put in, ensured that she progressed with remarkable speed.

She had just managed to immerse herself in a proposal for a composite genetic map for *Dolichovespula* when Karen appeared at her office door.

'Ummmmmm . . . Dr Trent?'

Laura stopped reading and looked up over the top of her spectacles.

'Sorry to interrupt, but there's a man here to see you.'

'What man?'

'Just a . . . man.'

'He didn't say who he was or what he wanted?'

'Nope.'

'Really? A man just turned up, asked to see me and didn't say why?'

Karen shrugged. Laura rolled her eyes, closed her file and followed her assistant to the corridor.

As she and Karen approached the reception area, Laura could see only one person waiting on the orange plastic chairs. The first thing she noticed was his shirt, which was a little too big for him, as if he were aware of the slightness of his build and wanted to disguise it. Above the collar was a hard face, grey with pencil lines that seemed to describe past difficulties and framed by lank hair that had needed a trim for at least six weeks. Despite this unimpressive appearance, the man had an air of unpleasant confidence that raised Laura's antennae. She was also intrigued by the deep, steel briefcase that sat between his legs.

'Thank you, Karen. I think I can manage from here,' Laura said as she continued to study the face, trying to eke out any aspect of it that seemed familiar. At her level, the entomological community was small and tight-knit, so if he was aware of her work in that capacity . . .

The man looked up, suddenly catching her eye. She tried to pretend she hadn't been staring at him but realized it was futile. She had better see what he wanted.

Watching her approach, he got to his feet, an effortful smile stretching his features.

'Dr Trent?' he asked, offering his hand.

'Yes,' replied Laura. His weak grip and American accent concerned her.

'Steven Bishop. It's an honour to meet you.'

'Er . . . Thank you.'

'You must be wondering who I am.'

'Yes . . . I'm sorry, have we met?'

'Not that I'm aware of.'

Bishop waited until two lab assistants had walked past and out of earshot before he continued.

'Is there somewhere private we can talk?'

Laura was surprised at the man's need for secrecy. The BEA was hardly MI5, but if this man thought privacy was so important, she was happy to oblige.

'How about my office?'

Bishop smiled, picked up his briefcase and followed her. Looking around at the blistered paintwork and ancient computers, he allowed the pity to show on his face.

Laura sat at her desk and gestured to the chair opposite. The walls of her tiny office used to be white but were now closer to chewing-gum grey, with a small patch of brown damp creeping its way out of one of the ceiling corners. Bishop squeezed into the chair and crossed his legs as best he could in the space available.

'Thank you, Dr Trent. I know your time is valuable, so let me get straight to the point. What I am about to tell you is highly confidential, so I hope I can rely on your discretion.'

'Of course,' said Laura.

What on earth was this all about?

'I run a NATO facility that researches and produces genetically modified insects. I can't say much more than that, but the reason I'm here is that we have just lost our resident entomologist, and we need to replace him as quickly as possible. Due to your background and the advances you have made in the field, we believe you are the ideal candidate, Dr Trent.'

Laura smiled. 'Well, that's very flattering, Mr Bishop, but there must be dozens of other people just as qualified to fill your post.'

'There are indeed dozens of other people with your qualifications, Dr Trent, but none of them is quite as brilliant as you. Your application of the human genome isolation to arthropods was nothing short of genius, and your paper on interspecies trait analysis was a quantum leap forward for the discipline.'

Laura was surprised into a moment of silence.

'You've obviously done your homework. In which case, you should know that I am at a critical stage in my current research. My subjects will require close analysis over the coming weeks. Leaving them for a substantial period of time would be out of the question.'

'I understand. You have obligations and responsibilities; I would expect nothing less. With someone of your standing there are bound to be obstacles in persuading you to take on other work, but if you'll permit me, there are certain factors that might make my proposal more attractive. Without being vulgar, the first is financial: we can offer you ten times your current salary, plus benefits.'

Despite herself, a light appeared behind Laura's eyes.

'Second, our facilities. Dr Trent, your equipment and computers look as if they could do with some ... modernization. Ours are state of the art. Beyond state of the art, in fact. We have the benefit of technological advances that have not yet been made available to anyone else. Whatever you think you are capable of here, you'll make far greater progress far more quickly at MEROS.'

'MEROS?'

'It stands for Military Entomological Research Operations. We're a scientific defence facility based in Venezuela.'

Laura laughed. 'Venezuela? I'm sorry, Mr Bishop, but that's out of the question. Aside from the work I have to finish here, I couldn't possibly uproot my son to go and work in South America.'

'Of course. I suppose the possibility that you might join us on a permanent basis was our most optimistic target. However, we still feel that any assistance you could give us, even on a consultancy basis, would be invaluable. We could make it worth your while, even if it were just the occasional short visit.'

Laura leaned back in her chair. 'I don't know, Mr

Bishop. The position does sound intriguing, but I'm not sure my part-time involvement would really suit either of us.'

Bishop nodded. 'I know that what I'm suggesting here is quite an undertaking, but if I may, there is one more thing which I hope can persuade you at least to come over and take a look at our set-up.' Carefully, he placed his briefcase on his lap, rotated the numbers of the combination lock and eased open the lid. Then he slowly brought out a large specimen jar and handed it to Laura as if it were an unexploded bomb.

At first she didn't see the significance. The contents looked like a thick twig, slightly distorted by the surrounding formaldehyde. She looked up at Bishop's encouraging expression and thought she must be missing something, something that deserved another look. She peered closer. The top of whatever it was looked familiar, but it couldn't be what she thought it was. That would be impossible, but . . .

What else could it be?

'Is this real?'

'Absolutely. I assume I don't have to tell you what it is.'

'No, the junction of the coax and trochanter is quite distinctive. But it can't be a wasp's leg. The insect would have to be the size of . . . *a rat*.'

Bishop gave the moment a little room before answering. 'Dr Trent, we are backed by quite substantial funding and expertise. Are you sure I can't interest you in a visit to our facility?'

Laura turned the jar around, examining the leg from every angle. The tibia was so clear she could make out the hairs that covered it like thorns on a rose stem. She was momentarily lost in imagining its owner.

'How big is the body?

'Big enough that I couldn't hope to bring it into this country without creating an international incident. A leg wouldn't be quite so provocative. So can I take that as a yes, you'll at least pay us a visit?'

Laura placed the jar on her desk. 'Well, I suppose with enough notice I can leave my experiments in good hands and arrange for Andrew's grandmother to look after him for a few days. Perhaps I could clear things for the end of next month.'

Bishop's ingratiating smile flattened.

'I was hoping you'd join us sooner than that. The sudden departure of our head entomologist has left us in a very difficult position. Is there no way you could come sooner? I'm actually thinking of the next few days.'

'Oh no, I'm afraid that's out of the question. I couldn't possibly find anyone to look after Andrew at that short notice.'

'Dr Trent' – Bishop's tone hardened – 'we'd be able to arrange for Andrew to be taken care of. We'd make sure you were adequately compensated. We could even make a donation to the budget of this facility. This is very important to us, and speed is of the essence. I'd really rather not leave without some sort of commitment from you.'

Bishop's change of attitude left Laura feeling as if the temperature in the room had plummeted.

'I . . . understand, Mr Bishop, but I just can't do it. There's too much to organize, and I don't think I'd be able to manage it all in time.' She stood up and handed the leg back.

Bishop stood, too. 'Please think about it carefully, Dr Trent.'

'I will. Of course I will. Now, I'm very sorry, but there are a couple of things I have to finish up before I leave for the day. If you'll excuse me.' She offered her hand.

Bishop shook it, fixing Laura with a look that left her in no doubt as to the extent of his disappointment.

'Thank you for your time.'

Laura watched him hurry back down the corridor, a mobile phone pressed to his ear.

2

In a sweaty clearing eighty miles east of Venezuela's Yapacana National Park, a matt-black C-27J Spartan cargo airplane squatted like an enormous moth. The surrounding area consisted of thick jungle, too dense to be populated by people but a fine home for some of the more obscure animals of the South American peninsula.

Where the west side of the clearing became trees there was a white building the size of a cottage which looked inadequate for the enormous aircraft it served. It was manned by a soft-bellied twenty-two-year-old African American called Taj, who spent most of his waking day at a white desk just behind the outermost of four security doors.

Three male and two female soldiers were carrying large boxes of equipment back and forth between the plane and the building. The scene was not unusual here, they loaded up the aircraft once or twice a month, but there was a feeling amongst the team that made today's preparations very different: the incident two days earlier had got to them all, and now every break gave rise to heated conversations which caused any downtime to last much longer than usual.

The process was further lengthened by the absence of Carter and Webster. They missed Carter's 200 lbs of muscle; he would shift those crates as if they were eggboxes. They were also without the smoothing effect of Major Webster's unquestioned leadership. In his absence, the command fell to Captain Van Arenn, and he was still simmering about what had happened.

'Yo, Cap, you want to get this shit loaded or what? I'm wheels up in two hours twelve minutes, and it don't look like you'll even be halfway done by then.' Gary Madison, a mercenary pilot who was unaware of the two deaths, was growing impatient. He did not know that pressing Captain Van Arenn in this way was unlikely to get the loading done any faster.

'Madison, talk to me like that again and I'll wipe your nose across your face,' said Van Arenn evenly. 'The job will get done. In the meantime we, meaning the proper soldiers, have shit to discuss, so step back and shut the fuck up.'

Madison knew that, whatever happened, they needed him to pilot the Spartan. 'Proper soldiers? You mean a bunch of shitcake wash-ups who couldn't hack it in the real army? Load my fucking plane, dickwad.'

The soldiers turned with menace to face Madison, but this was Van Arenn's call, so the next move was his. He smiled to himself before walking towards a surprisingly calm Madison.

'Hey, Van Arenn, you know I've got to fly this thing, so best keep your dumb grunt paws off me.' They all knew, deaths or no deaths, that nothing stopped the mission. Once it was in motion it followed its schedule to the minute or bad things fell from on high.

Van Arenn thought for a moment.

'When did you say we were flying? Two hours?'

Madison nodded, fear rippling his face.

'That'll give you just enough time to recover from this.' He dropped his right hand to Madison's khaki shorts, grabbed hold of whatever he could and twisted until Madison screamed, choked and felt every blood vessel in his face bulging through his skin. When Van Arenn loosened his grip, Madison slid down the side of the loading ramp and collapsed on the ground holding his sore, sore balls. The other soldiers laughed in appreciation while Sadie Garrett walked up to high-five her friend and spit on Madison.

'OK, everybody.' Van Arenn raised his voice. 'Fuck-tard here is right: we do got to load this machine. Let's get it done quick and meet up in the barracks if anyone else needs to talk things through.'

3

After an hour lost in pheromone biosynthesis, Laura checked her watch and saw that it was time to pick Andrew up from school. She would take him home, cook his tea and wait for her mother-in-law, Carol, to come to look after him for the evening. Every second Thursday was Laura's night to play bridge with three old schoolfriends, but they rarely went anywhere near a pack of cards, preferring instead to drink martinis and discuss unsuitable men to set each other up with.

She swapped her white lab coat for her beige mac and headed towards the car park. Reaching the doorway, she finally noticed the rain, which had been growing heavier as the afternoon continued. By now it was coming down hard enough to persuade Laura to cover her head with a couple of pieces of junk mail and half-run across the car park to her seven-year-old Ford Mondeo. Inside, she switched on the heater to drive out the solid cold. She sat for a moment, a long exhale marking the short time when nobody was depending on her to be responsible, then she started the engine and pulled out into the high street.

The heavier the rain, the heavier the traffic, so the ten-minute journey to Andrew's school took fifteen and was accompanied by the whining mechanics of her windscreen wipers dragging across the glass. Many of the parents had already been and gone and she was able to park right by the front gates. From there she could see the wide brick shelter that served as assembly point for fire drills and wet-weather outdoor-play area. It was also where children waited for their parents if it was raining or windy.

Laura squinted through the raindrops on the car window and saw that the shelter was empty. She gave a small sigh. Andrew knew this was bridge night, and that it meant that she liked to get home as early as possible. That way she didn't have to apply make-up and straighten her hair in front of her mother-in-law. There was something about doing that which felt disrespectful and Laura was keen to avoid the guilty mood it put her in before she left her son and went to get tipsy.

After five minutes waiting in the car, Laura looked at her watch for the ninth time and decided to go and look for Andrew.

As a former pupil of the school, it always took her a minute to adjust to the sights and smells that were so evocative of her daily life thirty years ago. Low coat hooks, enthusiastically colourful paintings and the stale odour of mass catering combined in a wave of nostalgia that made her forget for a moment why she was there. Turning a corner, she found herself standing by the open door of her old form room and couldn't help pausing to look inside as a thousand memories seeped through her. The distraction made it all the more surprising when a hand landed gently on her shoulder.

'Hello, Mrs Trent. What's Andrew forgotten this time?' It was Miss Halliday, Andrew's form teacher.

'Oh . . . er, hello . . .' Laura could never remember the teachers' names. 'Nothing as far as I'm aware, but he wasn't by the gates when I came to pick him up so I assumed he was inside somewhere.'

Miss Halliday, sweetly plump and middle-aged, dressed in a twin-set of muted earth tones, with spectacles that lay on the soft shelf created by her large, low bosom, looked confused.

'That's odd. I definitely saw him leave around home time. I had to remind him not to run in the hall, so the moment did rather stick with me.'

Laura and Miss Halliday both let the same thought blunder into their minds while simultaneously trying to keep it at bay.

'Well, I'm sure he's around somewhere, but just to be certain I'll alert the other members of staff who are still here and we'll search the premises. He's probably in the loo, somewhere like that.'

Laura smiled. It was too soon to be worried. 'Yes, probably.'

They began to search: Laura, Miss Halliday and several other teachers who broke off from their marking to help. The school was small, so everyone bumped into each other as they checked the same classrooms, toilets, cupboards and outside buildings. When they passed Laura she gave them each a smile of awkward gratitude before continuing down the corridor. The encounters felt like increasing constrictions around her. She looked forward to each one, hoping it would bring the final good news of Andrew's discovery, but as it failed to do so she found those smiles shrinking.

The situation perturbed her, but rather than expecting the worst, which she would have done if Andrew had been several years younger, she tried to think of a convincing explanation for what had happened. He was too old to be taken in by a stranger with a bag of sweets, and too bright to be unaware of the consequences of failing to meet his mum when he was supposed to. If something unexpected had come up which meant he couldn't be there, he had an emergency fifty-pence piece and her mobile number.

Now that twenty minutes had elapsed, Miss Halliday stood by the assembly hall and stopped each member of the search party as they came past. Laura was last to return. From the looks she saw on the teachers' faces, she decided not to ask the question for fear of having to hear the answer.

'OK, what do we do now?' she asked quickly.

'First, there's no need to panic,' said Miss Halliday.

'I'm not panicking. I just want to know what we need to do to make sure Andrew is OK.' The tension in Laura's voice was unmissable, accelerating each word as it crossed her lips.

'Right, well, we call the police and explain what has happened,' said Miss Halliday, trying to combine calmness with drive, and kindness with efficient detachment. 'We have a recent picture of Andrew from the class photos, which we will email to them. You should go home so we, or the police, know where to contact you. You can also telephone his friends from there.'

'Right. Yes, thank you.'

Miss Halliday looked gentle but serious as she took Laura's hand. 'Something similar to this happens about once a month and we've yet to have a significant problem.' She looked at the other teachers, who helpfully nodded their confirmation.

'Yes,' repeated Laura, distracted by the brightness of the powder-blue veins on the hand holding hers. 'I'm sorry, I just . . .' She said a single thank you to all of them, then hurried out of the study and back through the worsening rain to her car.

Driving home, she refused to let herself indulge in morbid speculation or self-pity. To keep her mind clear, she said her driving actions aloud. 'Change to second gear . . . slow down approaching junction . . . indicate right . . .' However, when she pulled up at the traffic lights three streets away from her home, she stopped speaking and covered her face with her hands. Even when the lights changed and two cars behind started blaring their horns, she took a little while to stare straight ahead through the formless shapes made by the rain falling on the windscreen, then continued her journey as if nothing had happened.

She concentrated on remembering that Andrew was a clever, confident boy who knew that his absence could cause trouble. There had been that time five years ago when she thought she'd lost him at the boat show in London, but he'd managed to find his way to the people at the PA desk and got them to call for her within a few minutes. Then again, he was not thoughtless enough to miss her at the school gates and just go home on his own without telling her. The one time she turned up half an hour late and was unable to call the school because the credits in her phone had run out, he had known to go back inside and wait for her there.

There was definitely something wrong, but she couldn't work out what, partly because the solution refused to present itself and partly because she refused to look for it. Every outcome appeared too improbable, so the possibilities kept pulling her back to a centre of incomprehension which, in some ways, was the best place to be.

She parked right outside the house and found that she couldn't move. In her peripheral vision she saw that none of the lights was on and the sight shrunk her stomach like a drawstring bag. In the end it took the thought that any minute now the police might be calling with news to get her to snap open her car door. On the path she had to force herself to cover the twenty feet to her house; she felt as if she were approaching the edge of a cliff. She found her keys disappointingly quickly and stuffed them into their locks. The front door whined open before her – she had spent far too long nagging Michael to oil the hinges; now she couldn't bear the idea of it opening in silence.

Inside, Laura was greeted by Crumble, her middle-aged tabby. He rubbed up against his owner's legs and wrapped his tail around her ankles, oblivious to her feelings. Laura barely noticed the soft pressure and firm purring as she looked up the stairs and called Andrew's name.

There was no reply.

She went to look in his room. He was not there. She called several more times and checked the other five rooms, but they were empty, and without her shouts the house was deeply silent and colder still. Now she was feeling the onset of dread, curling its fingers around her thoughts.

She called his friends. The seven possibles became definite nos, and with each one she could feel another dim light switching off in the growing darkness. She remembered how alone she had felt when Michael's boss had called her with the news of the loose scaffolding that had caused his death. That had emptied her from the heart outwards, and she always felt that the part of her that went missing that day would never return.

The phone rang. It was Miss Halliday wanting to know if Laura had heard anything. The answer was no, and it was met with a bruising silence that made it clear nothing could be said to improve things. She told Laura she'd be in touch if she had any news and asked her to do the same before hanging up and allowing that low hum of emptiness to rush back into the house.

Ten minutes later, Laura heard a knock at the front door. It had to be news of Andrew; nobody else would call at this time of day. Laura bounced to her feet and began thinking of how she would lovingly tick him off. At the same time another part of her recognized that the knock was sharper and more insistent than Andrew's. When she saw the size of the figure through the opaque glass, she knew it was not her son, and any elation she had felt disappeared as quickly as it had arrived.

'Hello, Carol,' said Laura quietly, looking at the damp indentations her mother-in-law's feet made on the doormat.

'Laura.'

There was a long pause when Laura did not know what to say.

'Well, aren't you going to invite me in?'

'Andrew's not here, Carol. He wasn't at school when I went to collect him. Nobody knows where he is.'

'Goodness. Are you sure? Yes, of course you are. Well, I shall make you a cup of tea and we'll both wait for him. He's bound to have just got into some mischief and . . .'

'You have to go home.' Carol looked wounded. 'In case he tries to go there or call you,' Laura continued.

'Yes, of course. What was I thinking? We'll keep in touch.' She was already halfway down the path. 'And don't worry. He'll turn up any minute, just you see if he doesn't.' She attempted a cheery wave, but Laura didn't see it because she had already closed the door and was on her way back to the living room to sit beside the phone and allow her imagination to taunt her.

The next sound to break the silence was a call from a policewoman who sounded like she was at the end of her shift.

'Hello, is that Dr Lorna Trent?'

'Yes, *Laura*.'

'Sorry?'

'It's *Laura* Trent.'

'Oh. I've got Lorna here.'

'Well, I assume that if you're trying to reach a *Lorna* Trent at this number but instead of a *Lorna* Trent there's a *Laura* Trent then maybe you've got slightly the wrong name.'

'So you're Laura Trent?'

'That's right. How can I help you?'

'It's Constable Watts of Lock Road police station here. I understand we've had a report of your son Andrew as a missing person, is that right?'

'Yes it is,' she said quickly, sitting up in anticipation.

'Right, well, we've no news yet. Obviously there's only so much we can do, but we have a photo of the young lad and we've got several officers assigned to the . . .'

Laura stopped listening, the voice growing ever fainter as she wrapped herself in the darkness again.

The policewoman wanted to know if Andrew had been found, because apparently that was the usual outcome at this stage. That made it harder for Laura to explain that he was still missing. She had the additional pain of feeling like a failure, one of the pitiful minority who could not easily find their child minutes after they had disappeared. She gave Andrew's details and the places he might be. Constable Watts told her they would take a look, do what they could, keep her informed, and it all made her feel one tenth of one per cent better.

'. . . So we'll give you a call if we hear anything.'

'Yes, thanks.' Laura thought about asking a few questions, just to keep her on the line and hold the silence back, but she was just too crushed to do something so active and pointless, and a small, rational part of her knew she should keep the line clear for Andrew to call.

By the time nine o'clock arrived with no sign or word of her beloved son, Laura began to weep. The possibilities of what lay before her finally made their way in and spread through enough of her to provoke a reaction. All the simple explanations had evaporated one by one and all that was left was a punishing feeling of inevitability. Laura sat on the stairs, looking at a photo of Andrew, smiling, in his football kit and let the tears fall.

Then there was another knock at the door.

4

Within three hours they had finished the loading. The spacious interior of the plane had become cramped as the crates were lined up at one end, halving the amount of room allocated to the soldiers. For now they were enjoying the freedom of the grass outside, lying across it in vests and trousers now a darker shade of the khaki they had been earlier.

'OK,' Van Arenn called. 'Now y'all take a shower. We could be forty-eight hours in that thing, with some hard work at the other end, so wash your stink off. We fly at . . . 2200.'

As the soldiers picked up their gear and ambled back to the white building, he went over to talk to Garrett. The others took this as their usual cue to whisper amongst themselves about how those two were definitely doing it, and how dirty she must be. The truth was a little different.

Sadie Garrett grew up in a trailer park outside Barwick, Louisiana. Prettier than most, with a dark sheet of shiny hair and a pert, fleshy body, she attracted the kind of bad-boy attention that got her drinking too young. By thirteen she was getting through a bottle of Cisco and forty Newport Menthol a day. By sixteen she had moved on to Oxycontin and the petty crime that surrounds it. After she was caught cramming herself backwards through the bathroom window of a trailer she was burgling, her daddy cut a deal with the local sheriff to keep her out of the county jail: he agreed to drive her to army recruitment and not come back until she'd signed up. In the end it worked out for everybody, as she found she liked discipline, routine, firing guns and, to an extent she hadn't really been aware of, showering with other women.

Van Arenn was from Fountain Hill, Arkansas, a town of a couple of hundred people and twice as many cows. At fourteen, too bored to take any more, he left his pop blind drunk on the porch, yet again, and never came back. He spent a couple of years hitching across the South, picking up odd jobs, easy to come by as his thick blond hair and arrogant eyes made him good-looking enough for middle-aged men of a certain leaning to pay ten dollars an hour just to have him in sight. He knew what was going on and didn't see the harm in it, and if he was ever hard up he'd go back to some of those places, top up the cash, steal a few things and head off again.

At sixteen he found himself drinking like his pop in a Mississippi roadhouse when a fat man decided to take him to task for looking shabby and steaming the place up with the smell of 'barbecued shit'. Van Arenn was stubborn enough to give a little back, but just as it might have turned violent, a small, quiet figure walked up from his table in the shadows and told the fat man to lay off picking fights with people half his size. When he was told to go fuck himself, the quiet man broke the fat man's nose and wrist, leaving him screaming on his knees, then calmly returned to his table. He was wearing a Marine's uniform, and that made a hell of an impression on David Van Arenn. Three days later, he had some good fake papers and a uniform of his own.

So he and Garrett knew each other before they'd even met. They belonged to a not-very-exclusive club of teenage wasters who had fallen into the army, but they were both from the South so they liked hearing each other's lilting drawl. When they found out they had both been dishonourably discharged for the same thing, well that just about sealed it.

They had both gone AWOL to see their fathers one last time before they passed away. After years of rotgut whiskey, Tyler Van Arenn had at last beaten his liver into submission. His son was supposed to be preparing for an inspection before the arrival of the Australian Ambassador, but he wasn't going to let that keep him from saying goodbye.

Garrett's daddy spent four days in a coma after his car was hit by the 4x4 of some drugged-up frat boys. She went AWOL from Camp Pendleton while delivering a printer to the admin block. She just drove right out of there, stopped twice for gas, and got to the hospital just in time to tell her daddy how much she loved him.

Ordinarily, they would not have been discharged for what they had done. The US Marine Corps prefers to resort to the stockade before spending all that time training two excellent soldiers, only to see them leave. However, in this case the Pentagon needed candidates for MEROS and these two young orphans with otherwise spotless service records fit their needs like air fits a balloon.

By 2159 hours the five soldiers were tucked into their seats, preparing their time killers and trying to find a position they could catch some sleep in. Exactly one minute later Madison closed the cargo doors and checked his instruments for take-off. He couldn't tell what hurt more: his balls or the ant bites that covered his buttocks since he'd slumped to the ground right on top of their nest. He'd spent most of the last few hours scratching himself crazy and looking ahead to a very long and uncomfortable flight.

The Spartan had been chosen for its load capacity and its ability to take off quickly and steeply from shorter runways, but it had also been modified in several ways to suit the needs of MEROS missions: temperature-controlled cargo bays had been installed to enable the transportation of live specimens; the engine had been overhauled to increase the top flying speed from 583 km/h to 792 km/h; and the fuel tank had been expanded so that the airplane had a range of over 8,000 miles.

The turbines roared into life and soon became the deafening assault that made this everyone's least favourite part of any mission. Once they were moving properly they could tune it out, and once they reached their destination they could get to work. Until then, it was a case of holding on tight while Madison tried to work the controls with one hand and scratch himself with the other.

5

'Hello?' Laura asked through her closed front door. She moved a few feet back; all she could see were two large figures, almost entirely blocking the light coming through the glass.

Surprisingly, an American accent answered. 'Dr Trent? Dr Laura Trent?'

'Yes?' Laura responded tentatively.

'We need to speak to you. It's about Andrew.'

Laura immediately opened the door. Two men in wet black raincoats and army boots loomed over her.

'Do you have any identification?'

The men fished a pair of matching fat black wallets from their inside pockets and flipped them out. They showed plastic cards with pictures of themselves beside an official-looking seal dominated by a pair of eagle's wings. Above that were words that plunged Laura into troubled confusion: Armed Forces of the United States.

'The American Army? What do you have to do with my son?'

'It would be easier for us to explain everything if we could just come inside.'

Unease crept through Laura like a spider, but she knew she had to find out more. Stepping back, she pulled the door open and gestured towards the living room. She felt uncomfortable, but the magic words had been uttered: *It's about Andrew* – and right now she would have let just about anyone in if they could back that sentence up.

The older man looked as if he'd been carved from teak. In his early forties, but looking good on it, he had warm, brown eyes that sat on his face like a cartoon bear's. His hair was dark, but flecked with enough ticks of white to give him an air of hard-won experience.

The other was in his late twenties, tall and broad, with smooth, wide features and light black skin. His head was a brown dome, shaved bald, and it made him seem unnervingly faultless, like a scaled-up toy soldier rather than the real thing.

They followed Laura into the living room and sat down together on a sofa not quite big enough for two men of their size.

The older man spoke first. 'Dr Trent, my name is Major Carl Webster. This is Lieutenant Jeffrey Carter. Let me get straight to the point if I may. We know the whereabouts of your son and we would like to reunite you with him as soon as possible.'

Laura looked at Major Webster with an unlikely mixture of bemusement, anger and relief.

'You know where my son is?'

'Yes I do, Dr Trent.'

'You *know* where my son is?'

'Uh . . . This afternoon at about 1600 hours myself and Lieutenant Carter did indeed persuade . . .'

'Where the *fuck* is my son?'

'. . . Andrew to accompany us, requiring the . . . uh . . . unfortunate disruption of his daily routine . . .'

'WHERE THE FUCK IS MY SON?'

Carter got to his feet and put his hands out to intimate that Laura should quieten down. 'Uh, Dr Trent, we would suggest that you calm down and . . .'

As his hands made the slightest contact with Laura's arms, she whipped them away.

'Get the fuck off me. What do you think you're doing?' Carter took a step back and looked to Webster.

'One more time. Where the fuck is my son?'

'It's not as simple . . .' Webster began meekly.

'Right then, I'm going to phone the police.' She lifted the receiver and dialled the first nine.

'I wouldn't do that if I were you,' said Webster, raising his voice slightly. 'I'm sorry, but having us arrested is not going to get you to see Andrew any faster.'

Laura stopped, closed her eyes and tried to control herself. The handset shook inside her steel grip. Her knuckles were white and the nails of her other hand dug hard into her palm. She knew Webster was right but her fury suddenly had nowhere to go.

'FUCK!' she screamed. 'Fuck you! What do I have to do to see my son?' Anger squeezed every word, pushing them out of her throat in a grating strain.

'Well, you, uh, have to come with us,' Webster replied apologetically. Carter couldn't even look up. Instead he hung his head down and concentrated on the worn paisley carpet beneath his boots.

Laura was seething, taking directionless paces around her living room. 'But . . . *why?* I mean, what could I have that you'd possibly want?'

'I'm afraid I'm not at liberty to explain the details of the situation right now, Dr Trent. I simply have instructions to ask you to accompany us immediately. Anything beyond that, I'm afraid, is classified. This is very important to us, and speed is of the essence.'

Laura shut her eyes so hard her cheeks ached. She could feel the throbbing blare of a headache building at her temples. When she opened her eyes again, she was looking at the ceiling, searching for words.

'Aren't you fucking *ashamed* of yourselves? The misery and . . . and . . . *worry* and all sorts of *shit* I have gone through tonight, it's all been down to you. Kidnapping an innocent child to get to me . . .'

Her tight, furious face froze as the realization made itself apparent.

'Hold on. Speed is of the . . .' She turned slowly to face them again. 'You're with *him.*'

The two soldiers tried not to betray the concern they felt at her words.

'What was his name . . . Bishop? The arsehole who came to see me today. Another bastard with an American accent. You're in this together, you fucking pair of shits! Is that what this is fucking about? *Really?*'

Again the two soldiers did their best to look impassive.

'You've kidnapped Andrew to get me to come to your fucking *insect lab* in Venezuela, is that it?' She

42

almost laughed at how ridiculous it sounded. 'Well, of all the fucking reasons. You are three disgusting fucking pieces of shit! How low can people get? And three of you! You'd better not have laid a finger on my son.'

'No, no, it was nothing like that. American military ID can be very persuasive to most people, kind of a consequence of everyone growing up on our movies. We explained to Andrew that you were doing something for us in a highly secret capacity and that he was to come with us to join you at our headquarters. Not that different from the truth, just a little, uh, alteration to the chronology.' Major Webster's voice trailed off at the end of his sentence.

'Look, arseholes, I want to see my son. Please just bring him in and I'll tell you whether I'll do what you want or not.'

'Um . . . Dr Trent, I'm afraid it's not that easy. We need you to come with us right now. You will see Andrew very soon but you have to come with us first – that's the deal. We are going straight to him, just via a small detour, you have my word.'

Laura looked at Webster, who could not bring himself to hold her gaze.

'And what? I'm supposed to trust you, am I? You pair of slimy shits who took my son, the only thing I have left in the world?'

Webster looked up and into her bright, green-grey eyes before offering a small nod. He was obviously hating every second of this.

Laura got up. 'OK. If I have to do this, I have to do this.' She shook her head in disgusted disapproval. 'Let me leave some food for my cat.'

'Um . . . better make it a lot,' said Webster.

6

As darkness closed in, Faisal Khayam and his goats were making their way up the foothills of the Hindu Kush. This far south, much of the sky was hidden by the jagged, red-brown mountains, bringing nightfall earlier and leaving the crags and hollows lurking in shadowy gloom.

Faisal looked up at the disappearing sun, then across to the west. At this time of day he would usually be on his way back to the thin blanket and thinner stew of home, but an afternoon dust storm and a lost goat meant he was now too far from his village to arrive before dark. Recapturing the animal was important; if he lost one more his father would force his cheap gold rings on to his thick, hairy fingers and wordlessly explain to his son just how valuable the family livestock was. And even if he had come back with the herd intact, there would always be another dozen lessons his father felt the need to teach him. By now, taking refuge in the hills had become a regular occurrence.

The tearing wind also reminded him that it was getting late. During the day it whipped a hot, dry gust across the rocks that left his face hard and sore, but at night it turned to a chill blast that shot through his patchwork of rags and gripped his bones like the fingers of a corpse.

Although every direction seemed to offer the same lifeless features, he knew what he was looking for: the jutting cliff that marked the western edge of the Fardeen Caves. They were spread throughout several square miles, but Faisal had used them often enough to know which ones were large enough to provide shelter for the goats.

Moving higher, he clambered over the last outcrop, driving the herd on as he went. The dull tinkling of their neck-bells combined with the clacking of clumsy hooves and occasional bleating to rise through the wind.

Looking ahead, Faisal could make out the black shadow of a cave at the lip of the ridge. Although it did not look familiar, the mouth was large enough to suggest that there would be room for the herd and, at this time of night, he could not afford to be choosy.

Faisal pushed through to the front so he could count the herd off as it walked by. Each additional number brought him closer to his thoughts of a night's rest amongst their warmth, and as the final few passed him he could also take satisfaction that none had been lost.

He gave the last one an encouraging slap and was surprised to find that it did not move on. Looking to the front of the group, he saw that the goats had stopped a few feet short of the cave entrance. He needed to know why, but there was not enough room to move to the front without sending one of them over the edge of the path, so he stood at the back, hoping to discover what could have disturbed them. He had fed them as best he could, they had just been watered, the unique stench that still hung dankly in the air confirmed they had managed to relieve themselves recently, so unless there was some kind of illness –

Suddenly the large male at the cave's mouth gave a long, drilling shriek that turned Faisal's spine to flickering rubber. Like a warning siren, it sent the others clattering back the way they had come, and Faisal was knocked to the ground as a hundred hooves scraped and dug into his legs and back.

The pain was bad enough, but now he was faced with the impossible task of chasing after his herd without the benefit of light. Aching and bloodied, he cursed loudly. He might find them all together the next morning, chewing on weeds in the shallow slopes below, but if he didn't . . . He thought immediately of his father's rings and the imprints they would leave on his legs and back. However he looked at it, the day was ending about as badly as it could for a twelve-year-old goat herder.

He used the faint, milky glow of moonlight to look down the slope and see if the goats had gathered somewhere close by. Although there was movement through the shadows, it was too quick and vague to be of any use. With little to see, Faisal wondered if he could pick up the sound of those dull bells, but all he could hear were firm gusts changing register as they collided with mountains and tunnelled their way through valleys. He picked up his bag and cursed again, then decided there was no point in trying to retrieve the herd now. He might as well get some sleep and continue the search at first light.

It was only approaching the rock-toothed dinginess of the cave that he realized how the herd made him feel safer, and how the absence of a friendly heartbeat, even that of one of his goats, made the night a little chillier. He pulled his *keffyeh* tighter around his neck and tried not to let the driving whoop of wind seem like anything more than a sweep of cold air.

But as each step into the emptiness gave him less to see and more to hear, the sound became impossible to ignore. The wind was growing louder, and it was changing from a smooth, hollow rush to something lower; a grumbling drone that almost growled.

Was it still just the wind? If not, what could it be? It didn't sound like a jackal or a lynx. This was constant, as if whatever was making it did not need to pause for breath.

It crossed Faisal's mind that he'd never been all the way inside this cave, so the sound could be some kind of running water, distorted by acoustics. If anything, that was more of a reason to continue. He was thirsty as well as tired, and the cool refreshment of a mountain spring would be just what he needed before settling down to sleep.

A little way in, the pitch of the growling changed and he was convinced that he was listening neither to wind nor water.

The sound had developed a higher tone and, more disturbingly, a rapid, chanting rhythm that swelled into every corner of the cave and sent a fear through Faisal that scraped his guts.

This feeling increased when the other sound slid its way into his ears: eggshells cracking and splitting beneath his bare feet. The breaking of the outer layer gave into a soft squelch as the insides released a light, sticky substance that felt like scrambled eggs.

With his full weight on the floor, the moisture oozed between his toes, rising up through the gaps and spreading across his thin bones. He stopped, paralysed, his left foot frozen in mid-step behind him. Instantly, he understood what the dampness suggested: something had died here recently.

The fear spread to his neck, stiffening it so he could not look down. These were not the corpses of birds or rodents, although they were about that size. They were too light, and he could not feel fur or feathers so much as something smoother.

He wanted to move, but the hypnotic sound submerged his senses. At last he inched his neck forwards to peer at his feet and could just make something out in the dim haze of moonlight. Whatever he was treading on, it was indeed smooth and rounded, with wide stripes of dark and light.

By now the noise was fierce and louder still, a purposeful hum that sent an insidious murmur through every part of him. It seemed almost to challenge Faisal to stop listening, to leave without finding out what it was.

Then, like a child's cry, the distant, howling bleat of a goat broke Faisal's concentration. It gave him the presence of mind to realize he had to get out.

But not soon enough.

He could only distinguish shadows struggling to become clear shapes in the darkness, so he could not tell how close or how many they were until it was too late. A blur of dark grey swirled towards him, combining with the noise to plunge him back into a trance of confusion. As the shapes reached him, the first thing he felt was the light *shh* of something brushing against his left cheek.

Then it landed. The weight was like a small bird on his back, but instead of two sharp claws digging into his skin, there were six. He tried to reach around to it but there was another pain, like a thin shard of glass sliding deep into his shoulderblade.

Then nothing.

He didn't feel his legs collapse beneath him, sending his knees to land hard on the floor of the cave. He didn't feel the wash of skittering breeze as more arrived to cover his face and body with their insistent wingbeat. And he didn't feel the mandibles digging their way into whatever meat they could find, taking firm hold and tearing wet chunks of flesh into their throats.

Although he couldn't feel, he could still see, and the sight that was to be his last was that of a dark triangle of wasp's eyes searching his own.

They peered, processed and guided until the rough, hard jaws beneath delved into the socket and pulled out the soft ball of moist tissue. Now there was just one eye remaining, but not for long: two of them fought over it until it was nothing but a churn of white-red mush, then they hurriedly passed whatever their mandibles could grasp back into the voracious gnashing of their mouths.

Faisal could feel and see no more. He was now but a corpse, moving in quick, shallow jerks as the wasps continued to pull the meat from his bones until bones were all he was.

7

Carl Webster couldn't remember the exact moment his military career had changed from the guns and tanks of his childhood dreams to kidnapping small boys and blackmailing their parents, but it made him feel nauseous and it never got any easier. This was the first kid since early '99, and he'd almost forgotten how it felt, but things were different then: more gung-ho and naïve, more whatever-it-takes-for-the-cause. This time, he and Carter had prayed that Bishop would not call, but when the number appeared on his mobile his stomach flooded with sickness and Plan B was set in motion.

Using the rear-view mirror, he looked at Laura, squashed up against the side window. She was staring at nothing, overcome by too many different thoughts to be able to concentrate on any one of them. They often reacted like this, and Major Webster could not honestly say it surprised him.

They had followed the usual stages of the procedure: Laura had informed anyone who knew about Andrew's disappearance that he was indeed alive and well and had come home late after visiting his dad's grave. He had miscalculated the fare home, which had meant walking several miles, getting lost on the way and of course he was incredibly sorry and thought that his mum had known that was what he was doing. The story had holes in it that could easily accommodate Major Webster's Land Rover but the people who heard it were tired and relieved and wouldn't think to ask questions until the next day. Laura also told them that she and Andrew would be taking a short break and that she would be back in touch soon. Again, not like her, but by the time her actions were questioned, she would not be available to provide any answers.

The roads they were driving on became smaller and scrappier until they were using all the Land Rover's torque and horsepower to negotiate a steep dirt track closely flanked by birch trees. Five minutes later, they came to a juddering stop. In the darkness, Laura could just make out a wide strip of tarmac that disappeared into the gloomy distance. There was a hut on one side of it with a corrugated iron roof, and it was here that Webster parked the car.

Laura looked out through the other windows for some clue as to what this place was and why they might have come here, but before she had a chance to speculate, a row of lights illuminated the centre of the tarmac and she heard the unmistakable sound of an approaching airplane.

At first she thought there must be a small airport nearby, but as the noise grew louder, finally pounding her ears with an overpowering scream, she realized it was meant for them. It touched down at the other end of the runway before taxiing in their direction.

It came to a halt just in front of the Land Rover, the

cargo ramp lowering a few feet from its front bumper. At the sound of metal on concrete Major Webster drove up the black steel incline and into the rear of the Spartan. The ramp started to rise before he had even applied the brakes, and they were manoeuvring towards the other end of the runway before he'd switched the engine off. Madison turned the plane around and within seconds they were speeding over the line of lights and back into the air.

As they gained altitude Laura followed the lead of Webster and Carter and got out of the car. The inside of the plane was like nothing she had seen before. It was off-white, with jutting beams of metal that stretched across the ceiling. Webbing and cargo jutted and curved in and out of dark recesses, and the far end was stacked with a dozen crates, leaving only a small gap between them for access to the cockpit. Behind the boxes the seats were set out in rows, like in a passenger plane. (The Spartan's original layout of a basic bench along each side had left the team exhausted and burning with cramp, so Webster had arranged for the interior to be refitted for a little extra comfort.)

To Laura's further unease, five of the ten seats were occupied by soldiers. Looking at them in the anonymity of their camouflage, she was trying hard but failing to think of a good situation that involved seven military personnel and an airplane. There was a seat on its own near the back that had a view of the dark nothing outside, so she slid into it and resumed her position, squashed up against the window.

None of the other soldiers acknowledged her, giving her no more than a second's glance as they turned to greet Carter and Webster. She was surprised to see that at least two of them were female, although it was hard to distinguish in the low fluorescent light, covered as they were with half-grapefruit headphones that made them all look alike. Andrew still infused her every thought, but against tough competition: the sensory and conceptual overload she had to process made her feel like she was underwater, straining to make her way to the surface.

An hour into the flight, Laura had no idea where they were. Even if she had paid attention since take-off, flying at night with nothing to help give her bearings meant she could be anywhere an hour's plane ride from Norfolk. Did that mean France, or Denmark? Ireland, or the Atlantic Ocean?

At two hours, she felt the engines winding down and the forward movement slowing. They seemed to be landing, so she looked out of the window for any clues to where they were and where they might be holding Andrew. She had imagined him in some US Airforce base in a desert somewhere, waiting for her in a cell, a plaintive expression on his smooth, soft face.

Only the immediate area was visible, and it was little different from the runway they had taken off from. A man on the ground attached a fuel pump to the side of the plane, they waited ten minutes, the man detached the pump and they were airborne again.

Shit. When was she going to see Andrew? Major

Webster took a glance back towards her. He caught her eye and tried an encouraging smile. The disdain in her face made him think he should try a bit harder, so he went to sit in the row in front of her.

In order to be heard by Laura but no one else, Webster had to half-yell behind his hand. 'I'm sorry to say this again, but you're going to have to trust us. We've got one more stop before we get to our destination, and I'll tell you now, Andrew is not there. We'd have sent you straight to Venezuela, but the need to find you coincided with one of our operations, so there was no one free to escort you to MEROS. That means you're going to see what we do first, which will take about an hour, then it's going to be another twelve hours back to where Andrew is. Is that OK? Is it better now you know?' Laura nodded quickly to get him to leave her alone then went back to staring out of the window.

8

Eight hours into the flight, Laura was aching all over. The seats were way below economy class, and she had to keep shifting around on the thin foam cushion to stop her buttocks going numb. One of the soldiers had brought her some revolting food: a weird plastic cake called a Twinkie and some tough sandwiches, curled up at the ends like rotten lino, which she was led to believe contained chicken salad but were actually filled with some kind of regurgitated beige mush. Everyone else happily guzzled Coke, a substance Laura could not stand, so she was given some mineral water that used to be cold and fizzy but now tasted like it had been siphoned from the bath of a flatulent pensioner.

For the second time the engines slowed and she felt the lurch in her stomach as they lost altitude. Was this just another refuelling? She could tell immediately it was not; the soldiers were far more active than on any of the other descents, unpacking and strapping on equipment and clothing ready for whatever was about to happen.

It was another dark landing on another remote runway. This time the terrain was featureless, with nothing but blank, flat land as far as the eye could see.

The soldiers collected their gear, dumped it together on the tarmac and got to work unloading the cargo.

Webster beckoned Laura over. 'We're just changing vehicles. The next destination is our last, but the terrain requires a helicopter.'

'Where are we?' asked Laura.

'Put this on.' He handed her a dark-green army jacket. 'The desert gets cold at night.'

They walked down the steps at the side of the plane and over to the landing pad where the Chinook CH-47 sat ready for take-off. Two of the soldiers were moving the larger crates with forklift trucks to speed up the transfer, while the others carried the rest of the equipment across by hand.

Within half an hour of landing, they had taken up their positions on the helicopter. Madison engaged the ignition and the quiet instantly turned to a deafening thunder as the blades of the chopper thwumped into life.

Laura had never been in a helicopter, so the journey, sweeping low across the plains then soaring up over the mountains, became yet another new and unwelcome assault on her senses. It was dark outside and she was disorientated as the Chinook lurched at sharp angles over jagged peaks then plunged through the turbulence of valleys.

After an hour, the slowing blades and loss of altitude finally signalled their arrival.

Major Webster barked a command through the intercom: 'Approaching target. Approaching target.

Prepare for full engagement and containment, T minus twenty minutes and counting.'

Laura peered out of the window and watched as the helicopter circled a small, flat plain in the foothills of a mountain range that faded into the moonlight behind it.

The soldiers, already indistinct, were now rendered anonymous by night-vision goggles that obscured most of their faces. Seven of them jumped on to the rocky terrain, taking various camouflaged trunks and boxes with them. Although it was alien to Laura, the soldiers moved without thought, as if this were as familiar as brushing their teeth. Not a second was wasted in mistakes or confusion as the equipment was unloaded and laid out in its proper place across the rocks and sand.

Webster waited until all the crates had been carried out before approaching Laura. 'I'm sorry about this,' he frowned above the whine of the slowing blades, 'but we need to make sure you are completely safe, so you're going to stick close by me and I'm not going to let you out of my sight. If you are in any way thinking of escaping, I should just tell you that we are in North-eastern Afghanistan, at least a hundred miles from civilization, and that's the kind of civilization that has little time for an English-speaking white woman.' He smiled, trying to puncture the blackmail of his last sentence.

'I know this has been tough on you, but I promise everything will become clear very soon.' He gave Laura a set of night-vision goggles, strapping his own over his forehead. 'Come on.'

They stepped down on to the plain in time to see the final preparations of the soldiers. Although Laura had no problem recognizing a gun, she had never seen anything like the weaponry being set up around her. One piece of equipment resembled a black metallic umbrella with blue lasers where the spokes would be; another consisted of a whirring disc at the end of a funnel which emitted a harsh, grinding drone whenever the trigger was pressed. Covering the entire area was a dense green fog that seeped from a device resembling a portable generator crossed with a Star Wars droid.

Once every crate had been opened and its contents removed, the froth of activity reduced to a simmer. One of the soldiers was making a few adjustments to some of the smaller devices, but the others had stopped moving with any real purpose and were now looking to Major Webster for further instructions. Seeing this, he strode towards them, his voice ringing out clear and sharp like a trumpet solo.

'OK, people, we have a tight homing of A-22s and A-24s. Recon has indicated that they have killed at least one human beyond the identified target, so be prepared for a greater degree of aggression. Mills and Garrett, take the light and ripple at point; Carter and Jacobs, gas; Van Arenn and Wainhouse, support and clean-up. One more thing: you may have noticed we are carrying a civilian. This is Dr Laura Trent. She is a genetic entomologist, the best in her field, and this is her introduction to what we do. Van Arenn, we're going to need a live, unharmed specimen.' He paused to see if there was any doubt in the eyes of his troops. Satisfied that they were prepared and confident, he gave a quick shout. 'All right. Let's go.'

Laura watched as two men she assumed to be Mills and Garrett primed their weapons and jogged steadily upwards, the foothills steepening into mountains beneath their feet. The other soldiers followed, masked head to foot in further protective clothing.

The mystery continued. Although Laura now knew her presence there had something to do with her expertise in insect genetics, her thoughts raced to think of what it was that connected the military with entomology. Were they wiping out crops to destroy supplies to terrorists? Had they introduced a host to breed out a beneficial species of parasite? Maybe they were tracking swarm patterns to see if they were registering any human interaction. Despite her situation, Laura couldn't help but feel a rush of excitement. She was being let in on a new and apparently secret aspect of her life's interest, and she wanted to know why.

Webster took her to the base of the path that led up to the caves then indicated that they should stop and wait at a small dip in the rocks where they would be sheltered from the wind. He offered Laura a coffee from his flask, which she declined with a wordless shake of her head.

Two hundred feet above them, the rest of the soldiers were approaching the target area. Mills looked ahead then changed focus to check the eye-mounted distance indicator that gave a more accurate idea of where the quarry lay. As they inched forward, Garrett stopped and raised her hand, halting the patrol. Amid the buffeting swoosh of the wind, they all listened for the familiar dense hum that signalled the beginning of the real work. They looked at each other, giving eerie, faceless nods to confirm what Garrett had heard.

Mills moved ahead until he came to the mouth of the cave. Checking the distance one more time, he looked back at Garrett and beckoned her forward. She removed a plastic casing from her belt and opened it to reveal a chrome ovoid with a black indentation at one end. Pressing this, she twisted the top 180 degrees, took one more look at Mills then placed it into a dark, round receptacle at the end of a brushed-steel tube. Sliding back a panel from the rear of the tube, she revealed a trigger, aimed for the centre of the cave and fired.

There was no loud bang, only a dense electronic drawl, as if the tiny beep of a digital watch had been stretched and amplified a thousand times. The ovoid shot into the depths of the cave like a cannonball, and the soldiers immediately retreated down the cave path, shut their eyes tight and turned away. The explosion of light that followed was so bright it illuminated Laura and Webster. The major barely acknowledged the eruption of bleaching white, but Laura jumped as if the mountain were about to collapse. Then the light disappeared as quickly as it had arrived, leaving the landscape unchanged.

The drone that rumbled from within the cave had been reduced to a few stuttering hums.

That was the signal for Mills to load his own weapon. It didn't have an official name, as it had arrived from the

Pentagon in the same way as all MEROS-specific technology: in an unmarked box with nothing but a serial number and a set of instructions. In spite of this, the soldiers needed to call them something and had christened this one the Ripple Gun. Cocking it like a 12-bore, Mills pointed it into the cave and held on tight as the flared end of its umbrella-like form whirred round hard and fast. His feet shook as if he were using a pneumatic drill, the revolutions turning faster and faster, grinding into his shoulder at one end, amplified by lasers at the other. It was sending out a wave of low-frequency vibrations that caused the ground to shudder like the tail of an earthquake. The effect was uncomfortable for humans, but for anything smaller it felt like time spent inside a washing machine; no permanent damage, but it would be a while before they knew which way was up.

The movement subsided, gradually dwindling to nothing. It always took the soldiers a minute to readjust to the return of calm, but when they were ready, Mills and Garrett stepped aside to let Carter and Jacobs take their places.

This was the point at which the mission became tricky. There were always targets that remained unaffected by the two preparatory measures, either buried in the depths of the nest or separated from the others on a search for food. Both Carter and Jacobs could see on their head-mounted motion sensors that several of them were indeed active, and it was their job to make sure these rogues posed no further threat.

Senses heightened, they stepped further into the

cave and drew identical weapons. Like all the small arms used by the team, these handguns resembled the equipment of conventional warfare but were advanced far beyond the use of something so crude as a bullet. Instead of a trigger beneath a barrel, the ammunition was dispatched by sensors attached to the user's synapses. When they came close to anything they were trying to immobilize, the gun pointed at exactly what they were looking at, assessed the distance and size of the target and fired at the point where it would cause most damage. It took some getting used to; with no need to aim or shoot, a strong instinct was removed from the process, but it was 100 per cent accurate and left no surplus ammunition at the scene.

The shells were like miniature canisters of enhanced CS gas, so they exploded on impact in a cloud of thin, freezing vapour that filled the air and clung to every surface. This was the main reason for the protective suits. Although not fatal to humans, the vapour could cause temporary paralysis, as it did for its intended targets.

Carter took the left side of the cave and Jacobs the right. Stepping forward as if on thin ice, Carter gently set down each tread of his sole with as little sound as possible. He wanted nothing to distract him or Jacobs from any more significant noises.

As they approached the nest, it became harder to keep the fear at bay. There had yet to be a mission in which all the wasps were incapacitated, so it was only a matter of time before –

The first one shot out of the corner to Carter's left.

He caught it immediately, sending a shell straight through its head.

The sharp report of his weapon made Jacobs turn and see if she should get involved. She needn't, but it meant she missed the one on her side: a clatter of frantic wings that headed straight towards her.

She moved her arm across to take a shot, but too late. It was in her face now, flapping across her mask, looking to get a grip on something.

Carter raised his weapon, but Jacobs' arms were too close to the wasp. A muffled *fuck* came from beneath her mask.

Several of them were using the distraction to rise up on Carter's side. Two headed towards him while another pair aimed for his back.

But Carter was fast and alert. He whipped his armed hand round in a wide arc that took all four of them out in less than a second.

Jacobs was still struggling, and Carter realized they didn't have time for this. It could penetrate her protective suit at any moment.

He waited for a safe opening . . .

waited . . .

waited . . .

crack!

The canister ripped the wasp in two. It fell to the ground in its still-twitching halves.

Jacobs calmed quickly enough to feel she had let Carter down. He could just make out a *sorry* from behind her mask.

No problem, he replied.

That seemed to be it. Looking around the cave for more movement, the sensors detected nothing, so Carter and Jacobs shut off their weapons, withdrew to a safe distance and allowed Van Arenn and Wainhouse to take their places.

Before clean-up could begin, Van Arenn had to secure that unharmed specimen for Dr Trent, a task that created twice as much danger as simply wiping them out. It meant they could not engage the pyroballistics until one of the little bastards had been captured, and all for that civilian who was drinking hot coffee down where it was nice and safe.

He had done it many times before: post-operational analysis had required specimen collection on every mission until three years ago, when they had managed to increase efficiency to a point where such precautions were no longer needed. In the early days, they had to see what changes, if any, had occurred to the wasps after deployment of the weapons. Now, they knew the alterations were not significant enough to require this measure.

As Wainhouse kept an eye on his motion sensor, Van Arenn removed a flat, square package from his backpack and inched forward. He would certainly come across them soon, but it was the element of surprise that made his job the riskiest. Mills and Garrett's light and ripple had a range that was almost perfect, but that margin of error was what could cost Van Arenn his life. Caves like this were the most dangerous, because no one could tell how far their depths snaked back, or whether overhangs and outcrops could shield the insects from the effects of the weapons. In addition, the CS gas could never be relied on completely, as it had to dovetail with any new genetic alterations. The rate of failure was low, but not quite low enough.

Van Arenn was among them now, advancing with as little disturbance as possible. He looked ahead to see the familiar signs: the nest structure, like a vast, crusty spread of brown honeycomb, and the first of them, lying on their backs, temporarily anaesthetized by the primary weapons.

His concentration was broken by the unusual feeling below his left boot. He looked down to see the bones of a human laid out in skeleton formation from the toes to the skull. Although Van Arenn had seen this sort of thing many times, the size of these bones made him stop a little longer. This one couldn't have been much more than a child. He had to stop himself thinking of the moment when the wasps had attacked, the fear of a boy who could do little as the skin and tissue was gripped then torn from his body, quickly, but inch by inch.

Ten yards in and the wasps were piled up to his knees, so he was wading more than walking. This was far enough. He looked down, trying to find a good-sized specimen with its wings spread out. They always looked better that way.

There was a perfect example on top of the heap,

just to his left. It had frozen in flight, each of its wings extended to the width of one of his large palms.

As he reached forward, he paused. At this stage, it was possible that one or two of them could be stuttering to life, but he couldn't tell for sure through the mask that covered his ears.

Ten seconds and I'm done, he thought, removing the tight plastic covering. It revealed a foot-square sheet of Perspex surrounded by metal tubing. Carefully, he slid it underneath the creature's thin, barbed legs until it lay in the centre of the sheet, then he moved the switch at the side, immediately transforming the flat Perspex into a transparent cube encasing the wasp.

Meanwhile, the sporadic sputter had become a more constant hum, but he didn't have time to look up. He moved the switch again to lock the structure in place then passed it back to Wainhouse.

'Cap—' Van Arenn could just about make out that Wainhouse had spoken, but didn't hear what he said. He was too distracted by what was in front of him.

They were moving, crawling and flitting amongst each other.

It was time to get out of there.

Van Arenn turned, catching his heel on a jutting stump of rock.

It only put his stride off by an inch, but that was the difference between finding a clear space to plant his foot and flattening a wasp's head with the edge of his toe.

The release of the dead wasp's alarm pheromone was instantaneous. The first effect was as if the volume control on the hum had been violently whipped clockwise, sending the noise to fill every forgotten corner of the cave.

Van Arenn knew instantly what he had done, as did the rest of the team. The mission had just gone from by-the-numbers to red alert.

This meant a recharging of the Ripple Gun. It would take about a minute for it to be ready again so that the soldiers could reassert their dominance. For that minute they were going to have to defend themselves with everything they had.

Van Arenn ran out to join the others, drawing his CS pistol as he went.

Carter and Jacobs had already reloaded and had been waiting for Van Arenn to clear the target area so they could get a shot in.

When he ducked beneath their guns, they emptied their clips at the rocks closest to their end of the nest, creating a CS barrier to bring about their primary aim: stop the wasps escaping.

They were too far away to see what was happening in the most populated area of the nest, so they just had to keep firing. This gave them the protection they needed, but it also created a cloud of gas. Visibility was reduced to just a few yards.

The soldiers watched, their weapons aimed at the swirling grey.

The hum of the wasps became the anonymous hum of the cloud.

How long would it take?

How many seconds had to tick by?

Each wisping curl made a shadow that drew the aim of a gun.

Each finger was poised with aching tension.

Pulses thudded with –

Three of them exploded from the vapour. Jacobs was quick, shooting the first through its left eye.

Carter got the next one. Jacobs' shot had been instinct but Carter's was very deliberate, sending a bullet into the jaws to leave a splatter of insides across the cave wall.

But the last one got through to Van Arenn. He had fumbled with his safety catch, leaving his weapon temporarily useless.

The wasp powered through to his suit, driving its mandibles into the arm. Carter could have shot it with ease, but he would also have blown Van Arenn's wrist in half.

'Shit!' Van Arenn gave a stifled yell from behind his mask. The gas was seeping into his suit.

He was coughing uncontrollably, waving his arm around in a desperate attempt to loosen the wasp. But it wasn't working: the mandibles had cut through to the flesh.

The pain seared through his arm like the blast of a blowtorch. The intensity of it grew as the jaws closed, taking in more of his muscle. He was going to pass out.

Carter got a grip on the wings, tore the wasp away and punched it into the cave wall. As he did so, Van Arenn collapsed in a heap of blood, mucus and violent coughs.

Carter and Jacobs dragged him away, the exposed flesh of his deep, jagged wound searing with the pain of the gas.

It was now time to finish the job. Wainhouse held on his back a large tank from which a metal-alloy hose wound its way around his waist like a silver anaconda. He stepped forward, pointed the hose at the walls, and pulled its trigger, emitting a spray that resembled a fine mist of molasses. Then he guided it across the wide span of nest, taking great care not to miss any potential hiding places.

This part of the job reminded Wainhouse of his previous life as a painter and decorator in Caspar, Wyoming. The main difference was that old ladies' parlours were not usually caked in the prone forms of giant wasps.

He enjoyed stepping on the paralysed bodies, feeling their exoskeletons crush as their internal organs became a sticky mess beneath his boots. It was like the satisfaction of squashing a dozen empty cigarette packets at once.

Soon he was in the depths. He could hear his breathing, mixed with the thick dripping of the spray and the occasional tennis-ball-landing-in-stew sound of a wasp falling from the wall with the extra weight of the liquid coating. He looked up to the ceiling and the giant sweep of nest that stretched away to the back of the cave. The mist was designed to break this down, leaving no discernible evidence.

Wainhouse continued to spray as he walked backwards

to the entrance of the cave. There, he bumped into Garrett, who had taken over from Van Arenn, and turned the hose off. The others were waiting just outside, relieved to see Wainhouse return. Operations never went wrong from this point. Once Garrett had given them the signal to clear the area, they knew the threat would soon be over. All that remained was for the fireballs to be deployed, and the mission would be finished.

Garrett did not enjoy replacing her friend under these circumstances, but she did relish the chance to use the pyroballistics.

She removed the smooth, black spheres from their casing. They had a fat weight to them, like huge ball bearings, and Garrett liked the idea that something that looked so perfect could cause so much destruction. She felt for the shallow indentations at either end and pressed them until she heard the solid spring release and felt the sphere rocking gently in her palm.

She held the first one up between thumb and forefinger as it vibrated with increasing force. This was accompanied by a hum that increased in pitch until – *Pyanggg* – the sphere leapt out of her grip and shot towards the back of the cave. The force of repelling electromagnets sent it to stop just short of the far wall, where it hovered a few feet off the ground, still shaking as if alive.

Another five followed, each powered by weaker levels of magnetism, so they didn't vibrate quite as hard. When they were released, they stopped closer and closer to where Garrett was standing, eventually forming a row of shuddering black globes that seemed impatient to fulfil their potential. All that remained was for Garrett to remove her mask and light a Lucky Strike.

She sucked deep and snapped shut her Zippo, taking one last look into the gloom. Then she flicked the cigarette into the cave and turned to join the others at a safe distance.

Not everyone on the team had seen what happened next before but they all knew the sound: a solid, metallic *clang* like a mallet striking a car door, followed by hundreds of tiny arrows firing into rock. The spheres were triggered by highly sensitive smoke detectors to give the team enough time to get away before the packed steel shards flew out and embedded themselves in whatever surface they found. Then it was just a short wait until they exploded, reacting with Wainhouse's spray to create the most efficient incendiary combination known to science.

A quick white flash lit up the entrance, and a second later everything in the cave was annihilated. Carter and Mills would go back in to check, but every time they had done so, the hiding place looked exactly as it would have done before the wasps arrived.

Outside, the team made its way back down the mountain to where Webster was standing with Laura. She had not spoken during the twenty minutes the others had been away. Each of Webster's offers of coffee and cigarettes had been refused, as she was intent on appearing anything other than friendly or dependent.

Webster saw that one of his team had been injured

and was now being helped down the mountain by two of the others. He removed his protective suit and ran towards them, fearing the worst. Van Arenn had taken his mask off and was leaning on Mills and Wainhouse as he blinked back a stream of hot tears.

'Van Arenn? You OK?'

Van Arenn had to hack through a series of coughs before he could speak. 'Just . . . some CS, sir. And this.' He pointed to the gash that was still pumping blood down his forearm and over his hand. 'Hurts like all hell.'

'Go back to the helicopter and get some first aid from Madison.' He turned to Carter. 'Any other problems?'

'Nothing out of the ordinary, sir.'

'You got the specimen?' Carter lifted it up to show Webster.

'Great.' He took the Perspex cube and headed back to where Laura was waiting further down the slope.

'Dr Trent. I apologize again for the inconvenience. I just hope you'll understand why we had to introduce you to the situation in this way.'

Laura raised her eyebrows as if to say *And?*

Webster held her look for a moment then brought the container up to her eyeline. It was too dark to see clearly what was inside it, so Laura's expression remained unimpressed. Little in her job surprised her any more, so whatever this was, it would hardly –

Carter broke open a fluorescent tube and Laura gasped.

It wasn't real. It couldn't be. She had seen the leg,

but could this creature really exist, be alive today, in spite of all the science she thought she knew? She wanted to say something, but the words stuck in her throat, which had become as dry as the desert she was standing in. She wanted to look at Webster for some kind of confirmation, but she couldn't take her eyes off it.

A wasp the size of a fist.

Although it didn't display the features of any one species, its overall resemblance to a common yellow-jacket meant that 'wasp' was the only way she could define it. She looked closer, and thought of the leg Bishop had shown her the day before. Again, she was amazed she could make out anatomical elements with her naked eye: the triangular configuration of the eyes; the petiole that divided the metasoma and the meso-soma and made clear the fascinating fragility of that tiny waist; and, most intriguing, the divisions along the antennae that were twitching into life.

Webster sensed her awe and slowly turned the cube round so she could get a look at the whole thing. It was so perfectly captured in mid-flight it looked as if Van Arenn had snatched it from the air. Bending down, Laura almost pressed her nose to the Perspex, admiring the perfection of the wasp's taut, brown legs.

Then, without warning, it burst into life, whipping its wings into a terrifying frenzy. Laura recoiled, and Webster made sure of his grip. He had expected this to happen, but nothing had prepared Laura for what she was now looking at. Sure, it was physically a wasp in every way, but somehow the size accentuated its more human characteristics. It was defiant, aggressive and very angry.

With a nod, Webster indicated that it was safe, so Laura cautiously returned to the side of the cube to continue her close-up assessment. It really did seem to direct its anger against her, ramming its head in her direction and making muted impact noises against the transparent barrier. That fascinated her, but not as much as the view from the underside of the cube: the wasp was deploying its stinger against the Perspex. Even though it could not embed itself, a thin, whiteish puddle of venom collected around its tarsal claws as it touched the bottom before flying into another rage.

'What is it?' Laura asked at last.

'Let's get back in the chopper,' said Webster.

9

Thousands of miles away in Colinas de Edad, the sun was slicing through the mist that enshrouded the tree-tops. Although it was now morning, none of the people working nearby was aware of it. Five hundred feet underground, the MEROS facility observed time like a Vegas casino. A few people were in the labs, some were asleep and others were enjoying the recreational facilities: a table-tennis table, a pool table and an extensive but well-used collection of DVDs. Two biologists and an experimental geneticist were sitting through the end of another showing of *Casablanca*, one of them about to go to work, the others to sleep.

MEROS had been built underground to keep its location a secret, but the people in charge soon realized there was another benefit: the lack of distinct days and nights encouraged a subconscious submissiveness in the inhabitants that made them easier to control. Not knowing something as fundamental as when night fell left them feeling dependent and cowed.

The interior walls helped to maintain the illusion of twenty-four-hour daytime. They were covered in bleached polycarbonide and permanently lit by white fluorescent strips that gave the rooms and corridors a harsh, oppressive glow. The sleeping quarters provided the only respite from the constant feeling that it was daytime and therefore some industrious behaviour was expected. There were no clocks, and with the lack of any nearby facilities for watch repair or battery replacement, hardly anyone had any idea what time it was. But that was of little consequence: in MEROS, the only timing of any significance was that of mission preparation, and on those occasions Bishop made sure everything happened during its appropriate fraction of a second.

The elevator was where any visit to the facility began. It opened on to a wide lobby area, whose featureless walls reminded all first-time visitors of a minimalist space station. The pristine white of those walls was interrupted only by the Perspex windows to the holding bay on the right of the elevator, and the retinal scanners beside each door, which could analyse anything from blood type to vitamin deficiencies in the time it took to blink.

At regular intervals the ceiling was dotted with innocent-looking transparent circles, each the size of a penny. These were the latest in video surveillance technology, designed to be mistaken for light fittings. They employed a complex arrangement of mirrors and fibre optics, providing video and audio surveillance of near-perfect accuracy, and covered 99.3 per cent of the facility.

The lobby area was the hub of MEROS and, as well as leading to the holding bay, gave access to the weapons storage, sleeping and eating areas, Bishop's office and the corridor to the labs.

Directly to the left of the elevator was the most sophisticated weapons-storage system in the western hemisphere. Based on the WS3, which was developed by the US army in the Cold War to hold nuclear weapons, the MEROS facility was designed to house anything from volatile explosives, such as HMTD or triacetone triperoxide, to custom-built guns and ammunition.

When it came to MEROS weapons, the rule was that it was better to have it and not need it, than need it and not have it. That's why there was also room for CS gas, cyclosarin, Desert Eagles, HM1018 High Explosive Air Bursting ammunition and all manner of prototypes, adaptations and hybrids which the Pentagon had created in conjunction with MIT.

Security was strictly monitored but, in practice, any of the soldiers could access the cache. They were unofficially encouraged to follow the procedural instructions for deployment and to familiarize themselves with the weaponry by practising with it up on the surface. This helped to pass the long periods of downtime – although many of the jungle's animals found the experience less beneficial.

The facility was highly automated, the air conditioning, heating, ventilation, water and electricity all maintained without the need for human involvement. This was most apparent in the scientists' sleeping quarters, which consisted of individual pods adapted from those of an Osakan capsule hotel. These self-contained bunks confined any mess and reduced the amount of building required. They were cramped and claustrophobic but they had not been built with comfort in mind.

Each pod contained a television, an air-conditioning unit and a control panel for the blind that covered the glass door. In the rest of the room was a row of lockers, a table and chairs and a small TV and video-games console that had taken a year of complaints to acquire. The soldiers' area was identical, except they had an X-Box instead of a Wii.

In between the two sleeping quarters was the rec room, which contained the pool and table tennis tables along with DVDs and a widescreen TV on which to watch them. It was also the scene of many heated arguments, as the soldiers preferred to watch blockbuster action movies, while the scientists argued for more cerebral choices, often involving subtitles and more intricate plotting.

The canteen served to produce microwaved, nutritionally balanced readymeals, delivered monthly and kept in a large freezer. Food was consumed in a square room containing four large plastic tables with benches on either side, long enough to ensure that anyone could eat separately if the mood took them. Favourite meals were eaten first, usually leaving a week of chili at the end of each month.

Steven Bishop's office was the only room furnished with a touch of humanity. Instead of stark white plastic, its surfaces were expensively shabby wood and leather, ostensibly to let visitors know that Bishop was both different and the boss. This effect was also achieved through the size of the room. It held a ten-person conference table at one end, for large meetings that never happened. The door from the corridor opened first to a vestibule, with the office door to the right and another to the left which led to Bishop's living room and decidedly non-capsule sleeping quarters.

Opposite the elevator in the lobby, the corridor scooped round into a warren of labs, the scene of any long-term experimentation. Although almost all the work in MEROS happened within a hundred feet of the elevator, there were many other laboratories, stretching back further than most of the soldiers and scientists were allowed to go.

The absence of the military personnel would normally leave the facility in a subdued state of low-level experimentation. However, a new resident had caused significant disruption to Bishop's routine: Andrew sat in a buffalo leather armchair across the desk from him, removing and replacing the cover of a memory stick. Although he was not aware of it, each click of the thin plastic seemed to twist a rusty screw further and further into the centre of Bishop's brain. It took thirty-five for him to snap.

'Will you please stop that?'

Andrew did as he was told. He was now so frightened and miserable he felt like a slight and tiny version of the boy he was when he left England.

The situation he found himself in became even more crushing when he remembered how excited he had been when the journey began. The moment those two big men approached him at the school gates, fixed him with those serious eyes and explained in deep American accents that they needed his cooperation, he felt important, like he was part of something real and grown-up.

That feeling multiplied when he climbed into the wide, dark car and it sped off through the rain. As he rolled through the gates of RAF Marham, he was fizzing with the thrill of it all: the blistering roar of the landing jets; passing through security with nothing more than a salute; and the sight of the fighter planes, toy versions of which he still played with.

But then he met the other man, the one who took him on a long, long flight to somewhere called Guantanamo Bay; the one who didn't let him pee until they left the plane; the one who forgot to explain how scary take-off and landing were, and didn't seem to notice when Andrew shook with fear at the screaming engines.

Bishop was a dismal child-minder: uncaring, uninterested and keen to keep his homeward journey unchanged despite the passenger he was looking after. Eight hours on a large, noisy plane slipped into another six on a smaller, even noisier one and, despite the sensation of the new experiences and places, thirteen of Andrew's fourteen hours of travelling had been as dull as stale bread.

And he wanted his mum. From the moment the two soldiers had left him in the driving rain with Bishop, trepidation had started to dissolve the excitement. But he had no one's hand to hold, no one's arm around him to pull him close and reassure him that, despite the way it looked, everything was going to be OK.

By the time the second plane skidded to a landing in the jungle, he was tired, lonely and fed up with so many strange new places. He didn't know when it was going to end, but that was all he wanted.

Bishop had hurried him into the small white building, down the elevator and into his quarters, where he had kept him out of sight since their arrival.

That was a day and a half ago.

Andrew's interest in Bishop's DVD collection had waned dramatically with the passing time. Sleep had been choppy hours snatched on a couch, and he was now leafing through old operations manuals and playing with the lid of a memory stick for want of something to do.

'Mr Bishop?' he asked softly.

Bishop grimaced at the inconvenience of having his work interrupted yet again. 'What?'

'When am I going to see my mum?'

Bishop looked up from the report he was writing. 'Huh? Very, very soon, I promise. Just hang on a little longer. Oh, what? Oh, don't cry! Don't cry, Andrew! For heaven's sake.'

He couldn't help it. Bishop had given him exactly the same answer on both planes, and several times since. Andrew had now stopped believing it.

Bishop had no idea how to deal with this situation;

he had thought it was going to be easy. Keep the kid shut away while he finished the admin reports, then wait for the team to bring his mom back from operations. If a demographic as dim as the world's au pairs could manage it, then it should hardly prove beyond the ability of a man who finished twelfth in his class at MIT.

But of course it did. Caring for a ten-year-old who had been parted from his mother was as complex as separating spiders' webs in the dark, and Bishop's feeble efforts were hardly making the best of things. And now the boy was crying, so he had to do something more than simply ignore him. It was time to make a phone call.

'Taj? Patch me into Hawk One ASAP.' As he waited, he did his best to pretend there was no small boy sobbing in his office.

'Hawk One, this is Bishop, state your ETA please . . . OK, thank you.' He replaced the receiver.

'Andrew, Andrew, hey, hey, hey . . . your mom is going to be here in exactly one hour. How's that?'

Andrew wiped his nose on his blue school jumper.

'Thank you, Mr Bishop.'

After a pause, he returned to fiddling with the memory stick, and Bishop prayed for that hour to pass at speed.

10

The Spartan was losing altitude again. The soldiers looked out at the trees below and started to put away their magazines and iPods. Laura's pulse quickened. She checked the view in every direction through the small window next to her, trying to take in as much of the surrounding area as possible. But even when they had descended beyond the clouds all she could see was jungle: dense, spinach-green treetops interrupted by patches of mist that clung to the broad leaves like wisps of white cat fur. It could certainly be Venezuela. It didn't matter. Just as long as Andrew was down there somewhere.

The wheels crawled to a stop at the edge of the tarmac. This was the cue for the soldiers to jump out of the side of the plane and fan out across the grass, stretching and groaning their way back to life. Despite her desperation to see Andrew, Laura was last to disembark, her movement to the exit blocked by soldiers who considered their comfort more important than anything the civilian could want.

The sun screaming into her face, the first thing Laura noticed was the heat. It was stifling, thick and close, something she had not experienced since an expedition to gather red-ant samples in Ecuador.

Shielding her eyes, she looked for Webster, who was by the pilot's door making his mandatory check of the flight log. Seeing her, he hurried through to the end of the list and returned it to Madison.

'Sorry about that. Andrew's just in here,' he said, ushering Laura towards the unassuming white building fifty yards away at the edge of the grass.

As they approached, the door opened, and there stood Andrew, looking around for any sign of his mum. Laura had thought about him so intensely over the last day that the sight of him released a thousand emotions at once.

'Andrew!' she called.

At first his view of her was blocked by the soldiers, but then he spotted her sprinting legs and started running himself.

When they reached each other, they hugged so hard it was all Laura could do to keep her balance.

'Thank God you're all right,' she whispered.

Andrew held her tight for a long time. When he finally broke off the hug he still gripped her hand.

'They didn't hurt you, did they?'

'I'm fine.'

'Good,' she said, putting her arm around his shoulders.

'Where have you been? They said you were helping out with some insect stuff, but they wouldn't tell me anything else.'

'I'll explain everything later,' she said, in a way that suggested concern.

'OK,' Andrew replied, a brief pause indicating that he understood.

He looked up at her, squinting at the sunshine. 'I missed you.'

'I missed you too.' She gave his hand a squeeze.

A figure dressed in the improbable formality of a slightly oversized white shirt and black cotton trousers had followed Andrew out of the building. He now stood a few feet away, content to allow the moment of reconciliation but not keen to let it continue indefinitely. At a pause in their conversation he moved forward a little further to cast a shadow over Laura's eyeline, causing her to release Andrew's hand and look at that uncomfortable, forced smile again.

'Mr Bishop,' she said, as if she were dragging the nails from his fingers.

'Dr Trent,' he replied evenly. 'Welcome to MEROS.'

'Thank you, but we're not staying.'

Bishop nodded with a degree of contrition. 'I do apologize for the circumstances of your arrival. Truly. If there had been any other way . . .'

'Any other way?' The steam was rising off her words. She glanced down at Andrew, who returned her look with a quizzical one of his own.

'Dr Trent, I am genuinely sorry. On reflection, I did the wrong thing. Of course, the two of you can return on the next flight out of here, and we'll never bother you again.'

'That's *incredibly* generous of you.'

'But as that might take a little while, perhaps there's some way in which I can make it up to you.'

'Mr Bishop, if you know of anything that can compensate me and Andrew for what we've been through in the last two days I will be *phenomenally* surprised.'

'I understand. I'd feel the same in your position. OK, well, you can wait for the plane out here if you like; one of the soldiers will be happy to get you something to eat and drink. But I have to warn you that refuelling will take a while, and then the pilot has to rest after flying for so long. Could be a good few hours in 40 degree sunshine.'

Laura glowered at Bishop. She could already feel her light English skin prickling with the heat. The humidity made the air feel almost solid, and the discomfort invaded her pores. Looking at Andrew, she knew they wouldn't last long out here, and she couldn't face another three hours sitting on the plane just yet.

Reluctantly, she followed Bishop into the small white building. As she walked, she took Andrew's hand. He immediately took it back and stuffed it into his pocket, a pleasingly normal gesture.

Bishop led them through the double swing doors of brushed steel and past Taj, who was leaning over his security desk. He offered a small wave of greeting, which Andrew returned, as they moved on past two sets of cameras to another set of steel double doors. The security system required Bishop to type in a pass code, allowing the perfect metal rectangles to slide apart with the merest of hisses. The next set of doors was opened by a pass card, and the set after that by a fingerprint scanner. They now stood in front of the elevator. Bishop ushered Laura and Andrew inside. There were no numbers to press. Instead Bishop swiped his card, the doors closed and the lift plunged downwards as if nothing were slowing its fall. This movement was accompanied by an appropriate noise, like that of driving in a tiny car at the same great speed.

'This goes on for miles,' Andrew said to his mum in a half shout.

'497 feet to be exact,' added Bishop.

The elevator continued to drop for what felt like the time it would take to reach the centre of the earth. Bishop tried to break the frostiness with what he thought was a reassuring smile, first for Andrew, then for Laura. Neither effort managed its intended effect, more the exact opposite.

The elevator slowed then came to a halt with a grinding groan which always managed to unsettle new arrivals.

Strangely, it was brighter down here than it was on the surface. As they were led from the elevator, Laura and Andrew blinked hard and tried not to feel like a couple of stains on a hotel bedsheet. Bishop led them to his office, opening the door with his thumbprint.

'Now, Andrew, if you wouldn't mind making your-self busy with a movie, your mother and I have a few things to discuss in private.' Andrew sighed and walked through the door to Bishop's living room.

For the umpteenth time since he had arrived, he

rifled through a collection that ran from *Apocalypse Now* through to *Zoolander*. Laura took *Pulp Fiction* out of his hand, replaced it with *Close Encounters of the Third Kind* and followed Bishop into his office.

11

On the surface, Webster was supervising the unloading of the equipment. He knew the flight had been longer than usual, so he didn't mind the soldiers taking their time and stopping for frequent cigarette breaks.

'So, Major, who's the civilian?' asked Mills as he lit up a Dunhill.

'You know better than to ask me that.'

'She sounded like a Brit to me. You thinking you might want to butter her muffin, Mills?' Garrett said. Everyone laughed except Mills.

'Well, no offence to those of you who can get five hours of debate out of one episode of *American Idol*, but at least she might be able to manage a decent bit of conversation,' Mills said, upping the poshness of his English accent a notch.

'Reckon so,' said Garrett, extending her southern twang in return. 'Say, Mills, do Brits keep a stiff upper lip when they're giving blow-jobs?' More laughter.

'Look, Garrett, I know you might find this hard to believe, but if it wasn't for *Great* Britain, you'd still be picking shit out of your arses with twigs.'

'Yeah, and if it wasn't for us, your name would be Fritz and you'd be wearing lederhosen,' said Jacobs.

'Fuck off, Jacobs. Our part in the Second World War was considerably . . .'

'OK, everyone, calm it down. It's been a long few days. Let's just get this stuff humped and packed,' said Webster.

For a while the only sounds were the clattering of crates and the occasional grunt from the soldiers. Then Webster went down in the elevator, and the rest of them took his absence as their cue to drop whatever they were carrying and prop themselves up against it to take in some rays. Now that the boss wasn't around, they wondered if they could get anything out of his lieutenant.

'So, Carter, who's the chick?' asked Van Arenn.

Carter made a zip motion across his mouth and tipped his wide-brimmed hat over his eyes.

'Come on. You know we're going to find out sooner or later.'

'Let's make it later, Van Arenn. Besides, the major never tells me anything. I only know what he told all of us: Laura Trent, bug lady. Beyond that, I don't know, and until something happens that changes my routine, I don't much care.'

They lay in silence until Garrett spoke.

'Seems pretty obvious to me anyway. She's here to replace the dead man.'

I 2

Bishop's office was messier and homelier than Laura had expected. Of course, there were no windows, but she was surprised to see a dark, fraying Persian rug covering a wooden floor. She liked his large oak desk and the deep leather armchairs and wide rectangular meeting table that matched it perfectly. Three of the four walls were covered from top to bottom in varnished bookshelves, used more for the storage of disorganized piles of paper than the books they were designed for. The last wall was covered in a gloomy Rothko print that seemed perfectly suited to its environment.

Without being asked, she sat down and looked challengingly at the man who had organized the kidnapping of her son.

Bishop arranged himself thoughtfully in his chair, as if there was a degree of spontaneity to what he was about to say. He had been through this conversation, or a version of it, on enough occasions to know just the right words to use and how to deliver them but, with the kid involved, this one was going to be more delicate than most.

'Dr Trent,' he said eventually. 'First and foremost, I must reiterate my apology. This has all been very sudden, and I understand that you have barely had a chance to catch your breath. You have had to suffer the kind of anxieties that should not deliberately be placed on anyone's shoulders, and for that I apologize again. Hopefully, it will become clear why we had to act in such an unfortunate manner. For what it's worth, Andrew has been fine company. He's a great kid; you should be very proud.'

'Look, Mr Bishop –'

'Steven, please.'

'Look, take it as given that I understand how sorry you are, that you didn't really want to abduct my only child and send me on some military mission to God knows where to see giant wasps. If you want to tell me about what you do here, fine. Otherwise, I'll just go back upstairs and wait for the next flight home.'

'Sure, of course, *mea culpa*. This must be very perplexing for you. One minute you're researching aphid breeding patterns at the British Entomological Association, the next you're in Afghanistan wondering what we've done to the common wasp, and now you're here.' He realized he was waffling again and sped up.

'You are in the office of the Chief Operating Supervisor – me – of the MEROS facility at Colinas de Edad, approximately forty miles from Venezuela's Brazilian border.

'Brief history: we were set up in 1998 by a cooperation of NATO countries to research the possibilities of genetically altering insects for military purposes. Of course, you're aware that nearly all genetic entomological research has been for the purpose of improving agricultural conditions, providing insects that can wipe out pests, pests inclined to prey on each other, that kind of thing. Well, there came a point when people were getting pretty good at that, even back then, so some bright spark at the University of Idaho submits a paper on the application of transgenic yellowjackets in natural pesticides . . .'

'Yes. Dr Paul Rober. That's a seminal work. I studied it for my PhD.'

'Exactly. Well, I don't know if you noticed, but buried on page 124 was a small paragraph about isolating the part of the genome responsible for the greater aggression in wasps.' Laura nodded.

'At the same time, at the University of Wisconsin, another doctor, who I'm not at liberty to name, was making some quite considerable headway in the area of manipulating the scale of insects. Those papers may not have reached you, because it is the Pentagon's practice to keep a very close eye on certain research. It's obvious when you think about it: some guy in the University of Nowhere invents some great way of turning chicken skin into an intercontinental ballistic missile – they want to keep that all to themselves. As I've been told on many occasions, there are only so many advantages you can get in these troubled times, so it's a good idea to keep your eyes open.

'Anyway, the Pentagon gets hold of Rober's research a little too late to keep it hushed up, but the findings at UW are buried quicksmart because some brainiac saw the possibilities in putting these two breakthroughs together.

'Now, we know that arthropods are nature's most efficient group in attack, defence and survival. If they were anywhere near our size, we would have been wiped off the face of the earth years ago. Thankfully, they are not and we can at least keep them at bay as we go about our lives. However, and this is where MEROS comes in, if someone were able to train or develop them in a way which would suit our needs, then they could give that someone a decisive advantage in physical combat.' Bishop moved around his desk to turn on an overhead projector.

'As time went on, and not without a little difficulty, we found that we could indeed use insects for such purposes. I'll go into this in more detail in a moment, but early experiments were not quite as successful as we had hoped. Critical functions, such as accurate deployment, post-operational containment, secrecy, etcetera, etcetera . . . there were many headaches and teething troubles, but the powers that be were happy to pursue the idea as another potential strand of warfare. The Pentagon likes potential strands of warfare.'

'Mr Bishop, I am still trying to take this all in, but the idea of training insects to kill people . . . the *optimism* of it. If you've managed to do it, and I assume that's what I saw in Afghanistan, that is a triumph of positive thinking over the most obvious prediction of utter, utter impossibility. I'd congratulate you, but I have a feeling you're about to tell me some things I'm not going to be entirely happy with.'

'Perhaps. Going back to the teething troubles, you

might remember the proliferation of this type of news story ten or fifteen years back.' Bishop clicked a switch on the projector to show various newspaper headlines about killer-bee attacks in Texas and Central America. Laura did indeed remember them; she had read the stories with avid interest. These particular ones tended to be of the gratuitous scaremongering type: low on facts, high on hysteria.

'Well, something of this sort did indeed happen, with the kind of regularity that almost shut this place down. We had things going pretty well – nothing like what you saw last night, but this was ten years ago, and we were pretty pleased with ourselves. The problem wasn't unleashing a swarm of the aggressive little bastards where and when they were required – until recently, it was clearing up the mess afterwards. As you might imagine, a thousand wasps are pretty difficult to keep track of, so in the early days their genetics were altered to ensure that they died within a few hours of their release – what we called the autocidal gene. It worked for a time, but then we realized we had failed to take into account their incredible evolutionary cycle. By the time we had altered wasp one thousand, wasp one was changing in a way that we just couldn't keep track of. The problem never became devastating, but we ended up with some cross-breeding between our wasps and those in the real world, diluting the danger and aggression of ours but increasing that of those on the outside. Minor casualties. The situation is now under control.' Laura looked incredulous enough for Bishop to stop talking and let her speak.

'Just so I've got this right: if you needed to kill someone in Mexico, you just unleashed a swarm of super-aggressive giant wasps on them? Did a gun not occur to you?'

'The wasps are rarely deployed on single targets. As you can imagine, a swarm of wasps is far more practically unleashed on a larger number. About fifteen to thirty victims is optimal, so terrorist cells such as the one that was using the cave you just returned from would be ideal. Our trump card is the fact that no one believes it can be done. Fifteen members of a Colombian drug cartel die in some backwater courtesy of a freak wasp attack? No one's going to blame the US government, at least not credibly.'

'I thought you said it was NATO.'

'I'll come to that. Five years ago, new advances in genetic research could finally be incorporated into further development in a way we could control perfectly.' Laura had been paying very close attention to every syllable Bishop uttered, but at this point she recognized something from her own sphere of research.

'The growth,' she said quietly. 'That was when genetic growth alteration advanced far beyond what we had known before.'

'Exactly,' replied Bishop. 'I won't patronize you by explaining that insect growth is down to the shedding of the restrictive exoskeleton during moulting. When insects are adults they no longer moult and . . .'

'Yes, Mr Bishop. I do have a PhD in genetic entomology.'

Bishop continued: 'But we didn't release the information that led to the real breakthrough in growth: Dr Heath worked out how to isolate the Juvenile hormone, which extends growth by preventing maturation. This was combined with a stimulation of the moulting hormone ecdysone to allow the insects to shed and grow without limit. The results in the early days went way off the scale, but further research involving the eclosion hormone and bursicon has allowed us to gain a great deal of control over the extent of the effect.'

'But some papers have been published that have alluded to that knowledge.'

'We decided to allow a little of our research into the outside world, because it could help to account for any oversized insects that went missing from here. Of course, the funding and technology were not really available to institutions such as the one you work at, so the chances of you actually breeding the kind of creatures we produce here would be minimal. But at least there would be less of a . . . *freakout* if one of them were found.

'The missions are now completed with far greater efficiency and there's almost no danger of our creations reaching anyone we don't want them to. They are all fitted with nanoscopic tracking devices as well as a propensity to nest that supersedes even their aggression, keeping them contained somewhere close to the area of original release.' Another slide showed this. The sight of a well-built marine surrounded by the vast, sugar-brown nest brought home the scale of what

Bishop was describing. 'The mission you have just returned from was clean-up from a deployment that took out a Taliban warlord with links to Bin Laden. No one will ever hear of it.'

'And this is just a way of offing the enemies of the US?'

'In the early 2000s, most of the other NATO countries dropped out of the programme and suggested that it be shut down. Unpredictability was becoming something of an issue, and with the increasing tenacity of the media, it was a potential scandal too far. There was also the fact that, as you say, most of the victims tended to be those who were anti-US, but then we were putting most of the money and time in, so that was justifiable. Following the reduction in NATO support, the Pentagon agreed to cease all military work and adapt the facilities here for less harmful genetic research. It seemed a shame to put all this technology and expertise to waste.'

'But?'

'But . . . they didn't. They simply continued the programme for their exclusive use. Just one of many US military operations that remain a closely guarded secret. Anyway, MEROS has been operating faultlessly for several years now. Your team of escorts in Afghanistan do all the clearing up with absolute efficiency and, if anything, the programme has become a greater success since the changeover. Not one insect lost, all targets successfully dealt with and no fatalities on our end.'

Bishop paused. He knew what effect his next sentence would have on Laura, so he wanted to make sure it was delivered with the importance it deserved. 'Except one: our chief entomologist, David Heath.'

13

The post-mission wind-down process had begun, which meant sleep, and lots of it; more than usual this time, following the detour they had made to pick up that lady civilian. After an average mission they'd sleep like winter bears, occasionally rising to play dominoes or X-Box and eat some indeterminate slop, then heading back to the bunk for another few hours of shut-eye.

This time, however, two of the soldiers sat up talking.

'I just think the whole thing's bullshit, man.' Garrett was pissed off and tired to the point of inarticulacy.

'I hear you,' said Van Arenn, picking at the dressing on his arm.

They were talking now because they knew they wouldn't be overheard. It was difficult to find a space with any privacy in such a confined setting. Talking in the barracks was a risk, but there was nowhere else in the complex not covered by surveillance cameras. The surface would have worked, but Madison was up there doing maintenance on the Spartan, and he was the last person either of them wanted to see.

Garrett shook her head. 'I mean, really bullshit. I tell you, Van Arenn, I want out.'

Van Arenn looked up at Garrett then spoke quietly. 'You sure?'

'It's not just what happened to Roach and Martin. I didn't take this on because it was supposed to be a walk in the park, but it's either so fucking routine that I want to goddamn shoot myself, or it's all guns blazing. And there's a part of this that looks to me like they don't know what the fuck they're doing, like more bad shit's gonna go down.'

'You don't know that.'

'Look, Van Arenn, you and me, we're gung-ho. We'll do what we're asked to do, no questions and no hoping we don't get picked like those other pussies.' She looked to where Mills was sleeping, with his pillow between his knees. 'But they just brought in this British civilian cold. What the fuck's she going to know about this place? Until she beds in, while we've got to deal with the new wasps, the whole thing is even shakier than it was last week. And like I said, I've had it with being a walking can of Raid.'

'And you think they'll let you go?'

'That's what Webster said when he picked me up.'

Van Arenn frowned. 'Yeah, that's what he said to all of us.'

'Well then, I give even less of a shit. I'll break out if that's what it takes. They catch me, bust me back to the stockade, I do a couple years then I'm free. I can go see the Cowboys play.' Garrett smiled at the optimistic simplicity of her plan. Van Arenn smiled too, but at his friend's naivety.

'You really think that's how it'll work out?'

'I don't know. What I do know is I'm not staying here till I'm drawing my pension, so if they're going to fuck me, better they get it over with.'

14

David Heath is dead?

Laura was stunned into a long silence as a rush of thoughts, feelings and memories were summoned from every corner of her mind.

'I'm sorry,' said Bishop. He picked up a remote-control unit and flipped it over in his palm.

Laura spoke in a small voice. 'What happened?'

'Well, I'd like to know that myself. He was working alone one night, trying, we *think*, to alter the current wasps for even greater strength and aggression. He was always talking about deploying fewer of them in order to minimize our exposure and increase the efficiency of the projects. As far as we can tell, he went too far.'

Laura considered this. It was just like Heath to behave in that way. She remembered a series of experiments he had tried in the mid-nineties where he attempted to replace the venom of an everyday yellow-jacket with the deadly poison of a huntsman spider. On each attempt the wasp died instantly, but that didn't stop him getting through 175 before giving up.

Bishop stopped fiddling with the remote and spoke tentatively. 'In the . . . uh . . . interests of clarifying the circumstances as much as possible, and to get your . . .

um . . . read on the wasps and their behaviour, I thought it might be best to show you the . . . CCTV footage of Dr Heath's final moments.'

Laura did not know exactly what this would entail, so she let her curiosity overcome her unease and turned towards the TV.

Bishop pushed the on button and the small screen lit up the room.

From the back they could see a middle-aged man dressed in a dark jacket, who Laura immediately recognized as her former tutor. He had his feet up on a Formica desk and was scribbling something into a notebook. In front of him was a computer monitor and its hard drive and, to the left of it, crawling on the desk like a pet, was a wasp the size of a lunchbox.

Laura leaned in. 'Is that what it looks like?'

'If it looks like a giant wasp, then yes. As you can probably tell, these specimens are about twice as big as the wasps you were shown on the mission. We don't know quite where such advances came from, but they were typical of his genius. And he had an amazing relationship with his subjects. The closest thing I can compare it to is a zookeeper and a tiger. I suppose time and familiarity can give you a certain sense of ease, but in Heath's case there was the additional matter of his control. He believed he was responsible for creating their personalities. That proximity to God can do strange things to a man's confidence.'

Gradually, the camera pulled out to show a wider view of the laboratory. As far as Laura could see, it was virtually empty. There was another chair, on which was stacked a large pile of notepaper, three pens in a mug on the near side of the desk, an empty bookshelf and, to her open-mouthed amazement, the earthy sweep of an enormous wasps' nest covering a large part of the ceiling.

'Shit,' she breathed.

Bishop pointed to the screen. 'You see that empty bookcase? When Dr Heath moved to this lab, that was full of textbooks, research documents and other papers. He let the wasps break it all down so that he could study their nesting patterns.'

Laura was still taking in the scale of what she was seeing, but within a few seconds, there was something different to focus on: at least a dozen of these massive wasps were crawling out of the dark holes in the nest and on to the ceiling above Heath.

If he had noticed this development or found it troubling, it was not apparent. He continued to concentrate on his notebook as if nothing out of the ordinary was happening.

Laura felt a cold dread spreading through her. She knew what the wasps were about to do, but she could not turn away. Their behaviour was horrific yet fascinating.

One dropped from the ceiling, and in a single movement gripped Heath's trapezius and sent its ovipositor into the space between his spine and his left shoulder-blade. It happened so quickly Heath hadn't even stopped writing as the poison washed into his blood.

Bishop spoke softly, attempting sensitivity and

empathy. 'I was the one who found him. To begin with, I thought he wasn't in the room, but it was very unusual for him not to be in his lab, so I took a closer look.'

Heath managed only to get to his feet before opening his mouth in an agonized scream that never arrived. He tried to steady himself on the back of the chair, but simply fell through it, landing on the floor to watch the swarm close on him.

'Initially what I saw was the nest, which I assumed was under his control in some way. Then I looked on the floor and noticed a bone, one of his ribs, I think.'

The first wasps had aimed for the exposed flesh: the face, hands and ankles. They changed from skin to blood, to muscle, to bone in a matter of seconds as the wasps churned through Heath like chainsaws.

'What was left of him was hidden behind one of the desks. We were only sure it was him because they hadn't managed to destroy his watch, a very distinctive Patek Philippe.'

Spatters of red flew up from the frantic grind of mandibles, then landed in small, viscous splashes to join the pool of blood collecting beneath the skeleton.

'I discovered that one of my best friends had been killed in the most terrible way. I imagine I felt as you do now.'

The footage cut to static as Bishop continued: 'However, despite the terrible loss of someone we all regarded with great affection, I have not had the luxury of being able to mourn him as I would wish. This facility is in constant motion, and it is my responsibility to ensure that even an event such as the one you have just seen causes as little disruption as possible. To that end, MEROS is now faced with some very serious problems, not least of which is that we are . . .'

'Without an entomologist,' said Laura numbly.

15

In the compression of this isolated underground complex there were fraught and incendiary aspects to the group dynamic. This was exacerbated by the fact that the personnel were divided down lines of deep and fundamental opposition: the soldiers represented the instinctive, physical side; low on intellect but possessed of a common sense learned from years in the field. The scientists, on the other hand, were intelligent, logical and considered; if they had a problem to solve, it would be done slowly and carefully, with thoughtful analysis of all the available facts. It was the heart versus the head, a battle that would never be resolved, played out daily. The soldiers cursed the scientists' foot-dragging attention to detail, while the scientists pitied the soldiers' impatience and their inability to find solutions that did not involve fists or a gun.

Each side looked down on the other, as they would have had they been the jocks and the nerds at school. The difference here was that each needed the others' help – but no one wanted to admit it, so they just continued to exist in dysfunction and attrition, leaving half of any potential friendships out of bounds in a place where you needed every warm shoulder you could get.

The other aspect of MEROS that made things tick

along like a dynamite truck on a road full of potholes was the impossibility of keeping a secret. Either through guesswork, someone overhearing or deliberately wanting to get under someone else's skin, anything of interest was soon known to everyone. With recent developments, something was in the air, and they couldn't help but tilt their noses upwards and have a good, long sniff.

George Estrada, head of genetic sequence programming, was sitting in the canteen in front of an abandoned plate of warm chili. He looked up at Lisa Keller, who was trying to pick the beans out of hers, not wanting to consume any of the glutinous meat.

'Yo, Lise . . . You seen Garrett lately?' asked George quietly. He was dark, squat and toad-like, with wide brown lips that looked as if they'd been spread across his face with a palette knife. At forty-one, he was one of the older scientists, with a Buddha paunch and balding crown to prove it.

'What do you mean?' Lisa said as she completed her pile of beans. She had arrived at MEROS a picture of blond, all-American super-health, but the lack of sunshine and exercise had left her the colour of putty and her toned body slackened like overstretched elastic. The hair was still fair, but with weeds of grey hiding within the gold. Before George had a chance to answer, they both said hello to Mike Irwin, Lisa's research assistant. He was on his way back to their table with his own plate of chili.

A frown dragged down Mike's face as he caught the

musty odour of stale meat. He dropped his plate loudly on to the metal table and spoke as he ate.

'Hey, either of you seen Garrett? She hasn't been that pissed since Madison hid her *Playboy*.' Still in his early twenties, he had piercings in his left nostril, right eyebrow and both ears. His dyed-black hair was spiked upwards, elongating still further his whippet body.

George smiled. 'Yeah. It's not just her. All the grunts are buzzing, and it's been going on since before they went on mission.'

Lisa shrugged. 'I've been pulling double days on prep, so I've barely seen them. They're crabby? How can you tell?'

'You know that pissed-off sneer they give us because they got concrete where their IQs should be? Well, it's sneerier. They're stomping around louder and talking in corners more and giving shittier looks when you catch them doing it,' said George.

'And your theory?' Lisa asked Mike.

Mike wiped his mouth with a paper napkin and sat back in his chair. 'It's obvious. Someone died.'

George and Lisa looked at Mike in such a way that suggested elaboration was now essential.

'There's only so many things that can happen around here that will rile those guys: the food's already shit; the work is shit – but, again, same old same old; it's not love problems because they're *all* sour, so unless they had a big orgy that went wrong, that theory is out. Which leaves us with death, backed up by this: when did you last see Roach?'

George furrowed his brow. 'Roach . . . yeah, I haven't seen Martin in a while, but Roach too. When did you last see either of them? They didn't go out on mission, and that's *really* strange.' His slight Mexican brogue elongated *really* into a few seconds of wonder that hung in the dry air waiting for a response.

Lisa broke the silence in an urgent whisper. 'Come on, that's not enough. They could be on manoeuvres . . . or something.'

'Manoeuvres?' said Mike. 'You think they go on manoeuvres? Unless they've got a bunch of bugs to clear up, they just man the surveillance room and dick around, maybe pump some iron if they're feeling constructive. You seen Roach and Martin doing that lately? If not, they've disappeared, and knowing how hard recruitment to this place is, Bishop and Webster didn't just can them. They had no choice but to let them go.' He paused to lean in for effect. 'In a fuckin' coffin.'

16

'Indeed, but if that were the only problem, we could continue as we are with little difficulty.' Bishop frowned and leaned forward on to his desk.

'The only record of David's progress is in note-books such as the one you saw him writing in. For ten years that hasn't been a problem, but now his latest findings are in the room with the wasps, and without them we're going in blind. Are they susceptible to cold, or immune to it? Are they going to die in two days' time, or can they sustain themselves indefinitely? Is their poison the same as usual, or something more advanced? The answer to any question that might be of importance is in that notebook.'

With a hint of a smile, Laura looked off into the middle distance. There was something karmic about the quandary they were in. Years of messing with the ances-tors of these creatures had created a generation ready and able to take revenge. The humans had all the control, the equipment and the science, and yet in just ten years the wasps had gained the upper hand. Laura couldn't help doing what she did every day at work: admire them.

'Do they differ from your usual wasps in any other ways?' she asked.

'Good question. One thing we avoid here is the nest

dynamic: queens, workers, etcetera. Removing that characteristic helps to keep them focused on their task. But when I went past the lab a couple of days ago, one of them behaved like it was . . . *in charge*. When it saw me, it immediately flew at the lab window, and the others quickly followed. Then, when it lost interest and fell back, the others did the same. We may have some unusual group-behaviour characteristics developing.'

'You used the word "it". Have you managed to breed the gender out of the subjects, or did you forget to use the word "she"?'

'They are all female, of course, otherwise they'd have no ovipositors with which to sting.'

'*Of course.*'

'But we tend to refer to them as "it" down here, because they strike us as objects of manufacture rather than natural living creatures.'

'That could be your first mistake, Mr Bishop. It sounds like these subjects have plenty of personality. You might want to remember that when you're trying to predict their behaviour.'

'Point taken. Thank you, Dr Trent. Anyway, to continue with the current facts : the first thing I did was call Major Webster and ask him to do what he could to contain the lab. He sent in two of our men – well, one male and one female – to retrieve the notebook and one of the wasps for study, and wipe out the rest. We didn't think it would be any more problematic than usual mission containment, but just to make sure we pumped in a good dose of insecticide.

'As it turned out, it was far from enough, and when the soldiers went in the wasps just . . . just *swarmed* on them as if the poison had had no effect.' Bishop paused, then looked away.

'So I locked them in.'

Laura let the horror show on her face.

'If the wasps had been able to gain access to the rest of the compound, who knows what would have happened? In these situations, containment is all. We watched as no more than fifteen wasps chewed the meat off those soldiers in less than a minute. It was like watching starving piranhas.

'The other soldiers were screaming to help their friends. Until I could get the door locked down it was touch and go whether they were going to break right in there and try to save them. They're a tight unit, and if they didn't hate me before that moment, they certainly did afterwards.

'It's not easy making those decisions, Dr Trent. Save lives by being an asshole, or place them in jeopardy by being the nice guy? No one considers the choice I had to make, just the consequences.'

'Tough job.'

Bishop gave a small shrug. 'I'm not telling you this to win your sympathy. I'm simply giving you an idea of the nightmarish time it's been for everybody. Understandably, some of the soldiers wanted my head on a plate, and Webster had to step in to make sure that didn't happen. Then they all had to fly on the mission you just observed. I guess that's it with grunts – they're used to their buddies dying in battle then having to carry on.

'But we are still left with the problem of what to do with the wasps, and the only knowledge we've gained is that they're incredibly dangerous and disturbingly intelligent. We could try all kinds of substances and infusions to attempt to kill them, but without the research notes it's damn near impossible to know for sure what, if anything, will work, so they've just . . . stayed there.'

'Doesn't that contain the problem? Let them starve.'

'We would, except we don't know how long they'll be able to hold out. Did David increase their ability to hibernate? It's certainly possible, and that makes things particularly difficult for us.'

'Why "particularly"?'

'Well . . . there's a way out, and we think they might know it. The heating duct is beginning to interest them. Normally, of course, none of our creations could hope to breach the casing, but the strength and intelligence of these wasps . . . well, we're concerned.'

'And you can't just seal it off?'

'It's a little more complicated than that. To seal it off, we have to shut it down, and that would put all the other experimental and holding labs at risk. Wasps are not keen on cold weather, as I'm sure you're aware. That's also the reason why we can't freeze that lab alone: the temperature at MEROS is set at a constant 21 degrees. That is the optimal temperature for humans and wasps to co-exist. The central computer will only allow the temperature to drop in an emergency, but that means freezing the entire facility. All ongoing experiments would be ruined, and there are many reasons why that would be less than ideal.'

'And if these wasps breach the ventilation casing?'

'Potentially, access to the rest of the complex and possibly the outside world, where they could attempt to procreate, and then . . . who knows?' There was a full pause while Laura and Bishop looked around the room, both trying to avoid asking the inevitable question.

Laura broke the silence. 'So how would I be able to help?'

Bishop pretended to think for a moment.

'We have to try *something*. You worked under Dr Heath for several years, so you must know how he thinks. At the very least, we'd like your read on the situation I've just explained. And if you could find a little more time, we'd also be keen to make use of your expertise through-out the complex, just to steady the ship a little before we find a more permanent replacement.'

The request Laura had turned down almost two days earlier now looked very different. She had already made the journey, and she might be placing these people at greater risk by refusing to help. She didn't want to let Bishop win, but the opportunity to find out more about these wasps was even more of an incentive now she'd seen them first-hand.

'OK. Whatever else happens, I want to leave with Andrew as soon as possible. But while I'm waiting to do that, I suppose I could help you out.'

'That is very kind of you. Above and beyond — particularly in light of the circumstances. And the moment we've arranged transport out of here, you and Andrew will be on it and heading home. I can't thank you enough, Dr Trent. This will mean an enormous amount to everyone here.' Bishop was beaming like a reprieved murderer.

Laura was businesslike in return. 'Perhaps you ought to show me these wasps.'

PART TWO
The Thorax

17

Bishop ushered Laura out of his office in a 'ladies first' gesture of oleaginous insincerity.

'I'll just look in on Andrew,' she said. Hearing this, Andrew switched *Seven* back to *E.T.* and pretended to flick idly through a six-year-old copy of *GQ*.

'Mr Bishop is just going to take me on a quick tour of the labs. We'll be back in ten minutes or so.' Andrew barely looked up from the article on shopping at Neiman Marcus. He had no idea what Neiman Marcus was, but he thought that if he looked interested in it his mum wouldn't check back anytime soon and he'd be able to get another half-hour of *Seven* in before she returned.

Laura and Bishop walked through to the corridor opposite the elevator.

'Welcome to the Thorax,' said Bishop, striding ahead. He pointed back to where they had just come from. 'We call the administrative area the Head. Kind of our little entomological joke.' Laura's expression remained unchanged as Bishop continued. He gestured towards the room to the left of the elevator. On one side of it, behind a window of Perspex, a thin, intense-looking Japanese man was deep in concentration. He was taking readings from a series of gauges on the wall and comparing them to what was written on his clipboard. Laura didn't recognize any of the equipment arranged on the tables behind him. There were several rows of what looked like miniature satellite dishes connected by rows of red lasers wired up to a central computer.

The man was joined from the other side of the lab by his assistant, a woman whose raked-back hair and lack of make-up failed to disguise a soft prettiness that didn't belong here. She opened a drawer and carefully brought out a plastic case containing one of the giant wasps Laura had seen in the desert. The two scientists examined and discussed the insect before placing it into another drawer.

Laura could have stood there all day, watching these fascinating subjects and the systems that enabled their investigation, however, Bishop was in a hurry.

'This is the holding bay. On a job, there will be up to one thousand wasps, depending on the number of targets. Of course, they all require meticulous preparation, and that's down to those two: Dale Takeshi has been here five or six years, and Susan Myers is two years out of college.'

'What did you do to blackmail them?' asked Laura, still gazing into the lab.

Bishop smiled. 'You may be delighted to know that we don't use the same methods to entice everybody to MEROS. Some of them actually come based on a patriotic calling or a devotion to the advancement of their field of science.'

'But most are blackmailed.'

'Most are blackmailed, yes. Moving on. Takeshi and Susan ensure that the wasps are ready to be deployed and in a proper state for transport: warm enough, docile enough, potentially aggressive enough, etcetera, etcetera. As you can see, there are holding cases and tunnels in place so that no one here ever has to touch a wasp. The delicate balance of genetics and, for want of a better phrase, 'state of mind' before the wasps are used is critical to the success of the ten to fifteen missions we complete each year.'

'Out of interest, what happens if you have a mission in a very cold region?'

'Well, we haven't yet managed to develop wasps that can stay alive long enough. However, we think the nest David was experimenting on when he died may be able to withstand temperatures lower than anything we've generated before. That could have been of great use to us; all it's doing now is adding to the pain in the ass. Thankfully, nearly all our greatest enemies exist in warmer parts of the world. One of the reasons why the Pentagon loves us so much.'

'And you just let these wasps loose by opening a box?'

Bishop gave a small chuckle. 'No, Dr Trent, we do not *let them loose by opening a box*. Although that part of our operations need not concern you, we use a container made of a highly volatile compound of our own devising. One hour's exposure to oxygen, and the container disintegrates. Then the wasps are attracted to a pre-applied pheromone that will have been admin-istered by another branch of the US military, generally

125

under the impression that they are helping us to track the subject, rather than kill him, or her.'

'Fascinating,' said Laura. To Bishop's panicked dismay, she then opened the door to the holding bay and walked towards Susan and Takeshi.

'Uh, this is Laura Trent, one of the finest genetic entomologists working today,' said Bishop quickly. 'Dr Trent, Susan Myers and Dale Takeshi.' They shook hands.

Takeshi removed his glasses and smiled shyly. 'I am pleased to meet you, Dr Trent. Are you going to be working with Professor Heath?' Laura looked around at Bishop.

'We're just discussing the best way to arrange that,' Bishop muttered.

'The professor is a bit of a recluse, so a little more one-to-one contact with someone would be helpful, if only to clarify certain aspects of the new developments,' said Susan.

'I'll see what I can do.'

'It would probably be beneficial to the . . .'

'I'm sorry, Takeshi, but we're in kind of a hurry here,' said Bishop.

'No, it's OK. What were you going to say?' asked Laura.

'Uh, well, it would probably be beneficial to be kept apprised of the changes that are taking place. The more notice we have of any alterations, the more efficiently we can take them into account and incorporate them into our methodology.'

'And if you're able to take a look at the aggression

levels sometime soon, that would also help. The recent ones have been harder to control,' added Susan.

'Yes, of course.'

With that, Bishop gave Takeshi and Susan something approximating a smile and manoeuvred Laura towards the door.

As soon as they were out of sight of the lab window, Bishop spoke quietly and urgently close up to Laura's face. 'OK, before you say anything, no, they do not know about Professor Heath's unfortunate accident. As you heard from Takeshi, they never really see much of him . . .'

'Never really *saw* much of him.'

'Exactly. So we made the decision not to worry the others any more than is strictly necessary. The soldiers had to know about it, but if the scientists were aware of the situation with the new swarm then we would not have such an efficient workforce and that would be something of an inconvenience right in the middle of a mission. If we can bring the problem under control without any of them knowing the details of what went on, then so much the better.'

Laura looked at him as if she were a headmistress who had just been lied to by an earnest pupil who was hoping, rather than expecting, to get away with something.

'What?' asked Bishop, attempting to prolong the pretence of his innocence.

'Nothing. Just getting a clearer picture of the kind of ship you run here, Mr Bishop.'

'Look, Dr Trent, the staff at MEROS are doing a valuable job that has its unpleasant aspects. If I can make it slightly less unpleasant by not telling them about every little negative occurrence that happens here, then I think that's excusable.'

'Well, I can't argue with that.'

The next area looked more like the conventional labs Laura was accustomed to working in, except that the equipment was greatly advanced. Every surface was pure white, so much so that Laura had to ask how they maintained such a sterile environment.

'It's remarkably clean down here. You know, I always wondered what the James Bond villains did with the builders who made the secret hideouts. Is it the same thing you do with the cleaners?'

'Hardly. These labs are all self-cleaning. You may not have noticed but, in the elevator, you were being sterilized. The environment here is micro-organism-free through the use of convection currents. They circulate the air through gaps in the walls into a cavity of microscopic incinerators, which destroy 99.9 per cent of anything they come into contact with, so no cleaners to kill. It's all part of the way this facility was built: automation wherever possible. It reduces the need for staff, something which has obvious benefits.'

He turned to the next window. 'These are the experimental labs where David's work was taken on and developed with a little more rigour. The stations at the front are used to conduct research with individual subjects, while the wider area behind it creates simulations of field conditions.'

Bishop pointed to a tall, thin man who was better dressed than the others, his white lab coat covering a brown wool suit whose cream pinstripes made him appear even taller. His face had a jowly length to it, as if it had melted a little in the heat, and it was topped off by a shining dome, cropped close in the few places where it had yet to go bald. As he looked up and made eye contact with Laura, he smiled with a warmth that was at odds with his otherwise unforgiving demeanour.

'That's Harry Merchant. He's in charge of the day-to-day lab work. He oversees the other scientists' testing of Heath's advances to make sure they are applied correctly. He's managed to isolate many emotional and behavioural characteristics of wasps in such a way that we can use them almost like the ingredients of a cake. A very complicated cake, of course, but to Harry it's so much flour and butter. The labs go back a way. Usually there's something like fifty separate experiments at various stages of development helping us to improve the methods we use to deploy the wasps.'

'And why are there so few people working here? I have more in my lab at home.'

'Well, we can't exactly advertise in the wanted column. This is a very specialized job, and as much as we keep an eye on all the rising stars of genetic entomology, there is a small supply against an increasing demand. Over the years, we have designed operations here to take that into account. Many of the experiments can simply be set automatically and monitored as required.'

Laura was glad to move on. They returned to the start of the corridor and now faced the elevator in the wide lobby area. The rooms to their right looked very different to the labs: darker, yet friendlier and more accessible. Laura could see a locker room, with doors beyond it leading off to other areas that looked similarly basic.

'These are the living quarters, where all the personnel except for myself are based. The scientists' rooms are on the left, while Major Webster's team lives and trains on the other side.

'Just quickly, the major is one of those old pros who can do his job in the dark and the snow because sometimes he has to. He's reliability personified and has run the military part of this operation since day one. SAS, Navy Seals, Israeli Special Forces, he's done years with them all. We only got him because he was going through his second divorce, needed a lot of money, signed up for a year and stayed ever since. There's usually ten in the team; unfortunately, that's down to eight, for the reasons you already know about. Those are the first casualties Carl has had to deal with for a long time, and he doesn't want any more. The team is at your disposal though, if you need them.'

A couple of days ago, Laura could not have envisaged a situation where she would have to make use of a team of highly trained soldiers; now, she could think of many.

'OK, that's the basic tour over.' Bishop unclipped a walkie-talkie from his belt.

'Major Webster, can we have you plus whoever is available to escort us to Station A.' He turned to Laura. 'Best to be on the safe side.'

They waited for Webster, Bishop rocking on his heels and Laura trying to see what was going on in Harry Merchant's lab. The closest person to the window was Harry himself, and Laura watched as he injected a wasp with a tiny syringe. He withdrew the syringe, and let the wasp go, keeping an eye on its progress as it pottered unsteadily around the glass cube that enclosed it. Obviously this was not what Harry had been looking for, but Laura was taken aback to see him reach into one of the gloves that was attached to the near side of the cube and squash the insect to a mustard-yellow smear. As soon as he did that, a small swarm in an adjacent tank flew towards what was left of the dead wasp, and Harry noted their behaviour on a handheld computer. It was at that moment that Laura realized how MEROS research differed from her own: all her experiments were carried out in such a way that the potential harm to any living creature was kept to an absolute minimum. Here there was something more purposeful; more of a sweeping stride than a gentle amble to greater knowledge.

She was of course aware of the alarm pheromone that was released when a wasp was in danger or engaged in an attack, which drew all the other nearby wasps to its aid, but she would never have killed one wasp to provoke that reaction in others. Harry looked up to see Laura watching the commotion, and his smile became a look of uncomfortable embarrassment, as if he had been caught doing something he shouldn't.

The awkwardness was cut short by the arrival of Major Webster.

'I thought it would be useful to have the major around when we go into the surveillance room to check on the renegade nest,' said Bishop. 'He can tell you anything that he and his team have already tried and perhaps give you his opinion on whatever measures you might suggest.' He then beckoned to Harry Merchant to join them. 'And I think Harry's read would also be useful. He knows what we can do here, so between the four of us we should work out whatever solutions there might be.'

Harry removed his safety equipment and stood beside the others before Bishop introduced him to the newcomer.

'Harry Merchant, Laura Trent.' He shook her hand a little too hard.

'Dr Trent, of course, from the British Entomological Association. I found your paper on the effects of photoperiods and host quality on reproduction most enlightening.'

'Thank you,' said Laura, disarmed.

'I know it must all be a bit much at the moment and, without wanting to sound condescending, things are a little different around here, but we'll do our best to bring you up to speed.'

'Shall we?' said Bishop, gesturing towards a locked door just beyond the barracks. Webster's palm print opened it to reveal an extensive internal security room. There were three banks of monitors, each covering a different part of the complex. A thin black microphone stuck out in front of the three chairs, currently occupied by an exhausted Garrett, Van Arenn and Mills. On Bishop's instructions for backup, Webster had roused them from their bunks, to a chorus of bitter cursing. The soldiers shared security duties when they were not actively involved in clean-up, but they all hated spending more time than necessary down here, especially when they were just an hour into a day-long sleep. There was hardly anything that actually required their attention, but they were employed and paid, so they were often given tasks that veered very close to the definition of pointless. As ex-army grunts they were used to nine parts boredom against one of extreme excitement, but it didn't make the boring times any more welcome.

Another issue was their current attitude towards Bishop. The deaths of Roach and Martin were fresh in their minds, so when the man they held responsible walked into the room, they were not inclined to hide their disdain. Bishop caught their sour looks the moment he walked through the door.

'Uh, on second thoughts, perhaps this conversation need not concern your troops, Major Webster.' The three soldiers turned to their commanding officer.

'OK, you three: stand down, but be ready to return at 1300 hours.' A welcome reprieve for the soldiers, who immediately made their way back to collapse on to their bunks.

'Now let's take a look at Lab 23.' Webster was already in the process of tuning as many of the monitors as possible to transmit what was happening in the area around the lab. Screen by screen, an entire wall was given to increasingly comprehensive glimpses of the corridor, the door and the view from outside the lab. The final three screens showed the inside, and a clear view of the wasps. Laura remained deeply disturbed by the footage Bishop had shown her, but this time, there was no Dr Heath, so she found herself able to watch the insects with a degree of professional detachment. Although the wasps were indeed the size of bricks, with wings as big as snowshoes, they moved with astonishing speed, flitting and hovering with the agility of their smaller counterparts.

She was also reacting as a human being, particularly when she saw the images from the final camera. They revealed an arrangement of gnawed bones which lay on the floor in roughly the poses in which David Heath, Frank Roach and Hayley Martin must have died: arms trying to cover skulls, knees tucked up into ribs and jaws wide open in the form of the grotesque screams they tried to give before the paralysis seeped into their bloodstreams. It was all too easy to imagine their last moments; knowing that death was inevitable but still praying for the horror to end.

The light colour of the bones was offset by the dark cloud-shaped stain that lay beneath them. The blood was mottled with clots and gore, as well as the results of bowels and bladders loosened through fear. Laura noted that there were no clothes to be seen, then looked up to the deep, wide nest and realized where they had gone.

Back on the floor, each bone was pitted like something a dog had spent a few days chewing, with the shadows of hundreds of scrapings darkening the white. The determined savagery this suggested sent a hard shudder through Laura.

Suddenly one of the wasps flew up to the camera, knocking it sideways and scratching the lens with its jaws. Everyone instinctively jerked backwards before remembering there was no threat and returning to their positions. As it dragged its mandibles across the glass they could see right into its mouth. It was like a machine, grinding and swallowing even when there was no food.

'It's probably attracted to the whirring of the camera, but that will give you an idea of the kind of aggression we're dealing with,' said Webster.

'By any chance, is that the one you thought of as the leader, Mr Bishop?' asked Laura. Webster looked surprised, then interested in how Bishop was going to answer this. He had not heard this theory and was not happy to be left uninformed.

'Uh . . . impossible to say, really,' said Bishop, without taking his eyes off the main screen. 'They all look pretty much alike to me.' He then took a piece of paper and sketched a layout of the room for Laura.

'It can get a little abstract looking at the same view

from six different angles. The door is here on the left. In the opposite corner is the computer with the nest above it. The . . . um . . . bones are mainly in this central area and the other computers are on the right-hand side.'

The wasps were agitated. Laura thought it might be because of the cameras, but then she spotted something on the ground in the corner of one of the shots.

'Can you move the cameras?' she asked. Webster responded by pressing a button and pushing a joystick, giving a panned view of the whole room. This immediately attracted the wasps, which then attacked the lens and body, causing it to judder violently.

'That one.' Laura pointed to a dark shape in the corner of one of the monitors. 'Can you point it more over there and zoom in?' They had to wait for the wasps to tire of attacking the camera and move away to reveal its view.

'Is that . . . ?' began Harry.

'I think it must be,' confirmed Laura. Now they were all looking at two of the wasps, their abdomens partly obscured by the edge of a table, fighting over something thin, fibrous, black and yellow.

'Must be what?' snapped Bishop.

'They're cannibalizing,' said Laura, staring at the leg sections and wing fibres the wasps were passing back through their mandibles.

'Why would they do that?' Bishop asked.

'They need to eat,' said Harry quietly.

'I assume you know that several normal species of

wasp live off insects. I suppose these wasps count each other as such. Other insects, such as woodlice, will eat their own, but I've never known this to happen with wasps. I suppose that's because, in the open, wasps can always find something other than themselves to consume, no matter how hungry they get, but here . . . Well, like Mr Merchant said, they need to eat.'

As the meal neared its conclusion, a larger wasp landed between the two and seemed to scare them off with its greater aggression and status. With the outer parts of its jaw, it grabbed the scraps and took them back to the nest.

Laura frowned. 'There may be another reason why they are doing this. I can only guess at their behavioural make-up, and we wouldn't normally see this in wasps, but we may be watching survival of the fittest in action. It looks like they're honing the quality of the swarm by removing the weakest and feeding the strongest. If there is a leader, a queen if you will, then she'll be getting fed by the others.'

'Well, at least it's reducing their number,' remarked Bishop.

Harry turned to Laura to see if she was considering the same possibility he was. 'Not necessarily.' Bishop looked at Harry first with incomprehension, then with fear.

'You don't mean they're . . . breeding?' Harry looked at Laura again, then she turned to Bishop.

'Possibly,' she said.

'No, not possibly. Impossibly. I mean, first off they're

all female, but even if we could cause same-sex reproduction, the one absolute in all the experimentation
we have undertaken to this point, the one hard, fast,
unbreakable rule is that they must be unable to breed
with each other. Even David would not have been so
irresponsible as to create anything capable of self-
procreation.'

'You don't know that,' said Harry. 'We have no idea
what these wasps are capable of. We have no idea if
they are a product of David's intentions or something
that went wrong. Perhaps he tried to achieve one effect
but happened upon another. It's a regular occurrence
in my labs. Until we get hold of that book' – Harry
pointed to a notebook wedged between the computer
monitor and the hard drive – 'we will not be able to
deal with them effectively. And, by the way, it's only a
matter of time before the wasps realize that David's
notes would make excellent nesting material, then we're
really in trouble.'

'Good lord,' said Bishop, 'this situation can actually
get worse.'

'Much worse,' added Laura.

'OK, we need a plan, and we're not going to leave
this room until we've got one,' said Bishop. 'All suggestions welcome because, at this precise moment, we
have zip.'

'Well, it's obvious, isn't it?' said Laura. 'Shut off the
heat. Shut it off now. You have no choice.'

'I can't sanction the destruction of all the work in
this laboratory on the off-chance that it will bring this

situation to an end. For all we know these wasps have been mutated to deal with colder temperatures.'

'Mr Bishop. You. Have. No. Choice.' Laura could not believe further persuasion was required.

'There must be another way. We have an obligation to exhaust all other avenues before we try something so potentially disastrous. I don't need to remind anyone here that we are required to provide these wasps for military use. It will be bad enough telling the Pentagon we were unable to contain one isolated problem in the facility, but if we explain that our action was something other than a last resort . . .'

'Will it be worse than what they're going to do?' asked Harry as he watched a wasp tearing the head off one of its sisters before using its mandibles to chew up the meat and pass it back through its mouth.

'Mr Bishop,' said Laura, 'these wasps will only get more dangerous, and quickly by the looks of things. You will still have the research and knowledge. This place can start again.' Bishop flashed a look to Webster, who pretended not to notice.

'*If* the cold works.' He paused and thought. 'No, I am not prepared to allow the end of this project and facility to happen on that basis. How long have they been in there?'

'From surveillance records, around two weeks,' said Webster.

'OK, then another hour or two won't make much difference. What about poison?'

'We've tried the conventional combinations of

acetamprid, pymetrozine and novaluron, but without much effect. We could up the dose; fill the room with chemicals. It just means that, with the current ventilation system, it might be difficult to enter for maybe a day, or we'd have to go in with masks.'

Bishop was delighted that Webster was even entertaining the possibility of sending more of his squad in. He had thought such a suggestion would be met with steadfast refusal. For now, though, in the absence of any further ideas, they may as well try pumping the place with insecticide.

'OK, that's the default idea. Major Webster, until we get something better, you can assume that what you have just outlined will be our primary course.'

Webster went to the barracks to put Bishop's orders into action, and Harry continued to look at the nest while Bishop escorted Laura back to his office.

She tried not to let it show, but the last few minutes had concerned her a great deal.

'Mr Bishop, I'd like to get out of here.'

'Excuse me?'

'If it's all the same to you, I'd prefer to take Andrew and wait for the next flight on the surface.'

'Dr Trent, you can't leave us now. Please. We've barely begun to explore our options.'

'Yes, well, that's all fine, but I'd rather not be down here while you do the exploring.'

'You're not afraid, surely?'

'Well, not afraid exactly, but I just want to err on the side of caution.'

'Dr Trent, let me assure you that we will have a great deal of notice before anything threatens the area outside that one lab. And even if anything did happen, we have security measures that could stop a million of those wasps. This entire facility is fully functioning, most of the staff have no idea what is happening in that lab. That's how contained this situation is.' He could see her wavering.

'You're here because you have the ability to find the best solution to what we're facing. Without your expertise, we have a much smaller chance of reaching a satisfactory conclusion. Please, Dr Trent, if not for me, then for the others. Don't desert us now. Give it just a couple more hours.'

She didn't have enough information to counter him without seeming callous and selfish. And he could be right: perhaps there was little immediate danger. Could she really refuse to give a bit more help? Turn her back on all the people she had just met, when helping them could be so easy?

'Another hour, Mr Bishop. Another hour and we're gone.'

18

'How are you doing?' Laura asked Andrew gently. Despite the great things Andrew had heard about *Seven* from his classmates, he thought it got a bit wordy, so after an hour he switched to *Terminator 2*. His mum had let him watch it before, so he knew there would be no difficulties when she returned to find him sitting in front of it.

'OK. How long do you think we're going to be here?'

Laura crouched down beside Andrew and rubbed his shoulder. 'Not long.'

'Does that mean three days or five minutes?'

'A couple of hours.'

Andrew scrutinized his mum's expression.

'Riiiight, 'cos even if it's a couple of hours, I'm getting really bored.'

'Of course you are.' *I'm not.* 'Look, sweetie, you know why I'm here.'

'Yes, you're the insect professor. You've got some insect stuff to take care of. This is like a big research lab in the jungle. I've got to hang around here watching DVDs while you do it, then we get to go home.'

'Yes, sweetie, I'm the insect professor and I've got some insect stuff to take care of, then we'll go home.'

'Can I do anything except sit here and watch films?'

'I'll see.'

Bishop opened the door and noticed the discontent.

'Anything I can help with?' He gave a cursory smile to Andrew, who did not smile back.

'Actually, there is. I don't want to leave Andrew in here watching more movies. What are the alternatives?'

'Well, there's a pool table across in the living quarters, but otherwise I could get Major Webster to send one of his crew here to pick up Andrew on their way to the outside. Maybe they can play some football.'

'How about that, sweetie? Would you like to go outside?'

'I'd rather play pool.'

'I'd rather you went outside. If you could sort that out, Mr Bishop . . .'

'Sure. The soldiers will be glad to have you. I'll make sure of it.'

'How does that sound, sweetie? Do you want to go with the soldiers?'

'OK. Could you stop calling me sweetie, though?'

As she watched the elevator doors close on Andrew and Lieutenant Carter, Laura wished she were going with them. Even though she was separated from that nest by a hundred yards and ten security doors, it felt much closer than that, and far more dangerous. Whenever she closed her eyes, all she could see were those voracious mouths feeding on Heath like piglets on a sow.

'Dr Trent.' It was Harry Merchant. He had appeared

behind her in silence and now stood over her like a camel, all height and teeth and smell.

'Mr Merchant,' said Laura, after a moment to take him in.

'I'm sorry to bother you, but with things as they are, I wasn't sure we'd get a chance to discuss some quite pressing entomological matters which I think you should be made aware of.'

'Oh?'

'Yes. Perhaps if you'd follow me to the lab. There are some specimens there which will make it easier for me to clarify certain aspects of how we operate.'

Laura looked confused. 'Well, if you think it's important.'

'I do indeed,' replied Harry, ushering Laura in the direction of his lab.

This was Laura's first chance to get a close look at the everyday lab equipment of MEROS. As Bishop had promised, it was far in advance of what was available at the BEA. The readings on the thermoperiodic and photoperiodic chambers showed they could be calibrated to one thousandth of a degree, a level of precision Laura did not even know was possible. Even the basic insect equipment – the aspirators, magnifiers, sliding boards and pinning blocks – all looked as if they had been removed from their packaging that morning.

'Is that a thermal cycler?' she asked.

'One of them. That's just for short-term experiments. The proper ones are over there.' He pointed to three similar but much larger units encased in brushed steel. 'They allow us to expand the range of any genetic research, both in time and physical size.'

Laura smiled. 'They make my one look like it's held together with chewing gum and shoelaces.'

'They're actually last year's models, due for replacement. What's really getting us going down here are the molecular dynamics simulators and visualization software.' He showed Laura to a desk on the far side of the lab. 'We fund a team of forty postgrads at MIT all year round to come up with this stuff.'

Laura shook her head gently. 'The things I could do with these.'

'With respect, I think we may already be doing them, but I'd love to get your perspective on any ways we could squeeze any more out of them. Perhaps later. If you wouldn't mind, the specimens I'd like you to take a look at are back here.' Harry showed Laura to an electron microscope that stood in a corner at the rear of the lab.

Gesturing towards the eyepiece, Harry said, 'As you can see, Dr Trent, the contents of this artificial environment are very dysfunctional.' Laura peered through the lenses, only to discover an empty petri dish. Momentarily perplexed, she paused before realizing that Harry wasn't talking about insects.

'Er . . . yes. That certainly appears to be the case.'

'And recent developments are not as unusual as you may have been led to believe.'

'No?'

'No. Similar incidents have been characteristic of the environment since its inception.'

'Really? That is worrying.'

'Well, I don't mean to alarm you. It's just that you might be able to make sense of things more readily if you are apprised of the available facts. You see, Dr Trent, some of us here believe that the introduction of a newcomer to the nest may force certain issues.'

'Such as?'

'Well, to be blunt, the destruction of this particular environment may be the most beneficial development for the subjects.'

'I would agree with that, yet I can't help suspecting that such a development would be difficult to bring about.'

'Perhaps so, Dr Trent. I just thought that you might like to know what some of us are working towards.'

Laura moved away from the microscope and looked Harry in the eye.

'Thank you, Mr Merchant.'

'I'd really prefer it if you called me Harry. I find the prevalent use of surnames down here both reminds me of boarding school and serves to dehumanize us.'

'I understand, Harry. Maybe we should go and see what Mr Bishop is up to.'

19

Harry and Laura arrived at the surveillance room separately, to avoid arousing suspicion. As it turned out, they needn't have worried; Bishop was far more interested in what he could see on the monitors. Beside him, Webster was controlling proceedings by using a walkie-talkie to instruct Wainhouse, who was standing in the maintenance room adding insecticide to a run-off duct that led to the ventilation system.

'OK, Wainhouse, send it in slowly for the first thirty seconds – we want to see how they're going to react.' A crackly *Roger that* was heard, and everyone in the room leaned into the monitor that showed the wide view of the lab with the nest visible at the back.

Two of the wasps were buzzing idly around the ventilation shaft, as their smaller versions might do on discovering a discarded wrapper smeared with a residue of melted chocolate. Wainhouse pumped the poison through the duct, sending a cold fog pluming into the lab and curling in on itself as it spread into the corners.

It took only a few seconds for the wasps to notice that something unusual was happening. The first pair buzzed louder and faster, simultaneously assessing this intrusion and sounding the alarm. Several more appeared from the nest to confirm that they had heard.

A few seconds afterwards they had all retreated into the brown honeycomb, leaving the lab looking still and empty.

A minute passed, and no one thought to tell Wain-house to stop. They were all transfixed by the wasps' behaviour.

'What are they doing?' asked Bishop.

It was difficult to tell that there were any wasps in the lab at all. The only clues to their whereabouts were some distinctive yellow and black markings striped across the many entrances of the nest.

'They're being very clever,' replied Laura, as the answer dawned on her. 'They're blocking off the holes in the nest to stop the poison getting in. If the insecticide kills the ones on the outside, and of course we have no guarantee of that, they will have died protecting the others.'

'But they can't just stay there for ever,' said Bishop.

'Well, not for ever, but a good long time. There's no reason why they couldn't just shut down and hibernate,' said Laura, taking her eyes off the screen.

'Then we're back to square one,' said Bishop. 'And that one's still moving.' He pointed to a hole where he could see the poison was not having the desired effect, even on the wasps whose spiracles were exposed to it.

'Can you not see? Do you still need persuading to freeze them out?' said Laura.

'Yes, Dr Trent. I still need persuading. I have already explained why that is not currently a viable option, so I would appreciate it if we could have some more constructive suggestions.'

His words were met with a muted response. Laura, Webster and Harry realized that any other ideas could detract from the option of freezing. No one wanted that to happen, but they also knew Bishop was not going to drop the temperature until the situation became critical, and possibly too late. Was it better to think of a less good solution to try to improve things, or stay quiet and hope the unlikely happened and Bishop gave in? In the end, the decision was made for them, as no one had any good ideas anyway.

Bishop didn't like the silence; every second of it made his failure here seem more likely. Perhaps if he reduced his requirements he'd have more chance of getting the response he was looking for?

'Come on! What about the notebook? If we could get hold of that, then we would at least know what we're up against. Can we incapacitate them long enough for one of the soldiers to go in there and retrieve it?'

'We could if we reduced the heat to a level that made them sluggish and disorientated,' conceded Laura.

'That is, if they get sluggish and disorientated,' Harry added.

Bishop was keen to push past that thought before it became another anchor. 'OK. Good. I think we can do that by turning the emergency freeze on temporarily. Harry, can we contain the other experiments so that they can be protected for that time? I'm talking about, what would you say, Major, ten minutes altogether?'

Webster nodded. 'We could also use a liquid-nitrogen canister to put some extra cold into the area around the nest, but we'll need the temperature to be as low as possible in the room to give my guys the best chance.' He looked to Harry. 'Can we cool the place down by ten degrees without jeopardizing your experiments?'

Harry thought for a moment. 'I guess so. We can incubate the important ones in separate, heated areas. It's just that, at this stage, these subjects are very delicate. It's not ideal, and we might lose a few but, against the greater good, I'm sure we can make it back up with no significant losses.'

'Great! That's what I want to hear: solutions, not problems. Thank you,' said Bishop.

Harry was worried Bishop was getting a little too optimistic. 'OK, but I'm just going to say that we don't know exactly how long these wasps are going to take to respond to the lack of heat. Liquid nitrogen will give you the best chance, but their size alone means they are going to be much less vulnerable than even the A-22s we've been sending on the most recent missions.'

'Sure, sure. We'll see where we are when the temperature comes down and take a judgement call then. OK, everyone?' Of course, no one thought this was OK, but rather than say so, they shuffled out of the security room while Harry arranged for the heating to be turned off.

20

Webster had to decide which two members of his team would have to risk their lives entering the lab. Before, this would have been simple, as none of the current squad had experienced any fatalities since arriving at MEROS. They knew there was dangerous work to be done, but they also believed it was never going to get critical.

Until the deaths of Roach and Martin.

These first military casualties had caused the team to reappraise the situation they found themselves in. Some were fine with the reality that they were indeed putting their lives at risk; after all, they were soldiers, and it was not an alien concept . However, there were those who had taken this job because they were not fully at ease with the business end of the military. They had considered this a softer option, a well-paid mercenary job that would set them up for retirement.

Webster had been aware of this during recruitment, but his choice had been restricted by the fact that this was not the most attractive of postings. He hadn't been spoilt for choice: weak soldiers or strong ones who lacked discipline.

Carter had lost his place as a Navy Seal through his final reaction to a series of racist provocations from his immediate superior. Sergeant Elias Wilkie had remarked that they had to throw something useless over the side of a navy dinghy to keep it afloat and it was therefore a shame that Carter's 'nigger-fuck mother' was not present. Carter had responded to this by breaking his jaw in three places and bringing to a premature conclusion an otherwise unblemished service record.

He was not one for excuses and refused to blame anyone but himself for what had happened. His only real worry was how to keep sending his mother the monthly cheque she relied on when he was locked up in Fort Leavenworth. That was when Webster stepped in. His offer was far from Carter's hopes when he had joined the military but, like most of those in MEROS, he had little alternative but to accept.

The recruits were not always so accomplished. Peter Mills, for example, was getting old. His discharge from the British Marines could have been for any one of a variety of reasons, from gross insubordination to being drunk on duty. Following a series of incidents that occurred as a result of his poor behaviour, he joined MEROS because no one else wanted him.

It was his failure to secure the ice screws on manoeuvres in Bolivia's Cordillera Central that led to the paralysis of the three men following him up Chaupi Orco. He expressed some regret, but by insisting that the true blame lay in faulty equipment, his fellow soldiers lost any remaining respect they had for him and it was felt he should move swiftly on to a new regiment.

Six months into his posting in the northern forests

of East Timor, he dozed off during his lookout shift. Ten minutes later he was woken by a bullet whistling past his left ear and the swift approach of a dozen enemy soldiers. Despite outnumbering their ambushers five to one, his section spent the next three hours pinned down under heavy fire, waiting for ground support to arrive. Although that incident did not result in any fatalities, for the second time that year he was left in no doubt that his colleagues did not want him fighting alongside them.

Fortunately for Mills, Webster had put the word out amongst his NATO contacts that he was looking for trained soldiers with few ties but enough skills that they wouldn't need carrying, and he soon found himself on a plane to Venezuela, where he had remained, unenthusiastic and unpopular, ever since.

Webster needed a minimum team of six to cover the different jobs required by operations. He had been keen to build up his team beyond that if he could, just in case they lost one – or two in the case of Roach and Martin. This meant that compromises had to be made and, although he could have done with another Carter, Garrett or Van Arenn, sometimes he had to stoop to a Mills or, to a lesser extent, a Jacobs.

Mary Jacobs was a lieutenant junior grade in the US navy when she jumped before she was pushed. She was from a naval family, which is how she ended up being commissioned, despite her obvious lack of commitment and her addiction to alcohol. She was the product of an absentee mother and father, both of whom served in the navy: father as a rear admiral and mother a commander. Packed off to a private boarding school from the age of five, she had her first drink at nine, and by twelve she was regularly knocking back enough cider to black out. The schools knew what was happening, but the parents were only intermittently available to each other, let alone her, so Mom and Dad's interest in improving things never seemed genuine enough for her to take it seriously.

By the time she was in high school, she already had a reputation as an easy girl who liked a drink and would do most things to get one. Pat psychology would suggest this was a classic cry for attention, but that didn't change the fact that she was often on her back or knees, stinking of Jagermeister. When she became old enough to enlist, it was the only solution her parents could think of and, happily for them, it meant they still didn't have to take any real interest in their daughter. If the navy couldn't tame her, they certainly couldn't, so she'd either work out there or they'd give up on her, convinced they had done all they could.

As it turned out, she took to her new career better than anyone had expected. With her undeserved commission, she went from ensign to lieutenant in a couple of years of near-perfect service. Then things started heading in the wrong direction. Accidentally posted to the same ship as her mother, she slipped again into a craving for maternal attention. At first she went about it in the right way, upping even her previous standards of dedication, but when this failed to gain any extraordinary recognition from her mom, she returned to standing out for all the wrong reasons: drinking, sex and flouting the rules. Initially this was treated with leniency, because of her service record and her mother's intervention. However, after an incident involving three petty officers (third class) and two bottles of Jim Beam, she was dishonourably discharged into an unexpected meeting with Major Webster. He believed she had the potential to step up when the situation required it, but he didn't expect much more from her than that.

Without the ability to pick and choose from the prime of NATO's armed forces, Webster often looked hard for whatever he could find amongst the candidates on offer. In Mary Jacobs' case it was whatever had made her the best in her class for more than two years. He knew there was something within her he could tap into, develop and bring to the fore. In any case, Jacobs had stayed pretty dry since arriving (partly due to the lack of access to alcohol; partly because she had simply opted out of her parents' lives, just as they had opted out of hers), and she had taken to the more physical regime with dedication, if not zeal. Another good-enough addition.

In the early days, Webster had worked with a limited crew as the operation ironed out its difficulties. No one knew quite how many soldiers it would take to accomplish whatever the scientists required, so Webster kept things small and discreet. The first five men he took on were killed, either by the wasps or during the clean-up process, which forced them to test out firearms innovations in the field. Since then, he had thought of the recruitment situation as ongoing, with those who failed to make it being replaced by others as and when they became available. Fortunately, that element of his job had all but disappeared as the wasps and weaponry improved. He had lost nobody in almost a decade and much preferred it that way, which was one of the reasons the current situation was straining him. Recalling what happened in those early years was not something he or Bishop wanted to do.

When it came to the trickier jobs, like this one, the first place Webster looked was to Van Arenn and Garrett, and they never let him down.

'No problem,' grinned Garrett. 'We just take a couple of pyroballistics, a liquid-nitrogen grenade, and problem solved.'

'Not this time,' corrected Webster, just realizing they had never had to deal with an internal situation before. 'We're not in some Colombian jungle or Pakistani cave here. Our ability to deploy the usual weaponry is severely restricted. We have the option of a manually operated nitrogen canister along with a reduced temperature in the whole facility, but that's about it. Plus, we just stuffed a cloud of poison in there with no ventilation, so you've got to go in with masks.' He looked for a reaction. There was surprise, but no apparent lack of gusto.

'OK. I like a challenge,' shrugged Van Arenn, looking at Garrett to check she felt the same way. Bolstered by her friend's attitude, she nodded in agreement.

'Well, this is more than just a challenge. I know I don't have to remind you what happened to Roach and Martin, and I'm sure you know from the others that we haven't managed to overcome these particular subjects with any of the usual methods. They are stronger, smarter and more aggressive than anything else that's been created here, so I want you to understand what you're getting into. It's not going to be as simple as opening up enough to get the nitrogen in and then closing it before they realize and get pissed off. They will see you coming before you get within ten yards of the door, and the way it's wired means that it opens all the way or not at all. We're trying to get that sorted out, but assume you are going to face real danger. We will be sealing off the area behind you in case any escape, which will make your retreat more problematic. And remember, we don't know if the nitrogen will have the required effect.'

'Sure, Major,' replied Van Arenn, seriously enough to convince Webster that they were not just going to steam in all bravery blazing and expect to leave in one piece.

'We just want you to get that notebook and get the hell out. OK, be ready in one hour.' He dismissed them and headed back to the control room.

21

Up on the surface, Andrew was sitting on the grass with Carter. The soldier had suggested throwing a football around, but Andrew wasn't interested in the American variety of the sport. Ever since his dad had passed away he had found it hard getting on with grown-up men. One side of him idolized them, because the only ones he really had any experience of were actors and sportsmen on TV, but the other side of him couldn't help blaming his dad for leaving him and his mum. However, he was bright enough to realize that Carter was a good guy, so he wanted to take this opportunity to talk to him.

'Are you a real soldier, Lieutenant Carter?'

'Sure. I was in the US Marine Corps before this.'

'So can you kill a man with your bare hands?'

'Sure I can. You heard of the Vulcan death grip?'

Andrew shook his hand.

'No Vulcan death grip? Man, what do they teach you in the Queen's army?' He said the last three words in the accent Americans use when they think they're imitating Prince Charles.

'I think they can kill people without even touching them in the SAS.'

Carter looked impressed. 'Wow, I think I heard

about that. So what about you? You know any good moves?'

'Not really. I tried karate, but it got kind of boring, but I'm a cub scout, so I know lots of survival stuff.'

'Oh yeah? Like what?'

'Like tracking, first aid, orienteering . . . that kind of thing. Check out my knife.' Andrew always carried a Swiss Army knife that his dad had given him for his eighth birthday.

Carter opened the various tools and examined each one before replacing it. 'Pretty cool.'

'Do you have a knife?'

Carter pulled up his trouser leg to reveal a seven-inch blade with a leather handle strapped to his calf. He unclipped the fastener and slid it out to show Andrew.

'The Ka-Bar. It's the Marine's knife. Dates back to World War Two.'

'And you need that out here?'

'Well, you never know.'

'Really? What do you do?'

'Uh . . . I guess you could call it security.'

Andrew looked concerned. 'Is this place under threat from terrorists or something?'

Carter gave a small chuckle. 'No, nothing like that.'

'So why do you need soldiers for security?'

Carter hadn't expected the conversation to take this turn. He wasn't sure what he was allowed to tell the kid, but he didn't want to seem like he had something to hide.

'Technical stuff. We're trained to work in specialist situations like this one.'

'So there's a place in the middle of the jungle that's protected by soldiers, and it needs an insect expert?' Andrew wasn't trying to drill for clues – he just didn't understand.

'I . . . guess so.'

'But . . .'

'Are you sure you don't want to play a little ball?'

2 2

'Of course I don't expect you to jeopardize everything you've been working on for all this time, but you have to see that you could end up with no MEROS and nobody alive. Please just freeze it down and abandon it for a week.' Laura was standing on one side of the big oak desk while Bishop sat on the other.

'Look, Miss Trent, I appreciate the advice you have to offer but' – Bishop increased the volume and aggression of his voice considerably – 'do not try to tell me how to run this place. I think my experience in maintaining the success of it up to this point leaves me best qualified to decide whether we abandon it or not.'

'Why on earth did you drag me all the way here if you're not going to listen to a word I say?'

'Your area of expertise is entomology, more specifically, Dr Heath's particular take on that subject. *That* is why I dragged you all the way here, and *that* is why I'm only interested in what you have to say about the behaviour of these insects, not how that behaviour might affect the existence of this facility.'

'But these people's lives, the lives of people on the outside . . . How can you be so cavalier?'

'I can make an informed decision. The degree to

which it is cavalier or not is a matter of opinion, and ours happen not to coincide. Thank you.'

'OK, then, I want out. I'm going to wait upstairs with Andrew.'

She expected Bishop to react with a desperate display of pleading, but he didn't even look up.

'Really? You know your pilot is down here, sleeping off the flight in the barracks? Are you really going to pop upstairs and hope he makes it to the surface in one piece? And that's just a practical question. Dr Trent, you don't strike me as the type of person who would leave so many to die when you could do so much to prevent it. Particularly when the current danger is minimal.'

Laura was burning to call his bluff, to tell him he'd got her all wrong, as she turned on her heel towards the elevator. But if she didn't do it now, she knew she'd be down here until the danger became significant. They both knew he had her; in fact, this was the moment Laura realized he'd had her all along. All she could do now was try and retain some dignity as she folded.

'Mr Bishop, if the danger becomes anything other than minimal, I hope they get you first.'

23

After prepping their weapons, Van Arenn and Garrett killed the rest of the waiting time by parading themselves around the pool table like a couple of feisty gorillas. While the other soldiers came and went from the rec room, they shouted and flexed and sent the pool balls flying across the table, just to show everyone, including themselves, that they weren't afraid of what they were about to face.

An hour later, Webster took them to where the main corridor of labs turned into David Heath's personal lair. Neither of them had been down this far before, so they only recognized what they had seen on the surveillance screens.

As per Heath's instructions, the further his labs stretched from the main part of the complex, the darker they became. He understood why Bishop wanted a blanched sterility to the rest of the building, but the project was his baby too, and that meant he could dim the lights, if that was how he wanted to work. It made this part of the complex feel more organic, like a deepening cave.

Otherwise, there was also a gradual change in the state of the labs: as they darkened, they also became stuffed with abandoned detritus. It looked as if Heath had worked for a while in each one until it became too chaotic, then simply moved what he needed to the next room and continued there.

Webster had not been this far back in years, and he was amazed to see what Heath had created: the walls were covered in the elaborate marker-pen flourishes of his diagrams and calculations; scorch marks, upturned tables and deep scratches in the window suggested that progress was made in explosive sprints; and, because of the sterile environment, several giant wasp corpses lay perfectly preserved around the desks and floor, like freakish taxidermy.

At last, they reached the doors that led to the nest lab. These were air-locked and windowless, so when Webster keyed in the code to open them, the light hit their eyes like a white wall. Since the discovery of the bodies, Bishop had kept the lab fully lit, as they would have seen from the surveillance footage, but with so much else of interest, it had been easy to forget. Garrett and Van Arenn blinked as if they had just woken up next to the sun, but Webster decided to make use of the pause as one last chance to address his troops.

'It's not too late to say no, and I will understand if that is what you wish to do.' He looked serious, like he meant what he was saying, but all three of them knew that he was really just giving them one more opportunity to give lusty confirmation of their full commitment.

'Sir, just let me at those fuckin' bugs, sir,' said Van Arenn quietly but firmly. He cast a quick glance in

Garrett's direction, smiled and looked back at Webster. Garrett mirrored the smile.

'Sir, that goes double for me, sir!'

Webster pulled a piece of paper out of his flak jacket. 'This here is where we are now,' he said, pointing to one end of his rudimentary sketch. 'You are going to head down this corridor' – he looked up to compare the real thing with the drawing in his hand – 'then, after ten yards, you will find yourselves here, at the east entrance to the lab. When you get past this door, it will be shut behind you and disabled. Although I'm sure we can trust you not to run through the doors with one of them, these wasps are smart, and we have to minimize any risk to the rest of the facility. Then you will reach the lab door here. Unfortunately, the nest is right above the notebook, on the opposite side of the room, so you are going to have to put yourselves in a very risky position. I suggest that only one of you does so, as we hardly need you both to carry off the notebook.

'We have managed to gain some control of the entrance. Initially, assuming the wasps are not pressed up against the windows in the door trying to get a good look at you, it will be opened for a count of three. This will allow you to prime the nitrogen and throw it towards the nest corner of the room. The door will then close, so we can see how the wasps react to the cold. If they react favourably, that is, suffer paralysis or death, the door will be opened long enough for one of you to retrieve the notebook and get out of there. That's the clockwork plan. If anything goes wrong, if the wasps are playing possum or their recovery time is quicker than we supposed, then you must try to leave, but you will not be allowed out with a wasp. I want to make that clear one more time. You're heading into the unknown, and we can only protect you so far.'

Webster continued loud and crisp: 'Good luck. We'll be watching you.' With a snap to attention and a swift salute, a gesture that was immediately returned in kind, he left Van Arenn and Garrett and headed back to the surveillance room.

When he got there, he found Laura, Bishop and Harry staring at the monitors . They moved aside to let him sit at the control panel. He settled down and leaned into the microphone.

'All right, outer door opening.'

He flicked the switch that worked the lock, and the doors opened as smoothly as butterfly wings. The two soldiers moved through the doorway and down the final corridor in a crouch so that they were below the level of the lab's window. From this position, they would be able to see the wasps but, hopefully, their arrival would go unnoticed. The spectators looked at the adjacent monitor for a clearer view of the approach to the lab.

Now Garrett and Van Arenn could see the wasps, but there was no obvious reaction to their entrance. The soldiers took this as a signal that the plan would continue as agreed.

Van Arenn confirmed what the others could already see. 'No movement, Major,' he whispered into his mouthpiece.

'OK. Approach the door with extreme caution. When you are there, we will commence a ten-second countdown to the opening, during which time you should prime the liquid nitrogen.'

'Roger that, Major.'

They covered the last few feet to the door, and Van Arenn gave a thumbs-up to the security camera.

'OK, Van Arenn, stand easy. Garrett, fall back to the opposite wall. We don't want you both on point.' Garrett gave a surly look to the camera above her then reluctantly slid back across the corridor.

'Good. Van Arenn, I am about to commence countdown. OK, you've got ten . . . nine . . .'

Garrett twisted the top of the canister, timing its deployment to ten seconds.

'Eight . . . seven . . . six . . .'

She primed the adhesive casing which would allow it to attach itself to the wall just beneath the nest.

'Five . . . four . . . three . . .'

She passed it to Van Arenn. Turning around, he fixed his attention on the door and the fact that he was about to pass the point of no return.

'Two . . . one . . . go opening.'

As the gap between the doors widened so did the veins of those watching, sending adrenaline rushing through every part of them.

Van Arenn took aim and pitched the canister across the lab.

'Close! Close! Close!' he said in an urgent whisper.

The doors slid back together, and the two soldiers

moved towards the window to watch what effect the liquid nitrogen would have.

The canister landed on the wall about a foot below the nest. It could hardly have been more perfect. The wasps were disturbed first by the sound of it landing, then the hissing of the escaping nitrogen.

Several of them appeared from the nest and hovered by the wall, trying to make sense of the noise and the shocking blast of cold.

It took another few seconds for them to react with anger at this attempt to breach their home. As with the insecticide, they retreated into the nest to take refuge and protect each other, leaving dark and light stripes where the holes had been.

Four pairs of eyes stayed fixed on the monitor, barely blinking. Another two pairs watched the action live through the lab window. All breathing was momentarily suspended.

After a minute had passed, Garrett muttered that it wasn't working, that if anything was going to happen it would have done so by now. Van Arenn ignored her and continued to stare through the toughened Perspex.

A minute later, Van Arenn whispered again into his mouthpiece.

'We are holding still, copy?'

Without taking his eyes off the screen, Webster replied.

'Copy. Affirmative Van Arenn. Hold –'

A wasp fell from its hole and on to the desk below.

'Van Arenn, Garrett, did you see that? Over.'

'Copy, Major. The wasp fell. Do you want us to go in now or hold back?'

It was a tough question. They could see from its twitching legs and antennae that the wasp definitely wasn't dead. And was this a one-off, or was the same thing happening to the others in the nest? Would this be the optimum time to strike, or would the two soldiers leave themselves open to attack from other wasps deeper inside? If they continued to wait, would the fallen wasp regain consciousness?

That was the call of one person in the monitor room, one person who desperately wanted this plan to work so that the pressure to shut down the entire facility would disappear. Bishop felt eyes turning in his direction. The loss of further soldiers on his word would be disastrous. He needed more to go on.

Just as he was thinking this over, he received a lifeline: a second wasp dropped. It was closely followed by a third and a fourth.

'Send them in,' said Bishop, as if he had been expecting this outcome all along.

'Van Arenn, Garrett.'

'Copy, Major.'

'We are going to commence the notebook retrieval ASAP. One of you stays on this side of the door unless the situation becomes critical.'

'Roger that.'

'I will count down ten seconds to the opening of the door, roger?'

'Roger that,' replied Van Arenn, taking another look

through the window. The wasps were continuing to fall.

'OK. And don't forget your mask. In ten . . . nine . . .' Garrett moved further away from the door to give Van Arenn the room he needed to spring forward as fast as possible.

'. . . Eight . . . seven . . . six . . .'

The blood in Van Arenn's head pumped louder and louder until it was drowning out the countdown.

'Five . . . four . . . three.'

He pulled the mask down over his face and crouched ready, like a sprinter on the starting block.

'Two . . . one . . . and open!'

The doors parted with a soft electronic sucking noise, and within a second Van Arenn had cleared the entrance.

He ignored the giant wasps twitching on their backs and burst through to the other side of the room.

There was the book, wedged between the hard drive and the monitor of Heath's computer. He jostled them apart and snatched it into his hand. Five more seconds and it would be mission accomplished.

Turning his back to the door, he felt a large, soft weight fall on to the top of his mask, and fear blasted through him like the nitrogen that was pumping out above his head.

What was that? A wasp? Was it alive? Properly alive and moving in for the kill?

It rolled off him and on to the floor. He looked down to see its pencil-thick legs scrabbling over his feet.

Van Arenn paused to decide whether or not he had to defend himself.

As he did so, two more shapes of yellow and black crept into his peripheral vision.

It had only been a couple of seconds since he grabbed the book, but he knew now that he had to cover the twenty feet to the door at speed.

His muscles snapped into position to run like hell but in that moment another weight grazed down the back of his mask.

He would have continued his run, but whatever had fallen on him had only dropped as far as his shoulder. He felt six small scratches, like cat's claws, on his back and neck.

At the door he could see Garrett screaming at him to get out of there, and he knew what he had to do. But then he felt something else: a thin, hot spike slid under his right shoulderblade and two grinding mandibles tore into the back of his neck.

Garrett seemed to disappear into the distance. Her melting image throbbed in and out of focus, replaced by three furious wasps flying towards him and three more flying towards her.

Raising his arm to defend himself, he succeeded only in loosening the clip of his mask. It clattered to the ground.

His vision dissolved into a washed-out blur of light and dark shapes increasing in size. Standing was now too much effort, and with a half-hearted reluctance he fell dully to his knees.

Back in the monitor room, Webster was yelling into his microphone, instructing Van Arenn to get out.

'Get the fucking door shut!' yelled Bishop.

Webster ignored him and watched Garrett hunkered ready in the doorway as she prepared to face the insects speeding towards her.

She knew that if she didn't save herself, she wouldn't be able to save Van Arenn, so she leapt up and slapped one of the wasps with a wide-palmed backhander. It collided with the other, leaving both of them dazed on the floor halfway between her and Van Arenn.

A third moved in, buzzing around Garrett's face, trying to get enough purchase to deploy its stinger somewhere, anywhere, on her body.

Meanwhile, Van Arenn was lost, able to process the loosest of visuals but unable to comprehend what was happening to him. That was just as well: nobody wants to be conscious when three wasps are ripping chunks of meat from their thighs and chest. His veins and arteries loosened to allow a growing soup of blood and tissue to collect beneath him.

Laura felt the cold horror reaching through her. 'Oh my good God,' she murmured, turning away.

Three soon became four, five, six and seven as the fallen wasps shook off the effects of the cold and took to the new set of circumstances with merciless vigour.

They quickly transformed Van Arenn's face into little more than the front of a skull, decorated with torn morsels of what was left of his forehead.

'Oh shit! Van Arenn!' Webster knew his cry was

pointless, but watching one of his good men die like this was too much for him to remain silent.

Although the image before his eyes would never leave Webster's memory, it was not the sight of the dripping gore that burrowed its way to the deepest part of him. More disturbing was the expression on Van Arenn's face: calm and willing, apparently not in the least troubled that he was suffering a death of unimaginable horror.

As Garrett parried the attempted thrusts of the third wasp, what was left of Van Arenn moved into her eyeline, sending a mixture of anguish, fury and her own strong instinct for survival flooding into her.

She knew she had to get out of there immediately to have any chance, but something told her the only way she could leave this situation with any honour was to get that notebook. It would mean Van Arenn would not have died for nothing.

Leaping upwards, she raised her fists and brought them together hard, the wasp in between.

Although they did not meet perfectly, they were close enough to obliterate the front of the wasp's abdomen and leave it spluttering like a helicopter with a busted tail-blade.

This released its alarm pheromone. Instantly, Garrett had become the sole focus of all the anger, aggression and malice in the room.

She knew what happened when you killed a wasp in the vicinity of others, but she had to get that notebook.

Her face steeled in focus.

'What the hell is she doing?' asked Bishop.

Laura had moved away from the others, and now stood at the back of the room, her hand over her mouth.

Webster stared at the screen in dread. Was he going to watch another of his squad die?

Then Garrett exploded forwards, running as fast as she could back into the lab.

Her move wrong-footed the wasps, and as she reached them, she dived on to the floor and tucked herself into a forward roll. By the time they knew where she was, she had grabbed the notebook and stuffed it inside her jacket.

Refusing to look at the wasps, she closed her eyes, crouched into a ball again and hurled herself towards the door.

For a second time she confused the wasps. Those who were smart enough to follow her collided with the ones who thought she was heading back into the room.

Her roll took her to the other side of the door, but no one had been quick enough to shut it behind her.

Looking up, she knew she was in trouble. This moment behind the open doors gave her time to take in the noise, the death and the terror that sped up her pulse even further.

'Shut the fucking door!' yelled Bishop. Webster suddenly realized he was closest to the button and slammed his hand down.

The doors started to come together, but two wasps were right behind Garrett and closing fast.

She turned just in time to see the nearest one. Grasping its wings, she wrapped her fingers around its compound eyes. She was shocked to see that it barely flinched, continuing the ferocious drive of its attack.

And now the second wasp was almost upon her.

She tightened her grip around the first one and used it to smack the other, sending them both flying back towards the entrance.

As they regained their senses to attack again, the doors slid closed on both of them, one at the thorax, the other at the abdomen.

A severed head dropped to the floor at Garrett's feet, then another slid stickily downwards at the point where the doors met.

The rest of the wasps flew against the door, their soft impacts giving her one last moment of fear before she shifted hastily backwards across the corridor.

The emotions rose inside her like poisoned gas. She had no idea what she was supposed to do next. As each breath took her closer to tears, she shut her eyes tight and covered them with her arm.

'Get out of there, Garrett!' Bishop shouted into Webster's mouthpiece. 'I want you through the other doors so we can seal off the whole area. One thing goes wrong with that entrance and we're back in the shit!'

She didn't react.

'Garrett? Come through the outer doors now,' coaxed Webster. 'Garrett?'

She was still staring at the door, ready for more of them to come for her. When she realized she was safe, she shut her eyes again, then reopened them to gaze with hatred at the camera pointing at her.

They all felt the blame aimed in their direction. Ultimately it was the work of the scientists that had created this situation. Without them, Van Arenn would surely be alive.

Garrett looked through the doors of the lab and saw two wasps picking clean the last of his bones. Then she looked down to study the remains of the insects crushed by the door. With a steady shake of her head, she slowly lifted her boot and brought it down on whatever was left, feeling immense satisfaction at grinding it to nothing but a stain.

To her left she noticed a glob of sloppy innards which had landed a couple of feet into the corridor.

She bent down, scooped it up and smeared it across the camera lens. The four people in the surveillance room recoiled.

'Well, we will be requiring a sample,' said Harry.

Garrett then walked to the outer doors, waited for Webster to open them and stomped through without looking back.

In the monitor room, stunned repulsion was all anyone could feel.

'Jesus Christ,' said Bishop, searching for a surface to lean on as he retched.

24

Van Arenn's skeleton became the fourth to litter the floor of Lab 23. It was impossible to tell where he ended and Roach, Martin or Heath began, especially after Garrett's boots had scattered the bones from one end of the room to the other. They were now an indistinguishable mess of collagen and calcium, as far from a respectable burial as it was possible to get.

The death had been a horrific tragedy, of that there was no doubt, but that did not mean time could be wasted. They needed to know what was written in that notebook, and that meant asking Garrett very nicely if she wouldn't mind handing it over.

Webster met her at the security door to the labs. She was walking quickly with apparent purpose.

'Garrett, I'm truly sorry,' he said, as she strode past without acknowledging him. 'Garrett?' He hurried to catch her up, but was just too far behind to stop her going into one of Harry's labs. She locked the door behind her and walked towards the gene sequencers. To get to them, she had to walk past two workbenches covered in row upon row of test tubes. Opening her arms wide, she casually swept them all to the floor in a monsoon of smashing glass.

The lab was well insulated, so all they could hear was the muted tinkle that came with each impact.

'Oh shit.' Webster was knocking hard on the Perspex window. 'Garrett! Garrett! Come on, open the door!'

'What's she doing?' asked Harry.

Before Webster could speak, Garrett answered for him. She turned to the thermal cycler that was closest to her, smashing its dial and readout again and again with her big black boots. She kicked the casing, too, but made little impact on the solid steel, so she returned to the glass covering of the display, adding spidery cracks to it with each impact.

As she kicked, she screamed from the pit of her stomach. It was impossible to hear exactly what she was saying, but the explosion of rage ripped open her face and tore through her eyes.

'Oh dear,' said Harry quietly. There was nothing he or Webster could do but watch and wait.

Next, Garrett pulled the sample cabinets over, sending them crashing to the floor, their drawers skidding through the broken glass. One after another they hit the ground in a series of rolling booms that made Harry flinch.

Bishop and Laura had come to find out what was taking so long. As Garrett turned her attention to the thermoperiodic chambers, Bishop banged on the glass.

'Hey! Hey! Garrett! Stop that!' He turned to Webster. 'How do we get in there?'

'We don't. It's locked from the inside.'

'For God's sake. Garrett! Garrett!'

If she could hear him, she didn't let it show. Moving on to the examination chambers, she wrenched the fire extinguisher off the wall and laid waste to the tall glass boxes.

'How long's this going to set us back?' muttered Bishop.

'We've got more than enough equipment in the other labs to make sure this won't be too intrusive,' replied Harry. 'I'd have thought the bigger question is how you're going to explain this to whoever allocates our budget. Those things don't come cheap.'

'I'm fully aware of the financial –'

Garrett cut Bishop short by upending a workbench. It supported a large genome sequencer, which landed with a rumble of colliding metalwork backed by an echoing crunch of broken glass.

Garrett gave another scream as she pounded the gene sequencers with her boots. There was nothing left to break, so she returned to the only thing left that could take another bout of her fury.

With little damage now being done, the frequency of her blows subsided. She delivered the last dents to the front panels, then bent over with her hands on her knees, shook her head and looked around at the carnage she had created. It would do for now.

She unlocked the door and rejoined the others.

'Take it out of my wages,' she called, as she walked down the corridor towards Bishop's office.

The others followed.

*

The office was filled with an awkward silence. Despite what she had just done, Garrett was giving off too much anger to be reprimanded. Her best friend, a man who made life down here just about bearable, had been torn to shreds and eaten in front of her. One wrong word from Bishop and she might decide to damage more than just lab equipment.

For a long minute, she stared at the bookcase, her shoulders rising and falling with each hard breath.

Finally, she turned and looked at Laura and Harry, then walked towards Bishop and stood over him as he sat in fear on the other side of his desk. Reaching into her army jacket, she took hold of the notebook, pulled it out and let it drop to the table.

'There's the fucking –'

At that moment the door opened and in walked Andrew. Everyone turned round, quickly enough for him to realize something was up and that he might have interrupted that something.

'Er . . . we've finished playing upstairs,' he said.

'Yes, OK, sweetie. Go and find . . . Mr . . .'

'Carter,' assisted Webster.

'Yes, Mr Carter, and play a bit of pool with him. Or watch a DVD. We have something important to discuss here.' Andrew nodded hard and fast and shut the door behind him.

'As I was saying, there's the fucking notebook,' spat Garrett. 'I hope it was worth David's life.'

'Well,' said Bishop, 'I'm sure Dr Heath would be pleased to know . . .'

'Not that fucking David! David *Van Arenn*. *My* fucking David, you asshole. You don't even know our names, do you, you piece of shit?'

'Garrett,' warned Webster.

'Now, look, Garrett, calm down, please. I understand you have been through a big, big deal. You have lost . . .' he looked at Webster for confirmation that he was saying the right thing '. . . your best friend, but it really has been for the greater good of the people within this facility and beyond. Your bravery . . .'

'Don't talk to me about my fucking bravery, shitfuck. And know this: I didn't do it for you, or this *facility* or whatever the fuck you want to call it. I did it for my *friend*, so at least he died for something. I really hope that book' – she looked at Laura – 'has got some fucking important shit in it.' And with that she walked out of the office, slamming the door behind her.

Back in the office, they all stared at the notebook, still unopened on the desk. It had the dimensions of a postcard, and was a hundred pages thick, black and the kind of leather you only found in London's more discerning stationers. The pages were edged in gold, like an address book, except for the large smear of half-dried wasp guts that encrusted part of the front, side and back.

'Dr Trent,' said Bishop in a small voice, 'I suggest you take a look inside.'

She picked the notebook up and opened it with a soft crack of hardening blood. The first thing she could see, to her relief, was that the pages were crammed with words and numbers and diagrams that seemed to reflect much of Heath's thoughts and research.

Bishop, Harry and Webster looked at her expectantly. Seeing this, she flicked through the pages to show them that there was plenty of information. Her action sent a spray of dried wasp over Bishop, who did his best to ignore it.

'Can we use it?' he asked.

Laura looked through the pages. 'Post-integration elimination of transposon sequences . . . phylogenetic distance . . . genome sequencing criteria . . . that's all language I understand, but it's the details, how he's referring to genes and genetic integration and sequencing methods that I'm not familiar with. I think it'll take a bit of deciphering. I mean, this is all as clear to me as English is to you but with the odd word that I'm going to have to work out through context, maybe with Harry's help.'

Bishop checked his watch. 'It's getting late. Let's go to the cafeteria, then you can get stuck in after dinner.'

This surprised Laura. 'What time is it?'

'Nine thirty,' replied Webster.

25

The soldiers, scientists and those in charge were separated into their usual mealtime divisions. Garrett was already seated, picking over a bowl of food she was never going to eat. Jacobs heated up her meal and took the next seat along.

'Fucking chili again,' she said, resigned rather than pissed off.

'Yeah, Jacobs, but this time it's got a special ingredient. Say . . . where is Van Arenn?' As George Estrada chuckled at his own joke, everyone on Bishop's table went ghost-white. Did the scientists know already? Webster looked across to them for clues. From the continuing laughter, they were sure George had just stumbled upon his remark. However, when Garrett snapped loudly to her feet and left, the other soldiers knew something was up.

The canteen returned to its usual calm, with gloomy silences punctuated by the occasional burst of conversation.

'What happens to the poo all the way down here, you know, when you go to the *rest room*?' Andrew loved using Americanisms; there was a coolness to doing it at school.

'Sweetie, not while we're eating.'

'No, I just mean, like you know when you do it in a plane, it falls out in a frozen block that lands on people's houses, here it must have to be shot up to the surface like in a cannon.'

'That's exactly what happens,' confirmed Webster. 'Then it fertilizes the jungle. Does it pretty good too. When we arrived there was only one tree, now look at it.' Andrew smiled.

Between mouthfuls, Laura flicked through the notebook. The early pages were full of Heath's first stabs at isolating the aggression gene. She found it fascinating to discover how he had succeeded in replacing junk DNA strands with duplicates of the characteristics he wanted more of. The density of his thought slowed her, but she also had to contend with the density of Dr Heath's incredibly ordered capital-letter handwriting. It was taking several minutes to get through each page.

His advances made her own research feel archaic, like papyrus compared to a computer. He had isolated and adapted genes that were thought to be inextricable and applied thinking from remote areas of biochemistry which advanced the state of the art.

And the creative thinking behind it was indeed an art: he had included perfectly proportioned diagrams of his findings, the work of a man who could have been incredibly successful in many different fields.

For better or worse, however, he had chosen this one.

26

In the barracks, Garrett was sitting on her bed, unable to think straight. It had all happened so fast, and now she had to deal with varying measures of anger, grief, desperation, despondency and fear.

She thought back to the conversation she had had with Van Arenn when they had returned from the mission. Had she tried hard enough to persuade him that this place was sliding into disaster? If she had been stronger, firmer, less of a pussy, would her friend be alive now?

On the other side of the barracks, Van Arenn's pine kitbox was jutting out from where he had left it in his capsule. Garrett walked over and shifted it out, sliding open the catches on the lid. As she looked through the photos and keepsakes, she felt an immense feeling of pity. The most recent picture he had was a two-year-old snap of Garrett posing on the chopper with the latest firearms consignment from the Pentagon. Beyond that, he had a beat-up black and white photo of a fat old man with glassy eyes and missing teeth whom Garrett assumed was Van Arenn senior.

To anyone other than their owner, the rest of the objects were a collection of junk: a bullet, two bottle caps, a wooden beaded necklace, a Lincoln penny and a cat's ID tag. In ten seconds, they had gone from meaningful to meaningless, and Garrett thought that was about as sad as it got.

There was no one in the room, so she lifted the box up and heaved it across the barracks, sending Van Arenn's clothes and trinkets flying. The wood was too dense to make much of a noise, but it left a wide triangular gash in the army-issue couch that took most of the impact. Bouncing off, it knocked quietly along the floor before coming to rest at the feet of Jacobs, who had just opened the door. She looked down at the box then up to Garrett, who was staring at the floor trying not to cry.

'Everything OK?' Jacobs said at last.

'Nope. Wasps got David,' Garrett replied, returning to her bunk. 'Ate him all up.'

'No shit,' said Jacobs softly. 'You need some company?'

'Whatever,' muttered Garrett.

This was a deeply awkward moment. Despite the fact that Jacobs was the only other female soldier, she and Garrett had never been close. Van Arenn was all Garrett had needed, so she had kept the others at a distance, being civil but no more.

Jacobs tried to ignore the silence by picking up Van Arenn's clothes and putting them back into his kit box. Sliding it back into the bunk, she turned to Garrett, whose eyes narrowed with bitter force.

'Sadie, if you need any help . . .'

Garrett looked up at Jacobs. 'I only need help with one thing, *Mary*, and that's getting the fuck out of here.'

27

As the inhabitants of MEROS finished up their food and got ready to go to work or sleep, Bishop took Webster aside.

'Carl, I suggest you get Garrett locked down. If she's feeling spiky about what happened to Van Arenn, she's liable to start turning the others against me. I don't know if we can stop that happening, but every second you can buy me could be the difference between chaos and control.'

'No problem,' said Webster flatly. He had been placed in similar situations before, and duty had always defeated his humane instincts. That was why they had chosen him. They knew that a little thing like *feelings* would not get in the way of his defence of the greater good, and Bishop liked to put this to regular use. He had been through too many similar incidents and made too many similar requests to think that this one was going to be a stretch.

As Webster headed off to the barracks, Bishop returned to the table.

'Dr Trent, Andrew, we have excellent guest facilities here. We never know when someone of importance might visit and stay here long enough to get a feel for the place. Please, let me show you to your rooms.'

He led Laura and Andrew to a small door just beyond the entrance to the barracks. Most people assumed that it was a storeroom of some sort, and none of the current staff, except Bishop, had ever seen the other side of it.

'When was the last time anyone stayed here?' asked Laura.

Bishop thought for a moment, then a moment longer. 'Do you know, I'm not sure anyone has *ever* stayed here. You might have the honour of being the first.'

The suite of rooms contained furniture, books and magazines, all from a time before Andrew was born. The living room was decorated in a dull collection of the minimalist earth tones that would have suited a boutique hotel of the late nineties. Someone had thought to add a CD player and a collection of discs, including the *Titanic* soundtrack and Madonna's *Ray of Light*. The walls were decorated with framed Damien Hirst knock-offs: a grid of coloured circles and a canvas of several butterflies trapped in pink paint.

Bishop gestured Andrew and Laura through to the bedrooms, which would have been pleasant enough, were it not for the feeling that they were walking on the grave of someone not yet dead.

'I guess I'll just leave you to it. If there's anything you need, please don't hesitate to ask. My quarters are off the rec room next to my office. There's a door at the back on the right. Major Webster sleeps in the barracks with his squad. Feel free to wake him if you need his help. I think we're all aware of the . . .' he noticed Andrew '. . . situation in which we now find ourselves, and its importance.' He walked backwards to the door and left them to it.

Andrew suddenly felt very tired, as if Bishop's departure had unleashed the sleep in him. Without a word, he headed off to the bathroom, peed, brushed his teeth and kissed his mum goodnight.

'I know you're tired, sweetie. We'll have a proper talk in the morning.'

Laura prepared for bed, then set about the notebook as if it were a novel she could not put down. She knew she had to sleep, but the call of just one more chapter was too strong for her to ignore.

28

From a quick glance at Jacobs' accusing face, Webster knew he was too late to hush Garrett up and that it was now only a matter of time before the rest of MEROS found out about Van Arenn.

Webster was relieved. When he had a choice to make that he didn't agree with, he preferred someone else to make it for him. Now he could do what he thought was right. Jacobs could see that this meant a quiet word with Garrett, so she took the hint and left them to it.

'Are you OK, Garrett?' Webster pulled up a chair and sat down opposite her, trying to catch her eye. She didn't react.

'I know you are a soldier and have been a soldier out there, but what you went through today . . . that was big, and I don't want you to feel like you've got to keep it all in.'

Garrett looked at Webster wearily. 'I don't feel like nothing, sir. I'm just trying to process a ton of stuff right now is all.'

'Please try to sleep on it. I know it's hard, but we'll work out what to do in the morning. And it's worth saying one more time that you did good out there. You gave us a shot and risked everything to do it. For a girl, your balls are big.'

She did not smile at this. Instead she got into bed and shut her blind.

29

Nights were the strangest time in MEROS. Most of the staff slept, despite the illusion of twenty-four-hour days, but some, mainly the scientists, used the time to get work done with fewer distractions.

In particular, Harry Merchant often ran the gene sequencers at night, setting them on the long series of calculations that might provide the next steps forward. It was not a task that required much thought or attention, so he usually spent the time working out how to process the next day's experiments.

Tonight, however, was different.

Tonight, he felt the arrival of Laura Trent, the deaths of Heath, Roach, Martin and Van Arenn, and the desperation of Bishop as a rough hand shaking him from his sleep.

Harry had been asked here personally by David Heath and had been so honoured to receive the invitation he had accepted without really enquiring into what it would entail. Ever since he had given up his post at the University of Kansas to 'have a little go at playing God', as Heath mischievously put it, he had been entranced by the opportunity to make unnatural history.

But, however thrilling the early days had been, the grim and inconvenient reality of the situation had gradually made its presence felt, like floodwater seeping under a door. By the time it all got too much, he was practically institutionalized, and the only things that gave him the impetus to leave were the kind of seismic events that now seemed to be a weekly occurrence.

The hum of the machines allowed him to tune out and focus on his thoughts. He started with Laura and her boy. He knew they would not be able to stay for any substantial length of time. Their arrival had been a last, desperate throw of the dice by Bishop, the move of a man who was clinging on to something by ever-slipping fingertips. Sure, she might get him out of this situation, but she and the boy would not, could not, remain here and, however they were going to leave, Harry wanted to join them.

His clandestine meeting with Laura earlier in the day had, he hoped, planted the seed in her mind that he was a kindred spirit, but he felt the need to reinforce it. If she ever found herself with a way out, he did not want to be forgotten. Equally, if he could think of a plan that required her assistance, he wanted her to know he could be trusted.

He checked the sequencers one last time, folded his glasses into his pocket and returned to his room. He had much to consider.

30

Sleep had overcome Laura like molasses. No matter how hard she had tried to continue reading, in the end it wasn't her choice. She sank into the wide leather couch, turned her eyes from the light and promised herself it would be for no more than ten minutes. Five hours later, she was still snoring gently into the cushions.

In his bed, Andrew blinked awake and tried to remember where he was. This pitch-black room was the sixth different place he'd woken up in over the last two days. Reaching for a light switch, he found one that instantly brought eight fluorescent bulbs to life and left his pupils aching.

Oh yeah. Here.

After a wash, he put on the same clothes he had worn since leaving England. Their clammy stiffness made him want to get moving, to think about something else. He ambled out into the living room, where it took him a moment to notice his mum tucked into the couch. He moved gently, turned off the light and slipped into the corridor.

With no one else around, he wasn't sure what to do, so he returned to the cafeteria for a bowl of corn-flakes with longlife milk. He ate alone until Carter walked in.

'Hey, little guy! What you doing here by your lonesome?'

'Mum's still asleep.'

'Oh. You want to go outside for a while? I'm heading up there for a run before I go on detail. Maybe you could show me some more scout stuff.'

'Thanks, Lieutenant Carter.'

'OK, just hang on a minute till I get some chili down.'

Carter scooped a ladle of corpse-grey meat-mush into a bowl. The sound, like muscle separating from bone, brought a look of amazed disgust to Andrew's face. Carter saw this and smiled.

'You should see what it looks like tomorrow,' he said, digging in a spoon. Five bites and the contents of the bowl were gone. A pint of coffee later, Carter and Andrew were in the elevator, Andrew trying hard not to breathe in Carter's stale breath.

31

Laura woke abruptly and eased her face off the sofa. Crease marks from the leather had left her cheek looking like a forgotten dishcloth.

The sharp raps came again.

'Hang on,' she slurred, feeling the wall for a light switch. The room flashed white and she fumbled for the door handle.

'Harry?'

'Dr Trent. I ... er ... I'm sorry to ... did I wake you?'

'I'm not sure. I didn't sleep too well. What time is it?'

'A little after seven.'

They stood there for a moment before Laura remembered her manners. 'Come in, come in. I think there's some ten-year-old coffee in that jar.'

Harry looked around the room and sat on a black leather armchair. Laura returned to the couch.

'How can I help?' she smiled, suppressing a yawn.

'Well, to put it bluntly, I'm concerned.'

'Aren't we all?'

'I'm sure, but as I said to you yesterday, I think the current situation may be coming to a head, and I'd like to help it do so.'

'OK. Any ideas?'

'A few. One in particular.' He paused to give some room to what he was about to say.

'I think I can release my wasps.'

Laura waited for Harry to make clear whether or not he was joking. His expression did not alter.

'How can you do that without making things worse?'

'I could open the incubators at the back of my lab then lock the door. They are maintained electronically, so the possibility of a malfunction is always there. I simply set them to unlock, and thirty minutes later the wasps will be wakened by the heat and out in the lab. Because the same area stores the genetic-data records, the soldiers will not be able to use their weapons. Bishop will have to freeze it down, and we will have to leave the facility when he does so. Under those circumstances, I for one would not return.'

'Is there a downside?'

'Only minimal danger to myself and the slight chance of arousing suspicion. However, the incubators are in their own area right at the back of the lab, so if I do it by torchlight I can't imagine anyone will even know I'm there.'

'Do you have a time in mind?'

'I could do it this morning. The earlier the better, really – less chance of prying eyes.'

'Well, be sure and let me know when you've done it. If there's a way Andrew and I can be on the surface when it happens, I'd prefer it.'

Harry looked confused. 'Andrew's already up there,

isn't he? I just saw him get into the elevator with Lieutenant Carter.'

Laura's eyes narrowed. She went to check the bedroom and found empty, rumpled sheets.

'I'm sorry. I thought you had given him permission.'

'No, it's OK. At least he's safe. Your plan sounds like a good one, Harry. Keep me posted.'

32

Garrett, Jacobs and Mills were huddled around a table near the back of the canteen.

'What the hell are we going to do?' asked Mills.

'Beats me, but we all know this place is fucked,' whispered Garrett, looking across to where George Estrada was happily chatting with Susan Myers. 'I'm not going to stay here any longer than I have to. I mean if you guys had seen these fucking things and what they did to Van Arenn, you'd want out too. Never mind the bullshit of being soldiers and what we signed up for. They've taken things up another fucking notch, and it's going to end in a big shit sandwich for all of us.'

'OK, everybody, think. I'd rather take my chances out there than handle any more of this. If it's like Garrett says, we need to get going,' said Jacobs.

'And how does that happen? The only way out is Madison and his sodding plane, and that's going nowhere without Bishop's say so, which leaves us with the impossible bloody jungle,' whispered Mills.

'Hey, I'll take the jungle over what's in there,' said Garrett. 'I know how tough it looks, but I'll give it my best shot if it means leaving this place behind.'

George and Susan got up to go to work. The soldiers eyed them with suspicion.

'And what about those guys?' asked Jacobs.

'That's up to them,' said Mills. 'I say it's every man or woman for him or herself. You never know, they might work out how to wipe these other wasps out with brainpower alone.'

'No, Jacobs is right,' said Garrett, picking at her porridge. 'If we leave them here, we're leaving them to die. I want to get everyone out.'

Mills responded with a short, cynical exhale. 'OK then, the first thing you're going to have to do is tell the nerds why we're off to catch the bus, then you've got to carry their dead weight through that fucking jungle. It's going to be hard enough for us to make it without slogging two hundred pounds of fat-arsed scientist with us. If that all sounds reasonable to you, go right ahead.'

'Fuck you, Mills. I just need to do some thinking,' said Garrett, getting up and leaving the table.

33

In the holding bay, Dale Takeshi was preparing the incubation containers for the next batch of wasps. Susan stood beside him, halfway through a speculative monologue about Laura's arrival.

'I just want to know what happened to Dr Heath. I mean, we don't see him for months – when was the last time you saw him? – exactly! So we don't see him for months and now this new head *ento* arrives without an explanation. It's weird, don't you think?'

Takeshi looked up to check she didn't really expect him to answer.

'Definitely weird. And those two soldiers, Roach and Martin, when did you last see *them*? So that's another thing that doesn't seem right. I mean, they just seem to think that it's OK to –'

Takeshi sshhhed her.

'What?'

He put a finger to his lips.

'What?'

'There.' A clear tapping noise rang out from behind one of the walls. 'It sounds like the heating system has slipped a gear again.' The sound stopped, then continued, louder this time.

'That's all we need,' said Susan. 'Heating goes down,

we lose a day.' Takeshi approached the wall, feeling around it for the panel that led to the heating vents. It was completely hidden and required anyone who needed it to press upon the exact square inch that flipped open to reveal the workings of the system.

'I think it's higher and to the left,' said Susan.

The sound was getting louder, but was no longer coming from the same place; in fact, there were now two different tapping noises, a few feet away from each other.

Takeshi stopped searching, stood back and gave the matter some thought. Meanwhile, Susan brought a chair across and stood on it, trying to reach the point at which she thought the panel would open.

'Maybe we need a screwdriver or something,' she said, jabbing at the wall.

Takeshi wasn't listening. 'I think we need to inform Mr Bishop,' he said.

34

After Harry left her quarters, Laura had a quick shower and returned to the notebook. It took a few minutes to retune her brain to the squash of Heath's handwriting and the magnitude of the ideas it conveyed, but soon she was working her way through it.

Heath had indeed been attempting to increase the wasps' aggression. Several pages were devoted to his trials in removing the gene Pet-1, which regulates serotonin, controlling the insects' propensity towards impulsive violence. Heath's notes went on to say that he had encountered problems with this particular gene, because it was also responsible for reducing levels of anxiety and depression. Knocking it out meant that the wasps were prone to aggressive rage when it was required, but they were agitated, anxious and harder to control. Laura found that Heath had experimented with many different levels of Pet-1, and suspected that it was its complete removal that may have left the wasps in their current state.

Turning the next page, she paused and stared straight ahead. Then she thought harder and felt a realization strike her so sharply it made her blink. She thrashed back through the book to find something she had noticed the previous night, then she read it again. And again.

'My God.'

She yanked her shoes on and hurried into the corridor. Looking in both directions, she moved across to the walls on the opposite side and pressed up against them, running her flat palm over their perfect white smoothness. Then she pushed into them as hard as she could, feeling how much they gave. They moved back a little, but she knew the real test would come when she gave them a knock.

What she heard flipped her stomach like a plunging elevator: a hollow sound that confirmed her fears. She had to find Webster.

Easing open the door of the barracks, the only soldier she could see was Wainhouse. He was sitting in one of the battered armchairs playing a violent video game.

'Oh, er . . . excuse me,' she said, feeling like she was intruding on something more important.

Wainhouse didn't react. He just carried on stabbing the buttons as if she hadn't said a word. Laura was sure she had spoken loud enough to be heard but, judging by his reaction, maybe not.

'Excuse me, I –'

'God*damn*!' spat Wainhouse, looking up. He was not happy that Laura's interruption had brought his game to a premature end. 'What?' he asked impatiently.

'I was looking for Major Webster,' said Laura apologetically.

Wainhouse pointed to one of the capsules and returned to his killing spree. Laura wasn't quite sure what to do. Approaching slowly, she stood in front of it until she heard Wainhouse behind her.

'He ain't gonna bite. Yo, Major!' he yelled.

With a loud *shhhrrriiippp*, the blind flew up to reveal Webster looking as alert as anyone can be after being awake for three seconds. He was dressed only in blue boxer shorts, so when he shunted himself forward to hang off his bed, Laura was momentarily distracted by his smooth, dense body.

'Dr Trent,' he said, grabbing a white T-shirt from a bag that hung off the end of his capsule door. He unfurled it over himself and jumped down to the floor. 'What can I do for you?' he asked, adding a pair of dark-green cargo pants from his locker. Laura looked awkwardly at Wainhouse, who was engrossed in his game, as if she had never entered the room.

'Come with me,' said Webster.

35

Taj was leaning back on the MEROS desk with his feet up and his fat brown fingers wrapped around a kids' adventure novel. He liked Willard Price, but he'd got through all those and was now making his way through the works of Enid Blyton. He wasn't stupid; just lazy, and the undemanding timekillers hit the spot day after day.

'God*damn* you, Uncle Quentin. You a shifty motherfucker,' he mumbled to himself.

The other way he passed the time was by eating junk food. It didn't take long for him to consume the chocolate bars he arranged to have flown over in the supply drops, but he did like to make sure he ate them in the right order.

Ever since his first memory of his Grandma keeping him quiet with a fun-sized Snickers bar, he had lived much of his life through the consumption of snack foods. In fact, their regular delivery to MEROS was his only condition on agreeing to come.

He had answered an ad for a minimum-wage security guard posted on Craigslist. The other applicants dropped out when they found out more details of what the job entailed, but a little blackmail over some low-level dope-dealing and his aunt's immigrant status meant that he was on his way to Venezuela within a week. As the job involved nothing but simple maintenance and utter secrecy, the arrangement was fine for both sides. Taj missed his family and the neighbourhood in Bed-Stuy, but the lack of pressure and constant supply of Milky Ways, Mars, Almond Joy, Junior Mints, Hershey's Kisses, Three Musketeers, Smores and Whatchamacallits made his position just the right side of bearable.

Outside, Carter was showing Andrew around the Spartan.

'These are the safety lights that tell us when we're close to the ground in the dark. Then we've got this rack of custom-built ammo boxes that reduce movement in turbulence. Did you fly in this kind of plane to get here or was it the Gulfstream, the G-100?'

'It was smaller than this one.'

'Yeah, that'd be the Gulfstream. That's the kind of thing Lil' Wayne flies in when he's touring.'

'Lil' who?'

'You don't know Lil' Wayne? He's a rapper. Anyway, I bet he kits his Gulfstream out better than ours.'

'Yeah, it was pretty uncomfortable. So, Mr Carter . . .'

'Call me Jeff.'

'OK, Jeff. How long have you been here?'

'It'll be four years in May.'

'And when do you get to see your family?'

'Not often.'

'What about for Christmas?'

'Depends on what's happening here. I've had to skip the last few.'

Andrew was amazed at this. 'Don't you miss them?'

'I miss my mom, and I know she misses me, but sometimes there're more important things.'

'I don't know what I'd do without my mum.'

'Yeah, I know what you mean.'

They both sat in the back row of seats, thinking about what they were doing here. Carter wondered how many more Christmases he was going to miss, while Andrew hoped that he and his mum would be on their way home today. He had a school football match on Saturday and he really didn't want to miss it.

Another chapter over, Taj reached down to his candy drawer and felt for his breakfast. His hands groped air as he remembered he needed to get a refill from the box in the storeroom behind his desk.

He marked his page and went to unlock the door. Switching the light on, he walked inside and checked his supply.

'Shit,' he said quietly, as he mentally totted up the number of bars he had left until the next delivery. He reached up and dragged another box off the shelf and on to the floor.

The smack of cardboard was loud enough to disguise the sound of a *clunk* in the lobby behind him.

It was followed by a long hiss as the CS gas shot from the grenade to fill the air.

Taj heard the sound and went to investigate. The

second he left the storeroom he was choking and coughing, trying to cope with a mighty wash of phlegm that sluiced through his nose like a stretch of rapids.

He could barely think to react, but he assumed MEROS was under attack. When a pair of hands grabbed him roughly from behind, he turned to see a man in a hazchem suit and gas mask staring into his streaming eyes.

'Don't . . . man . . . I can't let you in,' sputtered Taj. The hands pulled him out of the storeroom and into the open area in front of the desk.

Taj heard a voice say, 'What do we do with him now?', and looked up to make out the watery image of two more people in suits and masks. One put a finger to where his lips would be and pointed outside.

Did that voice sound familiar? Was that an *English* accent?

36

Andrew's words were swallowed by the echoed crack of an explosion, which left the entrance to MEROS obscured by a dense cloud of vapour.

A woman's muffled voice yelled, 'Go! Go! Go!'

A second later, two figures dressed in camouflage and gas masks emerged from the smoke, running at full speed towards Carter and Andrew.

Carter reacted quickly, pushing Andrew down behind the seats and looking for a weapon.

He could hear the shouting more clearly now and was certain Garrett and Jacobs were behind the masks. They were now just twenty feet away, and closing fast.

As they approached the rear door, Madison crept into the front with his Beretta PX4 9mm pistol cocked and a look of fear in his eyes.

From where he was folded into the back seats with Andrew, Carter could see the situation had the potential to deteriorate fast.

His first priority was to protect the boy, but to do that he had to calm Madison down and find out what the hell was happening with the others.

He soon discovered it was going to be harder than he thought. Garrett and Jacobs ran up the loading ramp to find Madison screaming at them.

'Get the fuck down! Get the fuck off my plane!'

He had jumped out in front of the cockpit with both hands shaking around his loaded gun. He obviously had no idea what he was doing or who he was doing it to.

Garrett held up her hands to calm him and nodded to Jacobs to do the same.

Everyone was now still and silent, the two soldiers standing with their hands raised, Carter and Andrew squashed flat a few feet away in the back row of seats and Madison refusing to lower his pistol, which was now pointing squarely at Garrett's head.

Carter broke the quiet by sliding slowly upwards with his hands raised. The sound of his jacket rubbing against the metal seat drew Madison's gun towards him.

'OK, OK, OK, Madison, calm down. We have a boy here, so no squeezing of triggers, please. Just lower the gun, and we'll find out what the hell is going on.' Madison did not move. 'Jacobs, Garrett, I have no idea what you guys are doing but, like I said, the new professor's kid is in here, so we need to avoid guns going off. Can you just take off your masks and tell us what's up? Madison, please put the gun down.'

'No way, Carter. Not till I get a clue from these assholes. Masks off. Slowly.'

Garrett and Jacobs duly obliged, gradually revealing their serious, defiant faces.

'Good. Now what the hell are you doing on my plane?'

'We're getting out of here, fuckface, and you're going to fly us.'

It was Mills. No one had seen him come out of the vapour after the other two.

He had used the confusion to work his way round to the Spartan's side door and waited for his chance.

In one quick movement he positioned himself behind Madison and pressed the muzzle of his gun to the back of the pilot's head.

Madison lowered his weapon, and Mills snatched it out of his hand, uncocked it and slid it behind his belt.

'Seriously, guys, what the fuck are you doing?' asked Carter, now that the danger had shrunk to something he could deal with.

Mills decided to be spokesman. 'You heard, Carter. We're getting the hell out of here. Madison is kindly going to agree to fly us to our safe base in the Dominican Republic, where we will live our future lives wasp-free.'

'OK. Makes sense. But why now?'

'It's fucked down there, Carter. 'Scuse me, kid,' added Garrett, noticing Andrew still squashed under Carter's wide palm.

She was preparing the weapons they had amassed for their escape. They had broken into the armoury and removed whatever they could carry: a couple of the specialist mission guns, several Glock 19s, some CS-24 explosive and three 120g CS gas grenades like the one they had, reluctantly, used on Taj at the MEROS reception desk. He was still desperately wheezing and coughing, staggering blind around the grass and trees.

Garrett continued, 'That new bunch of wasps – no

one can do anything about 'em and Bishop's still refusing to see sense and shut the place down.'

'So anyone who stays in there is toast,' said Mills.

'Hey!' said Carter. 'In case you'd forgotten, his mom's down there.'

'Sorry, kid,' shrugged Mills.

'So you all just going to up and leave the others to die? Webster? Wainhouse?'

'My mum?' said Andrew, his voice cracking. He forced himself up from under Carter's hand.

They hadn't been expecting this, and although Mills was mercenary enough not to be too bothered about the situation, the look on Andrew's face was yanking on Garrett and Jacobs' heartstrings like a bell ringer.

'My mum's going to die down there?' He said this angrily, his eyes filling with tears. 'I have to get her out.' He headed down the back ramp, but Garrett stopped him by grabbing his shoulders.

'There's no one going back into a cloud of CS gas like that, kid. Not without a mask, and the only ones we got out here ain't gonna fit you.' She pointed to a row of several hazchem suits which had been loaded on to the plane to replace the ones they had used on the last mission.

Andrew tried to prise Garrett's fingers from his shoulders. 'Let me go! Get off me!'

'Whoa, whoa, whoa. Calm down there. Even if you could get through the CS, you can't get your mom out without us. You need our IDs to get back inside the building.'

Andrew kicked Garrett hard in the shin.

'Kid, I'm being nice here, but you do that once more, you're going over my knee.'

Andrew stopped and stood huffing hard like a little bull.

Carter spoke up: 'Come on, guys, what the hell are you thinking? Garrett, I know you're sore about what happened to Van Arenn, but come on. Whatever beef you've got with Bishop, you can't just leave the others down there. If they're all screwed, then we have to help them get out, not run away like pussies. You know that.'

'We can't go back, Carter,' said Mills, sensing a worrying vulnerability in Garrett and Jacobs' silence.

'Mills, everyone already knows you're a weak bitch. You can go whenever you're ready. It's these two I'm trying to make see sense.'

Garrett ignored Mills. She wanted Carter to confirm that she was doing the right thing. If he wouldn't do that, she wanted him to point her in the right direction. 'We can't go back down there now,' she said.

'Why not?'

'Bishop will shut the place down and won't let us back up. We'll be fucked.'

'Why? He won't know what's happened up here. Taj is still throwing up in the bushes. You can go down there and get his mom, then persuade anyone else you find to come up here. That's got to be a better situation than what you've got now.'

'Yeah, Carter, but that's why we didn't handle it that

way in the first place: the persuading's going to take time and maybe get Bishop smelling a rat.'

'Come on, Garrett, you're better than that. We can see what five minutes gets us,' reasoned Carter. Mills sighed. Garrett was obviously leaning towards giving this a go.

'Please, Miss Garrett,' begged Andrew.

37

'Who is it?' snapped Bishop.

His door eased open to reveal Takeshi, whose usual quiet deference doubled in the face of Bishop's short temper.

'Um . . . it's the back of the holding area, sir.'

'What about it?'

'One of the motors has slipped a cog again.'

Bishop tried to look up through half a mile of dirt to the sky. 'Is there anything else, Lord? Busted latrine, maybe?'

He got up and followed Takeshi out of the office.

'Has the temperature dropped much?' asked Bishop impatiently.

'Not yet. We just heard the noise from behind the wall; a kind of tapping.'

'Tapping?'

'Yes. It sounds similar to the problem we had a few months ago, where it started slowly but broke down completely within a few hours. The difference this time is that the tapping is coming from two separate areas. That was why we thought we should inform you as soon as possible.'

'Right.'

They reached the holding bay, where Susan had

managed to find the panel, and was now trying to prise it open with a screwdriver. She looked round at Bishop and spoke quite innocently, her delicate smile accentuating the feeling that this wasn't really anything to worry about.

'Hi, Mr Bishop. The noise was loudest over here, but it stopped a couple of minutes ago and started again over there, so I'm sure it's just a loose connection in the heating duct or something like that.'

Bishop looked to where Susan was pointing. 'That's not where the heating system is located. Was it coming from anywhere else?'

'Around that corner.' She gestured in rough circles towards the point where two walls met the ceiling. 'I listened close, and there's really two different noises: kind of a dull hum, like the heating has gone or something, then when you listen closer at the corner, it's more of a scraping. We didn't think there was a room behind here, so at first we were kind of confused, but I guess there's all sorts of pipes and things that keep a place like this going.'

Bishop moved to the corner to listen.

'Like I said, the noise has stopped, so maybe it's just fixed itself already.' Takeshi noticed Bishop's concern, but Susan just carried on filling the air with words.

'Because, you know, if there's something up with the heating, then the wasps and experiments and all that might be in trouble. That's why we thought it best to come and tell you what's going on. We don't want the wasps dying on us, do we?' A dark look from Bishop silenced her.

Three ears strained towards the wall.

'I still can't hear anything,' said Bishop.

'Like I said, it might be all right now,' added Susan.

'Well, there's nothing we can do until we confirm what has been heard,' said Bishop.

'But even then what do we do? Should we get someone to fix it?' asked Susan.

'No, Miss Myers, I'll deal with it from here.'

There was an unpleasant pause, sharply concluded by a quick pitter-patter from the far end of the wall.

'Did anyone just hear that?' asked Bishop. A second later his question became redundant as the pitter-patter was replaced by a hard, muffled *thrumming*. Bishop dashed across to the noise and stood a few inches from the wall. He didn't have to listen closely; the sound was loud and distinct, and could certainly be a malfunction in any part of the machinery.

Then silence.

38

Webster had taken Laura to the canteen, partly for privacy and partly to get himself a bowl of cereal. Shovelling it into his mouth, he looked at her as if to ask why she wasn't already speaking.

'There's something in Dr Heath's notebook that I think we all need to know about.' She indicated the relevant pages.

Webster squinted. 'iaaP function was established by transformation to insert nopaline or octopine Ti plasmids . . . Sorry, Dr Trent, I'm going to need a translation.'

'Dr Heath has located and developed a gene that is necessary for indoleacetic-acid production. Under the right conditions, that would stimulate growth, which explains the increase in the wasps' size, but it might also have developed their internal acidity.'

'OK, now tell me why that's such a big problem.'

'Well, I assume you know how wasps make their nests, by breaking down materials, usually wood-pulp, but in practice whatever they can find. They chew these materials into a mush using their saliva. The increased acidity means they have a greater ability to do this.'

'Sure. We saw them using whatever was in there to build that nest. Weren't they having a go at the desk?'

'From what I've read in this notebook, that may very well be possible.'

'So synthetic substances aren't beyond them,' Webster reflected, without realizing the import of what he was saying.

'Major Webster, what are the walls of this facility made of?'

He almost said 'plastic'. Instead, he thought better of it and spent a moment considering what Laura had said.

'I understand from your silence that you know what I'm getting at. The next question is how thick are they and what is behind them?'

'Uh, it varies,' said Webster, collecting his thoughts. 'Some of 'em are pretty solid, but the dividing walls aren't more than a couple of inches.'

He and Laura shared a look of grave concern.

39

Bishop pressed his ear to the cold, white plastic veneer.

'I think I can . . . yes, I can hear a kind of scraping noise. Getting louder and . . .'

As he spoke, the part of the wall against which he was holding his earhole disappeared in the shear of a grinding mandible.

A split second later, the gap was filled with the dull, hard tip of a gigantic wasp antenna. It probed its way clumsily into Bishop's ear like a blind man's finger. He gasped loudly and scrambled halfway across the room, scraping his earhole with a fingernail as if trying to remove something that was still there.

Susan let out a thin, hideous scream that compounded the fear now filling the room like freezing fog.

'Get out of here and lock the door. We need containment!' Bishop shouted to Takeshi. 'And calm her down. The whole place will go crazy if they hear that.'

Takeshi didn't move. He was staring at the antenna, imagining the creature it belonged to. It was in his nature to react with considered calm and thoughtful logic; these circumstances were blowing a hole through that.

Susan continued screaming and ran for the door, her face spread wide in shock.

Bishop saw the situation slipping from his grasp. Her panic would cause the rest of MEROS to explode with terror.

Takeshi staggered backwards, collapsing on to the floor, trying to regain his thoughts. Sounds were coming from his mouth that were not words so much as grunted syllables. He got up and staggered towards the exit.

As Susan disappeared into the corridor, George Estrada ran into the lab with a look of petrified confusion on his face.

He caught Bishop's eye and gabbled his words. 'Sir, I–I thought you should know, there . . . there's a strange noise coming from behind the walls of our lab. It, uh, could be the heating, sir, and we thought . . .'

Bishop moved towards him, revealing the antenna.

George almost jumped in shock. '*Chingada Madre!* What the *fuck* is that?'

40

A burning shriek pierced Laura and Webster's conversation like a hot needle. Clattering the chairs aside, they ran into the corridor to find Takeshi leaning against a wall trying to control his shaking legs.

George was slamming shut the door to the holding bay, while Susan had stopped screaming and was now jabbering incoherently at Webster in an attempt to explain what she had seen.

Bishop was on the other side of the corridor, stabbing numbers into a panel on the wall.

'What's going on?' demanded Webster.

George pointed to the back of the lab, where Webster and Laura could clearly see the head of one of Heath's wasps poking through a hole in the wall.

'Check the other labs!' yelled Bishop. 'I'm bringing the Inshield down!'

41

On the plane, Garrett, Jacobs and Carter were having a hard time convincing Andrew that he didn't need to re-enter the complex with them.

'Look, I need to know my mum's safe, so I'm coming too.'

'Not if we say you're not, little guy,' scoffed Jacobs.

'Seriously, this gas mask wouldn't even fit you,' said Carter.

'And we need to move quickly. It'll give us the best chance of getting your mom out,' added Garrett.

'Nope. Don't trust you. I'm coming. Besides, the mask does work. I'm only just shorter than her.' He zipped up the hazchem suit and mask and, sure enough, they fitted.

'The name's Jacobs.'

A quiet *good for you* came from Andrew's mask.

'Mills, can you keep an eye on the kid until we get back?' said Jacobs, zipping up her own suit and covering her face with her mask.

'Why the fuck are we still having this conversation? We could be halfway to the Dominican Republic by now. We're giving a shit about the wrong things.'

'Great,' said Garrett, 'so the quicker you agree to look after the kid, the quicker we get the fuck in and out.'

'OK,' conceded Mills, 'just hurry it up.'

Carter and Garrett headed down the ramp towards the MEROS entrance, where Taj was recovering from the CS gas.

Mills grabbed Andrew, who put up quite a struggle as he was bound hand and foot and stuffed down between two of the rows of seats. Jacobs watched this for a moment then hurried after Carter and Garrett.

With a gun to his head, Taj opened the security doors to allow the three soldiers into the elevator. This was going to have to be fast and safe.

As the lift began its long descent, Carter and Garrett pulled off their gas masks and checked their weapons to make sure they were locked and loaded. They knew the chances of using them were remote, but they wanted to know the option was there if things got desperate.

'Hey, Jacobs, we're past the CS now. Aren't you hot in that thing?' Carter asked. Jacobs shrugged then dropped her weapon as if she was confused by the weight of it. That's when Carter noticed her fingernails.

'What the hell?' he said, whipping back the mask to reveal Andrew's determined face.

42

Webster bolted down the corridor. Only three more of the labs were in regular use, and two of them didn't have their lights on. Lisa Keller and Mike Irwin were already on their way out of the last one, looking for what had sparked off the commotion. Webster pushed them clear, locked the door and signalled to Bishop.

He punched the final number into the touch pad and watched as panels running the length of the corridor's ceiling opened and plates of sapphire glass began gradually to slide their way towards the floor.

'What's that?' Laura asked Webster.

'The Inshield. It's a last-resort fallback that seals off all the labs and this side of the complex from here to the elevator. It protects us from the wasps. We freeze the other side and get out when they're dead. Until then, nothing comes in or goes out.'

'But Andrew's outside.'

'Sorry. The guys will take care of him, but we're going to be locked down here for a few hours at least.'

With a low, ominous *clang*, the shield locked into the floor at the other end of the corridor. The noise made Laura turn.

In the lab behind her, a torch beam was waving frantically through the darkness. A moment later, the light switch was turned on. Harry was standing under the flickering bulbs which were coming to life in Lab 7. He turned off the torch and stood staring at the shield like it was his own gravestone.

'Major,' Laura said, tugging on Webster's sleeve.

He looked up to see what she was pointing at and felt an icy wash pass through him.

He turned his gaze to the corridor. None of the other scientists had noticed that Harry was behind the glass.

'Everyone in the canteen, now!' he yelled.

43

'You best stay the hell in this elevator while we get your mom out,' Garrett warned Andrew as they continued to plummet.

'Yes ma'am,' replied Andrew, knowing he didn't have to do anything he was told. While they looked for their friends, he was going to find his mum.

The elevator slowed. It had to decelerate so much, Carter and Garrett knew they still had a good twenty seconds to prepare.

'OK, Garrett. We've got to grab whoever we can and get them into the elevator before Bishop stops us. We see him, I sit on his ass till you get the others, and then I let him go.'

'Roger that.'

'And get his mom early. We don't want him going out on his own.' Andrew pretended he hadn't heard and stood facing the doors. Carter moved him to the back of the elevator and stood poised next to Garrett.

They had travelled in the lift often enough to know how fast the doors opened, so they readied themselves for the exact moment they would be able to spring out.

The elevator slowed to a stop. There was a beat to wait, then the doors *shhsssssshhed* apart fast.

Carter and Garrett jumped forward, spotting the

glass at the last fraction of a second. Turning sideways, they just managed to skid to a stop and avoid running into it face first.

'What the hell is this?' asked Garrett

'The Inshield.' Carter sounded worried. 'It's the security system that comes down if any of the wasps escape. It means nothing can get to the surface, including this elevator, until everything's guaranteed safe.'

'The wasps are out?' gasped Andrew.

'Maybe. There could be other reasons for it. We need to see what we can find out before we think about panicking,' said Carter.

'Should we try the phone?' asked Garrett.

'It goes up to Taj. Somehow I don't think he's going to be much help right now.'

'So we've got to stay in the elevator until they sort things out? Could be worse.'

Carter was silent. He didn't mind delivering bad news to Garrett – she could take it – but he didn't need Andrew to be more scared than he already was.

He looked around the small space they filled and realized they would both know sooner or later, so he might as well say it now.

'Yeah, well, the real problem comes in stage two.'

'What happens then?' asked Garrett.

'Everything this side of the glass freezes.'

44

'What's up?' asked Bishop. The scientists were safely out of the way in the canteen, so he went to find out what had spooked Webster.

A flick of the head in Harry's direction was all it took.

'Oh, good God,' said Bishop quietly. 'Do what you can. I'm going to call Paine.'

Laura looked expectantly at Webster, but he could only shake his head.

'We've got to do *something*,' Laura said.

Webster remained silent.

'But it won't be long before Heath's wasps try to get into this lab.'

'We'll deal with that when it happens.'

In the lab, Harry looked at the gene sequencers and took notes of the latest readings, jotting them down on a clipboard.

As he walked towards the last one, he suddenly froze.

'What's he doing?' asked Laura. She and Webster watched as Harry turned round very slowly to face the back wall. His brow lowered in concern as he walked cagily towards it.

'This doesn't look good,' said Webster.

Harry tapped at the wall. With no knowledge of

what had happened in the holding bay, he leaned into the cool plastic with nothing more than curiosity. He had no idea the noise that had drawn him had anything to do with the wasps.

'We've got to warn him,' said Laura. She waved, but Harry was facing away from her, and any sound she could make would have no way of penetrating beyond the Inshield.

Harry put his finger up to a place where he could feel a firm vibration. As he did so, that inch of wall was ripped away, replaced by the enormous jaws of a furious wasp.

With a hole in the wall, the sound was able to blast through: the wingbeat of a mutant wasp was drilling angrily at Harry's eardrums.

It had actually touched him, and the revulsion Harry felt at the contact made him stumble backwards into the sequencers.

'Oh, shit,' said Laura.

Harry was frantically searching for some sort of weapon. As in the holding bay, an antenna probed through first, followed by the mandibles.

The wasp was widening the hole just enough to get its head through when Harry ran towards it with a spray gun. He pumped the trigger and covered the insect in a fine mist of concentrated hydrochloric acid.

It had just the effect he had been looking for: the wasp's face melted as if it had been pushed into a fire.

'Go on, Harry!' Laura yelled. She turned to look at Webster, who did not share her enthusiasm.

'What is it?'

He was looking at the wall. It was covered in holes, each filled with the antenna or jaws of a wasp. Some were widening enough to accommodate a head.

Harry had noticed too, and was spraying as fast as he could, but then he looked back at the first hole. The acid was eating away at the surrounding plastic and the gap was growing larger.

Desperately, he searched for another weapon. He soon found a canister of liquid nitrogen and some rubber gloves. If he couldn't melt them, maybe freezing would work.

He splashed a little nitrogen over each hole, and it acted like glue: the insects were stuck to the wall by their frozen legs. In a fury, they tried to free themselves until the effort tore their legs off.

'Looks like he's stopped them,' said Laura.

'Yeah,' replied Webster quietly. 'But even if they don't get to him, I can't see how we can get him out before we freeze it. If we lift the Inshield, we release the wasps.'

'But you can't just leave him there.'

'I *know*,' said Webster. 'I know.'

45

In his office, Bishop was psyching himself up to make a call he would have crawled over several dead bodies to avoid. He picked up the receiver, breathed deep and dialled the three digits that connected him directly to the Pentagon office of Tobias Paine.

As usual, the phone rang only once before Paine answered in his distinct patrician tone.

'Steven Bishop. A rare displeasure.'

Bishop laughed this off. 'Good morning, Tobias.'

'Forgive my weariness, Steven, but I can't remember a time when you've called me with good news.'

'I guess that's because it's never been necessary to let you know when the place is running smoothly.'

'I suppose not. So, what's the trouble this time?'

'Well, it was all a result of attempting to make further progress in efficiencies, both, uh, economically and in minimizing our exposure as a facility.'

'Yes, yes. Feel free not to bore the living shit out of me if you can possibly manage it.'

'Uh . . . Sorry. Well, getting right to it, Dr Heath's created some superwasps that are advanced far beyond any of the previous iterations. They're larger, more aggressive and more intelligent.'

'Wonderful. I thought you said this was bad news.'

'Well, it would have been fine if we'd managed to harness them, but before that happened they turned on Dr Heath and killed him.'

A pause. 'Go on.'

'So I tried to get the reserve entomologist out here – the Brit? Laura Trent?'

'Wasn't there some kind of *issue* with her?'

'She's got a young son, so I couldn't persuade her to join us.'

'So?'

'So we kidnapped him to blackmail her into making the trip.'

'I assume you're not calling to inform me of a simple change in personnel.'

'Not exactly. The wasps got out. They've eaten through the walls and we've had to . . .' his voice shrank '. . . deploy the Inshield.'

Silence. Then, 'I see.'

'So we're just trying to work out the best course of action . . .'

'Allow me to assist you with that task. I want you to evacuate all non-military personnel.'

'We're already looking at that.'

'Then I want you to raise the Inshield and let the grunts deal with the wasps.'

'Raise the Inshield? But these wasps have already killed three soldiers. The idea that the ones who are left will be able to provide any resistance is –'

'Shut up, Steven. Freezing MEROS and restarting it again? That will take until next year. Do you have any idea how that will go down here? We have operations Fleming and Harper in the next month alone. How do you expect me to tell Jonathan that we have to cancel them because a few wasps got out and, rather than try to deal with them, you just wet your pants and ran away?'

'Tobias, it's a little more serious than that. I wouldn't be calling if there wasn't a very real and imminent threat.'

'A threat to what? Yes, Dr Heath has died and that is a . . .' he searched for the word '. . . *shame*, I suppose, but a few soldiers? That goes with the territory .'

'But Tobias —'

'If there are any further developments, call me again. Otherwise: do your job.'

'Tobias —'

'Am I understood?'

'Yes, Tobias.'

46

Bishop left his office in time to meet Laura and Webster coming back down the corridor. Wainhouse was making frantic gestures towards the elevator.

Webster hurried towards him, with Laura following close behind. As they reached the end of the corridor, she saw Andrew standing helpless behind the glass.

On the side that was going to be frozen.

With everything else that was happening, Laura had been grateful that she did not have to worry about her son. Now that single source of comfort had been wrenched from her and replaced with the cold darkness of its opposite.

She was torn between her instinct, which was to let the twisted rush of dread take over, and her need to make Andrew believe that this was not going to be as disastrous as it appeared.

In the end, she brought her hands to her face to mask the fear in her eyes, then realized how bad that looked and took them away again.

Shit, she thought, *shit shit shit shit shit.*

'Please tell me there's something we can do about this,' she said to Webster. She was trying in vain to keep her voice steady.

Before Webster could think of a reply that could possibly help, Bishop appeared behind them.

'What the hell are they doing in there?'

'We're trying to find that out,' said Webster.

'Please tell me there's something we can do about this,' repeated Laura.

'While we're on lockdown, the elevator can't go back up,' Webster said.

'But everything on that side of the glass is going to be frozen.'

There was a damp pause before Bishop spoke. 'No one expected this to happen.'

Laura moved to the glass in front of the lift. Andrew looked ashen. The initial waves of fearful shock were still pounding through her, so her attempt to appear calm came out only as helpless confusion.

Meanwhile, Bishop took Webster aside.

'Paine said to evacuate non-military and lift the shield, let your guys deal with the wasps. Obviously, that's changed now.'

'Yep. I think we're going to be lifting the shield with no evac, otherwise no one's going anywhere. Dealing with the wasps just went from hard to damn near impossible.'

Bishop agreed, like he was revealing a secret under torture. 'We'd better check on Harry.'

They walked up the corridor to Lab 7. Through the Inshield and the glass, they saw him facing the hole-ridden wall, looking for the next wasp that fancied its chances against him.

Some of the jagged gaps were blocked with frozen wasp heads. By splashing liquid nitrogen on the parts that had come through, Harry had created a macabre series of ice-sculptures which were strangely fascinating to look at. Cruel eyes peered out over vicious jaws, some with legs trying to prise their way forward; others with thick, lengthy antennae probing ahead.

But there would be no more of these. Harry's nitrogen had run out; he would have to search the lab for other means of defending himself.

The problem was that all the other harmful chemicals were corrosive, and he could see from the large, melted gap he had sprayed with acid there would be no point in using any of those.

His only other option was physical: he had smashed a beaker and was now armed with a jagged blade of glass, which he was using to stab the wasps that poked their heads through the wall. However, there were now so many of them, and they were smart enough to learn and adapt their behaviour. They would break down as much of the wall as possible, then take refuge in the cavity when Harry approached.

He knew it was only a matter of time before they made it through.

Catching a reflection of Bishop and Webster in the chrome piping at the back of the lab, he turned and saw their frustrated and despairing expressions.

Bishop shrugged hard and mouthed, *What the hell —?*, to which Harry replied with a *What am I supposed to do?* look of his own. Bishop closed his eyes, shook his head and walked off towards the barracks. Webster stayed to mouth, *Hang on. We're going to get you out of there.*

Hurry, was the silent reply.

47

The remaining inhabitants of MEROS had gathered in the mess room of the barracks.

The soldiers Webster and Wainhouse were making sure they had access to the kind of weaponry that would come in useful if the wasps managed to get out.

The scientists Takeshi, Susan, George, Lisa and Mike were still shot through with fear. And even if they had managed to calm themselves down, they had no idea how to contribute, so they sat on the couches worrying and speculating.

'See? This is what I meant,' said Mike, tapping his foot.

'What are you *talking* about?' asked Lisa, her eyes searching, her voice trembling.

Mike's words were coming with scrappy speed, the sentences running into each other, stumbling, then continuing at pace. 'I said – and I said it to these guys – that something was up. I bet you anything Roach and Martin are dead. I bet Heath's dead. Someone fucked up. I mean, did you see those wasps? Did you fucking *see* them?'

'No *cabron*, we missed them,' said George, lighting a red Marlboro with shaking fingers.

'Roach and Martin are dead?' said Lisa. Her arm was

rubbing Susan's tight shoulders as she sat, stunned into silence, on the couch.

'We don't know that,' Susan replied.

'Oh, they're dead all right,' said Mike. 'Just like we're going to be. No one here knows what the fuck they're doing, and we have superfreak wasps flying around all over the fucking place.'

'They are behind the Inshield,' said Takeshi calmly. 'We're safe here. We just have to get to the surface.'

'Oh yeah? What the fuck is the Inshield, and how come you know so much about it?'

'It's in the orientation pack you were given to read when you arrived,' said Takeshi. 'The Inshield is the final security measure. When it comes down, everything on the other side of it is frozen, then we will leave.'

'Yeah, 'cos leaving's gonna be a piece of cake. You see the elevator? Does that look like it's moving?'

Takeshi gave a small shrug. 'I don't know. Perhaps it would help if we all remained calm.'

'Easier said than done,' muttered Mike.

As Wainhouse organized the weaponry, he looked over to the scientists and wondered how much they were going to depend on him. If they couldn't get Garrett and Carter out of the elevator, it was going to be down to just him and Webster to make sure the rest of them lived. Looking unconvinced of their chances of success, he continued checking the weapons.

In the corridor, Laura was talking to Bishop. 'Is there no way of communicating directly with the people inside the elevator? At the moment, I'm writing everything down on bits of paper, and I know it would help Andrew if he could hear my voice.'

'The intercom in my office can do that. Press the blue button – but it's only one-way. Their emergency line goes up to Taj. And take the major with you. Maybe he can find out why Garrett and Carter were on their way down here, heavily armed, with your son in tow.'

Bishop walked into the barracks to find the scientists looking at him expectantly, and Wainhouse standing beside his cache of weapons with his arms folded. Silence greeted his arrival.

'OK, I know you will all have a number of questions regarding the situation we currently find ourselves in. Bottom line: without my knowledge, over the last few months, David Heath was engineering a strain of wasps larger, smarter, stronger and more aggressive than anything we have previously produced here. The ones you' – he pointed to Takeshi and Susan – 'saw up close and the rest of you have just seen through the window of the holding bay.' He paused for effect.

'Now, I have to tell you that Dr Heath was . . . over-come by these wasps.' Another pause. 'He was killed in the process of his research, in the line of duty, if you will. Then, as some of you also know, three of our military force were killed trying to deal with the situation. We have now reached a stage where these wasps have got into the wall cavities and come out into the labs. The decision has been taken to bring down the Inshield, which means the corridor, barracks, canteen and my office are the only areas available to us. The plan is to freeze everywhere else, kill the wasps and evacuate, restarting the facility either here, or elsewhere if that is not an option. Any questions?'

'How long is this going to take?' asked George.

'As this is the first time we have done it, that is currently unknown. Less than twenty-four hours.'

'And how do you know we'll be safe when the freezing is over?' asked Mike.

'The movement sensors beyond the sapphire glass will give us an idea of whether we can at least end the lockdown and leave the facility. People, I know this is bad, and it's ultimately my responsibility, but none of us . . . out here . . . is in danger. It's just a matter of sit and wait.'

Susan looked puzzled, then put her hand up.

'You don't have to raise your hand, Miss Myers.'

'Did you just say that the shield is made of sapphire glass?'

Bishop finally had something to look confident about. 'Specially toughened sapphire glass, which is around ten times harder than the regular stuff, so I don't think the wasps will be getting through it anytime soon.'

Susan continued to look puzzled, then put her hand up again, before Bishop's impatient expression made her lower it. 'What is it, Miss Myers?'

'Well, I only did one semester of Applied Materials, but isn't sapphire glass known for being brittle?'

'Excuse me?'

'Sapphire glass is very strong, as in resistant to scratches, but it is much more brittle than normal glass, so if it were subject to impact, it would be much more likely to break.'

A cloud of trepidation descended on the room.

'But they're just wasps,' Bishop said, with as much scorn as he could muster.

'Larger, smarter, stronger and more aggressive wasps, you said,' reminded Mike.

'But they couldn't possibly . . .'

'If they can get through the plastic of the walls, they can get through the Perspex lab windows,' said George. 'And if they get through that and are determined to have a go at the Inshield . . .'

Bishop could feel himself getting colder, from the face down. He had no answer and no way of testing this theory. If they broke any part of the shield glass, who knew how far that break would spread.

'But they're just . . .'

'They're just a few pounds of anger that can probably manage five or ten miles an hour,' said Mike. 'You'd better have a Plan B.'

48

'Can you hear me? Over,' Laura said carefully.

'It looks like you've got a yes,' called Webster. He was watching the elevator, and a thumbs-up from Carter, Garrett and Andrew told him all he needed to know.

'OK, Andrew, I'm going to explain exactly what is going on here. You've got to be really, really brave and listen to me so that this all works out the way we want it to.' Andrew was staring at Webster as if he were saying these words. In return, Webster was looking like the solidity Andrew needed.

'There are some big wasps behind the walls down here. We tried to keep them confined, but they got out. Now this area has been locked down with these glass shields so that we can protect ourselves, freeze the rest of the complex and kill them.' She took a breath as the difficult part arrived.

'Because of a timing accident, you are on the wrong side of the shield, but we're going to get you out here with us. Until then, you have to sit tight and wait.' Carter and Garrett looked pensive. Andrew looked scared. Webster saw Carter say something to Garrett then write a note, which he held up to the glass:

Can the wasps get in here?

Webster raised his hand to Carter and headed for the intercom to tell Laura.

'Well, we're not going to get away with keeping it from them,' she said.

Webster nodded and took the receiver. 'We don't know for sure if the wasps can get to you. Take the panels off the south side of the lift, away from where the wasps are. If you find concrete, then we know that's what the entire lift shaft is made from, and you'll be safe. If it's plastic, like the lab walls, we know we've got to get you out fast, OK?'

Webster returned to the elevator to find Carter and Garrett already attacking the panels with their knives.

Laura came at once and knelt down next to the glass. Looking into her son's face, she saw only the features his father had given him, especially those searching blue eyes. Andrew tried not to look worried, but his attempt at a brave smile collapsed into a helpless frown. That was about all Laura could take, and she turned away to protect Andrew from her tears. The next time she felt able to look at her son, Carter had a big arm round his shoulder and was no doubt saying the words she wished she could. Andrew looked at his mum and nodded to let her know that he could get through this.

For a moment, she believed he was going to be OK, that they would both get out of here and get back to England, but then the look on his face became one of utter terror.

Following his eyes, she saw what he did: the wasps

246

had torn through the wall at the back of the holding bay and were now butting up against its windows. It was the first room on the right ahead of the elevator, so they were now only a few feet from Andrew. Laura had not told him just how big the insects were, so his horror was multiplied by incomprehension.

He was rooted to the spot, confronting the thought of what could lie ahead: giant insects beyond anything he ever thought existed. Now that he could see into their eyes, a terrible reality fleshed out what his imagination had created. They looked so angry, evil and powerful that he couldn't see how they could be overcome. They had killed people much tougher and better armed than him. What chance did he have? What chance did his mum have?

They had already stopped trying to force their way through the window. Instead, they were using whatever grip they could find to keep their claws attached, while their acidic saliva burned through the Perspex.

Their jaws were wide open, and the spit they released was washing down the window, distorting the images of the yellow and black creatures behind it.

Andrew could see Laura talking to Webster with obvious concern. That worried him even more, and he gave an involuntary shudder.

Carter felt this and turned to Andrew, gripping his shoulders. 'Kid, I'm not going to let them get me, and if I'm not going to let them get me, I'm not going to let them get you. Are you listening?'

He said it louder: 'Are you listening?'

Andrew stopped staring at the wasps and met Carter's fixed eyes. 'Right, yes . . . Yes, sir.'

'OK. Now you have to do exactly as I say, and we will get out of here alive.'

Carter turned to the walls of the elevator on the opposite side to where the wasps were approaching.

'First, we're going to get these panels off. The intercom speakers will be the weak point. Work on them with Garrett.'

Meanwhile, Laura and Webster were doing their best to distract the wasps, waving at them and tapping on the glass near where they flew and hovered.

Bishop stood behind them, looking for the right moment to draw Webster away without arousing further alarm.

'Uh, Major, we just received another communication from Paine,' he said with an obvious wink. His attempt to sound genuine was poor, but Laura was paying too much attention to the wasps to notice. Webster turned and saw the deepening fear on Bishop's face, and immediately followed him to his office.

'The scientists have just pointed out an important design flaw with the Inshield. Sapphire glass is scratch resistant, but it's not too good when it comes to impact.'

'What?'

'If the wasps get through the Perspex, they can get through the Inshield.'

'And I just saw them. When they tried to get through the lab window the first thing they did was butt into it.'

'They do that on the Inshield, it might come down

in ten seconds or ten minutes. We can't know for sure, and that's the problem.'

'OK. Let's check on Harry, then we need to open this situation up to everybody. No shitting around. Facts on the table, has anyone got any answers, because we might be ten minutes from being wasp food.'

In the elevator, Garrett was wrenching the speaker off the far wall.

'Good,' said Carter, and reached in to pull back the surrounding panel.

Andrew and Garrett stood clear as he bent the metal away. It peeled off easily, with a tearing sound and a large clang, but before Carter could get to work on the next one, he saw Laura gesturing towards him and pointing at the wasps.

They had heard the noise from the elevator and had grouped together at that end of the lab, hovering against the glass and climbing the wall.

'OK, no need to panic,' said Carter quietly, continuing to bend away the panels.

As Laura watched, Bishop and Webster came out of the office, walking as fast as they could without running.

'We're going to check on Harry,' Webster told Laura. 'Then we need everybody in the barracks.'

They turned and headed back to Lab 7. Laura joined them.

When they got there, Harry was gone. There were now only a few wasps, which were exploring the equipment, searching for anything that might be food.

Laura was confused, wondering if there might be some hidden safe haven. Webster looked at the gene sequencers and thought the same. Could Harry fit inside one of those? But no inner workings seemed to have been removed to allow him the space he needed.

For Bishop, there was no such uncertainty. He remembered how he had found Heath and looked to the floor.

There it lay: Harry's skeleton.

This time, the wasps had not stopped at the meat. Harry's bones had been separated from each other and lay scattered across the floor of the lab as if by the force of a small explosion that had detonated from his pelvis. A few of the smaller bones, the ones from his fingers and toes, were missing. They were now inside the digestive tracts of the wasps which were searching for more food.

Laura looked away and crouched down, her knees unable to support her.

'Oh no, oh no,' she moaned softly, over and over.

With everything that had happened in the minutes since the Inshield had come down, she had almost forgotten about Harry. She thought he would have been able to last longer than this. There was an awful difference between how she had left him and what had happened since. It made her feel as if death was spreading through this place with an awful inevitability.

Webster was crushed. He had known Harry seven years, and although their friendship had not been deep, they had been through a lot together. He looked at the bones and saw beyond them to the man curled up in terror experiencing the horrific end he must have known would come.

Bishop was less affected. He had not seen the violence this time, and he was not to blame. For these reasons, this death had a smaller impact on him, and he was almost ashamed of the relief he felt. He also knew that they had to get back to barracks and decide what to do next.

He listened to the raised voices at the other end of the corridor and wondered how he might keep this quiet. Harry had been the scientists' first point of contact for anything important, and because they saw Heath so rarely, he was also a conduit for the respect in which they held the great man.

His passing would certainly reduce Bishop's authority over them, and drain away the remnants of what little morale they had left.

'I don't want the scientists told,' he said quietly.

'We have to raise the shield,' said Webster, not directing his words at Bishop. This was a statement and not for discussion.

Bishop needed no persuading. 'You find a way for us to do that without letting them out, and I'll do whatever it takes.'

'We need to try Taj. If there's a way round the security system, he'll know it.' Bishop ran to his office and picked up the phone.

49

'Taj. Bishop.'

Taj never used the phone receiver, preferring instead to switch on the speakerphone and leave himself free to walk around his reception area, eating food with both hands or firing paper darts at the 'O' of the MEROS sign that hung from the wall opposite his desk. Now he was waving his fat fingers around and expressing himself as if Bishop were in the room with him.

'Mr Bishop. I've been trying to reach you, but your phone's been tied up. There's been some stuff happening up here you gotta know about. Garrett and Mills and Jacobs are getting set to hijack the plane, and I think they on their way down to you.'

'You don't say,' Bishop replied.

'Damn straight. Assholes gassed me. Shook me up pretty good. You ever been CS'd?'

'Uh, no . . . look, I'll see to that. It's a bit complicated, but I'll work something out.'

'I've had to open the doors and air this place out. Someone still up here, though. I can hear them outside.'

'Yes, OK, OK, Taj. Just keep quiet for a moment, I need you to listen very carefully. The Inshield is down and . . .'

'The Inshield? What the hell happened?'

'You don't want to know, believe me. It's down, and we're still going to have to go through with the freezing, but before that, or during that, or I don't know when, we're going to have to raise the shield.'

'Don't tell me, the three who came down are stuck in the elevator.'

'Something like that.'

'Well, let me tell you, Mr Bishop, them folks can go fuck 'emselves, 'scuse me for saying.'

'Yes, Taj. One of them happens to be Andrew, Laura Trent's son. Another one of them is Carter. Did they gas you?'

'Not that . . . uh . . . I'm not sure, but the kid . . .'

'Exactly: *the kid*. So we have to raise the shield.'

'Yeah, I told them that would be a risk when they installed the security system, but nobody listens to Taj.'

'Yes, great. Well, here we are. We could simply freeze, wait and leave, but of course we can't just let them die. At the same time, we can't lift the glass, otherwise we'll all be dead. I know it looks impossible, but is there any way you can get the elevator back up there?'

'The only way is if I have your key card up here, along with mine, to override anything, and I guess that ain't going to happen.'

'Is there really nothing?'

'Well, sir, if you tell me what you want, I can do my best to make it so, but it looks like you're in what they call a situation down there. I could do what I can to lift the glass, but it doesn't sound like you want that, and if I try to get the elevator up here, the security system gets cancelled and the glass goes up.'

'That's kind of what I thought.'

'OK, I'm going to see what I can do, so stay near the phone and I'll call you back if I'm heading in the right direction.'

'Done.'

50

In the rec room of the barracks, Webster was standing in the corner talking to Wainhouse and Laura about trying to raise the shield. On the couches by the opposite wall, the scientists were speculating about the number of dead.

'Anyone seen Harry lately?' asked Mike loudly. Laura and Webster turned round too obviously and found themselves staring at Mike and Lisa in a suddenly silent room.

Mike raised his eyebrows.

'Seriously? Harry's dead?'

No reply.

'I'll take that as a yes. Who else?'

Wainhouse, Laura and Webster moved towards the others. With Bishop in his office, Webster could do what he felt was right, and that meant honesty.

'Roach, Martin, Heath and Van Arenn all died trying to contain the new wasps.'

George's brow furrowed into a series of fat hillocks. 'But if Heath and Harry are gone, who's going to . . .' He looked at Laura and his question was answered.

'But you're just a civilian. No offence, but if you haven't been down here before, you've got a lot to learn.'

'I'm taking a crash course,' Laura said.

This exchange was cut short by Bishop, who clipped into the rec room at a run. He failed to sense the mood and was speaking almost as fast as he was walking. 'People, we have a situation beyond the one we all thought we were in. As you may have seen, Carter, Garrett and Dr Trent's son, Andrew, are trapped in the elevator, which is going to mean there is some difficulty in implementing the final parts of the security plan. That problem, coupled with what we suspect about the glass in the shield, means that we need ideas, suggestions that can get . . .'

Mike jumped in. 'Maybe Harry could help. Or Roach and Martin. Let's get them to give us a hand.' Bishop looked to Webster.

'They guessed. I confirmed it,' he explained.

'Fine. I'll assume you're all up to speed then. As the person in charge, I do of course take full responsibility for what has happened here over the last couple of weeks. I accept that blame will be apportioned and certain processes will have to be put in motion. But, for now, we just need to make sure everyone who is still alive gets out of here in that state. I'd appreciate it if we could put other things aside for the immediate future and concentrate on what really needs our attention.' He looked at them as a group, challenging them to stand up to him.

No one did.

51

'OK, this is going to be easier. These panels are held in with screws, and I just happen to know that one of us has a screwdriver on them.' Carter grinned at Andrew, who gave a puzzled look in return. 'Your Swiss Army knife, please, Andrew.' Andrew smiled as the penny dropped and reached into his pocket for the red hunk of metal. Pulling out the correct blade, he handed it over to Carter, who made a show of admiring it.

'Well, maybe it's lucky you came along after all,' he said.

As Carter attacked the steel squares, Garrett moved out of his way. She couldn't help looking at the wasps that were still trying to get through the window to the right of the elevator.

It was difficult to see clearly, but their efforts were definitely having some effect: the Perspex was now riven with streaks that made it look like some real damage was being done.

'Jesus Christ,' she muttered. 'They are some mean-looking fuckers.'

Andrew followed her gaze. He found the insects hypnotic, especially the rhythmic way their mandibles came together as they scratched against the windows. Along with their acidic saliva, a fine spray of venom accompanied each tap of stinger on Perspex, warping the transparency. There was something disturbingly organized about what they were doing, as if they were certain of the ultimate consequence.

Andrew was brought back to what was happening in the elevator by Carter's voice.

'OK, last screw and . . .' The second panel fell to the bottom of the elevator shaft with a ripple of clangs, revealing white polycarbonide, the same material that all the MEROS walls were made from. He knocked on it with his screwdriver and got a dull tap in return. It seemed thicker than the lab walls but, with no concrete around it, the wasps' arrival on the other side would be a matter of when, not if.

The phone rang. As Bishop ran to his office and grabbed the receiver, Webster came out to check what was happening in the lift.

Carter showed them the plastic wall.

'Shit,' said Webster, trying to keep his voice down so that Laura wouldn't come out.

He looked across to the window of the holding bay. A wasp was poking its antenna through the Perspex.

52

'Hey, Mr Bishop, sir. I'm just calling to say that I've checked out the security system, and it's bad news. Whoever installed it made sure nothing goes in or out until it's all squared away safe.'

'Thanks, Taj. Don't move one inch from that phone, understand?' Bishop hung up and raced back to the rec room.

All eyes turned to him. 'OK, we can't lift the elevator without lifting the glass, so we're going to have to bite the bullet and freeze the other side.'

'Mr Bishop, if you think I'm going to stand aside while you kill my son . . .'

'Hey, hey, hey . . . just calm down, Dr Trent. Nobody said anything about that. We're going to work out how to get them out of there without them or us coming to any harm.'

'We'd better hurry,' said Webster. 'The walls of the elevator shaft are polycarbonide. We might have as little as twenty minutes before the wasps get in there. And they look like they're making some progress on the window of the holding bay.'

Lisa spoke first. 'We must have all kinds of insecticides and weapons to disable or kill these wasps. Why do we have to freeze the whole place?'

'Believe me, Miss Keller, if there was another way to deal with *these* wasps, then we would have found it by now,' said Bishop. 'Forget what you've been working on – these specimens are something else entirely, so any solution involving their control by conventional means is not useful. We intend to freeze them, because we know they are susceptible to the cold, and that's more than we can definitely say about any other methods of control.'

'If freezing works, why didn't you freeze them before, when, I assume, they were in a more controlled environment?' asked Takeshi.

'They were frozen to a certain degree that we, uh, thought was sufficient to kill them, but it turned out we only stunned them. Then we were presented with a series of, uh, unforeseen difficulties which made the completion of the task through the use of cold impossible.'

Wainhouse was steaming. 'Yeah, they turned Van Arenn into a main course, and nearly did the same to Garrett. Then they ate through the wall into the cleaning cavities, and now we're sitting here waiting to do something we should have done days ago, if some people hadn't been family-sized assholes about it in the first fucking place.'

'Thank you, Captain Wainhouse. Yes, tragic circumstances have surrounded the engineering of these particular specimens, tragic circumstances that were unavoidable . . .'

'Bull*shit*, Mr Bishop, sir.'

'Please! Can we just concentrate on finding a solution!' pleaded Laura. 'We're running out of time.'

Wainhouse folded his arms and looked at the floor.

'If you didn't reduce the temperature, how did you freeze the wasps before?' asked Takeshi.

'A canister of liquid nitrogen was attached to the wall near the nest.'

'Why not freeze them again?'

'OK, I thought I'd been clear about this, but I'll say it one more time for anyone who wasn't listening. The elevator is in the area that will be subject to freezing.'

'Yes, I understand that, but surely the wasps will react more to the level of cold than any human. It's part of their genetic make-up, and they're far smaller than even the boy. You could freeze the area to some degree, incapacitate the wasps, get everyone out of the elevator before they are affected, then replace the shield. Then you would be able to freeze the wasps' area to whatever extent you wished.'

Bishop thought for a moment, then met the expectant eyes of Laura, who obviously considered this to be a better solution than she had thought possible.

'Thank you, Takeshi,' said Bishop. 'That could be just what we need to do. However, there are two potential difficulties. First, I don't know if the security system is flexible enough for us to turn it on and off like that, but I can find that out right away. And second, we don't want a repeat of what happened when we tried to use a lower measure of cold on these wasps before. They insulated themselves and secreted some of their number away from the frozen part of the lab.'

'But if you freeze the entire area, then they can't do that again, can they, Mr Bishop?' asked Laura.

'No, for sure, but they can protect themselves by insulating each other. The question is, can we bring the temperature down far enough to really knock the wasps out? And can we be sure that degree of cold will not harm anyone in the elevator?'

'But we're talking about seconds here.'

'I know, Dr Trent, but we're also talking about introducing a sizable element of risk to the situation. Of course, I will do whatever it takes to save the three lives in that elevator but, under the circumstances, I don't know if it's really right to impose such jeopardy on these people.'

'So you'd be fine with it as long as everyone else is?'

'Absolutely.'

'OK.' Laura took a moment, then stood in front of the others. Trying to look everyone in the eye, she spoke clearly but with obvious emotion.

'You have just heard about the situation we are in. Although I'm aware you don't know my son, if any of you are parents, I guess you'll have some idea of what I'm going through. A few days ago, he was kidnapped, to blackmail me into coming here. I had no idea where he was, and I . . . can't explain how awful that was. I lost my husband two years ago, so Andrew is all I have left. When I thought he was missing, maybe even dead, well . . .'

She stopped, her thoughts mired in the memory of those few hours, then looked up again.

'The relief I felt when I discovered that he was alive was overwhelming. I need him. I mean, I can't go on without him. And we didn't ask for this.

She took a deep breath. 'The way I see it, the choice we have is simple: consign him, and Carter and Garrett, to a certain death and live with the knowledge that it happened despite our chance to choose otherwise. Or take a risk to save them. Should the worst happen, I am certain that, with the help of Mr Bishop and Major Webster, we will be as prepared as possible to deal with that.'

'Yes, ma'am,' said Webster.

'Uh, of course, Dr Trent,' said Bishop.

'Thank you. I suppose what we need now is a show of hands. Who would agree with Mr Bishop, Major Webster and myself that we should attempt to save these three lives?'

With varying degrees of enthusiasm, all hands were raised.

'Great,' said Bishop after a pause. 'Well, like I said, we don't know if this will work, but we'll give it our best shot.'

Laura nodded to confirm there was no way back for Bishop, and went to explain the plan to Andrew.

53

'They've been gone a long time, don't you think?' said Mills, half to Madison, half to himself.

'Twenty minutes? Yeah, I'd say so, fuckburger. What say you abandon the dumb plan and untie me? And while you're at it, maybe the kid would like some fresh air.'

Mills glowered at Madison. 'For calling me fuck-burger, you can stay put, but, sure, I'll take the mask off the kid.'

He only needed to bring the mask halfway off Jacobs' head before his expression changed from cocky to a bloodless grey.

'Jacobs, what the hell are you doing in there?'

'Mills, you simple sonofabitch. I may be the same height as that kid, and I may be flat-fucking-chested, but you must be the dumbest piece of shit in this jungle to have got that wrong. How many times did I have to say, "It's Jacobs"?'

'You can't make out anything through those masks. It sounded like you were saying "Don't make me" or something. Look, I'm sorry.'

He continued to untie the ropes, leaving Jacobs to shake out her burning wrists to the sound of Madison laughing to the point of asphyxiation.

'Hey, Mills! Are you sure it's me? It could be Webster,

or maybe Bishop in a Madison suit. Or even your mom. Ha! You dumb asshole!'

'This isn't helping you get untied any faster, Madison.'

'I know, but I wasn't expecting anything anytime soon, and that is the funniest thing I've seen since Garrett put that snake in your bio-suit.'

'OK, Madison, shut the fuck up. Jacobs, apologies again, but the question stands: do you think they've been gone too long?'

Jacobs paused to indicate that, even if she answered this question, Mills was a long way from forgiven.

'Yeah, it's been a good while. Best go ask Taj.'

'But he'll know we're doing something wrong.'

'Mills, he just finished a half-hour of coughing from the CS gas you exploded under his nose. I think he already knows there's something wrong. If there's something going on down below, then he'll also know about that.'

Madison laughed even more. 'Hey, Mills, this is definitely not the day to take an IQ test. What did you have for breakfast, a fucking lobotomy?'

Mills was starting to fume. Jacobs could tell from having been on missions and in barracks with him that he was about to snap and, sure enough, he gave Madison a noisy, open-palmed *crack* round the face.

'Speak again when you're spoken to, taxi-driver,' he said over his shoulder, as he and Jacobs headed to the open entrance of MEROS. Now it was Madison who was fuming.

'Would you think we'd need to threaten Taj?' Mills asked Jacobs as they walked through the muggy jungle air. He was ramming home the loaded clip of his Desert Eagle in an attempt to stop Jacobs thinking he was an incompetent prick.

'Could be,' said Jacobs. 'Just leave it to me,' she added quietly.

When they got within ten feet of the door, it snapped shut with a solid locking noise. Mills pushed and pulled at it, but with no success. Jacobs tried her security pass, and all the entry codes she had ever used, but it soon became obvious they were the reason the door was locked and it wasn't going to open anytime soon.

'OK, Jacobs, what now?'

54

Bishop was on the phone to Taj again, explaining the new plan.

'Sure I can do that, Mr Bishop, sir, but I'm guessing that we're talking about some split-second timing here.'

'That's right, Taj. I don't know how fast the shield will raise and lower, so I can't just say give it five seconds or whatever. We'll have to watch from down here and let you know what to do.'

'You got it. Just give me the word.'

'OK, stay by the phone. I'll begin the freezing process as soon as I've made sure everyone down here knows what they're doing.'

He replaced the receiver and hurried to the barracks.

'OK, people. As you can see, this area is not secure, so I'm going to ask you all to move to the safety of my office. We will have complete communication access to the outside world there and, yes, that does mean the Pentagon, although I'm sure it won't come to that. Major Webster, I am going to need you to assist both in getting everyone out of the elevator as quickly as possible, and in relaying to me the position of the shield so that I can tell Taj when to lower it. OK. If you're all ready, let's go.'

Everyone collected their belongings and moved across the corridor. This gave them another chance to see the wasps, two of which were now able to get their wings through the Perspex.

For Wainhouse and the scientists, this was the first time they had a good chance to see the bastards up close. Even though their everyday lives involved the control of giant insects, these were terrifying enough to wipe away years of desensitization to such horrors.

The thorny legs, as thick as cigarettes, gripped the rough edges of the glass. It was all too easy to imagine them taking hold of flesh, making it ready for the sting or the jaws.

And what jaws they were. Strong, sharp and thought-less, driving through whatever they needed to destroy until it was no more.

Susan turned away, trying to reduce their chances of infecting her nightmares. The others shifted along, feeling the fear scrabbling through their guts as they were drawn irresistibly to look.

The relentless way in which the wasps set about removing the barriers to further killing was truly fear-some. The Perspex was becoming a series of ragged, melted holes which were growing larger by the second. It would not be long before the wasps would be able to fit their abdomens through, then butt up against the brittle glass of the Inshield.

Bishop opened a control panel on the wall of the corridor and set the co-ordinates to freeze the areas on the other side of the shield.

'You'd better hurry,' said Webster, eyeing the progress of the wasps.

'No shit,' murmured Bishop. He jabbed in the last number and set the freezing to begin. 'It should take about five minutes. I told Carter to signal when the temperature gets too low for them. That is when you need to be there to drag them on to this side of the shield.'

'Roger that. And Dr Trent?'

'Will remain in my office with everyone else. What we really don't need is a combination of motherly distress and female panic. I'm going to use the phone in my office, but I'll bring it out here so that I'm as close to you as possible. I may even be able to see the elevator myself. Shit!'

One of the wasps was through and bumping up against the Inshield. It only had a couple of feet to get up some speed to fly as hard as possible into the sapphire glass.

Webster wasn't concerned. 'It'll be frozen before it can –'

A crack spread through the glass. Webster drew his Glock.

'Get back into your office right now,' he said evenly to Bishop. Bishop did as he was told, as Webster kept his eyes on the wasp.

Another bump, and the crack widened. This time it was audible, a soft thump followed by a small crinkle.

'Freeze, you bastard,' Webster said under his breath.

A third impact, this time from another wasp. Now there were two, then three butting up against the Inshield.

The cracks were inching across the glass towards each other.

Bump, *chinkle*.

Bump, *chinkle*.

Bump, *chinkinkle*.

At last, the cold was beginning to fog the glass, but would the Inshield hold?

A softer bump this time – barely audible. Webster couldn't be sure, but the wasps seemed to be less purposeful, more aimless.

Then one dropped to the floor.

Webster took this as a sign that he could check on the elevator.

Carter and Andrew were wiping the glass to make sure they could see and be seen. If they were aware of how close the wasps had come to breaking through, it wasn't clear.

Webster signalled to Bishop, who dialled up to Taj and told him to stand by. Meanwhile, the wasps continued to fade behind the greying condensation.

The insects were slipping from indistinct shapes into mere shadows, and Webster could tell that they were first panicking, then moving more and more slowly, stumbling around or flitting short distances. Most of them had made it through the Perspex to the Inshield and, as they dropped to the floor, they were forming a heap against the bottom of the glass.

There was no way of knowing whether any others were safe further away, insulating each other for protection as they had done before but, in the immediate vicinity, these wasps looked as if they were responding perfectly.

Bishop looked at Webster, who was staring at the insects.

'How's it going?'

'They're dropping like flies.'

Laura had made her way out of the office and was now standing in the doorway, anxious for any news.

'What did he say?'

'It's going fine. Please get back inside.'

Laura passed the information on to Wainhouse and the scientists, who were waiting in expectant silence. Carter and Garrett were looking at Andrew, for anything that might signal the need for action.

'OK, kid, there's no need to be a hero. Just tell us if you feel drowsy or there's pain anywhere,' said Garrett.

Andrew replied through a juddering breath of white-grey cloud. 'I–I–I'll let you know, G–G–G–Garrett.'

Another minute passed in silence. The tension was flowing through them like electricity.

Breathing quickened. Hearts thumped harder. Fists curled tight enough to make them shake.

Then Andrew gave the signal. He could only manage the words, 'I feel –' before passing out.

Carter whipped round and hammered on the glass. Half a second later, Webster signalled to Bishop.

'Taj, raise the glass now.'

'Yessir.'

Almost immediately the shield whined and rumbled its way out of the floor, inching into the ceiling. They all willed it on, praying for it to move faster so they could get out of there alive.

Then, just as it started, it ground to a snarling halt.

The sound of a slow-motion car crash echoed around the corridor, its piercing scrape ripping through the air before scratching and grinding over nerve endings and eardrums.

They could hear that the motor was still engaged in a straining effort to continue. It sounded like pain.

'Taj, are you still lifting?' snapped Bishop.

'Sure, Mr Bishop. Is there a problem?'

'I think the cold is jamming the mechanism. Keep trying, and if there's anything you can do to up the power, do it now!'

'Sure thing – increasing power.'

The grinding got louder until they feared the cogs and gears were going to wrench each other apart.

Garrett desperately tried to revive Andrew. Webster could only think to join Carter in getting his fingers under the shield to try and raise it.

Bishop watched as every atom of effort appeared on Webster's face in a network of inflated veins covered in a sheen of scarlet.

Then the loudest grinding scream suddenly gave way to a great *CRUNCHUNCH*. A gear snapped, sending the shield shooting up to the ceiling.

Carter was standing face to face with Webster, trapped in a millisecond of confusion.

The pile of frozen wasps now had nothing holding it back. Hard, slippery insects fell into the corridor, sliding across the floor in all directions. One reached as far as Bishop, who leapt back as if it were a grenade.

Carter flipped Andrew over his shoulder and ran into Bishop's office with Webster and Garrett right behind.

'Taj, drop the shield! Quick as you can!' They heard the gears reverse as Andrew was brought to Laura.

She grabbed his cold, still body. He felt dead. She looked up at Garrett, fearing the worst.

'His pulse is fine. He's just passed out. Keep him warm,' said Garrett.

She turned to help Carter and Webster deal with what was happening outside.

'What about these?' yelled Bishop, pointing at twenty wasps lying frozen on the floor in front of him.

They were either dead or about to react to the absence of the freezing air and rejuvenate, but Carter, Garrett and Webster weren't waiting to find out which.

They started kicking the wasps, as if they were so many oversized hockey pucks, back to where they came from.

Moving the insects was easy; the problem was the Inshield. Whether it was the intense cold, or the workings of a system that was rarely used, it had stuck fast three feet from the ground.

The guttural, piercing screech of the gears had restarted, providing a terrible soundtrack to the soldiers' efforts.

They soon got almost all of the wasps back to the other side. Just four were left when they heard the noise of the shield's motor being joined by another sound: the *barurummmm* of a large set of insect wings powering to life.

Looking over to where the noise was coming from, they saw a disorientated but rapidly thawing wasp stuttering into the air close to where Webster stood.

Immediately, it was joined by more.

'Get them through the other side!' screamed Bishop.

Terror shot through the office. Laura held Andrew closer and he gave a weak cough as he awoke.

Webster ran to one of the moving wasps and squashed it with a firm tread of his massive black boot, then he kicked the twitching corpse in the direction of the glass and moved across to do the same to the others.

'The shield's comin' down!' yelled Garrett. But the motor was slow, and there was still work to be done.

It was impossible to know how alert the wasps were, but with the shield still not low enough to cut them off completely, Bishop had to make a decision.

'Fall back to my office, now!'

The three soldiers ignored him. They were so close to total safety that the little extra effort seemed worth the risk.

Carter crushed another wasp, leaving just one to go. Garrett ran towards it, but they could now see a writhing scrabble of movement on the other side of the shield.

Her boot came down just as several more wasps

crawled into the corridor looking for heat. A few were even flying, rising awkwardly like newborn birds.

Bishop, Garrett, Carter and Webster ran for the office.

The roaring, spattering noise behind them pushed them forward like a strong gust of wind. They didn't look back. With the volume increasing, they didn't have to.

They were within a couple of feet of the door when a wasp rose up behind them and landed on Bishop's shoulder. He dropped the phone, smashing it on the floor, and flailed wildly as the insect climbed round to his neck.

Then they were face to face, and Bishop was consumed by horror, his senses drowning in tar.

The dark, latticed eyes searched Bishop's dilated pupils as the wasp became more and more conscious and remembered how useful its sting could be.

It pulled its abdomen away to give the barb room to drive home.

Bishop tried to squash it against the wall but turned too hard and slammed his shoulder instead. The wasp bucked its rear to lock the stinger fast, only to find Webster's concrete forearm smashing against its side.

It hit the wall by Bishop's head and landed on the ground next to him. Webster's boot came down, but too late: the insect buzzed aside and lost only a leg before whirling around to aim for his throat. Bishop quickly slipped into the office, leaving Webster to it.

Meanwhile, the other wasps were coming.

Webster had no time to work out how to repel the five-legged wasp, get into the office and avoid a situation that would make an agonizing death inescapable.

His hesitation cost him, allowing the single wasp to snatch a rasher of skin from his right arm as it tried to find enough purchase to bring its sting into play.

Before he had time to fully register the pain, he was already pulling his knife from its sheath and stabbing through the wasp's head.

Meanwhile, fifty thrashing wings roared to life behind him.

He looked back to see the swarm closing with single-minded purpose. The sound drove him to the door.

Turning, he lunged into the gap, which was just big enough for him to scrape through, and collapsed on to the floor of the office.

The door slammed shut.

A second later, an irregular beat of soft, insistent thuds could be heard from the other side.

PART THREE
The Abdomen

The Abdomen

55

The survivors were spread throughout Bishop's office. Some had found space on the floor, while others sat around his meeting table, trying not to look at each other. Bishop himself was slumped in the seat behind his desk, a migraine pounding through the side of his skull.

Laura was facing him, in one of his leather armchairs, still holding Andrew in a blanket. The other chair had been used as a soft place to deposit the explosives. With nobody moving or speaking, the only sounds in the room were the ticking clock and the butting of wasps against the wooden door.

'So what's happening out there?' asked Mike, his words competing with that invasive *thud-thud-thud*.

'Even if the shield has come down, there are now so many wasps on this side of it that we can't leave here safely. Eventually, the wasps will get through that door,' said Webster.

'Jesus,' muttered George, crossing himself. Mike shut his eyes, and Laura held Andrew tighter. That close-up they had all had of the wasps ten minutes earlier was the image in everyone's mind. It allowed them to see through the door to what was trying to get in, and that sent something raw and awful through their guts.

Susan looked over at Garrett's scars and the burgundy handkerchief that covered the wound on Webster's wrist.

'So . . . what are we going to do?' she asked. 'Wait here to die?'

'Taj will know something has gone wrong,' said Bishop unconvincingly. 'He will get help to us.'

Wainhouse stepped towards him, his face furious.

'Oh yeah! Fucking right he will! What's he going to do, send some people who don't know what they're doing down an elevator that doesn't fucking work? Jesus Christ! It'll be days before anyone gets sent down here – to find our goddamn *corpses*!'

Even though he knew Wainhouse was right, Webster didn't want him talking like that, but before he could reprimand him, Garrett jumped right in.

'Well, I'm going to go out fighting,' she said, loading ammo into the weapons Wainhouse and Webster had stacked in the corner.

'There has to be another way,' said Laura quietly.

'Well, judging by how solid that door is, I'd guess we've got about a half-hour to think of one,' said Garrett.

The silence that followed was dense, gently punctuated by those muffled knocks. They were soon accompanied by a hard scratching that scraped through the wood and down into the nerves of those who were listening. It reminded them that this time of waiting was not indefinite, and that every second that ticked by brought the inevitable a little closer.

At last, almost in a whisper, Webster spoke. 'We have to do it, Bishop. There's no choice.'

'What are you talking about?' demanded Garrett.

Bishop and Webster looked as if they were both standing on the edge of a precipice and each needed the reassurance of the other to jump off.

'The Abdomen,' said Bishop at last.

He hadn't used the word in fifteen years – not in this context, at least.

'The admin centre is the Head, the labs are the Thorax and, through there' – he pointed towards his bookshelves as the saliva in his throat thickened to cake mix, – 'is the Abdomen.'

'A way out? Why didn't you say? Why are we sitting here?' asked Garrett.

'It's been sealed off since '99.'

'Why?' Laura asked.

'Hey, can we just hurry up and get in there?' said Garrett. 'Who gives a shit what it is? It's got to beat waiting to die in here.' She grabbed at the books, pulling them off the shelves.

'Let him speak,' said Lisa. There was surprise at her talking over Garrett.

Bishop took in the pregnant pause, then his eyes met Webster's. They both knew that time wasn't something they could use indulgently, but the others had to know what they were getting into.

'Through there is the first MEROS lab. We had to seal it off when the insects took over.'

'What insects?' asked Mike.

'All kinds,' said Bishop. 'It was before we began concentrating on wasps. There were roaches, flies, spiders, centipedes, millipedes . . . you name it. All big, aggressive and under the kind of control we had ten years ago.'

'What do you mean, "took over"?' asked Laura.

'Heath kept trying different things, even though he had no real idea what the consequences would be. Eventually, he admitted that he was trying to dial up the rage as far as he could. It all went wrong when some flies killed a wasp. Of course, with their alarm pheromone, all the other wasps just went haywire. It was carnage. The lab technicians lost control. Mayhem. In those days, the facility wasn't set up like this, with contingency plans and glass shields.'

'He got us out,' Bishop said, looking at Webster, acknowledging the debt he still owed. 'Me and Heath. The insects were in charge. The electrics shorted and we couldn't even see what was happening beyond twenty feet. All we had to go on was the buzzing and the screams. I got this' – he pulled up his sleeve to reveal a six-inch scar of mottled purple – 'from a mosquito the size of a football. Major Webster came up behind me and shot it. We turned around to see Heath on the floor. He was using a scalpel to defend himself against two moths that were flapping around him like a couple of crows. We kicked them off and dragged him through the door.'

'What about the others?' asked Susan.

'We waited on this side for people to reach the door

so we could help them get out, but nobody else made it.' Webster was distracted by the memory.

Bishop's mind had replayed these scenes at least once a day ever since. Returning to the Abdomen was something he had never contemplated. Now his imagination churned with possibilities.

Had the insects died? There had never been even the slightest indication there was anything alive on the other side of that wall. The two or three times Bishop thought he'd heard noises – well, that was almost certainly just the weight shifting in one of the bookcases. And if the insects behind the wall were anything like these wasps were now, they'd have made their way through years ago.

But what *were* they like now? The genetic modifications had been primitive and the environment was artificial and without natural light – so what could survive? But that was just it: there was no way of knowing without going in.

'So we're talking about a potentially self-sustaining bio-environment,' Laura thought aloud.

'Something like that, Dr Trent. In your opinion, could anything survive ten years in a place like that?'

'Two days ago, I'd have told you that you couldn't get wasps the size of rats. Down here, I suppose anything is possible. I'd hope they'd all be dead through lack of oxygen or moisture, but that depends on how it's all set up through there. In theory, they could all be alive. But what's happened to them over the years, we can only guess. From what you told me about the early days of the juvenile- and ecdosyne-hormone applica-tion, anything is possible.'

'So our choice is the killer fucking wasps or the killer fucking giant insects? Is that what you're saying?' asked Mike.

'Maybe,' said Bishop quietly.

'Great. That's just fucking great! So we're fucking dead.'

'Hey, cool it. That talk won't help,' said Carter.

Garrett turned to Webster. 'OK, giant insects or no giant insects, what are we looking at terrain-wise when we get through there? 'Cos we've got to face it, whether it's disaster-movie shit or not.'

Webster sketched a map on the back of a Pentagon memo as he spoke. 'It's big. Three floors, each about the size of a football pitch.'

'Through there is a space as big as three football pitches?' asked Takeshi, incredulous.

'Maybe bigger,' said Webster. 'And the floors aren't normal height. They're more like twenty feet up. So we've got . . . yeah . . . I'd say maybe a hundred yards long and fifty wide. It's kind of like a warehouse with a couple of basements.'

'And where are we heading?' asked Garrett.

'Best-case scenario? We enter here. The point we are aiming for is here.' He marked the opposite corner. 'Now, that's the whole floor we've got to cover. If — sorry — *when* we get there, we've got a door leading to a staircase that's going to be five hundred feet to the surface.

'Simple, really, but between here and there, assuming no bugs, you're going to have to expect there to be all sorts of stuff in the way: upturned chairs and tables, broken glass, maybe holes in the floor, and about a third of the way in, we've got the room divided with thin walls, all in the dark. Hopefully, we won't have to know about the two lower levels but, just in case, their layout is the same as the first. If anyone ends up there, it just means that the escape stairs are that bit further to climb.'

'And *with* bugs?' asked Susan.

'With bugs? Anything. Any mutation you could imagine occurring in any insect could have happened in there – they could be super-sized and super-aggressive. Like those wasps and beyond. Let's hope they're all dead.'

Andrew let his imagination run a little before fear reined it back in. The wasps had been bad enough. If there was anything worse than them through there, then he didn't want to think about it.

He wasn't the only one. Susan and Lisa looked at each other with fearful pessimism.

'And why aren't they dead? Why didn't you just nuke the place and open up another lab elsewhere?' asked Mike.

'Money,' replied Bishop. 'The Head and Thorax used to be just the living quarters; all the research took place in the Abdomen. We had a lot more people in those days, because we were still feeling our way. This office was the way into the labs, nothing more. Rather than digging a whole new facility, it was cheaper and easier to downscale and reboot it all through here.'

'Now that everybody knows what we could be in for, I assume this looks like the best course of action to all of you,' said Webster.

However much they wanted to, no one could disagree.

'OK, Garrett, we're going to need a hole in that wall. I'd estimate there's a couple of feet of concrete. In an enclosed space like this, I suggest a tremor device to weaken it without causing too much of a blast. Nothing that will blow that door off.' He pointed to where the bumping noise continued. 'And maybe a few netspreaders across the blast points to minimize the fallout.' Netspreaders were guns which fired weighted adhesive nets to stop insects in flight. They were made of a flexible Kevlar composite that was virtually unbreakable, so they could also be used to provide temporary support and protection if required.

'Now, after the concrete, there's a polycarbonide hatch door with a circular window, about thirty feet of steel-lined corridor, then the final door to the Abdomen. When the tremor device weakens the concrete, we don't want anything that's going to make the corridor collapse, so use small charges.'

With Carter's help, Garrett pulled the bookcase away from the wall.

'OK, everyone, make like you're small,' she said, priming the explosives. As she did so, the others turned

Bishop's desk over and shifted it to the side of the bookcase to create a barrier.

'The timer's set to thirty seconds,' said Garrett, climbing into what was left of the space behind the desk. 'Fingers in ears, people.'

Laura covered Andrew, while the others arranged their limbs and bodies to minimize their exposure to the blast. Everyone tensed, as if waiting for a dentist's rusty drill.

The air in the room changed for a fraction of a fraction of a second before they heard the bang.

It tore through their eardrums, the pitch and volume expanding hard and fast before ebbing away and settling down to a fading echo.

It was as if all their senses had collapsed simultaneously. Deafness, blindness and an overall disorientation left them wondering if any of it was permanent. Gradually, however, the sounds seeped back into their ears, and they saw that the blindness was nothing but a thick cloud of dust that had everyone coughing.

Beyond it they also now saw the door, framed in broken concrete, daring them to enter.

No one had noticed that the sound of the wasps had stopped. Not that it would have made any difference; nobody was getting out that way. The corridor was the only path ahead. They got to their feet and moved slowly towards the door, taking a tentative look at where they were heading.

Laura gripped her son's hand and turned him to face her. 'Whatever happens – what*ever* happens – you stick with me, OK?'

'There's no need for that,' said Webster, raising his voice. 'We're all going to stick together. But if we do get split up, Garrett, Carter and Wainhouse: make sure one of you has George, Mike, Susan, Takeshi and Lisa. Group up now, and look out for one another. And don't make that face, Garrett, you may end up needing Lisa even more than she needs you. I will take Dr Trent, Andrew and Bishop. But I stress: this is emergency procedure only. We do not know what we are going to find .'

The quiet thudding began again.

Webster continued. 'But seeing as those bastards are still keen to join us in here, let's go.'

56

'He's not going to open up.'

Mills was lying on the grass outside MEROS helpfully explaining to Jacobs that her efforts to make contact with Taj were an exercise in futility.

Jacobs ignored him and tried again.

'It's been at least ten minutes,' he said in a sing-song voice. 'He's probably not even there.'

'Mills, the guy has just listened to a grenade go off in his ears. His hearing may not be 100 per cent.'

'Bollocks. He's just sulking.'

Jacobs shook her head and banged on the door again.

'Taj! Taj! Open up! Come on, we know you're in there. Just tell us what's going on.'

As she stepped back to ponder her next move, a tiny noise trickled through the door. She turned round and knocked again, with greater urgency.

'Taj? Is that you? Taj!'

Mills sprang up to join her.

They waited, listening closely to see if Jacobs had really heard anything.

Mills was again about to suggest giving up when the intercom barked into life.

'And what y'all want? Wanna gas me again? Wanna finish me off?'

Jacobs put her hand up to Mills. Their reply was critical and could not be fucked up.

'Taj, we had to get out of there, and we know you take your job real serious, so you wouldn't have let us out loaded with weapons.'

'You damn right, Jacobs.'

'Me and Mills didn't want to do it but Garrett, she said it had to happen. We still told her no and thought she'd agreed, but it turned out she decided to do things her way.'

'Oh yeah? So why you wearing your hazchem suits and masks? On the off-chance?'

'Nope. The plan was to keep anonymous, pretend there was a leak down there and that we were Webster and Carter needing to head out to the storage unit up here for supplies. Then we were going to get Madison to fly us out. Swear to God, casualties were not a part of the plan.'

A pause to avoid looking gullible, then: 'So what you want now?'

'The others have been gone a long time. We want to know they're not dead.'

A longer pause.

'Taj?'

'Yeah?'

'So, are they dead?'

'Nope. Got readings for them all on my motion sensor. Looks like they all in Bishop's office, but none dead, 'less you count Harry Merchant. He bought it in Lab 7 a half-hour ago.'

'So why don't you call down to Bishop?'

'Lost contact twenty minutes back. The Inshield came down, they needed to bring it back up to get the guys out of the elevator. Sounds like things got messed up.'

'With the new wasps?'

'Yeah, something like that.'

'Shit,' said Mills.

'So what we gonna do?' asked Jacobs through the door.

'We gonna wait, and you gonna do your waiting outside.'

'Fair enough.'

Jacobs and Mills took a walk back to the plane to decide on their next move.

'You know, I say we get the hell out of here.'

'It's not going to happen, Mills,' replied Jacobs.

They climbed up the ramp of the plane to find Madison's mouth covered in a dark red crust.

'Oh, you're back then,' he garbled through blood and missing teeth.

'Looks like it,' said Jacobs.

'You know, whatever shit you pull on me, I ain't taking *him* anywhere.'

'Forget it, Madison. We got bigger turds on our plate than your PMS,' Mills replied.

'What? You lost your buddies in a wasp accident?'

'Hey, Madison, your face looks a little swollen on the right side. Do you want me to even it up on the left or do you want to shut the fuck up?'

'Hey, Mills, untie me and we'll see who evens things up.'

'How about I don't and we see what you look like with your airplane rammed up your arse?'

Mills gripped Madison's jaw, inflicting obvious pain. Madison responded by spitting a phlegmy gob of blood over Mills' nose.

Wiping it off and taking a repulsed look at it, Mills drew back his fist, only to find Jacobs holding his arm with surprising strength.

'Chill the *fuck* out,' she hissed into Mills' ear. 'What possible situation can you think of where we will not need this man?'

Trying to maintain some dignity in the face of being humiliated by a woman and a tied-up man, Mills loosed himself from Jacobs' grip and stomped back down the ramp, repeatedly kicking Madison's plane on the way.

'Fucking asshole,' said Madison.

Jacobs exhaled slowly, shut her eyes and took a seat across the aisle from Madison. They sat in silence for a while, deliberately ignoring each other, until it felt pointless.

'So . . . are they really fucked down there?'

'Could be,' she replied quietly.

'If MEROS is screwed, I need to know. If there's any doubt, then I'm not going anywhere. Whether I'm airlifting corpses, survivors or the whole damn team . . .'

'Just shut up, Madison,' said Jacobs wearily.

'Hmmph, you and shitwipe down there go to the same charm school, huh?'

'Look, Taj says they've brought the Inshield down. That means things have gone very wrong. He's heard nothing for twenty minutes. That means things have gone even worse than that. My friends are down there, and there's nothing I can do to help them, so excuse me if I'm not minding my Ps and Qs. I'm in a bad place, and I need to work out how to leave it.'

Jacobs walked out into the clearing and looked at the grass beneath her feet. Somewhere down there, the people she was closest to were scared. Maybe they were trapped somewhere with no way out. They could be in pain. Some of them could be dead. She tried to imagine what it would be like if she were down there with them, if she were fighting for her life, or the lives of the people around her.

She looked back at Madison, bruised, pissed off and none too bright. Then she turned to Mills, who had gone back to lying on the grass. His tall, blond British arrogance crept right under her skin. The big gap between his talents and his opinion of himself made him halfway between a help and a hindrance. Then there was Taj. He was fine behind a desk, but if things had to get physical, 250 lbs of lazy fat was not what she wanted by her side.

She made up her mind: whatever the people underground needed to get them out of there, it would be up to her, and she was not going to let them down.

57

His fingers wrapped around the door handle, Webster peered through the window panel. The corridor was pitch black, offering no clues to what lay ahead. He looked back to Bishop, who gave his final nod of assent, and pushed the handle down.

As soon as the metal bar moved, a violent blast of machine-gun fire rang out through the door. Webster dropped to the ground, while the first bullets passed an inch from his hand.

The others dropped on to their fronts, doing their best to evade something they could not see.

Sound shot through them, filling the small room with cracking explosions of gunpowder and smaller but closer crunches of bullets on wood.

Nerves that were already burning were now stretched as tense as piano wire. The fear that came from being under attack was multiplied by not knowing where that attack was coming from.

Was someone firing at them from behind the door? Who? And why would whoever it was want them dead?

Then it stopped, just as suddenly as it had begun.

Everyone was still forcing themselves into a tight ball or flat against the ground. Surely they weren't safe already?

It took a few moments for Webster to trust the silence.

'Is everyone OK?' he asked, easing himself off the floor. The others had been away to the side, giving Webster room, so no one was hurt. They opened their eyes and looked up again.

'Sorry,' he said, getting to his feet. 'I forgot we mounted motion-sensor guns in the corridor in case any of them got that far. Turning the handle must have set them off. I guess we need to do something to run the bullets down. Everybody back.' He pointed to the furthest corner from the door and the others obediently squashed up into it. 'And brace yourself for some more loud noises.'

Satisfied that they were out of harm's way, Webster grabbed the handle one more time, pulled the door open and ducked. Another blast of fire came and went.

He knew there was still more ammunition, so he sat on the floor throwing protocol manuals into the corridor until the guns stopped shredding them to confetti.

After three increasingly hard throws got no response, he risked a very careful look through the doorway. Nothing.

'OK, people, I think we're good to go.'

Webster moved into the doorway with extreme caution. The guns had definitely stopped firing, so he beckoned the others out of their refuge and sent Carter ahead.

The corridor smelled stale, but only faintly. It was as if the molecules of death and horror were sleeping but not absent. The light from the office sent a gradually darkening illumination halfway down, enough to show that the space was clean and featureless but giving no indication of where it led. It was utterly silent, until it gave the softest of echoes from the noise of the boots that now inched across its steel floor.

Carter's left hand held a heavy-duty torch, which sent a wide wash of soft light across the span of the corridor ahead. His right hand was wrapped tightly around the stippled grip of his 9mm semi-automatic Glock 17, which had all three safety mechanisms disengaged and a full 19-round magazine locked and loaded. He stepped forward gradually, his senses on red alert, searching the inconsistencies of the torchlight for anything that might require his attention.

As he passed the spent guns, he stopped sharp and pointed his weapon dead ahead. In the darkness of the hatch window, he could just make out the milky glint of two eyeballs staring back at him.

He stood tensed, waiting for whatever it was to make a move. The eyes remained static and, in the shadows that surrounded them, he could not make out what they were attached to.

Taking another step, he blinked, and finally realized he was pointing his gun at a reflection of himself. With a little smile of relief, he lowered his pistol and covered the last few feet of the empty corridor.

He got to the far door, switched off his torch and peered through to the Abdomen. It was too dark to discern anything except for several hazy pools of faint blue light. He watched for a minute to see if there was any movement, but the vast blackness was perfectly still. He flicked the drop safety on his Glock and headed back to get the others.

He called to them as early as possible, just to make sure they didn't think his footsteps were anything to be afraid of.

'Hey, guys. Only me. Just Carter,' he said, emerging into the light of Bishop's office.

'Nothing to report. Not in the corridor, anyway. I had a look through to the Abdomen, but there were just some faint blue lights. Nothing moving.'

'If the blue lights are on, then the generator is still working,' said Bishop.

'What generator would still be working after ten years?' asked George.

'It's self-sustaining. Perpetual electricity. It's a version of the Elsasser model with a 24k gold conductor. It worked perfectly until we had to abandon, but I had no idea it would still be operating now.'

'Is that good?' asked Garrett.

'Could go either way.'

'Anyway, if that's where we're heading, it looks about as safe as it's going to look,' Carter said.

'OK, people,' said Webster, 'we need to take whatever weapons we can carry and get going.'

Garrett went in first, leading a line of eleven people through the corridor. When she got to the end, she looked back at Webster, the light from the office casting everyone into silhouettes.

'Whenever you're ready, Major.'

Stomachs writhed like bags of snakes and legs weakened as Webster shut the door behind them.

'OK, Garrett. Open it up.'

There was a central wheel on the door, which she took in both hands. Expecting resistance, she used her full strength to power through the grinding dryness. After some effort, the bolt slid aside. They were now just one hard pull away from entry.

'OK, Major,' she said, in a hoarse whisper, 'I'm opening the door.'

She eased it back an inch at a time, listening for signs of what lay beyond.

The first thing to hit them was the heat. The Abdomen's thermostat was connected to the generator, and the accumulation of warmth had given it the feeling of a jungle in August, a physical wall of sultry moisture almost pushing them backwards.

Next was the smell. Combined with the tangible humidity, no one had ever taken in an odour quite like it, and for that they were glad. It was a fusty combination of excretion, decaying flesh, dirt and bacteria.

Mike, Lisa and Bishop retched.

When they had recovered, Webster signalled to Garrett, and she pulled the door wide open.

It was time to go in.

58

Mills and Jacobs stood at the bottom of the Spartan's loading ramp.

'We need to speak to Taj again, find out what's going on down there. And let's untie him,' Jacobs said, gesturing towards Madison.

'*Untie* him?' asked Mills.

'About fucking time,' said Madison.

'What for?'

'Mills, this has gone far enough. He's done nothing wrong, and we're going to need all the help we can get.'

'But he's going to . . .'

'Kick your fucking ass. That's right, Mills.'

'Madison, if you want to kick his ass, you can stay tied up. We need you, and you'll need both of us. Keep it calm till we're out of here or stay where you are.'

Madison scowled. 'I can play nice.'

'Mills?' Jacob asked like a kindergarten teacher.

'One move and I'll put a hole in your spine,' said Mills, with all the menace he could muster.

They set Madison free and walked towards the MEROS entrance, which was still firmly shut.

'Taj?'

'Jacobs.'

'OK, we can carry on talking like this but, instead,

you could just let us in. Something has gone wrong, and the four of us need to do what we can to sort it out.' There was a pause while they waited for Taj to react, then the external security door slid open to reveal a suspicious face leaning over the desk.

'You'd better not try any shit.'

'OK, Taj, just so you know, we tried shit before because we wanted to get out of here. Now we want to get back in, and you're the only person who can help us. No more shit will be tried.'

Taj looked at them all warily, especially Mills. 'Haughty-ass motherfucker,' were the words he had used to describe the Englishman to Garrett just a week earlier. 'Acts like his shit come out in a goddamn Tiffany box.'

Madison and Jacobs were fine by him; they weren't exactly his best friends, but he had no problem with them.

'Yeah, well, dunno how much help I'm gonna be. Inshield ain't comin' up, so the elevator ain't gonna be movin'. If the elevator ain't movin' and I can't raise 'em on the intercom, we shit out of choices.'

'Has there been any more movement down there?' asked Jacobs.

'A bunch. Beats me where they gone, though. I'm getting readings a long way out the back of Bishop's office. Also got a bunch right outside it. Those ones ain't moved for a while, though.'

'So now your motion sensor has broken down,' sighed Mills.

'Could be. Could be there's another way out.'

'But there's nothing . . .'

Jacobs interrupted Mills before he riled Taj.

'Can we just get the facts straight? They lowered the Inshield, which means something big went wrong, and the elevator got stuck down there with Carter, Garrett and Andrew.'

'Right. Then they started the freeze, to kill everything behind the glass so they could get the wasps dead or stunned or some shit, make 'em harmless at least. Then they was getting me to raise the shield so the guys in the elevator could get out before they froze too much, then they was going to lower the shield again to keep the wasps dyin'. That was the plan. I got to raise the shield part way, then I thought Bishop was telling me to lower it, but he was spooked by something big time and that was the last I heard.'

'So they're fucked,' said Mills. 'They're all dead.'

'We don't know that,' said Jacobs.

'No, and I don't *know* Garrett's a dyke but, looking at the evidence, I can take a pretty good guess.'

'So you saying we should just leave them there? Let me fly you guys to Bermuda to chill?' asked Madison.

'No, I'm saying we might as well act like they're all dead, because it sounds close on 100 per cent they are.'

'Taj, have you got any contact with them? Access to security cameras, phone records, anything that can tell us what's happening down there?'

'Nothin' but the motion sensors. They got a half-mile range through anything. So, like I said: buncha readings out the back of Bishop's office and a lot right outside the door. Those ones ain't human, though.'

'Wasps?'

'Most likely.'

'And have the motion sensors ever been wrong before?'

'Not these new ones. Installed three months ago and state of the art. 'Less something gone haywire, Bishop's office got a back door.'

'I've been in Bishop's office, but I never saw another door,' said Jacobs.

'Me neither,' added Mills.

'Well, me neither, too,' said Taj, attempting to imitate Mills' English accent. 'But I tell you, if there's something back there, it's big. I'm getting multiple readings some hundred yards from the office.'

Jacobs thought for a moment. As hope went, it was a match flame in a tornado, but that was better than nothing.

'You got a plan of this place?' she said at last.

59

Standing in the Abdomen was a uniquely terrifying experience. As far as they could see, there was a long, dense darkness lit only sporadically by the faint glow of the blue lights. The illumination was too weak to give any idea of what the room actually looked like, other than its dimensions, so all they knew was that they were somewhere very big and very dark.

Given what Bishop and Webster had told them about what may or may not lie within these walls, this cavernous unknown multiplied the fear that hung over them like cold mist. The words had taken on a reality that brought the potential for death much closer.

At the head of the group, Garrett's torch provided some much-needed clarity, but it also created a series of leaping shadows, exacerbating the tension, which was already wound tight enough to snap.

The heat had covered everyone in a slick of perspiration that made hands slippery, while the crawling of sweat drops was often mistaken for the touch of an unseen creature. Panicked hands rose to cheeks and foreheads, ready to swat away wings, legs or antennae which turned out not to exist.

The sweat also came from overworked nerves that fizzed and pumped, particularly those of Bishop and

Webster. If the others were scared, it was nothing to what those two were going through. The last time they had moved across this floor, they had been literally running for their lives, hearing ravenous mouths and steely claws tearing through skin, bone and innards.

The last sounds they had heard were the wrench and churn of meat, the full-throated screams of helpless death, and the spatter of blood, gushing and landing, thickened by gore, all around them.

And then there was the guilt of their impotence. That was what had kept it all nagging away for the months and years since. They had had to watch friends die and decide that intervention was too risky, that their own lives were too important to be jeopardized.

Walking these steps again, it felt like something that had spent ten years fading to a tiny echo had just roared back to life. Bishop was overwhelmed by the return of the horror, the visceral visions of rampant slaughter that had invaded so many of his waking and sleeping hours. He could not see what remained of the corpses, but that was worse, giving free rein to his bubbling imagination.

Webster had been affected in a different way: unlike Bishop, he had seen plenty of death before he arrived at MEROS, so it was the action of leaving so many to die, rather than the violence itself, that had torn at his insides. No matter how many times he told himself there had been no choice, that it was escape or death, he had never shaken off the remorse.

Of course, none of them wanted to hear anything: sound meant movement, and movement meant that the nightmares were a step closer. But the silence added to the fear in its own way. It meant that there was nothing to conceal the random scuffles and knocks of so many people shifting around in the dingy chaos. Each accidental kick of a chair or scrape of a wall was filtered through unchecked imagination to become the unfolding of a pair of wings or the opening of a set of hungry jaws.

They kept to the soft blue glows as best they could, but these gave way to larger sweeps of darkness where the way ahead was lit only by the blurred greys of Garrett's torch.

Webster could not have given a more accurate description of the terrain, but it still left vast spaces of black that were capable of concealing anything. Small, careful steps were the only way to make progress, but with the only constant light pointing ahead rather than illuminating the ground, they shuffled through the murky detritus as best they could.

And no matter how quiet the room remained, it was impossible to escape the feeling that they were being watched, that something nearby was aware of them and waiting for the right moment to attack. Was that an insect scuttling in the corner, or just a reflection of Garrett's torch beam? Did that sound come from behind them, or off to the left? Were the acoustics distorting sound, or were pounding temples creating noises that weren't there?

From nowhere, a booming *BARUMM* of smashing, rolling and crashing arrived like thunder to the right.

Garrett quickly whipped her torch round to see a mess of sweeping, flittering shadows.

Lisa screamed and took a step backwards. As she tried to regain her balance, her knee clattered into a chair, knocking it over.

It sounded like they were being hunted from both sides and the darkness was concealing hordes of giant insects, recently woken and hungry for prey.

Susan started sobbing and held on to George, but he was just as scared as she was and didn't want someone clinging to him when he might need to run.

'Wait, wait, calm it down.' Garrett's voice was clear, but too quiet to rise above the scrabbling feet and panicked gasps.

'I said stop!' she yelled. The others were shocked into standing still. If Garrett was talking instead of shooting, maybe they weren't under attack.

They followed the torch beam to see an upturned table on the floor.

'I think that's our superbug,' she said.

Down the line, they were still a nervy mass of thumping hearts and dry throats, but it looked like Garrett was right.

Mike peered over at the table.

'What's that?' he asked.

Garrett moved her torch a little further to the right to reveal a white stick. Further still, and the stick became recognizable as a fibia.

With a tilt of her wrist, Garrett cast the rest of the

skeleton in the smoky beam of torchlight. It was scattered around the floor and, as more was revealed, it became obvious that this was not just one person's remains. Another yard to the right showed a second, then a third, skull. All were covered in years of dust and missing their jaws.

Suddenly, the scene revisited Bishop with alarming force. Even though he could see little, his memory filled out what was missing: visions of long-ago death, of moments when he had witnessed slaughter delivered without mercy. And those monsters: grotesque, ravenous, thoughtless. No matter how hard he tried to block them out, images of their malevolent faces appeared clear and true almost before his eyes.

Over to the left, he could make out a desk that had been smashed in two. A decade collapsed to nothing as he remembered how it came to be that way: it had taken the full force when a millipede the length of two men unleashed itself from its protective ball. Its football-sized head had reared up almost to the height of Dr William Schreiber, who had been able to do nothing but scream as it pinned him down and fed greedily on his face.

The screaming stopped when his throat was torn out, leaving his head to flop backwards on the strip of skin that was all that remained of his neck.

Bishop had watched as the millipede had clambered over the doctor's stomach and chest, chewing as it went.

The froth of tissue, blood and bone spattered across

the creature's hard, green skin was the sight that had taken longest to leave Bishop's dreams. There was something so remorseless, so driven about it, that he had found the scene forcing itself into his thoughts for many years afterwards.

He felt the bile churning in his guts once more but managed with some effort to keep it under control.

'We best get moving on,' said Garrett.

Laura put her arm round her son, gently but firmly manoeuvring him in front of her so she could keep a good grip on his shoulders.

The bones had scared them, but at least they looked old and neglected. And the burst of noise and activity didn't seem to have brought any insects out of hiding. In any case, they had no choice, so they all shuffled ahead, inevitably thinking about the ways in which the skeletons had come to be like that.

At the second blue light, they came across something that embodied Webster and Bishop's nightmarish description. Garrett stepped on it without realizing, but when she looked down, her exclamation of *Holy shit!* was a loud noise too far. It set off a ripple of fear along the line.

In the dark, Garrett wasn't aware that she had been responsible for the reaction. When she became so, she issued a series of loud *Ssshhh* sounds until there was silence again, except for the insistent throb of blood pumping through their chests.

'What is it?' asked Webster.

Garrett peered down again and looked at what lay

in the torchlight. 'Spider. Dead spider. All dry like it's been dead a long time, but it is fuckin' *humongous*. Like the back tyre off my daddy's tractor.'

George couldn't help looking over her shoulder.

'Jesus fuck me Christ,' he muttered, crossing himself. 'That is a big sonofabitch.'

'OK. I'm headin' on,' Garrett whispered. As each member of the group filed past, they felt grateful that the direct beam of Garrett's torch had gone on ahead. It left the arachnid near invisible in black-grey gloom. However, from the illumination of the nearest blue light they could tell that its legs were as wide as their arms, and that sent hard shivers of revulsion rippling through them.

Still the group continued to make its steady progress through the Abdomen, and still there was no sign of life. There were plenty of signs of death, but by now Garrett had come across so many dessicated insect corpses she had stopped mentioning them. The disruption to the group was taking its toll, so she tried to give each one a wide berth instead.

If she had had the time or the light to examine what they were walking over, she'd have seen how small piles of human bones had collected beneath the various dead insects. As their bodies had decomposed, the undigested ribs, skulls and limbs had slipped through the stomach lining and out on to the floor.

Those bones were the most troublesome obstacles they came across. Hidden in the dark, they were easily stepped on, causing some of the group to lose their footing and sometimes their balance, sending them flailing into clumsy, ignorant panic.

About halfway across the main hall, George trod on a femur and rolled backwards. The fright came over him like a white sheet, and he cried out, sending whips of fear slicing into the others.

Losing his balance, he reached out and grabbed hold of Wainhouse, bringing them down together. Wainhouse was unable to stop himself lurching backwards and tensing his trigger finger to fire off a volley of netspreaders towards the ceiling.

The explosions added to the terrified confusion. Garrett tried to illuminate the scene with her torch, but the moving shadows only suggested more possible horrors.

Meanwhile, the nets floated down from the ceiling, landing softly on top of Laura, Bishop and Wainhouse, who immediately assumed they were under attack from colossal web-shooting spiders.

Laura screamed, leaving Andrew terrified. The more she tried to disentangle herself, the more caught up she became. Her struggle made the thin adhesive cling even tighter, wrapping her hair and fingers together until she screamed again.

Webster and Wainhouse were deep in their own panicked confusion, but they soon recognized the distinctive odour of the netspreaders' adhesive and realized what had happened.

'Hey! Hey! Laura, Laura, Laura. Calm down, it's not insects. It's the nets from Wainhouse's gun. They fired accidentally.' Webster tried to find her and hold her by the shoulders, but he was also trapped in the nets, so he could only knock into her, poking out another shriek.

Andrew had heard Webster, though, and he did his best to get his mum's attention. 'It's all right, Mum,' he said, squeezing her hand. 'Major Webster says it's all right. Shhhh.' She was breathing hard, but understood what her son was telling her.

Garrett's torch confirmed that they were nets from Wainhouse's gun, but by then the fear and disorientation had left the group at a high pitch of terror.

'OK, everyone,' said Carter, loud and hard, 'I'm going to use the adhesive solution on these nets, so I need calm for the next five minutes.' His words brought everyone into line instantly, putting a stop to the random movements and desperate gasps that were fuelling each other.

Carter removed an aerosol from his backpack and got to work on Laura. Garrett held her torch up to help, and the others stood in silence. The task provided a welcome distraction, giving them a focus and a feeling that, if they had time to sort out something as small as this, the danger could not be so great as they feared.

Laura, Webster and Wainhouse were soon free of the nets, and a calm descended upon the group.

As they stood gathered around Garrett's torchlight, Webster spoke quietly but clearly:

'OK, everybody, it doesn't look like we've disturbed anything, or maybe there's nothing to disturb. Judging by how long we've been walking, we must be nearly at the other side, so let's get moving again and see if we can find the stairs.'

A darkness loomed over them as they moved towards the far wall. There were no lights on that side of the Abdomen, so they could not know for sure they were in the right place.

Webster took Garrett's position at the front and stepped forward to the wall, casting the concentric circles of torchlight across it.

'Hmmm . . .' he grunted. By now it was clear to Laura that he was not a man of excessive reaction. *Hmmm* could mean a serious disaster if said in the wrong way, and Webster's tone did not fill anyone with confidence.

'Bishop, you might want to take a look at this.'

Bishop made his way through the group, who stood in single file, forced into that formation by the partition wall of a lab and a dense collection of broken furniture.

Now they were all looking in the same direction as Webster, trying to work out what concerned him.

He pointed the torch upwards. To the group's disappointment, it definitely wasn't showing a smooth wall with a conveniently placed door through which they could all exit to freedom. Instead it illuminated a layer of something coarse and coffee-brown, riddled with holes large enough to fit a Labrador.

Webster was rubbing the rough surface. It felt like pumice stone.

'Wasps?' asked Bishop.

Webster shook his head. 'Did we ever have termites down here?' he asked quietly.

'I think so,' said Bishop, peering a short distance into the nearest hole. 'Masters of destroying whatever comes their way, as long as they can build their nest,' he said.

'That's a termite nest?' asked George, who had been eavesdropping on Webster and Bishop's conversation. He moved forward to see for himself. 'But termite nests in their natural habitat can be hundreds of times the size of the insect itself. This could be a mile high.'

'If it's a mile high, then it's through the surface, and I think we'd have heard something about that,' replied Bishop.

'Think so?' asked Mike. 'The jungle we're in has no people for miles around and plenty of places for whatever built this nest to hide.'

'No,' said Laura. 'If a nest of termites this big got out into that jungle, they'd have laid it to waste in a week. Something must have stopped them.'

She realized as she said it that she was sliding something unpleasant into all their thoughts: something had taken on these termites and won.

'Well, thanks a bunch for the insect lesson,' said Wainhouse, in his dull voice. 'What matters here ain't whatever killed these critters, 'cos it don't look to me like there's much of anything alive down here. What we've got to figure out is how to get through this to the stairs and get the hell out of here.'

'Yes, but the problem is whether we can get through this at all. It's obviously grown over the lights, so it might also be built around the stairs. That may mean our way to the surface is blocked,' said Takeshi.

'What about going up inside it?' said Laura. Bishop squatted down and looked into the nest. 'Come on,' she continued. 'If there's nothing alive down here, what danger is there to getting inside this thing, seeing how far it goes up and whether it connects to the stairs?'

One by one, they all looked to Garrett. Eventually, she noticed.

'Oh, I get it. Yes, I do all the crazy, scary shit, plus I'm a short-ass. Fine.' She undid her belt to remove her weapons and body armour. 'You can stop me anytime if I'm getting the wrong idea here.'

No one stopped her.

'Right, I'll take that as a "Get your sorry grunt ass up one of those holes 'cos we're either too big or too clever to do it ourselves." No fuckin' problem, amigos.'

Within a minute, she was down to a dirty vest, khaki cargo pants and her army-issue boots. Although she wasn't entirely visible, what light there was seemed to be catching a side of her no one had noticed before. Despite himself, George felt the stirrings of the world's most pointless erection.

'Which hole you think's a goer?' she asked anyone who might have an opinion. No opinion came, so Garrett chose the one closest to her. It didn't leave a lot of room, but whatever problems the size caused, she was soon out of sight.

While Garrett explored, Susan, Lisa and Mike examined the nest, knocking and scraping it.

'I don't want to meet whatever made this,' said Mike.

'If they were as devastating as regular termites at this size, it would have taken napalm to stop them,' Lisa mused.

Suddenly, a hollow scraping noise made them all look up in fear.

Webster drew his semi-automatic Walther P99 from its holster. The acoustics made it hard to tell which hole the noise was coming from.

'Someone get the torch pointed at this thing!' he snapped.

As the scratching got louder, Webster aimed the muzzle at one hole then another. It was soon obvious where the noise was coming from. Webster stood poised and cocked his weapon until . . .

'Fuck me, that must be what a rattlesnake's shit feels like,' coughed Garrett, dragging herself out of the nest. Webster lowered his gun and helped her.

'Stinks like month-old manure up there, like it ain't been aired since forever.'

'That's probably the case,' said Bishop, trying not to sound too patronizing.

'Anyway,' Garrett continued, ignoring him, 'there's only so far I can get. The tunnels are an OK size, but when they turn it's impossible to bend round the corners. You're going to need someone smaller than me if you want to get any further.'

No one said anything, but their thoughts immediately turned to Andrew. He wasn't Garrett, though. A small body wrapped around a dense core of fear, he was not ready to volunteer to climb into a giant termite nest. And even if he were, the chances of his mum letting him do it were less than zero.

'Another option is to blast it,' Garrett said cheerfully. She enjoyed using explosives.

'What we got, Garrett?' asked Webster.

'Thanks to Wainhouse, we got everything we need.' Wainhouse smiled in the darkness.

'Hang on, hang on, is any of this stuff . . . I mean, is it going to be very disturbing and . . . loud?' asked Bishop in a pointed whisper.

Garrett exhaled a derisory chuckle.

'Yes, *Steven*, it's going to be very disturbing and loud. That's what you get with C4 and Semtex: disturbing and loud. Something wrong with that?'

'Well, we still don't know what's around here. What if we wake something up?'

'Bishop, you whiny-ass –'

'We need to make this decision collectively,' said Webster.

'Well, sir, you got any other ideas?' asked Garrett.

'We haven't explored this whole level. We don't know what else we're going to find that could be of use.'

'You think they dug us another tunnel to the surface?' asked Wainhouse. 'Maybe one with a beer tap and some cable TV?' He wanted to match Garrett for cockiness, but he was talking to the wrong guy.

'Wainhouse,' was all Webster needed to say, and the soldier shrank back from the cheeky Garrett sidekick he thought he had become.

'We don't know how much explosive we need to

blow the hell out of a giant termite's nest, and we don't need a landslide blocking the staircase if we get it wrong. The explosive is a last resort. There could be a number of options, like maybe a way to the lower level that will let us come back up to the stairs. Split up, take a look around and report back here in ten minutes.'

He turned to Bishop, Laura and Andrew. 'You three stay here with me.'

60

'Times like this, I wish I was a little more organized,' Taj said to himself as he rummaged through the storeroom.

After twenty minutes of his fruitless searching, the others gave up hope of any useful discoveries and went to sit in the sunshine just outside the MEROS doors.

'I'm . . . waiting for the plans,' sang Taj, Lou Reed style.

Eventually, his search took him to the back of the storeroom, where he found several likely-looking boxes, which he dragged out and brought round to his desk.

'Yo, yo, yo. I ain't looking through these my lone self. Take one. First to find something good wins.'

They each picked up a box, found a quiet area and looked through its contents. Mills drew the short straw: accounts receivable and payable of equipment orders. Madison got the personnel records, which were of no use but certainly passed the time, especially Mills' psych evaluation, which suggested he was a latent homosexual. Taj had the post-operational reports of all the missions, written by Webster and Bishop, and found they read like drier versions of the teenage adventure books he read to pass the time.

Jacobs hit the jackpot: blueprints, structural plans, everything from the tensile strength of the materials used to the original architectural proposals that had been rejected. She understood their importance immediately but kept them to herself. If she let the others know what she had, she'd have to deal with too many dumb suggestions and time-consuming arguments from Madison and Mills.

Within minutes, she had found the blueprint to the complex. Taking a quick glance, she could see it was exactly what they needed, but she would have to lay it out to get a good look at it.

'Hey, what's that?' asked Taj.

'Looks like the blueprints to downstairs,' said Jacobs. They all gathered round to work out what they could see.

'Yeah, that's the canteen,' said Madison.

'How the fuck would you know?' asked Mills. 'How many times have you been down there?'

'Enough, gay-boy.'

'What did you fucking call me?'

'Gay boy. You read your psych report?' He grinned and waved the piece of paper in Mills' face.

Mills snatched at it, skimmed it and hissed 'Mother-fuckers,' before tearing it up in a rage, kicking Madison's box over and storming off towards the jungle.

'Nice one, Madison,' muttered Jacobs, looking over the plans. Madison didn't care. He didn't think a dumb bastard like Mills would be much help anyway.

'This is Bishop's room,' Jacobs continued. 'So this

must be the area you're talking about.' She pointed to the corner of the blueprints that showed what was behind the office. Her finger traced along the narrow pair of lines that led from the office to the Abdomen.

'What's this?' she asked Taj.

'Beats me. Some kind of heating duct?'

'But then there's this.' They all looked at the area the 'heating duct' led to.

'If that's another space, then it's bigger than the rest of the complex put together. And there's more.' She unfolded the blueprints to show two areas identical to the new one but drawn separately, unconnected to the rest of the complex.

Taj looked thoughtful. 'This would explain where those motion sensors are. Still don't know what the hell it is, but if it's a big slice of MEROS that we ain't never seen, then it makes sense they could be alive in it.'

Madison wasn't paying attention, but he was pretending to.

'So what is it?'

Taj whistled through his teeth. 'Ain't you been listening? We don't know. All ideas welcome, pilot man.' Madison looked awkward. He wasn't helping, and now he'd made that obvious.

Mills was still sitting on his own by the cargo ramp. Jacobs knew they were going to need him at some point, so she may as well coax him back now with a little flattery.

'Hey, Mills! You know anything about blueprints? Didn't you supervise some huts and stuff being built when you Brits helped out in Afghanistan?' It worked better than she had hoped. Mills sighed at their ignorant incompetence and walked over.

'Show me.' He took a look at the plans.

'OK. This means the areas are on different levels, and these lines might be stairs to connect them. What I don't understand is *these* stairs.' He was pointing out another set of zig-zag lines and the number 969.

'OK, so we've got more of MEROS than we thought. A walkway from Bishop's office connects to this big area. If Mills is right, then it's three floors deep,' said Jacobs.

'So what do we do?' asked Madison.

'No idea,' replied Jacobs. 'Maybe we should check those motion sensors and make sure the people in there are still alive.'

61

Each of the groups had aimed for one of the lit areas of Level One. Pools of foggy blue light hung like miniature clouds along the concrete walls, showing the monotonous features of the room.

The fear was distant now. They had spent long enough in the Abdomen to doubt there was anything there to threaten them, which meant their thoughts were directed towards escaping rather than staying alive.

'What are we going to do here?' Laura asked Webster.

'*We're* going to wait. You are too valuable to lose.'

'Am I? Why's that?'

'Huh?' Webster had not expected to be asked that question. 'Well, you're the best entomologist here, so your knowledge is the most useful. Bishop knows this place as well as me, and Andrew . . . well, he doesn't deserve any of this.'

Andrew was just out of earshot, using his Swiss Army knife to scrape away at the termite nest. Bishop noticed he was off by himself and, knowing that Laura would not be able to give an honest appraisal of the Abdomen while her son was around to be scared, took the opportunity to get her read on the situation.

'Miss Trent.' He had to act quickly, but his instinct

to prepare the ground before ploughing it up was too strong to suppress. 'You must find the potential of this environment to be quite fascinating.'

'I'm not sure that's the word.'

'Indeed, indeed . . . but I was wondering if perhaps there might be elements of your analysis that could be relayed to myself or Major Webster now that . . .'

'Now that what?'

'Well, it's just that I understand there may have been a degree of reticence about any overly negative . . .'

Webster knew they didn't have time for all this dancing around. 'Miss Trent, is there anything you want to tell us that you can't say in front of Andrew?'

'Oh.' She looked round to see if Andrew was within earshot. He had found another hole to widen with his knife. 'There *was* something that concerned me.'

'And what's that?'

'I can't see any reason why these creatures could not sustain themselves over a period of ten years. Given the elements that were set in place for the subjects' growth, and the fact that this environment was designed to accommodate humans for long periods of time, I'd say that the hardier survival abilities of insects would mean they could make a great deal of success of a place like this. They could grow, feed off each other and grow some more.'

'You think that's really possible?' he asked weakly.

'Absolutely. Except for one important factor.'

'What's that?'

'Lack of moisture. It's odd, though: even though

there doesn't appear to be an independent water source, the air is very humid. I can only suggest that whatever air-circulation system you have here is bringing in the precipitation from the jungle – but that wouldn't be enough for creatures of the scale you describe.'

It was too dark for Laura to notice the look that passed between the two men. Webster understood that Bishop wanted to maintain a degree of secrecy, but he also knew that this was definitely not a situation for withholding information.

'What if there were a substantial water source?' Webster asked.

'What are you saying?' asked Laura, lowering her voice.

'I'm saying that the levels below us were used for plant research, and those plants were grown . . .'

'. . . hydroponically,' Laura concluded. 'Of course. There's no sunshine down here. Where does the water come from?'

'There's a pump from a small reservoir on the surface. It serves the new MEROS area, too. That's why it hasn't been shut off,' said Bishop. 'The expense would have been too great, and everyone assumed this place would just wither and die.'

'And you're saying all this is happening on the floors below?' asked Laura. Webster nodded. 'That might explain why we haven't heard from them. If the only way up here is through a stairwell that's blocked by the nest, then we might be OK. Let's hope that *is* the case, because if you have heat, water, vegetation, genetic compounds we have no idea about, and uncharted interference with the juvenile and ecdysone hormones . . .'

There was a pause, before a small 'Yes?' from Bishop.

'Mr Bishop, this is all theoretical, but you have just described perfect conditions for almost limitless growth. Without those hormones, there's nothing to stop the insects reaching the size of . . .'

The scream came shrill and sharp, passing through them like a murderer's ghost.

All eyes turned in its direction, and a bubbling acid of fear poured into them.

It was Lisa. She continued to scream as Wainhouse squinted through the darkness to work out where she was. The sound was coming from the floor, so he bent down and moved closer, to see that she had fallen up to her waist into some kind of hole. Her fingernails scraped and scrabbled on the floor around her as she desperately tried to claw herself out.

And all the while the terrible screaming.

'Wait, shhh, calm down, calm down,' said Mike, who was crouching next to her. 'Lisa, have you just fallen through the floor or are there . . . insects?'

Lisa stopped screaming long enough to thrash her words out. 'I'm hurt! Oh God! I think I'm bleeding!'

'But have you . . . is it an insect?'

'No! No! Please help me! AAAARRRGGGHH!'

'OK!' shouted Wainhouse. 'She just fell through the floor. No insects. We'll get her out.' He held her arms to stop her falling any further.

'Jesus Christ! *EEEUUUGGHHH!* This hurts so much!'

On the floor below, the vibrations of the screams had disturbed the creature a little. The high pitch had sent a shivery ripple through its long, glassy-brown antennae and down into the hard, wide exoskeleton.

The antennae moved of their own accord, the ends twitching towards the sounds, stretching and sweeping through the air, trying to latch on to something they could use. Over the years, the pickings had become more and more scarce, but the creature recognized the opportunity for food when it came along. That was in its DNA, along with many other things.

It stretched its limbs, which were thin for a resident of the Abdomen but far thicker than those of the rest of its species. They unfolded like a deckchair, pushed through the leaves and found the solid floor, making a light scraping noise as they straightened out.

Now it stood, squat and flat, continuing to scan the dense, humid air, which had not undergone a change like this for so many years.

Mike and Wainhouse had succeeded in calming Lisa enough to keep her quiet, or at least quieter.

'I think I've cut myself. I think I might have fallen against something sticking out. My left side . . . Urrggghhh . . . my left side hurts from my thigh to my ribs.'

'OK, Lisa, hold on. We're going to try to get you out of there,' said Wainhouse.

'Be careful!'

'Of course, of course. Now give me your arms. Yeah, cross them over like that, it'll make it easier for me to pull you up.'

'Please be careful.'

'Trust me. OK, on three. One, two, three.' Wainhouse leaned back and gave a strong tug upwards.

'*AAAAAAARRRGGGHHHHAARRG-GGHHH!*' Lisa had barely moved.

'Stop! Stop! Stop!' she yelled. 'There's something in my side. *URRRGGHH!* Oh God!'

'Lisa, Lisa!' Mike knelt down by her and tried to hug as much of her as he could. 'Just hold steady, and we'll get you out of there as soon as we can, I promise.'

The creature could make out another wave of vibrations, and its search became more earnest. It had to make sure it was first to the source in case others had been alerted. Lower, quieter sounds followed the louder noise, and it began to salivate.

Like rusty machinery being oiled back to life, it felt movement returning to long-dormant parts. Its front legs searched for steady ground, but it had to be careful: if it disturbed anything else, it might have competition for the prey.

'Major Webster, sir!' Wainhouse hollered across Level One.

Webster ran across to the hole and crouched down beside Lisa.

327

She was exhaling in hard, shallow gasps, trying to cope with the pain, along with the realization that she would not escape from this without that pain increasing.

'Can you feel everything – your limbs, your feet?' asked Webster, squatting in front of her.

'Uh-huh,' gasped Lisa, blasting air through her gritted teeth like a weightlifter about to snap a barbell above his head.

'And where does it hurt?'

'My left side. I think it got caught on something as I fell through.'

Webster tried to peer into the part of the hole on that side, but the light was too poor to make anything out.

He could smell that slightly metallic tinge in the air that meant only one thing: blood.

'What is it?' she asked, her face a few inches from the top of Webster's head.

'Can't tell for sure. I think you're bleeding though.'

The glutinous red drips were slipping down her legs and on to the plants below.

It was the sound of these gentle *plops* that the antennae came to first.

As they brushed the leaves, a tear of blood landed on the end of one probing stalk, causing a reaction of surprise, then voracious recognition. The creature could still hear the sounds, and it sensed for certain that this was what it had been waiting so long for.

Lisa had fallen above a mess of foliage that grew and spread throughout most of Level Two. Many of the things that lived down there had made the dense vegetation either a home or a source of nutrition.

The cockroach was going to use it to climb.

'OK, Lisa, I can't see any way around this without it hurting some. I'm sorry, but we don't have what we need for a hell of a lot of situations here, and this is one of them,' said Webster.

The intense pain and loss of blood had taken all the fight from her. Another agonized grunt squeezed from her throat.

'I'm going to push you sideways off the jagged edge, and Wainhouse is going to pull you upwards, OK?'

'Uh-huh,' she gasped.

Webster put his hands in position around her ribcage, and Wainhouse stuffed his fingers under her arms.

'OK. One, two –'

She screamed.

She screamed so loud and so close to Webster's ear that he loosened his grip and took a half-step backwards. He looked to Wainhouse, but he had not moved.

'What's . . . ? Lisa, what's the matter?' he said urgently.

But her screams worsened: foul screeches of dragging metal and tortured animals emanating from her grotesquely contorted face.

'Lisa! Lisa!' No response.

The foot was gone, passed back through the mouth of the six-foot-long insect, and now the cockroach was gnawing hungrily through her left ankle.

329

Flesh and bones and blood slid over the mandibles as they powered hungrily through to her shin.

'Fu– Jesus! . . .' More screaming. 'Help me, please help me,' begged Lisa, with desperate, strangled effort. She grabbed Webster's neck and pulled him down to her face.

Over by the nest, Laura's hands covered Andrew's ears, but to no effect. The gurgling screams and terrifying pleadings made use of the clear acoustics to fill the room just as Lisa's bloody stump was filling the cockroach's jaws.

It was up at the shinbones now, inching its way towards the knee. Lisa could feel the deep scrawl of every scrape of the mandible.

The hard outer bone gave way to the soft marrow inside. It felt as if every atom was connected to a fish-hook and wrenched from her.

Then the cockroach started to pull.

It was trying to bring its prey closer.

Webster could see that Lisa was slipping and told Wainhouse to grab her under the arms again. He did as he was told, and a tug of excruciating agony began.

Just when they thought the noises could not get worse, they took on a desperation that made Lisa seem possessed. And there was no escape.

They were praying for something to bring this to an end. Everyone's ears were being subjected to an overwhelming torrent of sounds, as if they were standing neck-deep in rapids.

Garrett could not take it. She ran over to where Lisa

was, trying to make herself heard above the raw screams and pain-wracked moans.

'Major, we got to stop this.'

For the first time since she had known him, Webster lost his composure: 'What the fuck do you think I'm trying to do?'

That was when the second beast arrived.

The first cockroach knew it wasn't going to be able to keep its meal secret for long, which is why it feasted with such determination.

It had been too focused on chewing back the leg to notice the hard, thorny limbs creeping through the undergrowth. The second creature took advantage of this to get its mandibles working on Lisa's remaining foot.

Then she became unexpectedly quiet. The pain was still running through her like shards of burning shrapnel, but the stress on her lungs and throat was taking its toll.

It was hard to push out the same volume of air, and her vocal cords were not able to process it in the same way. She was screaming herself silent, and it made the others think the situation was improving.

She had lost so much blood her vital organs were shutting down. Her legs were ragged, blood-soaked bones, hanging down through the ceiling like torn branches. Blood continued to flow over the crunching jaws as they made short work of the marrow.

She became quieter still, but for a different reason: she was almost dead.

'What's happening?' asked Mike.

'How the fuck do we know?' answered Wainhouse, desperately scared and helpless, close to tears.

Webster was staring into Lisa's eyes, knowing he had lost her. As a soldier who had seen death in the field, he recognized the gradual flattening of the faculties before total shutdown.

'Lisa? Lisa?'

Without realizing it, he was shaking her, and in doing so he felt how limp and light her body had become. Slowly, he let her go, and she slumped a little further into the hole, although the jagged edge that had caught her torso did not let her fall far.

'Jesus, she's fuckin' dead! She's fuckin' *dead*!' sobbed Wainhouse.

Mike stared at Lisa, then collapsed to his knees beside her. He shook his head and tried to hug what little of her he could get hold of. Webster pulled him back.

'We need to get away from here. Right now.' His voice rose as he did.

'Everyone! Fall back to the nest!'

62

'So they're still alive in the new area,' Jacobs said.

'Looks like it,' confirmed Taj.

'How do you know these guys aren't them?' asked Mills, pointing at the other motion indicators.

'Every time someone comes in here, whether they know it or not, or like it or not, they get tagged.' He walked over to the entrance door and showed them what looked like a CCTV camera to record the elevator entrance.

'See this? It ain't a camera, it's a LITD, a Laser Integrated Tagging Device. It puts an invisible marker on the back of your neck, then my computer reads your DNA and checks you out through the FBI, CIA, Interpol, medical records, all kinds of shit.'

'Bloody hell . . .' muttered Mills.

'Then the tracking device reads where you are every three seconds – and I know how long it takes you to go for a dump. Look, here *we* are.'

They looked at the four lights on a three-dimensional model of MEROS. 'Cool, huh?'

'Why are their readings different to ours?' asked Jacobs.

'Dunno for sure, but I guess the signal I'm getting

from the new area is pretty weak. I can tell if there's movement, but I don't know who's who.'

'So they didn't programme the extra areas into the 3-D model?'

'I guess not, but they only installed it a couple of years back.'

'So maybe the other area is older than that. They brought the laser thing in and mapped out the known parts of MEROS to create the 3-D model, but not the rest of it, like it was out of bounds or something.'

'Makes sense,' said Madison.

'And when you go outside the 3-D area,' continued Jacobs, 'it still works out your position but can't place it anywhere on a map.'

'So they're moving around in an old part of the complex that is out of bounds. Is that Bishop's secret escape route now?' asked Madison.

'If it was, it wouldn't be that size. That's a lot of prime underground real estate. It must have been used for something else,' Jacobs said.

'And these dots here are other moving things which have just been sensed through vibrations or some other shit. They not tagged, and that's why they red instead of green.'

'But why wouldn't they be tagged?' asked Mills. Taj looked at him as if he was very stupid indeed.

'Wasps, motherfucker.'

'So these dots are another cluster of wasps?' He pointed around the middle of the new area: the cock-roach hole.

'Guess so.'

'And in the part we know about, we've got these three that are blue.'

'Yeah, that's Heath, Van Arenn and Merchant. They bought it,' said Taj. 'Blue equals dead, cos that's the colour you go when you die. A lot of them's still alive, though – I mean, considering there's a shitload of wasps on the loose.'

'OK, so we've established that there are live people in a big, probably disused part of the lab. I assume if there was an easy way out of there they would have taken it by now, so they need our help. Taj, is there anything – and I mean *anything* – else?'

'Like what?'

'I don't know … other maps, electronic controls that we can work from up here … a way of seeing if anyone outside here knows what's going on or what we can do?'

'The only one who phones out of here is Bishop. Dunno where the calls go, but he only dials three numbers, kinda like 911.'

'Can we do that? He communicated with you, didn't he? Does his phone line go out where yours does?'

'Take a look.' Taj shrugged, then showed them where the phone lines led into the wall.

'These have to go somewhere,' said Jacobs. 'Mills, check outside, see if you can pick them up.'

Mills followed the cables through the wall, out of the building and on to the roof.

'There's a satellite dish up there,' he said when he

returned. 'Why don't we just patch our phone into his line, press redial and see what happens?'

'Anyone got pliers?' Jacobs asked. At last Madison had a chance to be useful. He jogged back to his cockpit to get the miniature toolbox that sat under the pilot's seat.

It took them a couple of minutes to get the wires right, then Jacobs wasted no time in pressing redial.

'It's ringing,' she said.

63

In the Abdomen, everyone had collected in front of the termite's nest. Mike and George were pacing around, dragging hard on George's last cigarettes; Susan sat slumped against the nest, her head in her hands; Wainhouse was pointlessly checking and rechecking that his rifle magazine was fully loaded; Andrew's arms were tight around Laura, who was trying not to shake; Garrett was wishing she had never gone over to see what was the matter with Lisa; and Bishop stood with his arms folded, biting what little fingernails he had left. They needed reassurance, a plan, something to tell them what had happened to Lisa was not going to happen to any of them.

They looked to Webster.

But he was going through the same turmoil they were, more so, because he'd been right there as it happened. They were just dealing with the sounds; he had the visions of how her imploring eyes had begged him to save her, the smell of all that blood, and the feeling of her lifeless half-body in his arms.

And now he knew they were not alone.

If one of those things was still alive, it was likely there were many more. He didn't know what had attacked Lisa, but it had eaten a large chunk of an adult human in less than five minutes. That meant it was at the extreme end of what his imagination had conjured up over the last ten years. It had been bad enough when those creatures only existed in his mind. Now they were real and he was among them, with nine people to keep alive and no way out.

He knew the others were waiting for his lead. The pressure felt physical, pushing down on his shoulders until he could barely stand.

'Sir?' asked Wainhouse.

'OK,' he replied after a pause. 'Lisa is dead. I believe she died because there is something alive on the next level down, something substantial enough for us to regard it as a very real threat. Wainhouse, I need you to go to the hole and cover it with netspreaders. If whatever is down there is anything like our wasps, then that will give us at least fifteen minutes.

'Right. Everyone else. We're working against the clock, and we now know that Level Two is not somewhere we want to be. It looks to me like we've got one option: blast our way through that nest. Garrett, can you see any reason why that would not be possible?'

'No, sir, but if you want to keep out of Level Two, blowing the nest won't guarantee it. We got maybe twenty feet of nest covering another ten feet, maybe more, of concrete. Getting the poundage of explosive right on a combination like that is gonna be a tricky one. I couldn't say for sure, but if we need to blast through that much shit, the ceiling or the floor's gonna take a beating too. That way, you can choose: weaken what's above us and maybe get a cave-in, or weaken what's below and blow a hole through to Level Two. Worse than that, whatever you choose, I couldn't say for sure that you're gonna get it.'

'What if you rigged the middle of the nest?'

'That'll get us a weak top and bottom. Maybe a cave-in that comes down and crashes through the floor anyway. You want my chops for what it's worth? Blast the floor. We're bound to take out a bunch of them critters with the hole we make and, like I said, rigging closer to the top might get us a hole in the floor anyway.'

Webster looked at the height of the ceiling and imagined the consequences of a few tons of falling rock. Then he looked at the floor, imagining beyond it to the creatures stirring below.

'Fine. Yes, rig closer to the floor.'

'Aye-aye, Major.'

Garrett pulled out her detonators and placed them around the nest.

Webster turned to the centre of the room. He hadn't heard as much noise as he was expecting. 'Wainhouse! How're those netspreaders coming?'

Wainhouse was standing beside the hole fretting about what he'd been asked to do. Using the netspreaders to create a barrier over the still-jerking upper half of Lisa's corpse didn't sit right with him, but he knew he had no choice.

She had been pulled further into the hole, but her progress had been stopped by what was happening beneath her: there were now seven giant roaches battling each other for the right to finish her off.

She was waiting, dead and two feet shorter, to be dragged to her final disappearance down the throats of those insects.

Wainhouse could hear them – the moist, frantic chewing and shredding – and it was that, as well as a reluctance to desecrate the corpse any further, that made him hesitate. Then Webster's call snapped him back to the job.

Stepping away, he aimed at the crown of Lisa's head and shot three rounds in quick succession. Each net drove Lisa further into the hole, until the top of her head was almost level with the floor. She should have slipped all the way down, but the glue of the netspreaders held her up. It clung to the top of her head in a thin mesh cap that reached down to her eyebrows.

Then she started to move.

At first it was a shallow bobbing up and down and side to side movement that made Wainhouse watch with a quizzical expression. Then it became violent: a hard push upwards, stretching the Kevlar and testing the hold of each net. Then a yank downwards. More shaking, Lisa's head whipping around like a buoy in a storm, then another strong pull downwards.

She was being detached from the glue, but in a way that made Wainhouse's stomach turn. The strength of the adhesive was peeling Lisa's face from her skull. Each pull was like the tearing of a bandage from a fresh wound. Blood, muscle and skin came away with a *shhhrrriipppp* to leave a crisscross of visible white bone. Wainhouse stepped back and pulled his trigger until he had no more shells to fire.

His chamber empty, he turned towards Webster and yelled. 'Major!'

Webster ran through the mess of Level One to reach Wainhouse just as Lisa's skull disappeared, with a whipping twang of glue and Kevlar, into the depths of Level Two.

Now the sound coming from below was clear: a terrifying hissing noise that sounded like all the aggression and anger and horror they had feared concentrated into a foul whistling *SSSSSSHHSSSSSHHSSS* that pierced their bones.

But they still couldn't see what was making the noise. It was dark down there, and the webs of Kevlar had combined to create a solid barrier. Webster could just about make out a flash of movement that looked like a flickering wing. If it was making a sound, it couldn't be heard above the hissing, so loud and terrible it equalled Lisa's screams. Then it pushed its back up against the Kevlar. The brown translucent shell was unmistakable. The antennae, which now poked through far enough to touch his boot, confirmed it.

'It's a fucking roach,' muttered Webster.

'A what?'

'It's a giant fucking cockroach, and by giant I mean six feet, minimum. Shit, the timer just sped up.'

'It'll take them forever to get through the Kevlar, Major.'

'Could be, but it'll happen. They've got a taste for us now.'

'We letting the others know about this?'

'Hell no. They'll know something's up by this noise, but scaring any more shit out of them is not going to help. OK, the story is the Kevlar blocked our view. Looks bad but nothing to confirm – got that?'

'Yessir.'

They walked back to the nest, hoping they didn't look as unnerved as they felt.

64

The phone rang just once before it was answered.

'Bishop? What the hell is happening down there?'

'This isn't Bishop.'

A pause. 'All right, to whom am I speaking?'

They had put the phone on speaker so they could all hear but it had been agreed that Jacobs would do the talking.

'This is Lieutenant Mary Jacobs of the MEROS facility in Colinas de Edad. To whom am *I* speaking?'

Tobias Paine gave a quick snort at her impertinence.

'Ms Jacobs, what are you doing on Steven Bishop's secure line?'

'I'm sorry, but I still have no idea who you are. You can play the super-secret, I'm-in-charge card if you like, but that'll make this a very short conversation.'

Another pause was followed by a weary sigh.

'This is Tobias Paine, Undersecretary for Covert Operations, US Department of Defence. Now that you know who I am, I'd appreciate a little more information from you, if you don't mind.'

'No problem, Mr Paine. The reason why none of us are Mr Bishop is that we've had ourselves a bit of a situation. The Inshield is down. That's the fall-back . . .'

'Ms Jacobs, I know exactly what the Inshield is

because I signed off its installation. I am also fully aware that it has been deployed today. Bishop informed me of that state of affairs over an hour ago.'

'Congratulations. Do you know what happened after that?'

'Do tell.'

'We got about ten people trapped down there. They were pinned down in Bishop's office by wasps.'

'Are we discussing the usual mission wasps or the advanced wasps that David Heath was working on?'

'We're pretty certain that would be the advanced wasps.'

'Mmm-hmmm. Carry on.'

'Everything else we've got from Taj's motion sensors, so I'll let him explain.'

'Uh, hi, Mr Paine, Taj Kenton, Head of Security.' He expected at least a hello in return; instead, he got silence.

Taj shrugged. 'They stayed in Bishop's office for fifteen, maybe twenty minutes, then headed out the back to a part of the complex we didn't know about.'

'Hang . . . hang on. Say that again.'

'They left Bishop's office, but not through the front door. We don't know about any other way out, but maybe there's like a secret panel, like Batman's book-case?' Taj said this with an upward inflection, suggesting, along with the silence that followed it, that they expected Paine to clarify the mysterious exit. He didn't.

'Is that it?'

Jacobs gestured for Taj to continue. 'So they're in

344

this big room, alive and moving around, but not much else. We also picked up some other things moving around in there with them.'

'You don't say,' muttered Tobias.

'Mr Paine?'

'Yes, Ms Jacobs.'

'You know all this, don't you?'

'I am aware of the majority of what you have explained.'

'Then I'm guessing you know what this other area is and therefore how screwed they are.'

'There's an element of truth to that.'

'But you didn't know they were in there until we told you.'

'Possibly the case.'

'So I guess what we're asking you, if you know about this area, is how we get them out.'

Silence.

'Mr Paine?'

'Yes, Ms Jacobs?'

'Did you hear what I said?'

'I did.'

'Do you not want us to help them?'

'I would *love* to assist in any way I can, but there is a substantial element of risk to that endeavour.'

'Hey, we're OK with that. You let us know what the risk is and we'll let you know if we're willing to go for it.'

'The risk to you is not my concern, Ms Jacobs.'

'I don't follow.'

'Ms Jacobs, and the rest of you, without indulging in the kind of indiscretion that would cause me to commit a felony or a betrayal of my country, I think I can explain that the one absolute rule of MEROS is that its contents must never reach the outside world without being under complete control. I do not believe that would be the case if you were to attempt a rescue operation.'

'So you're saying we just leave them down there?'

'I would go one step further, Ms Jacobs. I would prefer it if you were to ensure the complete destruction of MEROS.'

'Are you shittin' us?' asked Madison.

'Ah, a new voice. To whom am I speaking?'

'Er . . . Gary Madison, sir. Pilot.'

'Thank you. Well, Mr Madison, I am not, to employ your vernacular, *shitting you*. You work in some capacity for a project that requires the strictest controls, and that, as I said, is the one absolute rule.'

'Even if it means sacrificing the lives of nine or ten innocent people?' asked Jacobs.

'I'm afraid so. Now, if we've all finished our little game of try to make Mr Pentagon go boo-hoo, what I would like to do is explain to you the steps that are required to annihilate the entire facility.'

65

Except for a couple of pounds she was keeping back for emergencies, Garrett had packed all the remaining C4 on to the nest. It was going to take a hell of a lot to put a good-sized hole in the concrete and she didn't want to risk going in weak with their only shot. All she had to do now was rig the detonator and they were ready.

'All set, Major,' she yelled. The hissing was now so loud she had to raise her voice to be heard. Webster pointed to the other side of the room.

'OK, everyone stand against the east wall. We're going to set the fuses on a two-minute timer.'

The only clear route to the other side of Level One passed within sight of the cockroach hole. As if it were a car crash, they all took at least a glance at the compelling sight of the jerking web of nets. It was too dark to see anything of the roaches but the noise cut through them like ground glass.

They had all suffered along with Lisa but now they could only imagine what was making a sound of that screeching volume. Susan visualized a cracking, clattering mess of hard shell and searching jaws just waiting for more prey. Bishop felt the approaching inevitability of nightmares becoming real.

There were ten of them now, their faces pressed up against the wall. Some were glad of the support as their legs shook and their bodies loosened with faintness. Garrett warned them to look away because the explosion would be bright and hot, not something they wanted to expose their retinas to after an hour in the dark. She also explained that there would be fallout from the explosion: lumps of nest, floor, ceiling, concrete wall, and whatever else lay between it and them.

'Don't know exactly what we're going to get out of this, but at the very least it's gonna look like the biggest Fourth of July you've ever seen being let off in your basement,' was how she put it.

Checking her stopwatch, Garrett shouted down the seconds from the moment Webster had primed the detonators. The others had no idea what would really happen or when until –

The light exploded in a shock of white. It led a quake of shuddering vibration that pushed them harder into the wall, bending their knees, and heating their backs like a roar of sunburn.

The flash continued to pulse out behind them. Hands over their eyes or not, they saw pure, inescapable white. It curled around them like needle-thin fingers that slipped in everywhere. Half-gaps and chinks were filled to the brim even though they shut their eyes tight enough to ache.

The sound was like being inside a thunderstorm: pitch-dark booms spread and throbbed around them, bouncing and swelling into every corner.

The heat, light and noise rose to a roaring peak then tailed off slowly, reverberating around the enclosed space before echoing to a silence that could not compete with the ringing in their ears.

Garrett blinked hard as she turned round. It was as if the house lights had come up at the end of a rock concert. The space was now lit by pockets of burning nest and she could see every part of Level One: its cavernous size; the thoughtless, rectangular arrangement of its grey walls and the chaos that had spread across the floor.

But all that was nothing compared to the shock of the human bones and dried-out insect corpses that littered the ground. There were so many that the Abdomen was a chamber of horrors where the evil masks of massive beetles and giant ants lay next to crushed bones and broken skulls. Now they could see clearly what had lived and died here, they could also see what might have survived.

Dealing with this alongside the confusion of dust blindness and the full ache of ringing in their ears was too much for some. Takeshi tried to steady himself on a table, but it only had three good legs, so he overbalanced and crashed to the ground. Susan held on to George for support, while Andrew clung hard to his mum. Laura simply couldn't take in all the death at once. She bit her lip and held her son tight.

Neither Webster nor Bishop had explained how many people had worked here, so the sheer number of skeletons came as a foul shock. The bones were strewn about the floor like giant grains of rice outside a wedding. Some told a story, like the four skeletons that lay beneath the dessicated remains of six enormous desert locusts. Skulls had been bitten in half, pelvises smashed into hundreds of pieces, femurs and tibia chewed like toothpicks.

Envisaging the massacre that had led to this scene was unavoidable. Like a battlefield that had been left for ten years, it preserved far more than its physical objects. Collectively, they observed a stunned, then respectful, silence as more of the grim remnants were revealed.

They also had no choice but to wait. The explosion had thrown up a murky cloud of dust that was inflating its way through the air. There was no point trying to examine the blast until it had settled.

Despite the explosion, the room had taken on an insidious calm. The hissing had stopped, the explosion had muffled everything that came to their ears and the fire had revealed the unknown horrors of the dark to be harmless, on this floor at least.

The dustcloud was slowing, so they watched as it settled, each passing second showing more of what the explosion had left behind. The highest parts cleared first, and they were relieved to see that there was little damage to the ceiling, only an angry black scorch mark that fanned out from the point of the blast.

The wall and its hard brown covering were revealed next. They watched without blinking as each new inch became visible, hoping to see a hole blasting back to a staircase free from obstruction. But the more they saw, the greater their disappointment: the explosion had made little impact. The north wall looked as it had done earlier, only a few feet further back.

'That could have gone better,' said George.

Mike and Wainhouse headed towards the nest to take a closer look.

'Wait!' shouted Webster. The dust was settling faster than they expected and now they could see why: the explosives had had their greatest effect on the floor. The cloud was falling into a wide, jagged-edged hole that stretched over thirty feet from the wall.

'Well, I guess that's something,' said Garrett. She moved forward to see if they were left with access to the stairs from Level Two.

'Hold on,' warned Webster. 'If the blast made a hole that big then the floor could be weak. Let's take this carefully.'

'Aye-aye, Major.'

As if they were making their way on to thin ice, Garrett and Carter edged ahead, testing the ground before giving it their full weight. The others followed behind in the same way, a chorus of dusty coughs.

Garrett inched past the cockroach hole. The Kevlar web had been blown clean away, leaving an uneven circle with a surprising amount of light coming from it, but nothing alive. There was no time to waste on what might or might not be down there, so she continued towards the wall.

The floor felt solid enough. What they couldn't see

were the struts that ran between the ceiling and floor of Level Two. Made of great steel girders, they had held up with no damage.

Carter looked over the edge. To his amazement, Level Two was clearly illuminated and full of broad green leaves and wide, twisting stalks.

'How come the lights are on down there, Major?' he asked.

Webster followed Carter's eyeline. 'Level Two was the greenhouse. I guess the generator just kept it going.'

'When we wanted to simulate jungle conditions in a . . .' Bishop was going to say *controlled* environment, but thought better of it, '. . . way we could use for experiments, we used Level Two.'

'Well, you did a pretty good job. It looks like an indoor rainforest,' said Carter.

'Hydroponics would explain the humidity,' said Mike. 'There must be metal halide or high-pressure sodium lights down there, and a hell of a lot of moisture.' George looked surprised at this knowledge. 'I paid my way through college by growing the best sativa on the Eastern seaboard,' Mike explained. 'But how come they're still burning after all this time?'

'LED-based innovations from our boys at MIT. Heat and light plus longevity – but I don't think any of us expected them to last ten years,' explained Bishop.

Carter leaned further over. He could see into the staircase on the level below, but only the part that led downwards. Further down, he could also see that the blast had taken out the floor of Level Two, revealing

Level Three. It was crowded with plants that looked like pure white versions of the bushes and creepers that surrounded them on the surface.

'And what was on Level Three?' he asked.

'That was storage,' said Bishop, moving next to Carter to see what he could see.

'Storage of what?'

'All the genetic compounds, including those that had gone wrong, just in case we needed to refer back to them at a later date.' He took a look for himself. 'Good Lord. I don't remember anything like that.'

The dust finally cleared all the way back, confirming that they would have to drop down a level to see if there was any access to the stairway.

'Well, shit,' said Garrett, shaking her head.

'I thought that hole was supposed to go backwards, not down,' said Carter.

'Yeah? Me too,' Garrett replied.

At the back of the group, Andrew and Laura could tell that this was not what the others had been hoping for. With all the debris and mess, they found spaces on opposite ends of the hole and moved in to take a look for themselves.

Laura stared in wonder at the insects that were now visible on the floor below. They didn't look like the blanched, thin corpses that had been lying on Level One for years. They were darker, more substantial, perhaps deceased only recently, possibly in the last ten minutes. It was impossible to say for sure, because the effect of the genetics was unknown, but it looked as if the inhabitants of the Abdomen had not only been living, they'd been thriving.

There was a woodlouse on its back. It was about half the size of Andrew, and its pseudotrachea were clearly visible. Laura could barely take her eyes off it. A praying mantis the length of a car poked out from under the foliage, its bristled coax resembling the blade of a hedge trimmer. Beside it were the antlers of a stag beetle. They were the same size as the antlers of a stag. If they were going to encounter living versions of these monsters, she didn't see how they could possibly get out alive.

A loud cracking sound broke her thoughts. She looked up to see Andrew losing his balance.

'Mum?' he yelled.

Mike was closest. He turned towards Andrew.

Another crack.

'Help him!' screamed Laura.

She started running.

Mike looked around and suddenly knew this was up to him. He broke forward but there was a table between him and Andrew. He leaped to hurdle it but caught his foot and crashed to the ground.

Shaking off the confusion, he heard another crack. Andrew's right leg dropped through the floor.

Meanwhile, Laura was vaulting over three upturned chairs, her only focus the boy in front of her.

Mike started running again. He caught the terrified look in Andrew's eyes as more cracks rang through the air.

'Andrew!' Laura was bolting across the floor. Her

only clear route took her round where the others were standing, unsure how they could help.

Webster moved Bishop aside and joined the chase.

Laura was level with him and they were both running towards George. He didn't know who he should let past, so he turned side on and hoped.

Laura got to him first and shoved him into Webster's path. They collided in a 400 lb smash that sent George flying backwards through the debris.

One more crack, then the floor broke away completely and Andrew was falling.

He spread his arms out to stop himself. His palms found the verge of the hole, but it was a sharp, jagged edge of concrete.

Scraping through his skin to the blood of his small fingers, the pain shocked him.

He reacted instinctively, lifting his fingers up and losing any grip he had. He tried to stop himself sliding downwards but the momentum and pain were too great.

Mike dived for the hole. Just reaching the edge, his hand stretched out in a desperate grasp. His ribs crushed a rack of test tubes, smashing them beneath him. Broken shards of thin glass stabbed into his chest and stomach, shredding it like the pass of a grater.

Ignoring the pain, he plunged his hand down and into the darkness. The tip of his finger found Andrew's palm, but for the briefest of moments.

He felt Andrew's blood-wet fingers closing around his, but he was falling too fast. The moisture made any contact slide away to nothing, leaving a red smear on Mike's hand.

'Muuuuuummmmm!' Andrew screamed as he dropped through the floor. Mike could hear the ragged thrash of the boy's weight through trees and branches. It continued, softer and more distant, until it ended in a deadened thud and a shout of pain.

Laura leaped over a glass partition wall. Tripping over her last stride, she landed full and fast on Mike's back. The pain of the deeper stab of glass shards was like the swipe of a lion's claw across his chest.

Laura hardly noticed. 'Andrew!' she screamed, scrabbling across to where he had fallen.

Mike's arm was still reaching down into the hole. He used it to pull himself forward and joined his voice with Laura's as she called Andrew's name.

There was just enough space for both heads. Although there was still light from the emergency electricity, it quickly dimmed to a green-tinged darkness as the dense leaves blocked the way.

'Aaaaandrewwwwww!'

'Ssshh! I think I hear him,' said Mike.

Laura half-turned her head to point her ear into the hole. The blood was pounding in her skull but she could still make out the sound:

'Muuuummmmmmm . . .'

It was surprisingly distant, struggling to reach them through a wall of leaves and branches.

'Andrew! Stay where you are. I'm coming!'

Laura crouched down and dangled her feet into the hole.

'Wait. I'll go,' said Webster.

Laura ignored him. Another glance downwards then she dropped.

Shhshhshhing and cracking her way through firm, wide leaves and bending branches, she tumbled to the floor of Level Two with Webster following right behind.

66

'Does that sound like something you can all manage?'

Tobias Paine had just finished explaining how to set off the nuclear detonation of MEROS. It involved passing through a series of security checks on the main computer then setting a code that would give them one hour to fly clear of the facility.

'Yes it does. What if we don't want to help you kill our friends?' asked Jacobs.

'I thought you might ask that. Let me explain the situation they are in. It might give you some idea of how unlikely it is they will get out alive.

'They are in an area called the Abdomen. It is where the initial research of MEROS happened ten years ago. The experimentation went wrong and the insects killed everyone except for Heath, Bishop and Webster. It was sealed off and the facility was restarted in the area with which you are now familiar.

'Lady and gentlemen, that area is almost certainly stuffed to the gunwales with giant insects who have had nothing to eat but each other for some ten-odd years; insects that have been bred for size, aggression and appetite, and the genetic compounds used for those purposes have been available to them, possibly creating mutations that would only otherwise exist in your most disturbed nightmares.'

'Yeah? And what if all the bugs are dead?' asked Madison.

'Was that Mr Madison again? Mr Taj has already told me that the motion sensors have picked up movements beyond those of the humans, but even if he hadn't, I'm now looking at the same screen as you.'

Jacobs mouthed '*the satellite*' to the others.

'If you'd been paying close attention to that screen during our conversation, you would have noticed that another of their number has perished. By what means we can only guess.'

'But we can still get the others out alive,' said Mills.

'And you must be Mr Mills. You appear to be English. Congratulations, but I'm afraid you *won't* be able to get the others out alive. Without my assistance there is no way in, and even if you managed to bypass that inconvenience, I will access the relevant codes here and activate the destruction remotely. The same conclusion will be reached, only with four more corpses.

'If you have their interests at heart, remember they are in grave danger, scared, hungry and with no means of escape. Let's get it over with, people.'

All eyes turned to Jacobs. Realizing that a decision had to be made, she leaned in to the phone mike.

'Mr Paine?'

'Yes, Miss Jacobs?'

'Go fuck yourself.'

67

The landing had been hard. It smashed Laura's ribcage like a truck, knocking the wind from her. Wheezing to her feet, her only thought was Andrew. His voice had come from the left, so she tore through the plants in that direction.

Pushing and yanking the leaves away, she called for him as she moved, praying for some kind of response.

'Aaaaandrew!' She walked more slowly, trying to quieten down the sound of the swishing noises around her and make it easier to hear him.

'Aaaandreeeeeeewwwww!'

She heard something. It sounded like *Mum*, but faint as a wisp of smoke. Was it off to her right?

No more sound. A moment's wait then: 'Aaaan-drewww!'

Silence. Or was that a rustle? Andrew or Webster?

More shouts. More movement. Where was she? She turned around. Light squeezed its way from the ceiling through the plants to bathe her in a green glow.

'Aaaaannndreeew!'

This time she didn't move. She could hear nothing but her own thumping heart. Her mouth was dry and it hurt to swallow.

'Oh God Jesus Christ where are you?' she whispered, looking frantically around her. 'Jesus where the hell are you Andrew where are you how am I going to find you where are you? Aaaandreeeeeewwwww!'

Louder this time. 'Aaaandrewwwww! Aaaandreww!'

Her thoughts raced ahead of her. *Where was he? He couldn't be gone? He must be safe. Please let him be safe. He can't be dead. Stop saying that. Not dead. Somewhere down here. Where? Where is he? Where am I? Jesus Christ!*

She broke into another run. Although she was fast and determined, she soon reached a twisted knot of trunks and vines she could not pass. She kicked and shoved them, beating them with her fists.

'Oh no! Oh God! Oh no! Oh God! Oh shit! Somebody! Help me! Where's Andrew! Help me find my child, my little boy! I love him! Help me, somebody, please!'

The tears were coming now, garbling the words through a web of saliva. She sank to her knees.

'Please. Somebody! Help me! Help! Help! Oh God, please don't let him be gone, dead, gone, dead . . .'

Then a rustle to her left.

She whipped her head round. 'Andrew?'

Getting to her feet, she moved through the undergrowth.

'Andrew?'

There was no reply, but another rustle came clear through the leaves.

'Andrew? Is that you?'

With each leaf she moved aside or bent back, the rustle became louder and firmer.

'Oh, Andrew!' Laura sighed, relief flowing through her. She didn't know how she knew, but she was absolutely certain that it was him; he'd have a few bumps and bruises but it would be him for sure.

Peeling back the leaves and stepping forwards, she smiled through her tears. It was all going to be fine. The panic was over. Just one more . . .

The screech was deafening and was joined instantly by a scream of utter terror from Laura.

She tried to move away by stepping backwards but stumbled over her feet and fell face-first on to a thick stalk.

And it was upon her. The Jerusalem cricket, as big as a Labrador, flexed its powerful legs to pounce upon her back.

She continued to scream as the mandibles dug into her shoulder and pressed slowly together, scraping and dragging through the flesh on the back of her ribs.

68

Mills stood with his arms folded. 'OK, Jacobs, you've pissed off the man with the nuclear button – what do we do now?'

'Let's start with you shooting out the satellite.' Mills shrugged and left.

Jacobs continued: 'Taj, I want to take another look at those blueprints. We're going to screw that sonofabitch.'

'Say what?' asked Taj.

Jacobs rolled the blueprints out across the reception desk.

'I don't know about you guys but for some reason killing the others just doesn't sit right with me. If we're going to get them out of there then we've got to break the remote connection between the Pentagon and here . . .'

She was interrupted by a burst of gunfire and the sound of the satellite shattering above them.

'. . . So now he can't remote-detonate, which means he's going to have to send someone to do the job instead. Madison, you've had to refuel around here, what are the closest bases?'

'Uh . . . Seven Islands in Bermuda, Garra del Aguila in Colombia . . . and Santa Cruz, North-east Brazil.

They might have others, but those are the nearest three I know.'

'OK, which is closest, and how long would it take to get a nuclear strike over here?'

'They're about the same, but I'd go for Santa Cruz. It's definitely strapped for nuclear. My man Nathan runs fuel into there, and he's seen the F-35s. Maybe two, two and a half hours when you factor in a few calls from the Pentagon and an emergency scramble.'

Jacobs set the countdown on her watch and waited for Mills, who strode back into the reception area looking pleased with himself.

'And what we gonna do with those two hours?' asked Taj.

'We're going to get them out. Something that asshole said made me realize there's another way in: 'With no means of escape'. He's saying that the only way into the new area is through Bishop's office. That's the only entrance and exit they ever had for thousands of square feet of lab space? No way. Let's not forget they only moved everything to our area after the old one went wrong, so there's not only another way out, there's got to be another way to the surface.'

'Great,' said Mills. 'And where the hell is that?'

'Let's all take another look at the blueprints, we might just find something we've missed.'

'There's only the stairs at the back of the Abdomen part,' said Mills.

'Yeah? Then maybe there's a clue in this number. 503. Could that mean anything good for us?' asked Jacobs.

Madison looked as if he was back in school, and in a class he was failing. Mills shook his head just to make sure everyone knew he was thinking really hard. Taj considered Jacobs' words for a moment before surprising them all.

'If that's feet, that's near as dammit five hundred, and we all know that's how far the elevator goes down, because we all took the long ride and asked the question. So we just look for where this'd be on the map and I'd say there's gonna be some kind of door, hatch, whatever, in the jungle.'

He folded his arms and stood back waiting for the others to appreciate his genius.

Mills and Madison were even more confused now. How did Taj beat them to it?

Jacobs smiled. 'Sounds like we might just have ourselves a plan.'

69

Webster was lying on his back in a crumpled pile of large green fronds. He had twisted his ankle on landing and the pain was enough to blanch his face and leave him groaning through his teeth.

He sat up on a tree root and pulled his sock down. The ankle was already inflating and had turned an angry shade of scarlet, but Webster had broken bones and taken bullets before; this might slow him down but it wasn't going to stop him. He grasped the broad stalk in front of him and dragged himself up, taking care to keep his weight on his good foot.

He ran through his choices: the most sensible would be to call for help and get Garrett down to winch him up. But that would mean losing Laura for sure, and he wondered how the sight of him hobbling around upstairs without her or Andrew would affect the others.

The other option would be to search for Andrew and Laura on his twisted ankle. Would he really be able to help them that much? He could barely walk, so even if he did find them, defending them from the insects and helping them get back to Level One would not be easy. He might even make things harder by needing their help more than they needed him.

But then, he was armed, and that had to be a big plus. He decided he would at least look for them.

'Lauuuuraaaaaa! Aaaaannnddrreewwww! Laauuur-raaa!'

He could feel the foliage deadening his call. With no response, the only thing he could do to improve his odds of finding them was to get moving.

As he took his first careful steps, he could hear Garrett calling for him, but there was no way he was going to drag her down here. Their best chance of survival was to stay on Level One, so he resolved to wait until he had moved further away before calling out again.

70

Laura was screaming in long, hoarse bellows of pain.

The metal shoulder-strap that hung off the back of her jacket was angering the Jerusalem cricket, which could not bring its jaws together to complete its bite.

The mandibles had drawn plenty of blood but had not yet reached the scapula or the ribs. To Laura it felt as if two blunt carving knives were pulling through her flesh, digging at the skin and causing mounting agony.

She was pinned across a hard, curving root as thick as her thigh, but just beyond that was a wide pool of water that made up part of the hydroponics system.

If she were forced any further forward there was a good chance she could drown, so she was doing her best to resist the pressure of the beast on her back.

She grabbed hold of the roots again but she was weakened by the blood loss, and now the creature was pressing her forwards with its strong back legs.

She looked up as far as she could to see the water just ahead. It appeared to be rising to meet her, getting closer to her nostrils and mouth.

Further the mandibles dug, sliding her onward with irresistible force.

The tip of her nose was touching the water now.

She could feel the tepid moisture as her hard breaths rippled the surface.

This is how I die, she thought.

Then she saw something else flop into her line of sight. Thin and brown, it bent in front of her, and she knew she had to grab hold of it.

Reaching forward, she just managed to get her right hand around it. *What now?* she thought.

Gripping harder, she was surprised to feel the pain in her back ease a little. In fact, the harder she gripped, the looser the cricket's hold became.

With one more massive effort, she yanked on what was in her hand.

The shriek in her ear felt like a long flow of sharp gravel. She had one of its incredibly sensitive antennae, and was inflicting hard waves of pain on the creature.

It snapped forward, aiming for the hand, but Laura moved out of range at the last moment and it bit hard into its own antenna.

Another God-awful screech came and elongated into a howl. Laura seized her opportunity and bent the other antenna back on to itself.

The cricket thrashed its head from side to side, squealing and screaming. This movement sent it off balance and it tipped on to its back, bent antennae in the air.

Laura slid painfully out from under it and coughed, feeling the barking agony of her back as her ribs shook.

She looked across at the cricket, seeing for the first time how hideous and powerful it appeared. But there was no time for fear. She had to finish it off, and fast, before its helpless noises attracted anything else.

Slumping over towards its head, she found its eyes and dug her thumbs deep inside them. She had to hold on tight, as the whipping and bucking continued with even greater vigour. She knew this wouldn't kill it, but she was harming it enough to make sure she could get away without it following her.

She slid her thumbs out of the black mush, staggered to her feet and stumbled away. Within a few paces she was out of sight, hidden by leaves and stalks. Taking a moment to lean against a deep green trunk, she tried to calm down.

The pause left no distractions from the pain. Along with the blood loss, it overwhelmed her and she felt something deep within ebbing away. Despite everything, it felt quite pleasant.

Torn, broken and bloody, she dropped to her knees, leaned forward against the tree and passed out.

71

'Fuck me, eh? Fuck *me*?' muttered Tobias Paine as he dialled the four-digit Pentagon extension.

'Good morning, Mr Paine, you are speaking to Sheila Berenson, General Facilities Secretary, Special Ops. How can I help you today?'

'Good morning, Ms Berenson, you can help me today by giving me the authorization codes for a twenty-two fourteen on MEROS.'

'A twenty-two fourteen?' She had been trained to respond in a calmly efficient manner to all requests but she had yet to receive one of this gravity.

'Yes, Sheila, a twenty-two fourteen. Would you like me to explain what that is?'

'Uh, no, sir. That won't be necessary.' In the face of Paine's patronizing tone, she immediately reverted to correct protocol. 'Could I have your password, please?'

'Certainly, it's cherry pie.'

She typed it in.

'That has been confirmed, sir. Now all I have to do is input my corresponding code and we should be . . .' Those words hung in the air long enough for Paine to think he had been cut off.

'Hello? Hello? Ms Beren—'

'I'm here, sir.'

'Well?'

'I don't understand. The codes have been sent, but I have no confirmation that MEROS has received them.'

'Are you saying that you don't know if the operation has been successful?'

'Negative, sir. The operation has not been successful. We have a reading here which tells us if there has been a deployment of nuclear weaponry. There has been no such deployment.'

'And what's the problem? This is a Code Red emergency, Ms Berenson.'

'Of course, sir. The problem is one of communication. We have lost contact with MEROS.'

'But I was just on the phone with them ten minutes ago. Does everything go through the same system?'

'Yes, sir; a satellite link.'

'So' – Paine rubbed his forehead and sighed – 'if this link had been disabled in some way, then a twenty-two fourteen would be impossible?'

'I guess so. But wouldn't a malfunction be more likely?'

'Perhaps. Perhaps not.'

72

'I'm going down there,' said Garrett, removing the heavier weapons from her shoulders.

'Are you sure that's such a good idea?' asked Bishop as carefully as he could. He knew that Garrett's default reaction was to do the opposite of whatever he suggested or wanted, but he also knew that her going down to Level Two would condemn her to the same fate as Andrew, Laura and Webster.

As far as Bishop was concerned – and he was not the only one – the three of them were not going to return. If a man as robust and experienced as Webster could not find his way back, then the others could forget it, and that included Garrett.

'Yes, shitcake, I am *very* sure it's such a good idea. I've lost one too many friends today and I'm running out. I know your motto is *Fuck 'em, especially if they're grunts*, but I happen to have a feeling or two rattling around in here.'

'Garrett, he's right.' The last person she was expecting to say that was Carter, but there he was, stepping in on Bishop's side.

'You must have a good reason for taking the side of this asshole, Carter,' she said. 'Let's hear it.'

'We can't just keep sending people down there

without knowing what we're up against. As far as folks I care about go, after my mom, it's Webster, so I want him back up here bad, but there's a reason he's still down there.' He pointed to what they could see of the foliage through the hole Garrett had blasted in the floor. 'That's the greenhouse from hell. We already know that whatever ate Lisa is down there, and now three more of us have gone and no one's come back. Don't you see? If we're going to get out of here, we've got to play the odds, and they're saying stay the hell out of there.'

Garrett considered this. 'I don't know, Carter. I can't let someone else die if I can do something about it.'

'Excuse me.' It was Takeshi. 'Perhaps there is a way you can help them without venturing to Level Two.'

73

Laura was finally coming round. Lying face down across a mesh of gnarled roots, her back was a throbbing wave of constant biting pain. When she tried to lift her head off the ground her shoulder joined in, sending that pain harder and deeper through her back like an axe blade.

Uppermost in her mind were thoughts of Andrew. They helped to repress the physical pain but presented an emotional agony that was far harder to manage. There was no way a boy as small and unprepared as her son could possibly have survived more than five minutes down here.

She wept. The tears came in dense sobs that shook through her and covered her face and hands in a slick of moisture. Her thoughts were swift black clouds, colliding in confusion as they shot around her head.

But the possibility of being found by another creature was also ever-present. She knew that she could give up and wait here to die, or she could cling to the tiny possibility that she might still find her son and that they could somehow get out of here and return to a home that now seemed impossibly distant.

Rolling over on to her good shoulder, she winced. She no longer felt as if she had a back; it was now just a fiery blast of excruciating misery. Her mouth was dry and claggy from the overpowering heat and loss of blood and her head pounded with the ache of dehydration.

Despite all that, she had to call her son's name.

The first effort was a pitiful croak that dissolved to nothing between her lungs and her lips. Much greater effort was required.

'Andrew,' she called in nothing more than a whisper. She shook her head, cleared her throat and gave it all she had.

'Andrew!' Much better. It was a decent shout now, so she repeated it over and over.

Was that a voice? wondered Webster.

The sound came again, straining to get through the density of the thicket.

He couldn't be sure, but in the absence of anything else to aim for, he headed to where he thought it was coming from. His wariness slowed him, encouraging caution and reminding him that another, hungrier beast could be on the other side of the next leaf.

There it was again. Two syllables. Could it be 'Major'? Was someone calling for him? His pace quickened as he forgot his ankle.

'Hello?' he shouted. 'Is someone there?'

I'm sure that was 'hello' thought Laura. And it was a man's voice. She tuned her hearing to Webster's tone and stood stock still listening again.

'Hello!' It was Webster.

'Major?' she shouted.

'Laura?' came the reply.

'Over here!'

'Say again!'

'Over here, Major.'

The rustling was now as loud as the voices.

'Here, here, here,' Laura said, until a giant leaf folded back to reveal the beautiful sight of a limping Webster. She was a picture of relief, but Webster couldn't help the shock showing on his face. Laura was caked head to toe in blackened blood-crust, some hers, some from the cricket.

'Jesus, are you OK?'

Laura looked down at her front. 'Oh, uh . . . it's not as bad as it . . . uh . . . looks . . .'

She turned and pointed to her back, which was an angry mess of torn jacket and dark, solidifying blood. 'You should have seen the other . . .' she said, but the last word barely made it out before she was sobbing uncontrollably. Webster shuffled closer and put his big arms around her. She leaned in, shaking as she tried to muffle her sobbing into his T-shirt.

'I'm sorry,' she said, separating herself from him and wiping a wet, bloody smear across her face.

'If anyone has a right to cry . . .' Webster began, then remembered Andrew and thought better of it.

A ripple of leaves flickered behind them. They both heard it and knew they had to move on.

'Can you walk?' asked Webster.

'I think so. I feel pretty weak, but my legs are OK.'

She looked at Webster's stick and the way he was keeping his left ankle off the ground.

'I twisted it when I landed,' he explained. 'It's getting better but it's still too much to walk on.'

'We can try leaning on each other,' suggested Laura. She stood next to him and put her arm around his waist, while he did the same to her shoulder. They felt solid enough to try moving in short shuffles.

'We have to find Andrew,' said Laura firmly.

'OK,' said Webster. He knew he had to get her moving. If by some miracle they found him alive, then great; if not then at least they might find the others.

'I have no idea where we are, though.'

Laura pointed in the opposite direction to where the cricket lay. 'I think that way might be . . . Did you feel that?' she asked quickly.

'What?' Webster heard the *shhhshhh* whisper of the ferns closest to him. Looking down, he could see nothing. Then from behind he felt the colossal strength of something closing around his thigh.

He looked down to see two jet-black claws pressing into him, as hard and thick as elephant tusks. He tried to force them apart with his free hand but they just gripped harder.

Webster gave out a strangled grunt, a gurgled mixture of agony and surprise, which made Laura look down.

Her first reaction was to shriek. She could only see the antlers but knew for certain they belonged to a stag beetle of colossal proportions.

Webster let go of Laura. All his efforts were trying

to resist the crushing force that dug into his leg. Another deep grunt strained his throat.Without Webster's grip to steady her, Laura stumbled backwards into the leaves. She landed on something hard just above the floor. It moved beneath her. She screamed again and scrambled to her feet.

'Oh God!'

She struggled to be heard against Webster's groans.

Grasping for him, she slipped and fell forward. Her hands landed on the antler. Its solidity and power were terrifying. She let go of it immediately and grabbed the bottom of Webster's jacket to steady herself.

The second her fingers took hold, she was swung through the foliage and high into the air, her shoes almost touching the ceiling.

Webster was underneath her, also off his feet. He had lost his grip on the antler and was trying to stay upright.

They hung briefly in mid air then came down hard, shredding and crunching through the plants until the floor rose up to ram into them. Laura felt a rib crack and gave a dark moan through gritted teeth.

By twisting at the last moment, Webster just missed landing on his bad ankle, but this meant his right knee took the impact instead, sending a web of pain spreading up his thigh.

Then they were moving, speeding through the big, solid stalks. The beetle was behind them, so they were being used as a battering ram, smacking into dozens of stalks and branches.

One impact after another left hard shocks of pain

flashing through them. Skin was scraped raw as they rumbled and smacked and rolled and whipped, upside down, backwards, forwards and sideways over the rough floor, into the legs of upturned tables, over scatterings of broken glass and through brambles of claw-sharp thorns.

Arms bent backwards then jerked forwards. Knees ground glass into bloody wounds. Fingers stretched until joints screamed, but still Laura held on.

Then it changed direction, digging the antlers still further into Webster's thigh and whipping Laura's neck sideways.

She did not know how much longer she could hold on. Webster's jacket was slipping further off his shoulders and her grip was severely tested every time the beetle swiped them through a tangle of stalks.

At last they slowed to a stop.

Although the pain and disorientation were overwhelming, they were most troubled by the fact that they were now in complete darkness.

Webster was so dazed he didn't even feel the antlers release him. Beside him, Laura's face was stuffed into a mound of soft earth. She tried to turn round but it hurt too much to move her neck.

In the pitch black, all they had to go on was the sound: a chattering, chittering, snickering noise.

They were in a nest.

'Major,' Laura said weakly. 'Major Webster?'

He choked out a strained gasp.

'Laura? You OK?' He coughed, wincing at the bark

of pain each constriction of his chest sent through him. There was movement all around them, and Laura knew from the sound that they were surrounded by stag-beetle larvae.

Like a group of rootling moles, the young beetles used their stunted antennae to explore what their mother had brought them.

Whatever Webster and Laura did, they could not get out of range of the rubbery teasing and probing. The movement, accompanied by those vicious, stridulating sounds, peeled back Laura's fear to its rawness.

They tried to push the antennae away, but there were too many. When they brushed one off, it was replaced by two more.

Webster's right shoulder had almost been wrenched from its socket, leaving him unable to move his arm. Scrabbling about him, one of the creatures pushed it off his chest. The pain was like a flare of fire. His useless hand lay on the floor as he tried to defend himself with the other.

Without warning, the larvae crawled off to one side. The noise became quieter as each one retreated to the rear of the nest.

Webster wondered what was going on but Laura feared the worst. She knew what these creatures were like in miniature with no increased aggression: voracious feeders mercilessly consuming their way to adulthood. These giant versions would not stop until the two of them were chewed, liquefied and sucked into their stomachs.

From nowhere the mother beetle's jaw came powering through the air, crashing into Webster's lifeless bicep. It just missed the main part of the muscle, but the rough stabbing was another torture. He gave a long howl that put the insect off, but only momentarily.

It retracted its mandible, taking bloody flesh with it. Webster howled again.

Laura could only imagine what was happening. She felt tiny eddies of movement in the air and heard the decisive *chomp* of the beetle's blunt dagger driving into Webster's arm. Beyond that she was blinded by the darkness.

The beetle moved in.

Rising up on its rear legs, it took aim at Webster's prone skull.

He rolled his head round to face the creature. Eyelids that had been matted shut with gore separated with crusted stiffness. Webster could see nothing, and the waiting multiplied his terror.

Then another sound.

It was so faint it could barely be heard, but it cheered Webster. He didn't even know why, but that tiny, faraway echo of a deep, electronic drawl made him feel like this might not be the end.

'Close your eyes,' he mumbled, his good hand reaching for Laura's. 'Close them tight, now.'

The brilliant flash, like the inside of a lightning bolt, shot through the entire Abdomen. Anything unfortunate enough to be looking would have felt a blowtorch burn searing through its pupils.

The light pulsed for minutes in waves of decreasing strength until it gradually faded to nothing and darkness returned.

Laura and Webster lay on the floor, their fingers intertwined, crusted with dirt, blood and plant sap.

'You still alive?' Webster whispered.

'Yes . . . You?'

74

Mills, Jacobs, Madison and Taj were hacking through the jungle behind the MEROS building.

'We're going the wrong way,' said Mills.

'I don't think so,' said Madison.

'What the fuck would you know?' Mills spat back.

'I know you'd be a hell of a lot happier with some nuts on your chin.'

'No, I'd be a lot happier with this rifle pointing up your arse.'

'You've got it on the brain, man, putting things up guys' asses.'

'Jacobs, we'd better find this door pronto before I break this fucker's face.'

'Calm down, both of you. Do you really think we have time to have a grade-school argument?'

'Aaaarrrgghh!' Taj's cry sent the birds ripping through the trees. The others ran over to where he was now lying on his back, clutching his foot.

'What is it?' asked Mills.

'Fuckin' toe!'

Taj went around barefoot, so if he were to walk into a large piece of half-buried concrete there would be pain involved and, as it turned out, a fair amount of blood.

'Maybe you should go back and get some antiseptic and a Band-Aid on that,' said Jacobs.

'Maybe I should,' winced Taj, limping off.

'So what the hell is this?' said Mills.

'My guess is it's the top of the staircase, blocked off with concrete,' replied Jacobs.

'Are we going to blast it off?'

'Yes, we are, Madison,' replied Jacobs. 'Here's where you thank us for bringing our escape kit. Mills, I think we need the CS-24.'

Mills smiled. 'Coming right up.'

'Is that explosive?' asked Madison.

'Well, we're not going to get very far with fudge.'

'Is there any danger of . . . ?'

'Of what?'

'I don't know. Could you mangle whatever is under here so bad that we can't get through?'

'If that happens, we blow it up again. We've got enough to blast our way through every inch of shit under here if we need to.'

Mills returned with the explosives and detonators.

'We've got to do this in stages. Pack on enough to get through the concrete first.'

'How much do you think?'

Jacobs picked up a chunk of explosive the size of a cigarette packet and felt its weight. 'I think that will do the job.'

Mills split it up into smaller sections and attached them by wires to the detonator.

'That's it: wide and shallow,' said Jacobs. Mills set a

short timer and they fell back to the plane to make sure Taj was safely out of the way.

Waiting for an explosion always got the heart pumping. Mills held up his watch for the others to see. They braced themselves as the last seconds ticked down, hoping everything had been set right so they wouldn't have to risk returning to a primed block of CS-24.

A distant bang followed by a shower of rocky fragments and a drizzle of dust told them it was safe to see what the concrete had revealed.

A blue hatch sat in the middle of a wide circle of scorched earth. It was still partially covered in a thin layer of concrete, so more work would be needed to get through it, but that was not what concerned them.

What occupied every single molecule of their collective attention was the soft, arrhythmic tapping that was coming from the other side.

'What you think that is?' said Taj, not at all keen to find out.

'Could be anything,' said Jacobs. 'Could be wasps, could be them. But just to be on the safe side . . .'

She ran to the back of the plane and returned with a couple of large nets made from the same adapted Kevlar as the netspreaders.

'Nice thinking,' said Mills. They laid them across the hatch and bolted them into the ground.

'Over to you, boys,' said Jacobs, gesturing towards the hatch wheel.

Taj and Mills stretched open a couple of the net holes and reached in to grasp opposite sides of the wheel. With the residue of concrete holding parts of it in place, the wheel was a stiff turn, but with a few grunts they got it going. When the lock was free and they could open the door, they looked to Jacobs.

'OK, guys, get on the other side so the opening is away from you. And be ready for anything.' She drew her weapon and pointed it at the hatch. 'On three, open that hatch real, real slow. OK, one . . .two . . . three!'

At the first try nothing moved, then the boys heaved again and the hatch opened a crack. Nothing flew out, so they opened it a little further.

The noise stopped. With a tear of concrete their next effort hauled the door wide open, leaving it flat on the ground.

Jacobs and Madison looked down the hole while Taj and Mills lay flat on their backs, knocked clear of the hatch by the effort it had taken to pull it open.

That's why none of them saw it: clinging to the back of the door was a termite, three feet long, with a bent wing and a broken leg.

Jacobs continued to peer into the staircase. 'I can't . . . Jesus Christ!'

Before she could aim her Glock 17, the termite tore through the net in a single bite and flew off into the jungle.

'Stop that thing! We can't let it get away!' yelled Jacobs. 'One of you stay here and make sure there aren't any more of them.'

Jacobs took off with her weapon drawn. She was closely followed by Mills and Madison, who sprinted through the undergrowth, following Jacobs' path.

At first it was easy to track. One of its four wings was also damaged, and that, coupled with its blindness, meant it had no idea where it was heading.

But then it was in the air, which gave it the kind of options no human could follow. Just as Jacobs was getting close enough for a shot, it took off into the sky. Mills aimed at it hopefully and missed by a long way, and the sound of the gunshot released hundreds of birds into the air, obscuring the termite.

'Goddamn you, Mills!' Jacobs exclaimed, coming to an exasperated stop.

'What? It was getting away. I had to try something. If I'd killed it you'd be patting me on the back.'

'Yeah, but you didn't, numbnuts, so she's looking to use your dick for dogfood.'

'Madison, I FUCKING SWEAR–'

'Quit it! We need to look for that bug. If it mates with a regular termite all hell could break loose.'

'If it mates with a regular termite a whole bunch of lube is going to have to break loose,' said Madison, chuckling at his own joke.

Jacobs rolled her eyes. 'OK, split up. We don't have much time, so if we don't find it, meet back at the hatch in five.'

Mills and Jacobs headed further into the jungle, while Madison stayed where he was. Moving slowly, he took to pointing his gun around trees like a rookie cop. He had spent little time in the jungle, so didn't know what to do when a spider monkey came screeching over his head. He almost shot at it, but it was too quick for him.

After a few minutes of walking, he realized that he was completely lost. He had let Mills and Jacobs run off without paying attention to where they had gone. Was it back up the slope or down towards the stream? Was that the tree they had stopped at or was it the one over there by those bushes?

'Jacobs?' He could not bring himself to call for help from Mills.

'Jacobs!' There was no reply.

She was probably half a mile away by now. And what chance did Madison have of spotting that termite? As far as he knew, it looked like every other bug and rodent in this jungle, only bigger.

But time was ticking on and he had no idea how to get back to the hatch. He turned to see if he could get a better view further up the hill.

As he swished through the bushes he heard a strange noise behind him. He couldn't place it, but it sounded like Taj demolishing a King-Size Snickers.

He turned to see that the top of the nearest trunk was shaking, even though there was no wind.

The eating noise stopped and the shaking turned to a swaying, accompanied by a whining *cree-aaaak*.

By the time Madison realized it was swaying towards him, he had just enough time to run to the side before it came crashing down, the widest branches skimming his back.

Seconds later, Mills and Jacobs arrived, ignored Madison and ran to the trunk. They both emptied their magazines as the termite was blasted, like a giant black egg, into a spray of cracked shell and sticky guts.

Satisfied there was no chance the thing was still alive, they holstered their weapons. Madison got to his feet and joined them by the tree stump.

Mills stood over what was left of the termite, grinding the guts into the jungle soil.

'I knew it'd come looking for a tree. Those things are hard-wired,' said Jacobs. 'Didn't think it'd be such a big one, though. It's like a goddamn chainsaw.'

Madison tried to look calm, as if he had been expecting the same thing. In truth, he was still trying to slow his heartbeat after narrowly missing getting crushed by a tree trunk.

'OK,' said Jacobs. 'Let's get back to the hatch.'

She jogged up the slope at a good pace. Mills was right on her shoulder, with Madison struggling to keep up.

When Madison finally reached the top of the slope, he found Jacobs and Mills looking around the hatch in confusion.

Taj was gone.

75

'Jesus, I'm never going to get used to those light bombs,' said Garrett, blinking hard.

'Me neither,' said Carter. 'Do you think it did any good?'

Garrett was on her way back to the hole, knocking into tables as her eyes readjusted from the searing white.

'Only if they heard the noise it makes before it goes off. Otherwise, they're trapped in a jungle of giant insects AND they're blind. But thanks for the idea, Takeshi. At least we gave them half a chance.'

Leaning in, she shouted for Webster, but there was no reply. That didn't stop her yelling his name over and over.

Gradually, the others were getting their sight back. The soldiers all knew that *Keep your eyes shut as tight as you can* was really good advice. But the scientists had never experienced it, so they just put their hands over their eyes and got a nasty shock when the light made short work of the cover from their eyelids.

'Don't move,' Carter advised Mike, who had just fallen over a table and landed face-first on a human skull. 'If you can't see, just leave it a while. It'll get better eventually.'

'That's reassuring,' mumbled Mike, rubbing his jaw.

George bent down to where Garrett was still shouting into the hole. 'Is there anything we can do to help out?'

'Sure. Shout for the major somewhere else. You can shout for the lady or the kid if it makes you feel better. We'll give it five minutes, then we're on our own, looking for an escape route.'

At a loss for anything else to do, the scientists were now calling down to Level Two. Bishop, Mike and George were bent down at the edge of the space created by the explosion, while Susan and Takeshi were at the cockroach hole.

Carter walked over to Wainhouse.

'That light bomb's gonna give us a little time. We should check out the blast hole, see if there's any way on to the stairs from the next floor down.'

'Sure thing,' Wainhouse said.

Carter kicked a few burning lumps of termite nest into the hole then watched with Wainhouse to see how far they would fall and whether or not they would illuminate anything.

The fiery boulders arced downwards through Level Two and on into Level Three, where they landed with a *phlumph* on the white leaves. The fire stayed on the top of the stalks and branches, as if they were the stiff bristles of a broom, then the foliage moved aside and let the brown chunk fall further amongst it. The bigger leaves seemed to envelop the flames and snuff them out.

'Did I just imagine that?' said Carter.

'Hey, this place is full of crazier shit than I've ever seen. That's *tame*,' said Wainhouse.

At the wall, the termite nest continued through the floor to Level Two. Carter edged closer to it, taking care to test the floor before giving it his full weight. He reached into a firm-looking nest hole and pulled down hard. It crumbled a little but felt safe enough. Moving his body round, he rammed his boots into more holes and climbed out over the sheer drop to Levels Two and Three.

One toehold broke away, but he was secure enough in the other three that it caused just a flutter of distraction. He then took the bolt gun from his belt, aimed it into the nest above his head and pulled the trigger.

A small *ptttwww* was barely audible above Garrett's shouting as a steel expansion bolt drove deep into the nest, creating an anchor for the rope.

Carter attached his grips then jumped backwards and dropped down towards Level Two. Looking around, he saw leaves behind and below him, and more nest in front.

'Got nothing here so far. Moving down.'

He slid further until he reached the solid ground of the level below. Balancing his toes on the outcrop of the destroyed floor, he peered into the darkness behind what remained of the nest. A glint of chrome told him all he needed to know.

'I got the stairs!' he called. 'It looks like there's still some nest around it but we should be able to get through.'

'You want me to come down?' asked Wainhouse. By

now the other scientists had gathered round to watch Carter's progress.

'Just hang on while I . . . what the hell –?'

He felt a scratching over his trousers, followed by the sensation of something about the weight of a mouse, then more of these. He looked down, ready to fire, but saw only a few beetles, nowhere near the size of the insects they had encountered so far. There was no need to use his weapons, but he didn't want them to climb any further, so he kicked out his foot.

The beetles responded by holding still and gripping his trousers with all six tarsal claws.

'Get . . . the . . . hell . . . off . . .' Carter muttered, shaking his legs.

'What you got down there?' called George.

'Some kind of beetles. They're not big, but I can't get 'em off and they're crawling up my pants.'

'Hey, make sure they don't get any higher. I think they like dark, sweaty places.' Wainhouse laughed.

'Ha ha. So where's your mom's ass when I need it?'

'Just bat 'em off.'

'I'm trying . . . just . . . can't reach.'

'Wait a second and they'll crawl up to you, *then* bat 'em off,' said Mike.

Carter stopped struggling and let them move further up his legs. They were quick and soon gripped the bottom of his flak jacket. He took a swipe and sent one spinning to the level below like a downed fighter plane. Another six were dispatched in the same way, and he was free of them all.

'OK – you done?' asked Wainhouse.

'Yeah . . . but there's . . . my hand is feeling kind of warm, like . . . Ow! Ow! God . . . damn!'

'What is it, Carter?'

'My hand, it's burning up like hell. Shiiiiit!'

'You'd better get up here now, man. I don't want you having to climb that rope with one hand . . .'

'Yeah, yeah, me neither. *Aaaarrfuckkkaar!*'

Now Garrett was at Wainhouse's side. 'Quick smart, Carter!'

'I can't . . . Mother*fucker*!' The pain was like forked lightning inside his fingers.

'We've got to get him up,' Garrett said, pulling Wainhouse round to where they could get hold of the rope. 'Hang on there, Carter.'

With a great effort, they drew the rope up the side of the nest. As Carter neared, she could see his hand clearly: a mess of ugly white blisters growing so fast they looked like boiling milk.

Garrett grabbed the back of his belt and wrenched him on to the floor of Level One. His eyelids were barely apart.

'Don't touch it,' he wheezed.

'Nerds, get over here! Now!' Garrett shouted.

Taking care to keep Carter's hand away from their skin, Wainhouse and Garrett carried him to a table where the four scientists were gathering to help.

'What was it?' asked Mike.

'Uh! Uh! It was like a beetle. Jesus Christ!' Carter gasped.

'Blister beetle,' said Mike. The others agreed.

'What's that? Is that bad?'

'Difficult to say without seeing how big it was. Maybe it had been bred to be more toxic, because I've never seen anything like this. It's a reaction to a poison called cantharidin. You can die if you ingest it but that's pretty rare for humans.'

'What can we do for him?'

'There's no known antidote.'

'No known fuckin' antidote? What's that mean?' asked Garrett.

'It . . . uh . . . means there's no cure for . . .'

'I know what the fuck "no antidote" means. I want to know what it means for Carter.'

'I . . . I don't know.'

'You don't know . . . You don't know . . . Well, that's just fuckin' great. Meanwhile, Carter's hand is a bag of pus. Remind me again, what the fuck are we dragging you geeks along for?'

'Calcium works on horses,' said Susan quickly.

'Well, why didn't you say so?' asked Garrett.

'We don't have any calcium.'

'But there's smashed labs all over this fucking place! Let's start looking!'

Takeshi, Susan, Mike and George searched the floor around them. Bishop didn't even move.

'Jesus! Split the fuck up!'

Garrett had raised her voice so loud they all shot off like they'd backed into a cattle prod.

'We won't have long before the bugs recover from the light, so hurry up.'

'Carter, how you doin'?' He was veering close to unconsciousness.

'Garrett?'

'Speak to me, man.' She held his good hand.

'Garrett . . .' The lids were drooping over his shining eyes. When they shut completely, Carter's whole body went limp.

'Oh shit. Is he dead?' asked Wainhouse.

Garrett tore open Carter's shirt and listened for a heartbeat. 'Got a faint one, but it's all over the place. Fuck! This we do not fucking need! Stay with us, buddy.'

Carter could not hear Garrett. His body was trying desperately to fight the poison that was flowing through him.

Garrett looked around at the fires burning across Level One. They reminded her of the checkpoints she'd crossed in Iraq. You drove up to them in your jeep, and they'd put anything in your way to make you stop: Iraqis dressed in US uniforms, roadblocks of burnt-out cars, even kids pretending to play. But the orders never changed: you just drove through, because if you didn't they'd shoot you where you stopped. It was a no-win situation, because you didn't want to kill a kid, but you didn't want to die either. Whatever happened, you were going to lose.

MEROS had always been heading this way, and she had been given a front-row seat for the whole show.

Now there was no Webster, no way to Level Two, no stairs to climb and a warehouse full of deformed super-insects to contend with. The final curtain couldn't be far away.

'Garrett? Are we ever going to get out of here?' asked Wainhouse.

She didn't even look up.

76

Tobias Paine was driving down Rhode Island Avenue towards Jonathan Stern's Foxhall Road estate. He hated coming here, because it reminded him how much further he had to go. Despite attending the Spence School and Yale, his family's money was not quite old enough for him to truly belong in the upper echelons.

Jonathan, on the other hand, had the right education, family and accent to ensure that his passage to the top of government was inevitable. Back at Yale he'd have been one of the boys who made sure Tobias was spoken to with civility but excluded from the invitation to summer in Hyannis Port.

He turned his BMW 850csi into Jonathan's drive and eased up to the door. It was opened by Jonathan's butler, Harold, who showed Tobias upstairs.

'Toby.' Jonathan Stern welcomed his friend with a firm handshake.

'Great to see you, Jon. How you doing?'

'Never better. G&T?'

'Maybe not. Got the car outside.'

Jonathan looked out of the drawing-room window and made a barely audible noise to indicate his disdain at Tobias's arriviste choice of automobile.

'Well,' he said, turning back to face his guest, 'it sounds like you might be in a spot of bother, so I'll dispense with the chat about the Redskins, and Charlotte and the kids, except to say we're still on for dinner at Marcel's Thursday week.'

'I appreciate that, Jon.'

'So I understand you need a little favour. How long's it been since the last one? Six years?'

'Something like that; since the battalion went missing in Grenada. That could have been a bit embarrassing.'

'Indeed. Well, no one's going to find *them* in a hurry.' They shared the kind of smile that suggested they were referring to a time when they'd skipped out on a bar tab, then sat down on Jonathan's matching cherry-leather wingbacks.

Tobias got straight to the point. 'Jonathan, I'm afraid it's MEROS.'

'Shame,' Jonathan tutted. 'The bughouse has proven very useful over the years. Those Saudis will certainly think twice before lowering their oil prices again.'

'Indeed. Well, unfortunately, for reasons I won't waste your time on, the wasps are out in the compound. All fallback methods have been exhausted so I'm afraid I'm here to ask you to approve a remote nuke.'

Jonathan raised his eyebrows in such a way as to suggest that he was only really doing it for effect.

Tobias continued. 'Believe me, I wouldn't be asking if it wasn't absolutely necessary. I've already tried sending the bomb from here but the comms link is down and I can't get the signal through.'

'I understand, but a nuke's a pretty big ask, Toby. Can you give me anything else?'

'Not much. There were a few people still alive down there when I made the call. Not sure the grunts I spoke to were keen to follow department protocol, you know, just in case it meant them deep-sixing their friends.'

'So there has also been a security breach?'

'I wouldn't call it that exactly. But if we can get the bomb on the way sooner rather than later, then the people I spoke to will not be able to escape and tell tales that might be awkward for us.'

'Thank heaven for small mercies. So . . . ?'

'So I just need a four twenty-seven to override the approved system and call on an independent strike from the nearest airbase.'

'Mmmmm . . . Well, much as I'd like to help, I'm afraid things aren't quite as simple as they used to be. You know how it is: post 9-11, they're keeping a pretty beady eye on any off-piste activities, especially those that involve a thermonuclear explosion.'

'But surely you can . . .'

'Oh, *I* can still do whatever I want. It's just that I can only pull my gun out of its holster so many times before the bullets run out. Do you see what I'm saying? So the question is, why should I do it this time?'

'You know we've got a zero-tolerance escape policy on MEROS.'

'Indeed, but I also know you could fill in the appropriate paperwork and ask General Klein through the proper channels.'

Tobias smiled nervously. 'You're kidding, right?' Jonathan's expression did not change. 'MEROS isn't even on Klein's radar. If I have to explain to him about giant bugs and expendable civilians, he's going to make me jump through hoops then ask a whole bunch of questions we'd both rather he didn't.'

'True. But the buck will stop with you, Tobias. Nothing solid connects me with MEROS.'

'Jonathan, please.'

'I don't know, Toby. This isn't like asking for a napalm hit in Columbia; this is serious. I haven't ordered an unscheduled nuke since Clinton was in the White House. I'm afraid the simple truth is that if you want me to go out of my way for you, then you're going to have to do the same for me.'

'Of course. How can I help?'

'We've been having a little difficulty with the governor of Wyoming. To cut a very long story short, he doesn't see things our way on the subject of military funding, seems to think it might be better to buy one fewer warhead and use the money for a couple of dozen hospitals or something equally ridiculous. Problem is he's got the ear of half a dozen senators, a factor that could flip the vote on our next budget request. It would not be inconvenient if he were unable to carry out his threat.'

'A MEROS hit on American soil? That is a giant ask.' Tobias frowned, then thought a moment longer. 'And if you gave me the nuke then I'd have to use MEROS B, and that's not fully operational.'

'I'm sure a resourceful man like yourself could find a way of accelerating its progress.'

Tobias knew he had to agree, but he also knew he was going to be cleaning up after that decision for a good long while. In the end he had no choice.

'Consider it done.'

They shook hands again.

'My assistant will email you in fifteen minutes with the codes. Good luck, and give Charlotte and the kids my best. You can see yourself out, can't you?'

77

When the termite flew off, Taj stood beside the open hatch wondering if anything else was going to fly or crawl out of it, and what he would do if that happened. He had no weapons and was in no shape to go running after another giant flying insect. He didn't even have a shoe to swat it, so he just waited a few feet away and hoped that would be the extent of his duties.

He was watching the pattern the sunlight made on the trees when he noticed a strange bird-call. It took his attention because it was unusually sonorous, echoing gently towards the end of each cry. He turned round, trying to see which tree it came from and what the bird looked like. Then he froze.

It was coming from the hatch.

With visions of monster spiders and horror-movie millipedes, he sprinted away and took refuge behind a tree. As he watched, his heart inflated like a bullfrog at the back of his throat.

The sound got louder and louder.

'OK, Taj, you not a pussy like they think. You can do this. Check this thing out,' he whispered to himself.

His eyes were locked firmly on the hatch as he waited to see the giant legs of some kind of beast clamber into the light.

'Then again,' he whispered, 'if this mother shoots poison out its eyes then I am getting the fuck out of Dodge.' His fingers were gripping the tree bark as he tried to keep still.

He stopped breathing, focussing everything on that square yard in the centre of the trees.

Then the sound stopped. Taj continued to stare at the hatch.

A bird clattered from the tree, giving him the closest thing he'd ever had to a heart attack.

He was shaking now, wound up like a jack-in-the-box, ready to go off at the slightest provocation. Making a huge effort, he clung again to the tree, damping down the noises he was making as he wheezed and shook.

He had stopped whispering to himself, but the thoughts were coming like a rockslide:

Why the hell they leave Taj alone up here? They know I got no shoes and my foot all bleeding. They gonna come back up here and find me all eaten up by some freak bug, then they'll regret it. Gonna miss old Taj. Gonna wish they didn't go chasin' after no Goddamn termite. Gonna make sure they —'

'Hello?' came a tiny, plaintive voice.

'Shit,' muttered Taj. He set off for the hatch at a run.

'Andrew?' he called as he got closer. There were only so many small boys with English accents around here.

'Hello?' came the reply.

Taj jumped over the flat metal door and looked down. It was indeed Andrew. His cheeks were torn in a dark criss-cross of blood, a red-and-purple swelling ran from his temple to his eye and his lips opened into a long cut that had also removed two of his front teeth.

Tears turned the blackened blood red and he shook, inhaling hard.

'You, uh . . . there's some bad shit down there, huh?' Taj asked.

Andrew just stood there sobbing, then he put his little boy's arms around Taj's big, fat belly.

'OK there, buddy,' said Taj gently. 'You all right now.'

Reaching down with his enormous arms, Taj lifted Andrew up and held him against his chest like a baby, then turned down the slope and walked back towards MEROS.

Swiping his card through the security check, Taj took Andrew to his desk and placed him gently in his wide leather swivel seat. He looked at Andrew's face again, and thought of TV footage he'd seen of people who had witnessed a bombing. The blood and cuts were bad enough, but the real damage was in his eyes, simultaneously shell-shocked and terrified.

'Uh, you stay right there. I'm just going in here' – Taj pointed to the storeroom – 'to get the first-aid kit, see to those cuts, OK?' Andrew didn't reply. He'd stopped crying, but was still breathing in gasps.

Taj rummaged around to find the kit as quickly as possible, throwing aside anything in the way. He grabbed it from a high shelf and hurried back out to Andrew.

As he prepared the cotton buds with antiseptic and selected the right kind of plasters, he wondered what might make the kid feel better.

'Hey, er, Andrew, you hungry? You want a Snickers or some shit?' Taj wasn't sure, but he thought he saw a nod, so he slid his cardboard box along the desk and tipped it out beside Andrew. The noise and bright colours seemed to distract him for a moment.

'I knew it,' said Taj. 'Kids love candy. It's in the DNA. Take your pick, little man.'

Andrew chose a Baby Ruth and tore it open, cramming the contents into his mouth, while Taj fetched a Coke and a Sprite from his personal fridge.

For the next few minutes, Andrew ate while Taj cleaned his cuts and covered the worst ones in gel fibre plasters.

'The others gonna be back soon,' said Taj. 'They gonna head on in there and help out your mom and everybody else.'

Andrew stared blankly ahead.

'Hey, come look at this,' said Taj. He rolled the chair over to the motion sensor and showed Andrew the screen.

'This tells us what's happening downstairs. These dots show everyone who's still there, kinda scattered about right now, OK?'

Andrew looked at the monitor, so Taj assumed he'd heard.

'Now, what we don't get,' he said, indicating the bottom of the screen, 'is that this is the MEROS we all know, and that there's Bishop's office, right? So what's all the rest of it?'

Andrew traced the line of the corridor to the Abdomen. 'This was the way in,' he said, his voice like a kitten's mew.

'And this?' asked Taj, moving his finger over the space at the end of it.

'The . . . Abdomen.' Andrew shut his eyes and began to cry again.

'Hey, hey, hey, little man. I tell you, this is all fu—sorry — *messed* up. I know you been through some bad stuff, else you wouldn't look like that, but we got to do this. Got to go in there and help get your mom out. You understand?'

Andrew's eyes opened a little wider. 'Yes, yes! Please! You've got to help my mum.'

They could hear footsteps approaching on the grass outside.

'No problem,' said Taj, ''Cos these are the folks gonna do it.'

Mills strode in first. Andrew's chair was facing away from him, so he could only see Taj. 'Hey, fatso, where the fuck did you go? We need to get in there and . . .' Taj turned the seat round to show the small, wide-eyed boy with the cuts on his face.

'Jesus Christ!' said Jacobs as she walked through the door. 'Andrew?'

'Please help my mum.'

Jacobs looked to Taj.

'Kid was in the hatch. Came up after you went looking for the termite.'

Jacobs moved around the desk to take a good, concerned look at Andrew. 'Are you . . .?' She realized how pointless the question was going to be.

'Look,' said Taj, 'Andrew and me have had a talk. We know you gonna go down in there and he's going to help you any which way he can. We got the readout on the motion sensor and my man here gonna tell us what it all means.' He gave Andrew a wink.

Taj turned Andrew's seat round to face the monitor and the others gathered behind him.

Pointing at the screen, Taj spoke quietly. 'OK, we was just getting started. This is a corridor, huh? And this – what d'you call it? – the *Abdomen*?'

Andrew looked at the screen and took on a look of panic. 'You've got to get my mum out of there,' he blurted. 'Now. You've got to do it now!'

'OK, OK. Let's just take it easy,' said Jacobs, putting her hand on his arm. 'We're going to do exactly that. All we need is an idea of what we're going into so we can prepare ourselves, OK? This is the only way we can help your mom. Now take a couple of deep breaths with me, like this.' Jacobs held Andrew's gaze as she inhaled and exhaled. Andrew followed her, taking on the calm.

'Good. Now, I'm just going to ask you a few questions and we'll go get your mom right away.'

'Look, what the hell's down there, kid?'

409

'Mills!'

'Jacobs, we don't have time for this! Let's just get strapped and get in there. We know it's a bunch of giant fucking bugs. What more is he going to tell us?'

'He can tell us how many . . .'

'Garrett blew the nest up,' Andrew said.

'What's that?' said Jacobs.

'Here,' said Andrew, indicating the area on the screen that corresponded to the back wall. 'The termite nest blocked the way out so Garrett blew it up. There's a big hole down to the floor below.'

'How many floors are there?'

'Three, I think, but I only went down to Level Two. Level One had nothing in it, but one of the women got eaten when she fell through the hole.'

'Say *what*?' said Madison.

'*Eaten?*' said Jacobs. 'What the hell is down there?'

'Everything. She fell through the hole and she wouldn't stop screaming. I heard the others talking about it and they said it was definitely cockroaches. Giant cockroaches ate her.'

'Paine wasn't bullshitting,' said Jacobs, looking deeply worried.

'After the nest blew up, I fell through the floor. It's Level Two, where all the insects are. Insects, spiders, everything. All in big leaves and stuff, like a jungle. There's lights but you can't see much because of the leaves. I think Major Webster came to look for me but . . .' The fear returned to his face as he was overcome by the memory.

'Go on, honey,' said Jacobs.

'Something bumped into me. I couldn't see it but I screamed and it screamed back. I tried to get away but it came after me and nearly got me.' He showed them the sole of his trainer. It had four scrappy gouges at the heel. 'Then I stabbed it with my penknife and it stopped following.'

'You did good, Andrew. What happened then?'

Andrew shut his eyes tight. Tears came from the creases and sent rivulets of bright red through the dark crusts on his face.

'Other big insects?'

He nodded again. 'I carried on and tried to keep quiet. I don't know what I passed, but they were big and long like a centipede.'

Andrew was hurrying through his story. Either he knew they were in a rush or he didn't want to dwell on what had happened.

'How did you get to the stairs?' asked Jacobs.

'I had to climb something that felt like the nest. I fell down the other side through a door. One of the lights was on. I could see the stairs. I went up them but there was something ahead of me. I don't know what, but I scared it and it did this.' He pointed to the gash across his face and looked down, more tears dripping on to his knees.

'It was too big and the wings were right in my face. I couldn't see. It just kept coming at me. It was making this noise like a crow and trying to bite me. Then I grabbed one of its legs and ripped it off with my knife.

It flew up the stairs, but I lost the knife somewhere. I waited further down. Then I heard you.' His little body was heaving as if he was going through those moments again.

After what felt like long enough, Jacobs said, 'We have to go back in there and get your mom out, and anyone else who's alive.'

'I can't go back in there,' Andrew said, quickly terrified.

'Relax, honey. Not you. We'll go in. You can stay here. We're not going to be long.'

Taj pointed to the screen. 'You see these dots? These are the people who are still alive. The blue ones are people who have bought it, and there's still only one of them since your mom went through. If it was one of the scientists then that means your mom's alive, 100 per cent.'

Andrew pointed to the dots that represented the wasps. They had got through to the corridor, and now only the Abdomen door separated them from the people.

'What are they?' asked Andrew.

'Other things,' Taj replied. More and more of those dots were becoming clearer throughout the Abdomen.

'Madison, you and Mills are coming with me. Taj, no offence, but you're not ready for this. Andrew needs a friend, and an eye on the monitor would help.'

'Yo, I think I'm modest enough to admit I might not be your best play.' He winked again at Andrew. 'Although my kung fu alone would be more than a match for whatever is down there.'

Andrew grabbed Jacobs' arm. 'If you see my Swiss

Army knife, could you bring it back? It's red with ten blades and I really need it.'

'Sure thing, kid. OK. Let's get all the weapons we can carry. We're going to bring them out alive.'

78

'What was that?' groaned Laura.

'Light bomb,' Webster replied, his voice a croaky strain. 'Someone above must have set it off. Can you see OK?'

'Just about.'

'Good. It'll take longer for the insects. I'd say we've got fifteen or twenty minutes while they're all stunned.'

'Do you have any idea where we are?'

'I'm pretty sure it's still Level Two. Even on that trip, I think I'd have noticed a twenty-foot drop. But whereabouts, I have no idea. Do you think you can walk?'

Laura tried to lean forward. Her ribs screamed through her. 'Jesus!'

'What?'

'My ribs. I might have cracked a couple on my left side.' She rolled over on to her right and rocked forward on to her knees. 'But I think I'll be OK. What about you?'

'My arm is pretty messed up, but I think my ankle's gone down a bit, so nothing that's going to stop me moving. It might not feel like it, but we were lucky.'

Webster eased on to his front, looking for a way to move that didn't fill him with pain. After trying every angle, he realized he was just going to have to grit his teeth and get on with it.

He stopped for a moment and turned to Laura. 'If we find Andrew . . .'

'I don't want to talk about it.'

'OK,' Webster said quietly.

They shuffled their way out of the nest, Webster suppressing a moan as he knocked his arm into the horns of the stag beetle.

'That sounds bad,' said Laura. 'Are you sure you're OK?'

'Let's just get moving.'

'I think it's this way,' said Laura. 'The larvae moved in the other direction when the mother came back. They would have gone further into the nest for protection.'

In great pain, she eased herself past the giant beetle and shifted herself along beside Webster so that he could follow her.

79

Garrett had given up on Webster, Laura and the kid. If it was going to be her and Wainhouse trying to save the geeks – well, she couldn't see how it was going to happen.

George turned to her. 'So, what now?' The silence cranked up the discomfort still further.

'Who you asking?' Garrett asked eventually.

George shrugged. 'I wasn't . . .'

''Cause I'm just about shit out of ideas,' she added.

'OK, Garrett, I'm asking anyone. Let's get it out in the open: no way through to the stairs on this level and no way on to Level Two without more of that.' He pointed to Carter's hand. In the absence of laboratory calcium, Susan had found some blackboard chalk and mixed it with water to calm the inflammation. It had had little effect. 'But we've got to do *something*.'

'Unless Bishop's keeping a secret fire escape up his ass, I don't know what that something is.' Bishop looked up. 'Yeah, you. You got us the hell into this mess, any ideas how we're going to get out?' Garrett asked.

'What about back the way we came?' asked Takeshi.

'You do know it's full of killer wasps, don't you?' said Wainhouse.

'Certainly, but if we have two routes and we know one is impossible, it only makes sense to try the other.'

'That's a little too Zen for me,' said Wainhouse, hoping for a laugh from Garrett. It didn't come.

'Do we have any more weapons that can clear the space on Level Two?' asked Susan.

Garrett shook her head. 'We've used up the good stuff. Only basics left,' she said, tapping her semi-automatic rifle.

'So we're fucked then?' said Mike with sarcastic brightness. He pretended to think for a moment.

'You know what we could do?' he said. 'We could send Bishop here down to Level Two so he can check things out. It's dangerous, but it's a risk I don't mind taking.'

'Me neither,' said Wainhouse, getting to his feet. Bishop looked up to see everyone except Garrett staring at him.

'What's that going to solve? What do you think I can do down there?' he asked, now feeling very anxious.

'I'm not sure I care,' said Wainhouse, moving towards him. 'If I'm going to die because of you, I wouldn't mind watching you cop it first, shitcake.'

Susan spoke up. 'He's right. What's the point? We'll be no better than him if we just send him off to die.'

'Let's take a vote on it,' said George. 'Anyone who wants a little thrill in our last half-hour in this hole, say "Aye".'

George, Wainhouse and Mike said their 'aye's with bitter menace.

'That ... that's three against three,' Bishop said. Takeshi, Susan and Garrett had remained silent.

'You know what?' said Wainhouse, his face inches from Bishop's. 'Maybe I don't give a shit about the vote.'

'Leave him!' snapped Garrett. 'We might find a way out of here that he can help with. We keep him alive, whether he deserves it or not.'

Wainhouse looked darkly at Garrett.

'So we're back to being fucked,' he said.

'What was that?' said Susan.

'What?' asked George.

'Stop moving, everyone!' Susan's complexion was skimmed milk, her small voice unsteady. They all listened.

'I can't . . .' began George.

'Shhhh!' hissed Susan. 'There!'

The sound burst out from the floor below and they all turned to see a blackfly, big as a baseball and loud as a chainsaw, swooping in gentle curves above them. The insects would have been affected by the light bomb to differing extents, depending on how much protection they had had from the glare. This fly reminded the seven they were on borrowed time. Soon the rest of the insects would wake up and want to explore the commotion on Level One.

'That's all we need,' said Garrett, pulling her rifle from her shoulder.

80

Pain and weakness were gradually slowing the progress of Laura and Webster. They had stopped twice to see if they could tourniquet his arm with strips of leaves. The second time, Laura insisted on doing it and felt the sticky mush of the coagulating blood. Webster stifled raging screams as she tied the leaves off with a piece of torn trouser-leg. Her lack of medical experience meant this was done with little precision. Webster thought her efforts were actually hurting more than the stab of the beetle, but he did nothing to remedy the situation but gasp, 'A little looser,' into her ear.

Reaching a wall, they found that Level Two had its own set of blue lights. It was all they had to go on, so Webster tried to use them as markers. He smeared a little blood on the wall next to each light so they knew where they'd been. But it was hopeless: as soon as they found themselves pushed away from the wall by a barrier of plants, they had to change their route to avoid the dense trunks that would not let them past. By the time they reached another blue light, it was not the one Webster thought they had been aiming for.

Occasionally they ran into insects. The first scared the life out of Webster when he moved a leaf to reveal its malevolent eyes staring up at him. It took a

419

second to accept that it was too stunned to move, but Webster was still shocked at the sight of this armchair-sized spider, enormous claws curving out of its mouth.

'That must be one of the mutations,' he said.

Laura peered over his shoulder. 'Sorry to diappoint you, but that's an amblypygid. They're not poisonous, but I'd rather not be in reach of those claws when he comes round.'

They moved on and almost stumbled into a scorpion. Like the amblypygid, it was not moving, but they could see the life behind its eyes as it waited to rise and kill again. It was so big that, although they could see its huge claws, they could see no more of its body except for the giant sac of poison that hung from its tail ten feet above them.

'Thank God for that light bomb,' said Laura. 'That's the Arizona bark scorpion, one of the most venomous species in the world. If they were trying to make killers, they chose their subjects well.'

They moved quickly on.

By now they had been walking for about fifteen minutes, with no obvious progress.

'Major, do you have any idea where we are?'

Webster sighed and looked down to Laura's clear blue eyes.

'No. I'm sorry.'

'Maybe we need to try something else.'

'I just don't know what. These insects are going to

wake up soon, and our only chance has to be trying to find the way up.'

'What if we follow the wall until we get to the hole the explosion made?'

'I've tried that. We get maybe ten yards before getting blocked off, then we have to move out into the middle again, where we're lost.'

'OK. Well, let's keep going. It's got to be better than staying here.'

'Sure,' said Webster. She was right, but they were running out of time.

81

Despite being a hundred times the size, it moved exactly like a real fly. Rubbing its forelegs together, it snapped its head quickly from side to side. The scientists watched closely as it buzzed from surface to surface. It stopped next to Carter's hand and bent forward to examine it. Something, perhaps the poison from the blister beetle, put it off and instead it flew down to the cockroach hole and disappeared inside. Garrett ran to the hole to see if she could get a shot in, but it was long gone.

'Did you see that? Proportionately, it's far bigger than the wasps,' marvelled George.

'Amazing,' said Susan. 'The integument still operates even at that size.'

'The integu-what?' asked Wainhouse.

Mike turned to him. 'It's what makes them so strong and flexible. And if that part of them has survived all the experiments, then maybe everything else has.'

'So what?'

'So it might help us. If they also have the same visual processing as normal insects, then they will only be able to see us clearly if we move.'

'But we've got to move,' Garrett said. 'We've got to get the hell out of here.'

'I know, but it doesn't hurt to remember things that might make them leave us alone,' said Mike.

They were distracted by another sound: from the other side of the room, they heard a soft paradiddle, getting louder. One by one, they turned in the direction of Bishop's office. By now most of the fires had either died to embers or gone out entirely. A near-darkness had returned that sapped the room of visibility. However, the entrance had a blue light above it that made it just possible to see the door, which now showed a small, jagged hole.

'The wasps!' shouted Bishop.

'Nobody move,' whispered Mike.

Nobody did, except Garrett. Slowly, she brought her automatic rifle up to her shoulder and set it to fire a single bullet.

Closing her left eye and lowering her right to peer through the sights, she was now looking straight at the hole that was growing around the door lock.

She knew that if her shot was off she might just blast a hole in the door and release the wasps, so she did not squeeze the trigger until she was absolutely certain of her aim.

Only Susan had seen Garrett raise her weapon. The *bang* of the primer igniting the propellant sent an explosion of shock through everyone else.

Her shot was true.

The bullet ripped through four wasps then flew down the corridor and into Bishop's office, shattering his coffee machine.

The sound of the wasps stopped, then began again with less purpose, as if they had regrouped and were only warily restarting the process of breaking down the door. This gave Garrett another chance to take aim.

'What the fuck was that?' said Bishop in an angry whisper.

'That was me shooting wasps,' said Garrett, in a manner that suggested he ought to be grateful and shut the hell up. 'I'm buying us time. Now get to the ropes and head down to Level Two. None of us checked –'

Her instructions had to wait for another pull of the trigger and the chaos that followed.

'. . . Excuse me. None of us checked the stairs in Level Two yet. Watch the hell out for the insects, but right now that's our only way out of here, and time we ain't got. I'll cover these fuckers while you do it. Hopefully this confusion's going to keep the others off your ass.'

'Wait,' said Bishop. 'Listen.'

'I am listening. I can hear big fuckin' wasps.'

'Shut up!'

It was faint, but it was definitely Laura and Webster, calling their names.

'Where the hell are they?' asked Garrett, moving around the floor. 'Major! Keep shouting! We're gonna find you!'

At the next call, they looked towards the cockroach hole. Webster and Laura's calls were still faint, but this was where they were loudest. Garrett dropped down and dipped her head through the floor.

'Major?'

'Garrett?' He sounded like he was talking through a pillow.

'Major? Where the hell are you?'

'Garrett. Look for a blue light. Can you see a blue light?'

'A blue light? Hang on.' She swivelled herself round until she had taken in 360 degrees of the floor below. 'Yes! A blue light. I can see one, twenty feet away. Wave your hand in front of it so I know I'm looking at the right one.' Webster did as he was asked.

'Yes! Major, I'm looking right at you. Follow my voice and we'll get you up here.'

'Keep talking, Garrett.' This was followed by the swish of leaves and the bending and snapping of twigs and branches.

'Keep talking? You got it, Major. The fuckin' wasps are at the fuckin' door but I just shot a bunch of 'em. Carter got fucked by some crazy poisoned beetles but he's still alive, and it's good to know you're alive cos I fuckin' need you up here if we're gonna have even a half-chance of getting the fuck out of this place. We're not a hell of a lot closer than when you jumped down the –'

'Garrett, we're right underneath you but we need help. There's a good trunk right here but it's not enough for us to climb up. We're going to need someone to come down and help us.' Webster was looking right at Garrett, who returned his relieved smile with one of her own.

'You got it, Major, I'm sending Wainhouse with a rope.'

Wainhouse had appeared at the hole while Garrett was talking. He had a huge grin on his face. This was hope, and he could feel it filling him up as the despair shrank away in response.

'You two had better clear the way,' called Garrett. 'He's coming down.'

Garrett tied one end of the rope to an enormous filing cabinet that was lying on its side nearby and the other end to Wainhouse. He dropped into the hole and Garrett eased the rope out to let him down.

By now the others had gathered around.

'George, Mike, I'll need you two to pull this up when Wainhouse ties them two on.' They were grateful to be useful, and when Wainhouse gave the signal, they pulled Laura up in a few seconds.

She never thought she'd be so glad to see Level One of the Abdomen. Her appearance, bloody, pained and filthy, forced the others to imagine the horror of what she had been through.

Webster was up almost as quickly. His injured arm was a cause for concern, but he assured them he was OK in spite of it. He too was caked in blood and dirt.

'How did you find us?' asked Garrett.

'We heard your gun firing and realized we were close to the hole,' said Webster.

'If I'd known finding you guys was that easy I'd have shot a few rounds off as soon as we lost you. By the way, you look like the worst shit I ever did. What the fuck happened?'

Webster shook his head. 'I'll tell you another time.

But I will say this,' he said, looking around at the few insects that were now flying through the air around him, 'we need to get the hell out of here before the rest of them wake up.'

They only had to wait for Wainhouse, who tied the rope back on and was winched up to the lip of the hole.

He had one foot on the floor of Level One, ready to lever the rest of himself up, when he felt something touch his other foot.

As he looked down to check what it was, two enormous spiked claws sliced up from below, slashing him in half from collarbone to pelvis.

Before he fell to the ground, the whip scorpion took hold of his left side and tossed it through the air to come crashing down through one of the glass lab dividers on Level One.

Everyone turned to look in the direction of the noise, leaving the giant beast to slip through the darkness with what remained of Wainhouse firmly clenched in its grip.

It was an unusually repellent creature, even at its normal size. With eight thorny legs as big as drainpipes and two giant pincers, this one looked as if its only purpose were to cause the death of other things.

A rushed scuffle to see what had smashed the glass further disguised the scorpion's movements. The soldiers and scientists arrived just in time to see the last squirts of blood spraying over the base of the exposed spine.

'What the fuck?' said Garrett. 'Is that Wainhouse?'

Although it was obscured by the growing darkness,

the visceral horror of what they found grabbed them all by the guts and swung them round the room.

The confusion added to this, as no one could understand how Wainhouse had been so brutally attacked without them realizing. What had done this, and where was it? Were they all in danger?

Because of their injuries, Laura and Webster lagged behind the others. As they limped along to the source of the noise, something flickered in the corner of Webster's eye.

He looked across to see the reflection of a weak flame on the whip scorpion's shiny back, but he could hardly make out what was going on.

'Laura!' he said loudly. 'Over there!'

Laura looked to where Webster was pointing but could not see what he was talking about. Suddenly, the creature, as large as a dining table, raised itself up and starting shovelling Wainhouse into its mouth with voracious greed.

Collapsing forward with fear and revulsion, Laura gasped. Webster had already moved towards the cache of remaining arms to select his weapon.

He took the Daewoo USAS-12 that he'd kept as a souvenir from an operation in Korea and flicked off the safety.

He had to move a little closer to work out exactly what was going on, but he'd already made his mind up to shoot.

Taking aim, the blast blew out the rear left leg and cracked the shell of the abdomen.

In angered shock, the whip scorpion gave a guttural screech. Tensing its glands, it spewed a thick cloud of acetic acid from its rear.

Takeshi was closest to the warm mist. He managed to turn away, but it made no difference. The acid began dissolving him from the back, melting first his clothes, then his hair, then burning through his skin slowly enough to stretch out every millisecond of agony.

He had effectively shielded the others, but as he screamed and screamed and screamed, he fell to his knees, the acid exposing his tissue from behind.

It looked as if a guillotine were slicing him in wafer-thin sections. His skull and scapulae were visible, surrounded by angry scarlet tissue and the browns and whites of his rapidly disintegrating organs.

From the front, however, he looked completely normal: excruciatingly agonized but visibly undamaged. In the dark, Mike and Lisa could not understand what was happening to him.

He toppled forwards, showing them his meat-raw innards. Susan's screams joined Takeshi's as he continued to melt away.

The smell was overpowering as the evaporating remains of the clothes and skin rose through the air.

Bishop wanted to be sick, but his stomach had emptied long ago.

Garrett moved through to the side of Takeshi's remains and, along with Webster, pumped the giant scorpion with whatever was left in her gun. They took out six of the legs, leaving it immobile, but as they were attacking from the rear, they couldn't find the head shot that would kill it.

In anger and desperation, it was making an appalling shriek like the screams of hundreds of dying birds. There wasn't much left of Wainhouse's torso, but it dropped the mangled scraps as it tried to turn to face its attackers.

More bullets pumped through its sides and it gave up, slumping to the ground. Its abdomen was now a broken shell oozing a mess of glutinous moisture.

Webster and Garrett stood over what was left of the scorpion and Wainhouse. To their left, Takeshi had completely disappeared, and the acid was now eating away at the floor beneath him. The hellish smell of melting flesh combined with the acrid stench of burning concrete to make eyes water and stomachs convulse.

'How does this shit keep getting worse?' muttered Garrett to herself.

Susan's screams had subsided a little, but that only made the buzzing at the door audible again.

Garrett reloaded her rifle.

82

A soft *ding* announced the arrival of the nuclear launch information in Tobias's inbox.

The instructions gave him an email address and a series of codes to send, and he wasted no time in tapping them in.

After pressing the return key he watched the screen and wondered if that was it. Had he just sent several men and women to their deaths? Would there be any kind of –

The reply took the form of a series of sporadic beeps, followed by a black screen. Then his computer spoke:

'Good morning, sir. This is Comsat liaison,' said a computerized male voice with the tone of a cheery smile. 'Operations of this nature may not be conducted in such a way that they can be intercepted. That means no writing. I am an officer at the Pentagon, but you are hearing a distorted version of my voice that has been filtered through multiple encryptions. Yours will sound the same to me. If that is clear, how can I help you today?'

Tobias looked carefully at the screen and leaned in warily.

'Do I . . . do I just speak in here?'

'That's right!' the voice replied brightly. 'Your computer is equipped with a microphone.'

'Uh, OK . . . I have an authorization code for a D-22 on Colinas de Edad.'

'Certainly, sir. I now need confirmation of your identification.'

'Sure, er . . . comsat. hazlit, fourteen, niner, astro.'

'That is affirmative, sir. May I have the authorization code from yourself, and details of the second contact from Mr Stern?'

'I have both codes, including the override sequence that allows me to present Mr Stern's numbers.'

'Copy that, sir. Go ahead.'

'Twelve, one, twenty-six, seven, one, four, zero, eight, sixteen, eight, three, niner.'

'Affirmative, sir, a nuclear strike will be launched on the MEROS facility immediately. With the time it will take to engage the pilot, and judging by the travel distance, we are looking at an ETA of approximately one hour, over.'

'An hour? Can't you assholes move any faster than that?'

'Sir, Colinas de Edad is a remote facility. Our nearest airbase lies 146 miles away from it, north-north-east. So, negative, sir. We are unable to get there any faster. However, I believe that there is a remote satellite detonation system that we could attempt to make use of.'

'No, that's OK. Just get the plane in the air quick-smart.'

83

Garrett lined up her rifle for a third shot. The hole was getting wider, partly because the wasps could attack it while she was reloading and partly because her second shot hadn't been quite as good as the first. It had clipped off a small piece of the door as it went through. The bullet took out another three wasps, but that still left a dozen trying to get in.

Webster had everyone crouching on the floor, as still as they could be. Many insects were scuttling and buzzing up to Level One, but they were more interested in each other than the humans that lay motionless, almost invisible amongst them.

After what had happened to Wainhouse and Takeshi, the mood was desperate.

As a group, they were broken and empty, clinging to a glimpse of hope that was disappearing far into the distance.

Garrett's finger was poised on the trigger, ready to squeeze off another round. She came to the end of the quick, silent prayer she said before each shot and her neurons immediately sent the message to fire down her arm and into the bent knuckle at the end of her index finger.

As she fired, an apple-sized aphid bumped her

gently on the elbow. The impact was not great, but the shot required absolute precision, which was now impossible.

The weapon she carried, adapted from an Israeli Tavor 21-C, discharged a 6.5mm, 5.9g round at 854 metres per second, and that bullet was now flying on a trajectory three degrees higher than she had intended. All she could hope for was a small entry hole with several dead wasps behind it.

What she got instead was a high-spread impact that took out three wasps and half the door.

'Incoming!' yelled Garrett as she joined the others on the ground.

This was it: hard enough to fight in a bright, enclosed space, any attempt to repel the wasps in a room this cavernous and gloomy would be completely futile.

Death was now inevitable.

The wasps' entry was a percussion of terror. Every corner of the Abdomen was filled with the furious collision of gossamer ripping through the air.

The dense heat, the foul smell and the terrible, inescapable sound were overpowering, as was the absence of light, creating apparitions that brought fear from the shadows.

On the ground, the scientists and soldiers hugged themselves into tight knots of dread and waited to die.

84

The staircase at the back of MEROS was now lit with a series of green flares. Jacobs, Mills and Madison had no idea how many they'd need for five hundred feet of darkness, and they had weapons to carry, so illuminating their route wasn't the priority. Mills said that it was better to run out of flares than firepower, and the others agreed. Their progress was fast but wary. They knew they would not have much more time before Paine was able to initiate the nuclear wipeout from the Pentagon. But they also knew people were dying down there, and the thought of their rescue plan going off course because of one big bug made them check their speed just a little.

'Fuck, how much further down is this fucking place?'

'Hey, taxi driver, I don't suppose you get a lot of exercise sitting in that chair all day.'

'No. And I don't get the cardio workout you get from jerking off guys, either.'

Jacobs shook her head, amazed that these two could be quite so pathetic at a moment like this. But maybe that was what they needed: a bit of banter to lighten the mood before going up against whatever was down there.

It also helped them to forget about the bomb that could be heading their way.

'I've got enough work trying to keep your mother

and sister happy. And don't forget we've got to go back up, you fat fuck.'

'Sssh!' The banister felt rougher, first like pumice then more like coral. The stairs had changed from a monotonous smoothness to a series of bumpy obstructions that grew larger with every step.

'I think we're close,' said Jacobs.

'What is this stuff?' asked Mills.

'Beats me, but I don't think it was part of the original design,' said Jacobs.

They set off another flare, the first for a hundred feet, and saw that the dark concrete steps were now strewn with a covering of brown ridges and holes. Looking ahead, they could see less of the staircase and more of this substance that covered it. Two flights down, it became too dense for them to continue, with gaps which only a small boy could get through.

'No problem,' said Mills. 'I've got enough C-22 to blast that into the next century.'

'Yeah, probably not the best idea, what with us being in an enclosed space that will funnel the heat and smoke of any explosion upwards. Plus, we don't know where the others are. Killing them ourselves after they've survived this long is something we should really try to avoid,' said Jacobs. Madison smirked in the green half-light of the flares.

'I'd suggest non-explosive ballistics like bullets to break this stuff down and see if it'll get us through.'

'Also no problem,' replied Mills, steadying his rifle.

85

Upstairs, Andrew and Taj were staring at the motion-sensor screen.

'There! There's movement.'

'C'mon, Taj, what does that mean?'

'That mean they're not dead.'

'Who's not dead?'

'You know I don't know.'

'But these two are blue. That means that another two have died, doesn't it?'

'Uh . . . I'm not sure.'

'But you look at this screen all the time.'

'Yeah, and that's why when you asked me ten minutes ago if they was all dead, I said no. They was just staying still, 'cause this gives a reading when there's "no movement, like dead", instead of "no movement, like standing still".'

'And those dots are two more dead.'

'OK, OK . . . yes, that's two more dead, but there's still eight left.'

'But one of them could be my mum! My mum and Webster, because they both went down to Level Two looking for me!'

'Hey! Not so fast, littl'un. Yes, your mom's down

there. Yes, two more died. But you're jumping to some dumbass conclusions right now.'

'But one of those could be my mum, Taj!'

'Yeah? And what's the use of talking in "coulds"? If it was my mom in there and there was eight of 'em still alive, I'd be thinking she was one of the eight, 'cos the odds of that is much higher than she's one of the two dead. Don't that make sense to you?'

Andrew's face was a frown of consternation.

'I suppose,' he said quietly.

'Damn right you suppose! Damn right, little man. Taj will tell you this for nuthin': you give up before every single one of them lights has turned blue, you giving up on your mom. How would she feel down there if she knew that? Huh?'

'Yeah, I see what you mean,' Andrew conceded.

'You best see what I mean. Now come on and keep that chin all the way up. They gonna see this out and we gonna watch it happen.'

86

At Jacobs' suggestion, Mills had tried one bullet first, just to see what would happen. It went through the nest like it was stale sponge cake, but only to a diameter of his .223 ammunition.

'OK, how are we going to make that work? I'm going to run out of bullets before we make a hole big enough to look through, let alone crawl through,' said Mills.

'Just let me think.'

While Jacobs stood looking thoughtfully at the nest, Madison peered into the hole Andrew must have climbed through.

'Helloooooooo! Anybody there?' he shouted.

'Thank God we brought you along,' said Mills.

'Do you have any grenades?' asked Jacobs.

'Sure. Fire or frag?'

'You're carrying an incendiary grenade?'

'Be prepared, that's what I learned in the Scouts.'

'Yeah, that and how to give a reach-around to the scoutmaster,' said Madison.

'Do fuck off, you enormous . . .'

'Frag. Incendiary will send a fireball back up here. I'd suggest you throw it down one of these holes, but they might stop five feet in, so what we need is some bullet holes close together in a circle formation to create what we know will be a long tunnel for the grenade. But aim for a long diagonal that will hit the floor halfway across. If it goes straight it might come out the other side and hit one of the others.'

'Easy,' said Mills. He pressed his Glock to the nest and fired it off in a small circle, leaving the narrow tunnel Jacobs was looking for.

'OK, now drop the grenade in, and we take cover back up the stairs.'

'Shouldn't we give Madison a head start?'

'I never knew you cared,' said Madison, taking the hint and bolting up back the way they had come. Jacobs followed, leaving Mills to drop the grenade.

He pulled the pin on the M67 and listened for a second to make sure it rolled, then he sprinted up the stairs.

Ten seconds later the explosion reverberated around the stairwell as fragments of shrapnel streamed through the nest. The weak, dessicated structure had no chance, collapsing like so much polystyrene.

But as the brown chunks disintegrated, the termites were revealed. The ones that weren't killed by the blast fell to the ground then flew screeching into the darkness of the staircase towards the three soldiers.

'Don't let them get past you,' warned Jacobs.

Mills fired off his AK-47, killing or maiming most of the swarm. The ones that got past were dealt with by the boots and handguns of Jacobs and Madison.

'Woooah . . . is that the shit they're having to deal with?' asked Madison after the last one had gone.

'That's the shit Andrew had to deal with, with a

pocket knife, in a tunnel, and that's the shit we're going to deal with right now. Come on, let's go, time's running out,' said Jacobs, heading down the last flight of stairs.

They came out at the back of Level Two and could barely see anything. They had one last flare, which Jacobs lit and threw into the middle of what was left of the floor.

'Fuck me,' said Mills in a hoarse whisper.

The insects were flowing and seething amongst themselves, a sprawling morass of chattering jaws, clackering limbs, roaring wings and the tear and grind of flesh as they attacked one another. Sounds of aggression and submission, intimidation and death coursed through the air; a foul burst of noise as ugly and brutal as the creatures that made it.

Madison, Mills and Jacobs were poleaxed by the reality of what they had to face. The creatures that had crawled through their imaginations had not even come close to these beasts which writhed in front of them, clambering and scraping their way to kill or be killed.

They could just about keep enough distance and cover of darkness to be ignored, but that would only last so long. These claws and jaws and stingers and antennae would soon seek them out, and they would not be able to keep that kind of force at bay for long.

87

Captain Tony Fox stood at the back of the Swoose Goose bar in the US airbase at Santa Cruz. He was only five foot six, but what he lacked in height he made up for with ability. Since his first term at the Academy he'd been known as Fantastic Mr Fox for taking down his tutor three training missions in a row. He was the one they all looked up to, even when they were six inches taller than him.

To his right, First Lieutenant Henry Wells was dancing with his groin pressed up to the buttocks of a lissome Brazilian stripper. Surrounding them, fifteen other airmen cheered the couple on with a version of 'Happy Birthday' that was peeling the paint off the walls. More jugs of margaritas were ordered, more bottles of Bud cracked open and more shots of Patron lined up.

Captain Fox joined in with the singing, but he was drinking nothing stronger than soda water. It was his misfortune to be this afternoon's emergency pilot on call. No one in that position had been scrambled for over three years, but it was a hard and fast rule that the pilot on call was ready to go at any moment, and that meant no booze.

In eight minutes' time the responsibility would shift to Captain Mark Jenson, but that possibility disappeared when the emergency link came through with the codes of Tobias Paine.

A call was placed to the bar, and Janie Weathers, the Goose's landlady for the past nineteen years, frantically signalled to Captain Fox that he would be required to take off immediately. *At least I didn't spend the afternoon sober for nothing*, he thought as he pushed past the birthday boy and into the blazing afternoon sun.

After changing into his flight kit, he went to find his F-35 Lightning 2. It was supposed to be as ready as he was, sitting close to the edge of the runway, canopy up, waiting for its pilot. Fox ran across the tarmac looking troubled, until one of his flight crew came out of the north hangar and beckoned him in.

'What the hell's going on?' Fox snapped as he walked towards his jet. 'I'm supposed to be wheels up in five.'

He saw his usual AMXS crew working with his payload, but there was another man with them. He was older than Fox, with a granite face and dark suit that made it plain this was going to be no ordinary mission.

'Captain Tony Fox reporting for duty, sir.'

The man stood and removed his reflective aviators. 'Major Kenneth Finn, WSO. Son, I apologize for the unusual protocol today but this is an unusual situation. These men are attaching a B61 Mod 11 nuclear-bunker buster to your JDAM. You understand that I won't be explaining further and that I will be expecting you to carry out your mission as normal, but of course you have to know what you're carrying in case you need to bail. Not that we expect that to be the case.'

'No, sir.'

'OK. It's going to be another couple of minutes, then you're gone. Good luck.'

'Thank you, sir.'

They saluted each other, and Major Finn headed back to the control tower.

Captain Fox understood why he was being told, but it didn't make any difference to him what he was carrying. If he'd had a problem with it, he'd never have joined up, let alone made it this far.

He climbed the eight thin, steel rungs to his cockpit and eased his helmet over his head. As always, a shudder of excitement passed through his shoulders. He wanted to be cool and dispassionate, but flying the finest, most advanced Joint Strike Fighter in existence was the reason he had decided to make the Airforce his career.

It was the first aircraft designed to be unstable in order to enhance its manoeuvrability, so it took real skill to work it. It also used a side-stick controller for the same reason, along with HUD and JHMCS for enhanced weapons deployment. To someone like Fox, it was a pilot's plane, and that suited him just fine.

The ground staff cleared the runway, removed the fuel line and signalled him for take-off. He rolled the plane gently over the tarmac then waited as the F110-GE-100 Turbofan kicked in.

A second later he was on the move, rammed into his seat to blast backwards and forwards simultaneously at full force.

MEROS was now on a very real countdown. In a little over an hour, anything living within a mile of Colinas de Edad would be gone for ever.

88

'The way I see it, we've only got one hope,' said Jacobs.

From her backpack she took out the umbrella-like form of the Ripple Gun. Madison had watched it being loaded on to his Spartan many times but had never seen it in action and had no idea what it did. He watched as she cocked the barrel and spread the spokes out before handing it to Mills. It took real strength to handle, so this was a job for him.

'This better work on these big-ass monsters like it does on the mission wasps,' Jacobs said as Mills strapped the gun around his shoulders. 'Run it for as long as you can.'

Pointing it into the Abdomen, he held on tight as the spokes started to spin. When the lasers appeared, Jacobs and Madison took a step back and looked away. Without the usual protection of his safety suit and goggles, Mills had to shut his eyes and hope that the machine's powerful judder didn't leave him aiming in the wrong direction.

'UUUUURRRRRGGGHHHHHHHHH!' he yelled as the pain and the vibration combined to send him bouncing off his feet.

Jacobs and Madison were bouncing, too. Jacobs had never seen the weapon used for this long before. It was

convulsing violently, like a tumble dryer on a trampo-
line.

'AAAAARRRRRGGGHHHHH!' It rumbled up
and down over Mills's shoulder like a giant thumb
intent on rubbing his humerus out of its socket.

Just as Jacobs thought it might be doing permanent
damage, Mills was knocked off his feet. The jerk caused
him to let the trigger go, and the rumble tailed off to
a stillness.

Without the vibrations to shudder through their
ears, they could now hear that the sound of the insects'
movement had disappeared.

There was a brief moment of disturbing quiet,
suddenly replaced by one almighty crash after another.

Bees the size of dustbins dropped from the ceiling.
Vast beetles plummeted like gargoyles falling from a
roof. Ants and cockroaches crashed from the wall to the
floor, making the Abdomen feel like the epicentre of
an earthquake for the second time in as many minutes.

On Level One the people were running for cover.

A cockroach's rear leg sliced down the back of
George's lab coat, ripping it in half and cutting an inch
deep line down the length of his back. It was like being
slashed with a machete. Blood seeped through the rest
of his shirt and coat while the pain sent him to his
knees in a puddle of roach guts.

Mike and Susan dived under a lab table that took
the thunderous weight of a white-kneed spider crashing down; its enormous legs were left flopping around
them like curtains. Susan screamed as it lost balance

and slid to one side, leaving the spider's dark eyes staring her in the face.

Garrett and Webster covered Carter with upended chairs. This shield worked fine until a tiger centipede lost its grip directly above them and plunged to the floor with enough size and weight to squash them flat.

Garrett reacted quickly, blasting everything she had into the huge length of armoured sections. This sent it off course, and it landed with a deafening crash just to the left of Carter's prone body.

To reduce the chances of anything landing on him, Bishop had run for the corner furthest from the blast hole. He thought that fewer insects would have made it all the way over there, so he pressed up against the wall and watched the others cope with the rain of creatures that was crashing across the Abdomen.

He was right that this was the area least populated by the inhabitants of Level Two, but in the darkness he could not see the black form of the enormous rhinoceros beetle hanging above his head. Its round, solid shell and big black horn were hanging by just one tarsal claw, so when Bishop backed up against the wall with a relieved thud, the vibration sent the giant insect falling towards him.

He had no idea what had happened until all 200lbs of it landed right on top of him. The impact was full and jarring, sending waves of bruising pain from his shoulders to his knees. Miraculously, no bones were broken, but he was badly winded, with mild concussion and a pair of shoulders that throbbed with a deep ache.

Laura was running across the Abdomen, avoiding the hailing insects by the smallest of margins. She knew she had to find cover, but couldn't see where it would come from.

To her right, in a pool of guts, stood the wide dome of the whip scorpion's shell. Laura gave the matter a millisecond's thought then slid into the pool of leaked innards and curled herself into a ball under its dark hardness.

The stench was what she imagined a recently opened grave would smell like: fusty and stale, yet pungent with a foul sourness that seemed to cling to her olfactory receptors. Her stomach leaped and lurched, but it was a small price to pay for safety.

By the stairs of Level Two, Jacobs, Mills and Madison were pleased to see that the Ripple Gun had had the desired effect. The floor in front of them was carpeted with upturned bodies offering an occasional faint twitch but nothing of the malevolent threat of before.

On Level One the noises of crashing and gunshots had stopped. Everyone was still wary, but it seemed the danger had come to an end.

'Hey!' yelled Jacobs, stepping out into the floor of Level Two. 'Any of you assholes still alive?'

'Here! We're up here!' They heard Webster's solid voice from above.

Garrett got to her feet and moved towards the blast hole. 'Where the hell are you?' she called.

'Down here. Sorry about the Ripple. It was the only

449

thing that looked like it had half a chance of making a dent down here. Is everyone OK?' replied Jacobs.

'I'll round them up,' Garrett replied.

The first one she saw was George, lying on his front in his reddening lab coat. His face was a tight grimace as he tried to avoid moving and worsening the pain down his back.

'Shit, man. You OK?'

'How . . . how bad is it?' he asked, gingerly getting to his feet.

There was no time for bedside manner right now. If you could talk you were doing OK. 'You'll live,' said Garrett, already jogging on to the others.

Laura extracted herself from the mess of guts and hobbled to her feet.

Garrett screwed her face up in disgust. 'I'll tell you something: we get out of here, I ain't sitting next to you on the plane.' Laura took the hint and removed her jacket, to reveal a cleaner T-shirt underneath. It didn't help the smell much, but it might stop everyone else throwing up.

Susan and Mike came out from under their table and made their way over to where Webster was looking after Carter.

'Hey, anyone seen Bishop?' called Webster.

The others shook their heads.

Garrett wished it was someone else she had to spend time and energy looking for, but she wasn't callous enough to leave him without checking out whether he was dead or not.

Just as she was about to give up, she heard a groan from the back corner.

'Bishop? That you?' She walked up to where the sound was coming from but still couldn't see him. Now she was standing right by his head, so when he groaned again she knew he was somewhere under the rhinoceros beetle.

It had to be Bishop who needed all the help, she thought, straining to lift the giant insect off him. He was only just conscious, so she hoisted him on to her shoulder and staggered across Level One carrying his weight.

'That's all of 'em, Major,' she said as she dumped Bishop on the ground, with the minimum of care.

'All here!' called Webster.

'Good. OK, now we've got to get a move on. Bishop's friend Paine is going to blast this place to the Stone Age in less than a half-hour, so get your asses down here so we can climb those stairs. Oh, and Dr Trent, Andrew is alive and just fine on the surface.'

'Alive?' she said, almost choking, afraid to ask the question in case the confirmation did not come.

'Sure. Wouldn't kid about a thing like that.'

Laura couldn't stop herself from crying with relief. She had never given up on her son, but the thought that he could have made it up to the surface alive had never even crossed her mind.

Susan and Mike inched towards the edge of the blast hole to see Jacobs, Mills and Madison standing on the floor below.

It was the first time it looked as if they might make it out of there.

'OK, let's get moving,' called Jacobs. 'We've still got to get you guys on to Level Two, up a long-ass flight of stairs, on to Madison's plane and in the air before MEROS becomes a burning hole in the ground.'

This was not going to be easy. Between them they had enough injuries to lay low a platoon, but they had no choice but to get on with it.

Even with his twisted ankle and torn bicep, Webster knew he had to take charge from up here. With a little help from Garrett and Mike, he manoeuvred his good leg and working arm on to the nest, taking the ropes to get down to Level Two. He held them taut so the others could make it down more easily, particularly the scientists, who hadn't touched a climbing rope since some embarrassing gym classes in high school.

'Garrett, go down the rope and get the others to pull you into Level Two, then help these guys as they follow you.'

Garrett did as she was told and was soon down with Jacobs, Mills and Madison, holding the rope tight for the next person.

Laura went first and, after a loose slip on the edge of the nest, she was down and safe. Susan couldn't be persuaded to go next, so George grabbed the ropes and managed the descent with great pain, but no problems.

When they helped him on to Level Two, Jacobs felt his back. It was drying, but the blood was still partly moist. She wiped her reddened fingers on her jacket and tried not to let the revulsion show on her face. If you got injured in the Abdomen, you really got something world-class, but it was better than being dead, like Wainhouse, Takeshi and Lisa.

Susan and Mike stood at the edge of the hole with Webster. Behind them was Bishop, who was staring into the middle distance.

'Come on, Susan,' said Webster, gently, but with an undertone of urgency.

She knew she had to do it but winced as she moved on to the face of the nest. She shifted across in tiny steps with Webster holding on to her. He let her go only when the others could reach her feet and pull her down.

Watching Susan manage it safely both embarrassed and galvanized Mike into taking the ropes. He dropped down easily and, within a couple of seconds, Mills and George had grabbed his feet and brought him in safely.

Webster turned to Bishop. 'OK, Steven, you next, then I'm bringing Carter down.'

'Huh? You have to do Carter first. I'm still all . . .'

'No one's 100 per cent, Steven, but Carter's a risk, and if that means we have a problem, I want to know everybody's down. Get yourself on the rope.'

Bishop didn't move.

'Now, Steven.'

'I . . . I can't do it, Carl. I just can't.'

'Steven. Don't do this. You heard Jacobs. Paine could push the button at any moment. These people have to get out of here with five hundred feet of stairs to climb and we're all waiting for the insects to come back to life. Look over there.' On the opposite side of the hole, a cockroach was stumbling to its feet.

Steven looked pathetically at Webster. 'Help me, Carl,' he pleaded.

Webster was furious, but there was no time to mess around. He grabbed Bishop with his good hand and the crook of the opposite elbow and lifted him on to his shoulder. Bishop actually whimpered as the group on Level Two watched in confusion. With great effort, Webster pulled himself and Bishop on to the rope and started on his way down.

The descent was pain from all directions. The hand on his good arm burned as he tried to use it to slow himself, while the strain in his torn bicep was blaring like a siren. His thighs, wrapped around the lower part of the rope, felt an uncomfortable heat and pressure that spread through his groin, and his eyes stung as he blinked back drips of salty sweat.

He couldn't afford to let up on any part of his grip, so he slid his way down slowly, like ketchup easing from a bottle.

As he came to the edge of Level Two he felt a jolt. The weight had dislodged the pins in the nest, dropping him down a couple of feet in one go. He was now face to face with Mills and Madison, who grabbed Bishop and took him off Webster's back.

'What happened to you?' Garrett asked Bishop.

'Nothing,' he muttered.

Webster wasted no time in climbing back up the ropes. He pulled himself on to the floor of Level One with one arm and grabbed Carter, slinging his massive frame over his shoulders with a pained grunt. He didn't want to stop to think about what he was trying to do; he just drove on, knowing he only had a few more moments of effort to endure.

The strain of carrying Carter made Bishop's descent seem like carrying a child. The lieutenant was a dead weight and some fifty pounds heavier. The sweat was now a slick film that covered every inch of him and he had to keep wiping his face to see what he was doing.

He could not keep the same slow control he had done with Bishop. Movement came as a jerky series of stops and starts, a quick drop ended by a hard squeeze. The others watched as more and more of Webster became visible. First his boots, then the bottom of his trousers, his knees, his belt –

Then everything else passed by in an instant.

One of the expansion bolts had pulled all the way out, leaving him swinging by his good hand with Carter slipping off his wet shoulder.

The loose pin had dropped them further down but it had also sent them swinging in a wide arc away from the others.

When they came within reach of Mills and Garrett their momentum gave them too much speed to be caught and they continued on another loop, Carter slipping further down.

Webster could feel every ounce of his lieutenant's weight, and every inch that was sliding off his shoulder.

Then the balance shifted and the pressure became too much. Webster knew he couldn't save himself without letting Carter go.

The rope swung round to the others again, but it was still too fast and whatever grip they could get was wrenched out of their hands by the speed of the swing.

Out over the hole, Carter's body slipped level with Webster's until it became completely detached, his arm sliding ever so slowly off the Major's back.

He dropped into thin air, plummeting towards the dense white undergrowth of Level Three.

At the last moment Webster whipped his hand out to catch Carter's.

Their fingers met and Webster managed to close his around Carter's in a desperate grip. For a split second, he thought he had saved him, but then the sweat gently eased their hands apart.

Now there was no way back. Carter fell through the air like one of the giant insects, landing with a *swooosshh* of leaves, a crack of branches and a thick thud on the floor of Level Three.

The white plants made it easier to pick him out, but he was a long way down.

Ignoring the danger, Webster flipped himself round so his head was as low as possible, his face grazing the tops of the blanched leaves that obscured Carter from view.

'Carter!'

Webster was amazed to see that his cry got a reaction. Carter opened his heavy-lidded eyes and looked up as his head rolled heavily forward.

'Get me some more slack on this rope!' yelled Webster.

Garrett knew they couldn't let it out any further

without sending Webster crashing down to join Carter, and then how would they get back up?

To her right, she spotted a firehose and ran across to it.

With one hard tug she emptied a spray of smaller insects from the end and fell flat on her back. The rubber had perished long ago and there was no chance of any of it holding their weight.

Webster continued to yell Carter's name, every shout helping him regain a little consciousness. His eyes opened wider and he stared ahead as if trying to focus. Then, with a huge effort, he leaned forward until he was almost sitting up.

Hearing Webster's calls, he looked above and saw a blurred vision of the major hanging upside down amongst the blanched plants that rose above him. He could just about make out the sound of his name and some other drowsy words asking him to do something he couldn't understand.

Distracted by the shouts, he didn't notice that the vines were coiling their way around him.

'Major, we can't pull the rope out and there's nothing else to use.'

Webster ignored Garrett and slid further down the rope.

He could see that Carter was now covered in a weave of thin tendrils. Then he felt something light brush against his fingers. Looking down, he saw that the tallest plants seemed to be stretching higher, as if reaching out for him.

He whipped his arm away and rubbed where he had been touched by the unpleasantly cool stems.

In the darkness he tried to confirm exactly what he thought he saw. The pale, writhing shapes of the stalks were flowing amongst each other like a nest of serpents, shifting and slithering with horrible purpose.

Carter was being eased backwards, forced to the floor by the weight and strength of the stems and leaves that wrapped themselves around his wide chest.

'Carter!'

Looking up again, he wondered why his torso felt so tight.

Webster watched the plants reaching around Carter's head, mummifying him before slipping carefully into his nostrils, ears and mouth.

'Carter!'

There was the smallest muffle of reply as the last breaths left his body.

He was gone, lost to the white stalks that were filling his throat, forcing their way into his oesophagus so there was no longer room for air.

They continued to slip further down, finding the stomach before filling it up and rupturing its walls then exploring the rest of his organs.

The tiny white tendrils that had slipped into his ears pushed through the drums until they found their way past the cochlea. Then they pushed harder until they poked at the rubbery moisture of Carter's brain.

Whatever had invaded his nostrils had reappeared at his eye sockets, easing out the damp tissue and straining the fibres that held the flesh in place. Then, with a muted wrenching, the eyeballs detached and rolled across his face to be gathered up greedily by the plants around his chest.

Webster shut his eyes hard, as if trying to squeeze what he had seen out of his thoughts.

Then he felt something tighten around his wrists.

Looking down, he saw that they were both covered in thin, white, fibrous stalks that were continuing to wrap themselves around him like leather straps.

The pain in his bicep was crashing through him in waves. He tried to pull free but couldn't find the strength.

'Shit! Help! Pull me up! Pull the rope up!' The others did as they were asked but the plants would not ease off their hold. Webster's hands felt cold and numb.

The dense beat of his pulse tried to force blood into them, but his arteries were being squeezed flat. His right fingers had gone stiff and he was worried he would soon lose them.

'Do something! Shoot them!' he yelled.

Madison pulled his weapon first. He took hasty aim and emptied his whole magazine into the ground on Level Three. Some of the bullets passed into Carter's corpse, but none freed Webster.

Garrett shunted him out of the way. She raised her rifle to her eye and ran through her prayer at top speed:

'Lord let me shoot true and straight deliver me from my enemy and let me continue to do your good work for as long as I have your strength amen.'

Two bullets ripped through the ends of a plant that

had attached itself to Webster's wrists. One snapped completely and the other was left thin enough for him to tear his arm up and free.

Mills and Wainhouse hurriedly yanked him up to Level Two as more plants reached up for him.

'Fuck! Fuuuuuck!' Webster bellowed.

The others watched as he hobbled around, smashing any insects he could find with the butt of his rifle. Some were killed, some lost limbs, others were knocked over the edge and down into the plants of the floor below. Then he gave a massive, lung-emptying yell, which only stopped when he caught sight of what was poised at the edge of the top of the hole.

The wasps had arranged themselves in a row, like birds on a wire, and were silently watching their quarry.

'Nobody move,' said Laura.

89

'Uh-oh,' Taj said, shaking his head. Immediately he regretted opening his big mouth.

'What?' asked Andrew.

Taj couldn't bring himself to answer. 'That's another one dead, isn't it?' Andrew said, jabbing his finger at Carter's blue dot.

'Yeah, that's another one dead.'

Andrew looked like he'd had the life punched out of him.

'Don't be makin' that face,' Taj said. 'I thought we had a deal. Why you gonna think that's your mom when there's all these alive?'

'But that's easy for you to say. That's not your mum down there. You didn't see what I saw.'

'OK, then, little man, this dead one here, it's your mom.'

'Don't say that!'

'Why not? It's what you thinking.'

'No it's not!'

'Yes it is. You looking like the whole world just caved in on you. You wouldn't think that if this one here was Mills, would you?'

'No, but . . .'

'So you think your mom copped it.'

'I bloody do not. Just shut up, will you?'

Taj gave Andrew half a smile. 'Now that's what I wanted to hear. That's not her, am I right?'

Andrew's voice was quiet and reluctant. 'Yeah.'

'Am. I. Right?'

Louder this time: 'Yes. OK?'

'Cool. And what you haven't mentioned is the good news: Mills, Madison and Jacobs are down there and they all got together now. See?' He pointed to the cluster of 'live' dots near the stairs of Level Two.

'But if they got down, why haven't they come back up? And why aren't they moving?'

'What do I look like – Superman? Gonna use my X-ray vision to see through that floor? There could be a million reasons. Like maybe one of 'em's injured and they all checking him over. Or there's something they need to work out about the climb before they get going. Jacobs and the others went down there fully strapped, so I'll tell you one thing: it ain't 'cos there's a bug in the way.'

'Maybe it's got something to do with whoever just died.'

'Oh . . . right . . . you think they having a memorial service. Maybe pouring out a forty for him.'

Andrew looked confused. He could hardly spot Taj's sarcasm if he had no idea what he was talking about.

'What's a *forty*?'

'You don't want to know, my friend. All I'm saying is they ain't organizing a wake.'

'Maybe it's Webster and they don't know what to do without him.'

'Maybe it's Bishop and they don't know what kind of party to throw.'

Andrew smiled and Taj felt that warm feeling again. Taking the kid from frightened despair to seeing the funny side of things in just a couple of minutes was a tough job well done.

Andrew looked at his watch, but it was pointless because the only time that mattered was the countdown on Taj's wrist. 'How long have they got?'

Taj looked at his watch, which showed they had twenty-three minutes left.

'They got time,' he said quietly. 'Now keep watching the screen.'

90

Nobody dared move.

The wasps stayed at the lip of the hole, their eyes and antennae focused on Level Two. It was as if they knew their prey was somewhere in the vicinity but they couldn't pinpoint where. The movement of the other insects provided a distraction which meant the humans could not be located with any accuracy.

It was hard to keep still with these creatures moving around them. Millipedes slithered between their legs, flies landed on their backs and spiders stumbled into them. The sound of beating wings had accumulated to a roar that brought to mind dozens of revving engines. Mosquitos swooped and arced through the air, criss-crossing with hornets, flies, beetles, termites and more. There were also the genetic corruptions, foul hybrids that flapped uncontrollably or walked like cripples, one or more of their legs or wings now useless.

Trying to stay still was a tall order.

'What the fuck are they doing?' asked Mills, looking up at the wasps. They were still the only insects to show any interest in the frozen humans.

'Don't move. Shut up,' said Laura, barely opening her mouth.

A single wasp flew down and across them like a

general surveying the field before battle. It seemed to know they were down there and wanted to take a closer look.

'The other insects are confusing them. They know we're here but they can only make out moving objects. If you take a step they will recognize your shape and know where we are,' she continued out of the corner of her mouth.

'So we're just going to stand here? We need to move,' said Madison, his stifled voice like an amateur attempt at ventriloquism.

'We move, we die,' said Webster.

'We got just over twenty minutes. We don't move, we die,' replied Jacobs.

'We've got five hundred feet of stairs to climb before this place goes nuclear. I'll take my chances with a fucking bug,' Mills shouted quietly.

Before anyone could stop him, he turned around, crouched behind the others and scuttled back towards the stairs. Nobody else dared move even an inch.

Mills had not seen what these wasps could do. In fact, he had seen very little of what any of these creatures were capable of. He was used to clinical operations where they overcame the insects with state-of-the-art weaponry and relative ease.

Assuming he had the others as cover, he moved swiftly towards the stairs with enough weapons to ensure his escape.

The floor was covered in small mounds of dried termite nest that had survived the explosion. These were difficult to see in the cloaking darkness, especially when combined with a frantic mess of oversized insects.

As Mills made his way through these obstacles he did not notice his boot treading on the tail of a centipede. The shifting movement made him lose balance and he went crashing to the floor with the full weight of his collection of guns and ammo.

Up to that point his escape had been obscured by the standing figures of Bishop and Webster. But now his position was clear and the wasps were keen to investigate.

In his arrogance and ignorance, Mills still didn't recognize the danger he was in.

Then he heard that distinctive *spridding* sound getting louder. Even amongst other similar sounds it stood out: higher in pitch, louder in volume and more urgent in tone. But Mills simply dismissed it as the noise of any one of this menagerie taking to the air.

Collecting himself and cursing under his breath, he resumed his escape.

As he came to the entrance of the stairwell, he believed he was completely safe.

Then the sound came so much closer and was so much louder that he was forced to stop and listen.

With single-minded focus the wasp swept past the frozen people, its right antenna almost grazing George's cheek, before speeding onwards.

No one could give a warning. The others remained still and silent, like a row of shop dummies.

A second later, the soft breeze of the wings was beating inches from Mills's ear.

Finally he knew that the sound was meant for him and his spine collapsed from the inside.

As that ear-shredding *brrrrrrrr* tore through his brain, the mandibles gripped like pliers, cutting sharp and swift into the base of his neck, the exact same place those exact same mandibles had gripped Van Arenn.

Then, as easily as before, the ovipositor slid in smoothly under the shoulder blade, the jaws passed the neck meat back into the mouth and the poison gushed through Mills's bloodstream.

The others bristled as the company of wasps flew through them to feed on the carrion of the soldier. He was face down on the floor now, his expression that familiar confusion that froze before the frenzy took over.

Clothes were ripped from skin, and skin was ripped from muscle, which was ripped from bone. They feasted with the relish of animals that had waited a long time and worked very hard for their meal, taking satisfaction in a job, or part of a job, completed.

But now they were finished and they knew, *just knew*, there was more nearby.

There were now eight wasps crawling and hovering around the humans, extending their antennae to find the very specific signs of life they had been hard-wired to search out.

Laura shuddered. The wasp that had finished off Mills was stroking its antennae against her leg to see if there was anything significant about those tiny spasms at her ankle.

It was still clumsily feeling its way, giving no indication it knew what it was touching. Laura shuddered again, harder this time.

The wasp showed more interest, as if a switch had ignited another part of its brain.

It started tentatively, the antenna fingering further up to the point where Laura's left thigh joined the knee.

She did all she could to keep still, but her leg had begun to wobble.

It was the sign the wasp had been looking for. Gripping Laura's trousers with its claws, it started a slow but purposeful ascent up the back of her thigh.

She tried not to scream but the shudder became stronger.

Laura was now gently but insistently rocking her entire body back and forth in a failing attempt to suppress the pounding horror.

She knew she was losing this battle, but the harder she tried to stay still, the more exaggerated her movements became.

Her face was riven with the contortions of silent desperation. The back-and-forth sway was now joined by a small wave of side-to-side motion.

And still the wasp continued its climb.

Laura could feel it on her lower back. It was hanging heavily off the bottom of her loose T-shirt.

Every so often a sharp burst of wingbeat would run another icicle of terror down her spine. The wasp gripped harder with all its claws to keep balance and gain height.

Laura remembered how Van Arenn had been killed. If the wasp reached her trapezius, she knew she would die before she had the chance to see her son again. It was beyond a miracle that they had both survived this far. Now they were so close to being reunited, to end it like this was too much to bear.

The climb of the wasp was like a chilling countdown, every step another effort it no longer needed to make.

The others stood completely still, even Mike, the only one with a view of Laura's back.

He was trying to think how he might prevent her death without harming the wasp and releasing the defence pheromone that would whip the others into furious action. They currently posed no threat, watching what was happening to Laura in a scrabbling, buzzing huddle.

At last the wasp reached Laura's neck.

It would take two more steps before it was in position to sink its stinger into Laura's shoulder. She shut her eyes tight and wondered how long she had to live.

If she was going to die then couldn't she do something? Couldn't she just reach around right now and jam her fingers into those black eyes or rip off a wing? The paralysis of fear meant she could not. Besides, she knew that doing anything like that would bring the livid attention of the rest of the swarm.

Now the wasp was in position. Laura's face was soaked with tears and she finally gave a whimper.

This seemed to please the wasp. It took another step and climbed over Laura's collarbone, moving its head as if sniffing at her neck.

The last embers of the nest fire were burning out nearby. They cast a sepia glow over Laura's tortured face, the malevolent eyes of the insect just visible in the half shadow below.

She could feel one of the wings, surprisingly firm, tracing across the nape of her neck like the edge of a finger.

At last the wasp moved backwards over Laura's collarbone and took a good look at what it was about to sink its mandibles into, almost as if it were raising a knife and fork.

Then the claws ripped out of Laura's back and a furious buzzing burst from behind her.

She was still alive.

How could that be?

Slowly, she opened her eyes. There was no weight on her shoulder, no mandibles at her neck.

To her left there was a frantic thrash of wingbeat. She couldn't see what was going on until a wasp rolled into one of the orange rectangles of firelight. It was obscured by three flies, which were pinning its wings down with their claws and snatching at its flesh with their mandibles.

Around them, the other wasps were trying to escape as more flies tore into them.

'Robber flies,' Mike whispered.

Laura peered closer, a huge smile covering her face.

'What the hell's a robber fly – except for my new best friend?' asked Garrett.

'Natural enemy of the wasp,' said George.

'They gonna win this?' asked Webster.

'Who cares?' said Jacobs. 'We've got eighteen minutes left to get up those stairs and on to the plane.'

91

Andrew and Taj watched as another dot turned blue. Andrew took on a look of desperate worry but Taj knocked it back with an admonishing glare which declared the subject closed.

Looking back at the screen, they couldn't understand why the dots had stayed still for so long. Andrew knew they were near the stairs, so he wondered what was preventing them from escaping.

Taj kept taking subtle glances at his watch, wishing the passing seconds would slow down.

'Look! They're moving,' said Andrew, as if he had just spotted Santa Claus.

'They are that. Looking good, looking good.' Half of Taj's face was taken up with a grin. He'd never known something with such high stakes come in at such long odds.

Andrew was tugging at his T-shirt. 'How long are they going to be? If they make it, I mean.'

'Wow, uh, I'd give 'em fifteen minutes,' said Taj hopefully, checking his watch for the hundredth time. 'They gonna be taking those stairs three at a time, that's for sure.'

'Shouldn't we get over to the hatch?'

'I think so. And don't you worry, the first one out gonna be your mom.'

Andrew had managed to keep everything in when his dad had died, but this time something turned the taps on full blast. He was standing in front of Taj, only able to give a jerky nod while the tears dripped off his chin.

Taj wrapped him in a big hug. It wasn't his usual thing, especially for a kid he hardly knew, but he remembered his grandma doing it when the time was right and he knew how good it could feel.

When they separated, Andrew gave a draggy sniffle and left a big trail of snot on Taj's shirt.

'We best get over there now, you know. I bet Jacobs told your mom that you up here, so you'd best be the first thing she sees.'

Andrew nodded and they set off for the hatch.

92

Although the wasps were definitely the hardest obstacle to overcome, they were by no means the only one. The rest of the Abdomen was fully active, and anything aggressive enough to believe it could take on a human would be keen to give it a go.

This became clear as soon as the celebrations began. The elation was cut brutally short by a wild scream from Mike: a Siafu ant caught his movement and sank its razor-blade jaws into his shin.

'*AAARRRRRGGAAARR!* Someone help me!' he yelled. As he moved his leg into the sliver of available light, he realized he had a substantial weight attached to him.

'Fuck,' said George as he caught sight of it. 'Siafu.' The smaller versions were well known for their tenacity: once the jaws clamped shut, they would not let go, even if the ant were decapitated. This one was the size of a rat, leaving George with only one option.

He turned to Webster. 'Give me your knife,' he said urgently. The major handed over his ka-bar immediately. George knelt down next to Mike and wasted no time in cutting the ant's body off, leaving the head and jaws stuck into the leg like a pair of scissors.

'Sorry, man,' George said, as Mike continued to

grunt in pain, 'you know the Siafu. We can't get that out until we hit the surface. Better grit your teeth.'

They could all feel each second thumping by like the boots of a marching army, but they also knew they couldn't just run up the stairs and hope to make it out alive. They went back to standing still as Webster took charge one more time.

'Jacobs, what have we got to blast our way out?'

'Not a lot. The explosives might screw the stairs up, so all we got left is a shit-load of old-fashioned semi-autos and a flamethrower you're going to have to take off Mills's back.'

'OK, I'll use the fire on point to clear the way ahead. Whoever's used a semi-auto before, use one now; if not, grab a handgun. We can't risk you guys firing weapons with massive recoil in a confined space. Garrett, I want you at the back taking out anything that follows. OK? Let's move.'

The soldiers grabbed the M-16s and AR-15s, loading their clips and slamming them home. Then they took the safetys off the Beretta 92Fs and M1911 Colts and passed them to the scientists.

'Just aim and squeeze the trigger like you seen in the movies. Ain't nothin' to it,' said Garrett to a clearly nervous Susan.

Now that everyone was armed, Webster took aim with the flamethrower and sent a vast cone of fire into the stairway. He knew it would attract some of the insects, but he had to clear the way and give everyone a view of where they were heading.

'Let's go!' Webster shouted, jogging towards the stairs with a small limp rolling off his ankle. He sent another blast into the bottom flight, burning up what was left of the nest. He also set fire to a swarm of bulldog ants the size of mice, which burnt out quickly.

Jacobs, Laura and the scientists were following about ten feet behind, with Bishop at the back of this middle group.

Further back, Garrett and Madison were fighting a rearguard action against the insects that had been attracted to the fire. The sound was putting some of them off, but others, fuelled by their unnatural boldness and aggression, were coming at them at full speed.

'Get up there,' Garrett shouted to Madison. 'If we don't get into the stairs, we're never going to get out of here. We need a smaller gap to funnel them into.'

Madison ran into the stairwell while Garrett fired behind her. The insects sensed prey and were following in numbers, but the spray of bullets took care of them with messy efficiency.

Further up, Webster was wondering if the flame-thrower was such a good idea after all. It gave great protection, but it left the stairs full of giant burning insects, which thrashed around the enclosed space. Gravity meant that most of them came down the stairs, leaving Webster to keep them at bay with the butt of his rifle. Twice his jacket caught fire, and the time he took to smack the flames out was slowing the ascent even more.

On the sixth flight the decision was made for him: the flamethrower ran out of petrol, so he gladly ripped it off his back and switched to his M-16.

Progress was faster now, as the insects were thinning out and the ones he came across were killed instantly with a couple of well-placed bullets. The few that got past him were dealt with by the boots and handguns of the scientists, who felt a vague sense of shame at how much they enjoyed firing their weapons.

At the bottom of the stairs, Madison and Garrett were catching the scientists up. Some insects were still following, but there were fewer now, and the occasional burst from Garrett's AR-15 took care of them.

'Hey, Garrett, you got any more ammo? I'm all out.' Madison was one flight ahead, so there was little need for him to keep firing, but he didn't want to go on unarmed.

'Sure,' said Garrett, climbing up the steps behind him. They were right next to one of the flares Jacobs had set off earlier, which made it easier for Garrett to see what she was doing.

'Anything down there?' Madison asked as she rammed his new clip home.

'Nothing big. A few ants here and there. My boots work fine on them.'

They both heard the soft, rhythmic thumping, but couldn't tell where it was coming from. As they hadn't been under much of a threat for a while, they both looked up the stairwell to see if one of the scientists was coming down.

It didn't sound like that was happening, but now the thumps were getting louder.

Garrett looked down the stairs just in time to see the jumping spider, as big as a dustbin lid, bounding towards them.

Madison had his back to it, so all he saw was Garrett's terrified face, her arms flailing towards him, pushing him sideways.

With a fraction of a second to spare, she shoved Madison out of the way, but that meant that she could not raise her arms to defend herself.

Madison watched as the spider's giant fangs plunged straight into the middle of Garrett's chest.

She was knocked on to her back, smacking her head against the metal steps.

Madison brought his gun up and drilled a volley of bullets into the spider from the side, missing Garrett but turning the arachnid to a furry mush.

Using all his strength, he wrenched what was left of the beast off Garrett's chest. Great gushes of blood lashed up in a thick fountain, pumping directly from her heart.

'Garrett! Garrett! Talk to me!'

She looked dead, but just as Madison was about to give up hope, her eyes opened weakly.

'Garrett?'

'Madi . . . son.' Blood was pouring out of her mouth and down her neck.

'Oh shit, Garrett. I've got to get you help.' He started to move, but her hand rose weakly, just catching his.

'No . . . you go. You go . . . fly the plane.'

Her eyes shut softly and her head gave a small *clank* as it fell limp on the metal stairs.

Madison grabbed her by the shoulders. 'Garrett! Garrett! Oh fuck!' As he felt her lifeless body in his arms, he knew she was gone, and he knew she was right: he had to get out of there to fly them to safety.

Shaking his head and choking back the lump in his throat, he grabbed the banister and sprinted up the stairs.

Ten flights up, they were all running, or going as fast as they could, injuries permitting.

Although her back, ribs and shoulder were still send-ing hot shocks of pain through her, Laura was using thoughts of Andrew to block them out and pull herself up faster and faster, a wash of perspiration clearing the blood and dirt from her face.

Webster was driving upwards, ignoring the sharp stab of pain his ankle gave him every time he put weight on it. The swelling had reduced a great deal, but not enough for a climb like this. His torn bicep was also screaming for attention but he just kept on look-ing forwards, concentrating on the next flight.

The ant head clinging on to Mike's shin was so pain-ful he had to keep stopping to have another go at pulling the jaws apart. The effort was pointless. These ants got stuck fast at half an inch long; this one was a hundred times the size, so it would take more than a hard yank from Mike to remove it. Like Webster, he just had to accept he could run in pain or die.

The slash on George's back seemed to pull apart a little more with every step. It was as if the skin were trying to knit together but the motion of the climb would not let it. This was on top of a general lack of fitness: the Marlboros and beer were definitely making themselves felt. Jacobs could see he wasn't going to make it on his own, so she dropped back, put his arm over her shoulder and gave him the lift he needed.

Susan was the only one of the original group with no serious injuries. It hadn't occurred to her to help the others up to then, but she saw how Jacobs was supporting George and went to do the same for Mike. The physical assistance made a difference, but in the rush to avoid being left behind, the feeling there was someone else with you was equally motivating.

Madison ran past Bishop. He knew there was no point in telling anyone what had happened to Garrett, but he also knew he had to make sure the plane was ready for take-off as soon as possible. If the others were safely up on the surface and he was still on the stairs, that would be a huge waste of effort. He jumped up the steps and dragged himself higher by pulling on the banister.

Overall, it was an effort that strained every sinew, every blood vessel, every muscle, but the reward was too good to give up. It would mean that the last six hours had not been for nothing, that they had a chance at a life which had only recently seemed so remote.

Bishop was the only straggler. He looked at the walls and the stairs of the building that surrounded him and was overcome by a sadness that tempered the relief of survival. Was this really the end? Was he really going to leave this place that had been his home and his life for so long?

The last few weeks had seen him go through more pain, horror, death and revulsion than most people would go through in ten lifetimes. But something made him think he had dealt with that problem. Now it was time to get back to normal.

Maybe Paine would understand that MEROS was too valuable to destroy. Maybe he could persuade the others that it was worth saving. Maybe things weren't as bad as they seemed.

He continued up the stairs, but with little enthusiasm.

93

Captain Fox eased back the throttle and banked over the hills between Aracadinya and Cabadiscana. There were small villages below, which must have found the sight and sound of an F-35 Lightning 2 JSF both strange and fearsome. It was a grey bullet of searing metal, almost invisible against the gathering clouds, but its whining roar filled the sky like an elongated thunderclap.

Fox checked the Synthetic Aperture Radar system to view the terrain ahead. It was time to change down from supersonic and lose altitude. Although it was unlikely the Venezuelan government would be paying close attention to these areas, as far as international aviation tracking went, this mission was non-existent.

The Pratt-Whitney F135 engine slowed under smooth control. Fox then applied a little more pressure on the right pedal and yawed in a southerly direction. He was less than 100 miles from the target so he checked his instruments and prepared to switch to the internal electro-optical targeting system. He was still too far away to make a direct ID of MEROS but he wanted to test the F-35's capabilities in the head-up displays.

Reaching forward, he moved the cursor on his screen towards the target and designated the B61 Mod

11 for a small white building in a clearing at the end of a jungle runway. Then he moved the cursor and selected a nearby copper mine instead. Playing God with a nuclear bomb gave him a guilty thrill. The idea that a swipe of his index finger and a push of his thumb would end the lives of whomever he chose was a perverse but undeniable pleasure.

His head-down display informed him that the distance to target was only 50 miles. He switched the monitor back to MEROS and looked ahead: nothing but dense dark green, interrupted by the occasional smear of white-grey mist. He hoped the terrain stayed that way. On a similar mission two years earlier, intelligence had sent him to destroy a supposedly isolated cave in Yemen. It turned out to be located half a mile from a bustling village. Sending down that bomb haunted him to this day. He liked to think they had been upwind of the explosion and that the villagers had not been infected by the fallout, but he knew it was unlikely.

His training had suggested that it was inadvisable to imagine the details of what he was attacking, and the radar system made that easier. It had the appearance of a very basic video game, reducing buildings and the people within them to a series of coloured shapes that gave no indication of what lay within.

MEROS was now one of those shapes: a white triangle, for the next fifteen minutes, at least.

94

There was nobody else within eight flights of Laura. Her thighs pumped like pistons, eating up the stairs in leaps and jumps. Much of her climb was in darkness, but she could just make out where she was going from the dying flares that Jacobs, Mills and Madison had left on their way down.

It had been almost thirty-six hours since she had entered the complex, twice that since Andrew had gone missing, but it felt like weeks. Even before the Heath wasps had escaped she had doubted she would ever be able to return home, but oddly enough the disaster that had followed was what had made it possible.

Perspiration poured down her front and back while the inside of her mouth was dust-dry. How many more steps could there be? How much time was left? She prayed nothing had happened to Madison, and climbed faster still.

Near the summit the steps curved in a different direction with shorter flights and she felt the first whisper of cool air from outside. It was joined by a faint haze of natural light that showed the stairs to be a dark blue rather than the black they had seemed as they passed beneath her feet. As she made her way up the last steps she heard voices from above. It was impossible to know who was talking but she could understand the tone, a minor disagreement between a high voice and a low one.

'They should be here by now.'

'They on their goddamn way! Now chill! Listen!'

Taj was interrupted by the faint clang of Laura's boots on the metal stairs. Andrew immediately tried to run into the staircase, but Taj held him back.

'Leave room. They all got to get out.'

The clangs became louder until it was obvious they were coming from the final steps.

Andrew broke free from Taj with a fierce kick.

'Andrew, Andrew, Andrew,' was all Laura could say as she buried her face in his neck and hugged him so hard his ribs ached.

She had lost him twice in the last three days and both times she thought it was for ever. As she held him again, she resolved to remember everything about this moment: his scruffy brown hair, his shining eyes and the way he held her like he would never let go again.

When at last they separated Laura saw Taj looking awkward.

'Thank you for looking after him . . .'

'Taj.'

'Taj, of course.'

'Must have been plenty, uh, I mean to say you must have been through a lot, Dr Trent.'

Laura looked at Andrew and rubbed the back of his neck as he smiled up at her, squinting at the sun streaming in behind her head.

'Yes . . . it's been quite . . .'

Just when she thought that no words could do the experience justice, Webster came through the hatch, closely followed by Madison.

'Sorry, but we have to get to the plane now,' Webster said. 'There's a minute left on Jacobs's clock.'

They ploughed through the trees: Madison running ahead, and Webster, Laura, Andrew and Taj tight on his heels.

The way through the jungle was not easy: ripples of earth, thick with trees and creepers, undulated down the steep slope.

Leading the way, Madison caught his foot on a tendon of root and went flying. Landing hard, he somersaulted down past stumps and trunks, twice missing concussion by the width of a finger.

Trailing his hand behind him, he managed to grasp a tight mess of vines. The momentum wrenched at his knuckles but he finally came to a stop just before a row of rocks that would have split his head like a pineapple.

Webster caught him up. 'You OK?' Madison didn't even reply. He just got back up and bolted through the bushes.

A hundred more yards of flat jungle and they were at the clearing. Thumping boots swished through the foliage and on to the grass.

Madison was already jumping through the Spartan's side doors and grabbing his headphones.

'Thirty seconds!' warned Webster, looking at his

watch as the others took their seats. 'Paine had better be late.'

They all took seats by the windows and watched the jungle for the arrival of the others.

'Come on . . . come on . . .' whispered Webster.

Madison gunned the ignition and the twin turbo-prop engines swept into life. They were already at the end of the two-thousand-foot runway, so Madison did not need to manoeuvre the plane into position.

'Come on!' snapped Webster.

Suddenly the cockpit alarm blared in Madison's ears.

'Shit! I have incoming, north-north-east, approaching at low altitude and high speed. This looks like the one, Major. I can try to taxi slowly, but we can't really wait any more.'

'Hang on, Madison!'

One by one, the others appeared from the trees: George, Susan, Mike and Jacobs limped and staggered across the clearing. Webster ran out to help them along and they were soon up the steps and into the plane's side door, gasping hard and sweating harder.

As Madison powered up the engine, Taj called out from the back row. 'Hey, Jacobs. Looks like your calculations were a little off. My watch is at zero.' There was a smattering of relieved laughter.

'Glad to be wrong, Taj.'

'OK, we ready to get the fuck out of here?' called Madison. Webster counted them off then looked around again.

'We're missing two.'

Madison got out of his seat and appeared at the door to the cockpit. 'I'm sorry, guys. Garrett bought it on the way up. I didn't see any point in saying until we got out of there but she made it very clear she wants us to live, so let's talk about it after I get us safe.'

He returned to the cockpit, leaving a stunned silence behind him.

Webster couldn't believe what he had heard, but right now he had to push his grief aside. Who else was . . . ?

'Bishop,' said Mike sourly.

'We can't leave without him,' said Webster.

'Major, pretty soon I'm going to have no choice,' called Madison.

'How long?' replied Webster.

'ETA of two minutes. That gives us thirty seconds before I have to lift off, but I'll gun the engine as hard as I can.'

'Come on, Bishop,' said Webster through gritted teeth.

'Hey, I say we leave the asshole. You really want to risk this, Major?' asked Mike.

'You really want to leave a man to die?' Webster shot back.

A second later, Bishop was out of the jungle and into the clearing. Webster frantically waved him towards the plane.

But he wasn't running. He ambled on to the flat grass and looked ruefully at the plane. Then he gave the smallest of waves and walked back towards the white building.

Webster wanted to stop him but he knew they had no time to wait for that. There was something in Bishop's eyes that seemed impossibly empty, as if they were transparent. It didn't feel right to leave him in that state, but on this occasion they couldn't do anything else.

'Take her up,' he shouted to Madison, sadness in his voice. If anyone had been standing close enough to Bishop, they'd have heard him talking:

'It's OK. The blast will be a half-mile underground. There'll be no danger. I just can't leave my post. And I'll be in touch. When we've sorted this place out and we can get MEROS functioning again somewhere else, I'll get hold of you all and we can continue what made this place great, continue the work, continue our valuable contribution to . . .'

Either he realized nobody was listening or he didn't know how the sentence was going to end. He turned back to the Spartan again and waved at no one in particular, as if they were all his good friends, moving on after their final year of college.

With a melancholy smile on his face, he looked back to the entrance of MEROS.

Behind him, the Spartan was accelerating down the runway.

Three miles to the north-east, the F-35 was coming in low. Captain Fox tapped the cursor on his screen and the B61 Mod 11 was on its way.

The Spartan had covered half of the runway, and was nearing take-off speed.

'OK, everyone,' yelled Madison. 'I'm picking up

something else. Smaller, coming in faster. Brace yourselves. I'm going to do my best to avoid it, but I've got
to get airborne first.'

As he spoke, the Spartan's wheels lifted off the
concrete and into the air.

Fox was gaining altitude so he could come back
round and check that the bomb had hit its target. As
soon as his nose lurched upwards, the Spartan appeared
on his radar as a hostile craft.

'What the hell?' he said to himself, then switched
on the mike in his oxygen mask.

'Candyman to base. Candyman to base.'

'This is base, copy Candyman.'

'I've got a rogue hawk approx one K from target,
please advise, over.'

'We see it, Candyman. Hold fire until instructed
otherwise.'

The bomb was heading straight for the Spartan.
Madison could see it coming but didn't have enough
lift to bank out of the way.

He was yanking the control stick back and right as
hard as he could, sending the plane into a steep climb.
The elevators on the tail were fully tilted, and the pedal
was pushed into the floor.

They were a hundred yards apart now, and closing
at a thousand miles an hour.

The plane kept banking and climbing.

The bomb kept burning through the air.

At the moment of impact the Spartan lifted another
inch. As it rose, the bomb's tail fins scored the back

wheel of the plane, puncturing the tyre, then passing on.

Everyone felt it: a wavy bump that flicked the tail out again, sending the plane upwards at a perilous angle.

'I can't . . . fucking hold . . . it,' grunted Madison, gripping the control stick like he was on a rollercoaster.

Behind them, 400 kilotons of bomb plunged through Bishop's spine and into the doors of the white building.

The explosion was instantaneous. Thousands of tons of earth flew upwards as if wrenched by a giant earthquake. The jungle, clearing and runway seemed to jump in the air as the violent shockwave whipped through them.

The Spartan, still yawing perilously to the left, took another hit of pressure. The explosion of dirt flew up around it, rattling the tail and sending a plume of dust around the back windows. The plane lurched again, throwing Susan and Mike out of their seats.

'Hold on . . . everybody!' grunted Madison.

It was his will against the force of the nuclear explosion. The Spartan was gaining distance, but it was heading into a flat spin that could easily send it diving back into the jungle.

Laura and Andrew gripped their seats as cargo crashed and flipped around them. George took a fierce knock to the head from a flying toolkit, drawing a trickle of blood from his temple.

The roar of the engine was so loud it invaded their

ears like a white-hot sledgehammer, driving out the ability to think, but expanding the fear.

'AAAAARRRRGGGGGHHHHHHH!' screamed Madison.

With that scream, the plane seemed to reach a peak. Surrounded by dust and pointing upwards at sixty degrees with a noise of tortured metal, it dropped ever so slightly.

The sound calmed a little and they began to escape the dirt.

Blood returned to white knuckles, and teeth that were clamped tight slowly loosened and separated.

They could hear Madison breathing hard, but slower.

'OK, everybody. I think we're going to make it.'

The F-35 banked round over MEROS. Flying directly back over his approach route, Captain Fox watched a little pocket of Venezuelan jungle transform from verdant foliage to a blinding flash of brilliant white in the blink of an eye.

'Candyman to base, the toad is in the hole, repeat, the toad is in the hole, over.'

'Base to Candyman, we copy. Return to base immediately.'

'Roger that, base. I still have the rogue hawk in my sights. Should I engage, over?'

'Negative, Candyman. Return to base as instructed. Over and out.'

Captain Fox was happy to obey orders, but he didn't think it would hurt to let the Spartan know he was there.

He switched to supersonic and blew past the larger plane at a distance of ten metres before heading north-east to his base.

'Jesus, what the fuck was that?' yelled Madison as the F-35 shot past. It was one last ripple that had to be dealt with. Like a storm wave hitting a fishing trawler, the turbulence sent the Spartan tossing from side to side.

'Asshole!' Madison screamed at the disappearing bomber. A little more attention to the control stick and the plane settled down.

'OK, folks, I think that's it. I got nothing on my radar, so we should be looking at a flight time of approximately four hours to the land of no fucking bugs, but many, many mojitos.'

95

Laura looked out at the jungle. She had only arrived yesterday – or was it the day before? She checked her watch. Its face had been shattered somewhere along the way. It was the only thing her husband had left her, and she wondered if there was a point when it might have been broken saving her from a set of grinding jaws or an intent stinger.

On the plane, there was a shellshocked silence. There was nothing to say beyond looks and gestures as several of the passengers collapsed with exhaustion and sank into a treacly sleep.

Looking across, Webster caught Laura's eye. He slipped out of his seat and came over to where she and Andrew were sitting.

'Hi,' he said, just loud enough to be heard above the sound of the thundering engine.

'Hi,' replied Laura.

There was an awkward pause while Webster tried to articulate a million thoughts. In the end, Laura spoke first.

'So what happens now?'

'We're going to head to the base in Costa Rica. It's not a hardcore military operation and we've got friends there who'll make sure we can all go on to where we want to be. I assume for you that's England.'

'Definitely,' said Andrew, just in case his mum was thinking of anything else. Laura put her arm round him.

'And what about you?'

'Me? I don't know. MEROS has been the closest thing I've had to home for a long time. Got no roots elsewhere, so I might hang in Costa Rica for a while until something comes up. I hear there's good fishing there this time of year.'

There was another pause as they both avoided being the one to speak next and willed the other to do it instead.

'Well, I just want to say thanks,' said Laura.

'What for? Kidnapping Andrew? Dragging you out to the land of giant killer insects?'

'Obviously. No, for keeping us alive. Without you we'd still be down there.'

'Without me you'd never have been there in the first place. I owe you a lifetime of making up. You too, Andrew.' Webster reached into his trouser pocket. 'Maybe I can start with this.' He pulled out the chunk of bloody metal and passed it to Andrew.

'My knife!'

'It was on the stairs. I saw you playing with it yesterday. Figured you'd want it back.'

Andrew checked the blades.

'Thanks, Major Webster.'

'Any time.'

96

Tobias Paine stood in his garden smoking the cigarettes that his wife would not allow in the house. He took another look at his watch and realized that, if everything had gone to plan, MEROS no longer existed.

Perhaps there would be questions to answer, enquiries made about the efficiency of his operation. Why was he unable to provide the military resource that was required? Where were the results of all that funding? And, most importantly, when would the bugs be available again?

But that was the benefit of working in covert operations: within reason he could do things his way without having to justify himself. He could redirect finances. He could wipe out jungles. He could kill.

But what was that nagging feeling in the back of his mind, the one that made him suck just a little harder on that full-strength Winston 100? It couldn't be guilt, could it? Not when he ordered and arranged death every day.

No, it was definitely not guilt. It was something much more unpleasant than that. Like an oily arm around his shoulders, it was the inescapable sensation of failure.

He had been given another responsibility and, just

like those times at college when he hadn't quite made the social grade, he had come up short.

And why? Well, it was that prick, Bishop, of course. He might have been his wife's brother, but the man was an idiot. No matter how many times Paine had found positions for him, he had never been repaid with anything approaching competence. At least the posting to MEROS had meant he no longer ruined family Christmases with his execrable attempts at humour and questionable personal hygiene.

Paine exhaled another lungful of smoke with a raw snort. He had certainly got rid of the little shit now. Harriet would be . . . dismayed, but it was definitely for the best. They could all make a fresh start; pretend he never happened.

And once the current difficulties were dealt with and the ashes of Colinas de Edad swept under the carpet, he would be free to move on, unencumbered by mediocrity, compromise and the growing pains of something that had progressed by trial and error. With MEROS out of the way he could now concentrate on the next stage of the bigger picture, the endgame that he had dreamed of from the very beginning: MEROS B, the second bughouse, new and improved with 100 per cent more everything. It would be his shining achievement, his crowning glory, and it would not fail, because it would not be under the control of someone as pathetic as Steven Bishop.

No, this time he was going to take a personal, hands-on interest in its success. He had very big plans for the continuation of the MEROS project, plans that would make this incident seem like a minor hiccup, plans that would make the world sit up and pay attention, finally allowing him to take what was rightfully his: wealth, power and a place in history.

He couldn't wait.

He took one last drag on his Winston and flicked it through a triumphant arc into the flowerbed.

97

Several square miles of jungle that had suffered little interference for thousands of years vanished in less than a second.

From the physical impact of the missile, a chain reaction began that had no regard for nature or history, laying waste to thousands of years of both in the blink of an eye.

As the hydrodynamic front moved outwards, radiation rapidly heated everything in the surrounding land to an equilibrium temperature. Waves of thermal radiation sent millions of degrees of heat sweeping from the hypocentre of the blast at a speed of 600mph, sending a thunderous wall of flame to annihilate everything in the surrounding miles. Even the rocks and earth were vaporized instantly, reduced to atoms in the expanding shockwave.

Then the fireball roared upwards into a mushroom cloud that curled in on itself like a frowning skull and hung over the bombsite as if overseeing the devastation below.

When at last the smoke cleared, MEROS was a vast, empty hemisphere that pulsed with radiation. Aside from the distant crackle of flames, the air sat heavy with an empty silence.

In the following weeks, the only changes came with the weather. Rain darkened the soil, wind whipped the ashes of the jungle around in whitish eddies and the sun brought life to nothing.

When the rainy season arrived, a monsoon lashed the giant scoop of dirt.

Without trees to break the storm, the gusts tore through the air, sending the rain down in hard, heavy drops to hammer the ground.

The water pooled in the bottom of the crater, and soon the downpour was churning the surface of a lake of mud.

In the half-darkness of wet earth, bruised clouds and shadows of frothing rain, it was impossible to make out the whip-thin, grey, translucent rod that rose through the water. It slid upwards, thickening as each new inch was revealed, until it protruded some ten feet from the water.

It hung still in the air, water collecting at its tip and dripping into the mud in slow, plump splashes. Then, like a shark's fin slipping through the surface, a second shaft of slim, leathery flesh joined the first.

Through the driving hiss of landing rain, a furious scream rang out in the darkness.

It was hungry.

Acknowledgements

I'd like to thank everyone who was kind enough to take the time to read this book during its development. You helped take it from a mewling, underweight neophyte to the strapping bruiser you see before you. Biggest thanks must go to my wonderful wife, Gabi, who had to read it enough times to more than justify divorce proceedings. Then, in chronological order: Mum, Dad, Vicky, Toby, Sean and Sian, each of whom gave me invaluable advice and encouragement. Also, thanks to my brother Andrew who set me on the path of a good story well told from an early age.

My eternal gratitude must also go to Robert, my agent, who took me on in spite of some very good reasons to chuck my manuscript into the nearest incinerator. Here would be a good place to admit to him that I may have fibbed slightly when I suggested that other agents were interested in me. None were. If it wasn't for him, it's very likely that this book would not exist.

Equally deserving of my thanks is my editor, Alex. Not only was he kind enough to want to publish *Instinct*, he also made many of the most beneficial suggestions that brought about its improvement. Having said that, he sometimes attributed these to a nameless team of people back at Penguin, so thanks to them, too, whomever they may be. And thanks to Sarah, my copy-editor, who cheerfully smoothed off the rough edges on my behalf.

Finally, I'd like to thank Arsene Wenger for his contribution to my happiness over the last dozen years.